A

A Dorset Girl

A
Dorset
Girl

Janet Woods

**SIMON &
SCHUSTER**

LONDON • SYDNEY • NEW YORK • TOKYO • SINGAPORE • TORONTO

First published in Great Britain by Simon & Schuster, 2003
This edition first published by Pocket Books, 2003
An imprint of Simon & Schuster UK
A Viacom Company

1 3 5 7 9 10 8 6 4 2

Simon & Schuster UK Ltd
Africa House
64–78 Kingsway
London WC2B 6AH

www.simonsays.co.uk

Simon & Schuster Australia
Sydney

A CIP catalogue record for this book is available from
the British Library

ISBN 0 7432 3947 4

This book is a work of fiction. Names, characters, places and incidents
are either a product of the author's imagination or are used fictitiously.
Any resemblance to actual people living or dead, events or locales
is entirely coincidental.

Typeset by SX Composing DTP, Rayleigh, Essex
Printed and bound in Great Britain by
The Bath Press, Bath

Dedicated to my husband, Trevor,
a gem of a Dorset man.

*

The author is happy to receive feedback from readers.
She can be contacted via her website.

http://members.iinet.net.au/~woods

PROLOGUE

Wales. 1815

The girl was a slip of a thing, her patched skirt and faded bodice hung loosely on her slender frame. A shawl, the wool hand-spun and woven by her grandmother, was clenched to her chest in a tightly fisted hand.

Beneath the grey drabness of the gown, the small bulge had been noticeable only to the most sharp-eyed of the village women, until they'd honed their tongues to match.

The girl's face was pale, pinched around the mouth. Her eyes, burning with her shame though she kept her head held high, were of a peculiar greenness, a gift from her ancient warrior ancestors.

'Get you gone, Megan Lewis!'

Behind her on the chapel steps stood her father, stern in his own righteousness and resolve. She would not look back. Behind her, a bad memory, the travelling preacher, his mouth thundering with the teachings of the Lord, his loins hot and thrusting with the instrument of Satan's punishment.

'Shame on you, sinner.'

Behind the lace curtains of a neatly kept cottage were

1

her stepmother and sisters. Prayers would be said for her soul, then for as long as they lived she would never be mentioned again.

She bit back on a sob, resisting the urge to pull the shawl over her head. Led by her stepmother, the village women had hacked the waist-length locks from her head. She felt naked without it, the black tufts were spiky and rough between her fingers.

A clod of earth hit her between the shoulder blades and she stumbled.

'Your mother was too proud for the likes of us,' Aunt Wynn hissed with snake-like malice. 'Descended from the marcher lords, she said she was. A pity it is that she isn't alive to see this.' Wynn stood next to Grandmother Lewis on the doorstep, a spinster, her youth withered by the lack of a man's interest, unattractive in her brown plumage.

The older woman was still tall and upright at sixty. Her shock of white hair was pulled into a coarse linen bonnet, the black coals of her eyes were clouded over, her mouth crabbed inwards over her gums. 'Megan . . . is that you, our Megan?' Her voice had a high-pitched fluting strangeness to it.

Megan shivered. 'It is me, Grandmother.'

'I burned a lock of your hair, *cariad*. The smoke showed the future.'

'And what is that future, Grandmother?'

'You will go forth into misery, but the man who caused it will be cursed. Your life will be hard.'

'And what will become of my child?'

'Her Llewellyn blood will strengthen her, but she'll never be accepted as one of us.'

Wynn's breath sucked sharply in. 'Llewelyn blood, is it? A lot of good that will do the bastard when the mother is already condemned as a temptress. She carries the devil's child, not the preacher's.'

'Hush, Wynn, don't be so hard on her, the girl has troubles enough to face, as does her child.' The old woman stepped forward and whispered against her ear, so Wynn could not overhear.

Wynn tugged uneasily at her arm. 'If you're filling the girl's head with pagan prophecy, come away in, before the chapel elders hear any words of blasphemy.'

Tears streaming down her cheeks, the woman's bent old fingers clutched at her daughter's arm. 'Give Megan my piece.' She turned and went inside, her head bowed.

Wynn came to the gate and held out a bundle. 'Be grateful she is losing her wits, mind, for you'd not be offered a crumb from my table. Here's a blanket and some food for your journey.'

'Thank you, Aunt.'

Wynn avoided her eyes. 'Despite being my own brother's child, you will never call me aunt again. From this moment on you are nothing to us, you no longer exist and, God willing, we'll never meet again. Good riddance to you.' She walked inside without looking back, banging the door shut behind her.

The road from the village wound steeply upwards. When Megan reached the top of the hill she turned and looked back. Nobody stirred. No dog barked. The doors and windows of the cottages were closed. The village where she'd been born and raised was nestled into the border marches, as it always had been. But it was closed up, the backs of its inhabitants turned to her – and Megan felt like the stranger she'd become.

Over the peak and ahead of her, a track winding down. Then what? England? She'd heard there was work in the towns, and she could spin and weave.

She shivered as a cloud moved over the sun. Her grandmother had spoken of misery.

The woman was old, known for her strangeness. Some called her fey. But Megan, smiling with all the optimism of a girl nearing eighteen years, suddenly experienced a sense of freedom.

The road ahead was strewn with stones. Summer was in decline, but enough warmth was left in the day to lull a fool into believing the weather would be fair for ever. Although her heart was heavy, Megan's clogged feet began to dance over the ground.

It was a while before she stopped to rest. The horizon was a smudge of grey and purple. She must find shelter for the night, the shepherd's hut in the distance, perhaps. She headed towards it, into the long afternoon shadows.

There was a crusty loaf, a slab of cheese and a slice of mutton wrapped in a clean rag inside the blanket. There was also a small cloth pouch. Inside, a few preciously hoarded coins jingled as she tipped them into her hand. Amongst them shone an intricately patterned silver cross on a chain. She turned it over, painfully mouthing the few letters she'd learned at her mother's knee before she'd died.

'Siana,' she whispered, and a lump came to her throat. It was her grandmother's cross.

4

1

Straightening up from the tub, Siana Skinner stopped humming long enough to gaze over to where her mother was hanging a pair of patched corduroy trousers on the line. They hung, empty and baggy-arsed, dripping into the long grass.

It was early; the sun had just cleared the horizon; the air was still. Unless the breeze came up they'd be lucky if the washing dried by nightfall. If the trousers didn't dry, it would fetch her a clout from Bill Skinner and worse for her mother, especially if he'd been drinking. She prayed for a good drying breeze.

'Josh,' she shouted towards the cottage, 'when're you going to scythe the top off this grass? The seeds are sticking in the wash and I have to pick them all out when it's dry.'

'Josh has gone already; he's earning a penny or two running messages today over Tolpuddle way, and wanted to make an early start,' Megan Skinner told her.

Siana's smile faded as she gazed at her mother. 'Our Josh will get into strife running messages for those troublemakers. A haystack was fired last week, and I

5

hear tell the authorities have got their eyes on the Tolpuddle men.'

Her mother supported her back with her hands. She was carrying the infant low, Siana thought.

'A pity there aren't a few more who have the welfare of their fellow workers at heart. Not like some I could mention, who're always out for themselves.' And Siana knew she was referring to Tom.

'All the same, we don't want our Josh to get into trouble.'

'I suppose so, but he's got his head screwed on tight, and has got the right to earn a little for himself. One of these days he'll wed and have a family to support.'

Siana laughed. 'Get away with you, Ma. Our Josh is only twelve.'

'And you're seventeen. I was expecting you at that age.' She shook her head. 'Lord, it seems such a long time ago. Marry in haste, repent at leisure, they say. I hope you do better'n I did.'

Head slanted to one side, Siana gazed dreamy-eyed at the rolling green hills stretching off towards the coast. They lived a mile away from the village of Cheverton Chase, situated inland, five miles from both Wareham and the bustling harbour town of Poole. When the wind was strong you sometimes caught the pungent odour of salt and seaweed in the air.

'One day I'd like to wed a man who treats me nice. I'd like to have a dress covered in flowers to wear to church on Sundays and a room specially for sitting in. A house with an extra bedroom and a pump in the yard would be lovely, too.'

Putting her hand on her hip, Siana paraded up and down, her chin in the air. 'I'll send you an invitation to take tea with me.'

Megan laughed. 'I'll be Mrs Gentry coming to call in these old rags. Look you, girl, this shawl belonged to my mother, and I swear this skirt was the one I was wearing when I was marched out of the village all those years ago.'

'One day I'll buy you another,' Siana said fiercely.

Her mother smiled at the thought. 'Well, I don't see why you shouldn't have all them things. You have the looks and the wit, and you speak like a little lady since you've been going up to the rectory.' She shook her head in warning. 'Just remember to keep your hand on your ha'penny, my love. A man respects a maid who says no to him. Proper gents like their women to be untouched on the wedding night. The other type they keep for their sport.'

'I'll remember, Ma.'

'And be careful that Tom doesn't get the chance to force himself on to you. I've seen the dirty beggar watching you. I thought marriage would have cured him of his itch, but it hasn't. He's like his father in that way.'

Siana bit her bottom lip as she remembered her stepbrother's threat when he'd cornered her the week before. He'd given her a painful squeeze. 'One of these days I'm going to have a taste of this little pie you've got under your skirt. Just see if I don't.'

'If he got the notion into his head, I don't know if I'd have the strength to fight him off.'

'It's not his head you have to worry about, and he'd be counting on you putting up a fight. But there's one little trick you can use if you have to,' and Megan leaned forward to whisper something in her ear.

Siana grinned. 'It's a pity you didn't do that to his father.'

The light went from her mother's eyes as she said dully, 'We're married; he has the right to me.'

'Why did you wed him, Ma?'

Megan's eyes filled with memories. 'It was winter. I was on my way to sign in at the poorhouse when you decided to be born. The only shelter I could find was a cow byre, and thank God I didn't have to share it with the cows for they'd long been slaughtered. He heard you crying and found us there, nigh on frozen to death. Took us in, Bill Skinner did, and gave you his name. Turned out he needed a mother for his young uns. We needed a home, so I stayed.'

'Did you love him when you married him?'

Megan's mouth pursed, then she gave a bit of a smile. 'He was a bonny-looking man then, all right. One thing led to another and before I knew it I was pregnant and the banns were being called. I don't know whether it were love or not but it were a mighty powerful feeling.' Her hands covered her stomach. 'Been pregnant ever since, with only our Josh and Daisy and nine dead uns to show for it. Yonder cemetery is full of little Skinners. Unhallowed ground, mind. They didn't survive long enough to be christened.'

'Perhaps this one will live,' Siana said gently.

Megan shrugged. 'Perhaps. I remember Bill had to

get permission from a magistrate to wed because of my age. Told them I was an orphan, he did.'

'And were you?'

'Might as well have been with all those blood relatives in Wales casting me out of the village. Pious in their praying, no charity in their hearts, that lot. There's a name for such as them.'

'Hypocrites?' Siana suggested.

Megan's work-worn hand caressed her daughter's face. 'There's clever with words, you are, *cariad*. You must get that from your father's side.'

'What was my father like, Ma?'

Megan's face tightened. 'He was a rapist and a sinner, for he took from me by force. Said I tempted him with my pagan ways. The village women were worse. Except for my grandmother, the witches didn't believe me. Those with daughters to marry off had their eye on him, see. Couldn't have done them any good though, for your grandmother Lewis cursed him afterwards. The women cut off my hair, spat on me and cast me out for something not my fault.'

'Did Bill Skinner know who he was?'

'Bill never asked.' She shrugged. 'He was a different man then. He picked you up as gentle as if you were a lamb, sets you in my arms and says, "You and the infant'll be all right now, missy."' A faint smile touched her face. 'Poverty drags you down, though. He took to the drink and turned violent. But men can be fools when they take the fancy for you. If you can get one with means all the better. Who wants to be miserable in poverty when you can do the same in comfort? If I'd known what was ahead then, I would have kept on walking.'

Her mother suddenly looked tired and gaunt, older than her thirty-six years. Her hair was dull and stringy, its raven darkness threaded through with pewter. Her eyes had lost their youthful gloss, but were as dark and green as the pine trees in the forest.

Siana was glad she'd inherited her ma's looks. Megan Skinner still possessed the remnants of a wild beauty, but the never-ending cycle of drunken beatings and pregnancies had robbed her of her strength and vitality.

Thank God Josh and their babby sister, Daisy, had survived.

Daisy was crawling in the long grass, stalked by two kittens and giggling every time they pounced on her. Siana marked her sister's position, in case she tired of the game and fell asleep. Daisy was a placid, easily amused child. Siana adored every inch of her flaxen-haired little sister, and Josh was a lovable, but cheeky scamp.

Gazing at her mother's swollen stomach and her puffed-up ankles, Siana experienced a moment of unease. Although today seemed to be one of her good days, her mother had been lethargic and ill for most of this pregnancy. She ran out of breath quickly, and was carrying the child low, so her back pained her all the time. Siana wondered if she'd survive this birth.

'Go and put your feet up, Ma. I'll finish off the wash and mind our Daisy until it's time to help out at the rectory.'

10

It was a secret between them, her job at the rectory. Half of the money she earned was handed over to her mother for food, the other half was saved for her by the rector himself.

Then there were the reading lessons, and the books she was allowed to borrow from Reverend White's library – books she kept hidden in a secret place and read when she could get away from the battle of everyday survival. She memorized the information and stories she read so she could tell them to Josh, swearing him to secrecy in case her stepfather found out and put a stop to it.

'You're a good girl, Siana.' Her mother came over to where she stood and unpinned a little cloth pouch from inside her skirt. 'I've got something for you, a silver cross which once belonged to your great-grandmother Lewis. She had the sight. "You will go forth into misery, but the man who caused it will be cursed," she told me. "Good will come out of bad. You'll give birth to a daughter blessed by the gods. The child will have troubles to face, but the sight will be strong in her. Her pagan heart will beat a rhythm with the soul of the earth and it will bring her much happiness."'

Siana smiled for she'd heard the prophecy many times and, as a result, had always felt a strange kinship with her great-grandmother. She had not known about the cross, though.

'I named you for her and have been keeping the talisman safe all these years. Keep it hid, else your stepfather will have it off you and will sell it for what the silver will bring.'

As Siana looked at the celtic cross shining in her

palm she felt that sense of connection with her unknown ancestor. Her hand closed over the object and she shut her eyes for a few moments, seeking something more solid for her mind to grasp. She found something the opposite of solid , but satisfying, all the same.

'*Siana . . . Siana . . . Siana.*'

The name seemed to come whispering through the grass and was strangely comforting. She turned her face to the growing warmth of the sun, to the slightest kiss of dew against her cheek. When she opened her eyes again, she found the day clothed in a golden light. The grass bowed before the breeze, the long slender stalks were resilient, their ears fire-tipped, as if an army marched through the field holding flaming arrows aloft.

Her stepfather's trousers bulged fatly with air and flapped about, so they looked as if they might leap off the line and dance. She felt light, reassured, as though someone had taken her under their protection.

She gazed at her mother, saying with a sense of wonder, 'I think I felt my great-grandmother near.'

Daisy, suddenly discovering herself lost in the forest of whispering, waving stalks, let out a howl of distress.

Siana turned towards her then back to her mother, her eyes appealing to her, for there was something a little frightening about what she'd experienced. 'Did you hear her call too?'

Megan gave a faint smile, not bothering to pretend her daughter referred to Daisy. 'What you felt is inherited from her, Siana mine. She believed we were descended from the marcher lords, and they had a mighty powerful way with them.'

12

'And are we?'

Their eyes met in complete understanding. 'So they say, but the knowing of it is one thing, the proving another.' A kiss landed on her cheek. 'Tell no one of it, for what people cannot understand they try to destroy.' When Daisy began to grizzle, Megan said practically, 'Fetch our Daisy here for a cuddle. I'll give her the last of the milk and she'll settle down for a nap whilst you go about your business.'

'You'll be all right on your own, Ma?'

'I'll be all right. The babby isn't due for a month.'

Siana watched her mother go into the house before she turned back to the washing tub.

When she checked later, she found her mother asleep, Daisy snuggled against her chest, her thumb in her mouth. It was easy to sleep when hunger drained the energy from you.

2

The rectory was a good two miles from where Siana lived, on the other side of the village of Cheverton Chase.

Siana's long legs carried her rapidly over the hill and onto the path leading through the woods. The woods and everything in them belonged to the squire. On the left edge was Croxley Farm, tenanted by her step-brother. Further on was the labourers' cottage lived in by his sister. Having grown up tormented by the pair's bullying ways, Siana despised Hannah and feared Tom.

Except for the wind soughing in the branches above her head, it was quiet and peaceful when the shade of the trees enclosed her. She took a careful look around in case either of them was lying in wait for her. Standing quite still for a moment, she listened to the birds and the wind. As she absorbed the earthy odour of dampness into her body, she sensed someone watching her.

Her eyes snapped open in alarm, to discover a squirrel poised for flight on a fallen tree. The creature took her breath away with its polished red coat, bright eyes and bushy tail. For a moment they stared at each other, then she laughed with the sheer joy of the discovery of it. Chattering in alarm, it spiralled up a tree and scolded her soundly from the safety of a branch.

'Don't worry. However hungry we get, I'd never let you end up in the cooking pot,' she whispered, smiling at its nonsense. 'Just be careful you don't come across Tom for he'd kill you for the fun of it.'

Beneath her feet, the roots of trees were entwined fingers of mossy greenness. She avoided the boggy patches. Although her boots were stout, they were old army boots passed down through the family. They would have to do Josh a turn after her, so she was careful not to slip or get too much muck on them, which would crack the leather even more.

The rectory was a short way past the church. It was a small church, built from local stone, the square Norman tower dwarfed by yew trees. The church had been built by the Forbes family two centuries earlier, and was carefully distanced from Cheverton Manor so the bells wouldn't prove disruptive to the landowner.

The village itself consisted of a muddy, narrow lane flanked by low cottages. Most of the dwellings had a sty housing a pig or two, or some chickens scratching in the dirt. There was a handpump for water set in the middle of the lane. A perpetual and unhealthy stench permeated the village. It attracted flies, which swarmed over the children in summer. Cramped as the Skinner family was, Siana was glad she didn't live in the village.

Up by the quiet woods the world seemed far away, her troubles few.

When she reached the rectory, she straightened her

hair, then knocked at the back door and waited to be admitted into the kitchen.

Siana smiled at Mrs Leeman as she slipped her arms through the white apron the woman held out for her. She liked coming to the rectory. The house had an upstairs with five big bedrooms, and the downstairs had a drawing room, a library and a dining room as well as the big kitchen.

Her ma wouldn't know what to do with such grandness, she thought. Their whole cottage could be swallowed up by the drawing room with spare lengths around the edges for a garden, even though the Skinners' was a bigger cottage than those in the village proper.

She had come by the job quite by chance. Drawn by the woman's cries for help, she had come across the reverend's housekeeper in the woods. Mrs Leeman had been gathering blackberries and had tripped over a root and badly wrenched her ankle.

Siana had supported her, carrying her home on her back. Then, because the woman was upset and in pain, she had completed Mrs Leeman's tasks for the day before fetching her employer from the church. After a whispered conversation between them, she'd been offered some work until Mrs Leeman recovered. When the woman had, Siana was given a permanent few hours' work a week.

There was an unexpected bonus. A few weeks later, she'd been discovered laboriously spelling out the words of a book in the library when she should have been dusting. Far from being annoyed, the Reverend Richard White had offered to teach her to read. That had been over six months ago and Siana was making good progress, although she lived in dread of her stepfather finding out she was working. One day he was bound to.

It was Siana's job to iron all the linen, using heavy, black smoothing irons which were heated on the range top. She was careful not to burn herself, or the linen, and kept the edges straight and neat and the folds sharp, as the housekeeper had taught her.

Mrs Leeman smiled kindly at her. 'The reverend said he'll have time to listen to you read after you finish your work.'

Siana's heart leapt as she eagerly went about her tasks. After the ironing, there was the silver to clean. She polished the little cross her mother had given her as well, admiring it before securing it back inside her skirt. Who would have thought she'd ever own anything so precious and pretty?

After the silver it was the turn of the heavy furniture, brought to a deep glow by an application of beeswax. When it was polished, it seemed as if she'd lit a fire inside the wood for its ruby depths seemed to contain leaping flames. The house smelled lovely as she polished the curving hand rail of the staircase.

Mrs Leeman was baking. Delicious smells wafted through the house, setting Siana's stomach rumbling. She hadn't eaten since the night before, and her supper would consist of thin potato soup with cabbage and, if she was lucky, a dumpling floating in it. The last of the mutton would go to her stepfather.

She sat back on her heels, admiring her handiwork and indulging in her favourite daydream. One day she'd live in a house like this, with pretty ornaments on the mantelpiece, lace curtains at the windows and food in the larder. Her daughters would never go hungry, and would go to school like proper little misses in white cotton pinafores over muslin dresses. On Sundays they'd wear ribbon-trimmed straw bonnets to church.

She jumped when somebody gently coughed behind her. Rising, she curtsied to the reverend, keeping her eyes lowered out of respect and staring at his black, polished shoes. 'Good day to you, sir.'

'Good morning, Siana. Join me in my study in ten minutes and we'll see how your reading has progressed.'

The reverend was a kindly looking, short man with pale cheeks. Middle-aged, he wore round glasses which gradually slipped to the end of his nose as he bent his head. He never thought her questions foolish, but answered them with patience, afterwards asking her if she understood, and explaining again if she didn't.

The lesson progressed smoothly, she read a passage from the King James bible with hardly a hesitation, before solving some sums he'd set down on a piece of paper. 'Good, you've grasped the concept of fractions,' he murmured before enquiring, 'How is your mother keeping, Siana?'

'She's very tired, sir. Carrying this babby has fair knocked the wind out of her.'

'Baby.'

'Sorry, sir. Baby then.' She smiled; correcting her pronunciation had become a habit with him.

Mrs Leeman knocked at the door. 'Master Daniel has arrived, sir. I've shown him to his room.'

18

'Thank you, Mrs Leeman. Ask him to join us when he's ready, then bring us some refreshment.'

Mrs Leeman looked uncertainly from one to the other. 'All of you?'

'That's right, Mrs Leeman. I've decided to invite my favourite pupil for tea today.'

Mrs Leeman bobbed a curtsy and gave him a faint smile. 'I'll make sure there's plenty of bread and butter on the plate then.'

'Cake, Mrs Leeman, we shall have cake. I'm sure this young lady would enjoy a slice, wouldn't you, Siana?'

'I don't rightly know, sir. I've never eaten cake before.'

'Then you have a treat in store.'

Had Richard known, it would have been equally a treat for Siana to eat bread baked from milled wheat and spread with butter.

Siana had natural grace, Richard White thought as Daniel Ayres was introduced. If she was shocked by meeting the lad she gave no indication. In fact, she gave every indication she was unaware of the connection between them when she bobbed a swift curtsy.

As for Daniel, he smiled ironically at the gesture and lifted her hand to his lips, not in the least disconcerted by her ragged gown. 'I'm delighted to meet a *relative-by-marriage* to my mother.' The distasteful emphasis was marked.

She gazed blankly at him for a moment, then spots of colour rose to her cheeks as she noted the ironic inflection of his words. In an almost hostile voice she hastened to inform him. 'Tom Skinner is not my brother; he's my stepbrother.'

'My pardon.' The pair joined glances in a moment of mutual understanding, then Siana withdrew her hand. She stood awkwardly for a moment or two whilst Daniel gazed questioningly at her.

Richard drew her attention with a gentle cough and indicated the chair with a nod of his head. Realizing manners dictated she be seated first, she scrambled to comply, appearing slightly flustered as she folded her hands in her lap.

'Perhaps you'd pour the tea, Siana. Find a seat, Daniel; you've grown so large, you're blocking the light from the window. How are your studies progressing?'

Daniel looked slightly put out. 'I've reached the levels required, and have been assigned to a local attorney to acquire practical experience, as my father arranged. I should like to travel abroad before I practise at the bar, though.'

The elaborate silver teapot in Siana's hand hovered in mid-air. 'How wonderful, Mr Ayres. Which countries will you visit?'

Daniel shrugged. 'Oh, Italy and Greece, I suppose,' he said carelessly.

Her eyes began to shine as she said rather formally, 'I should like to visit Rome and see for myself the artistic works of Michelangelo.'

Daniel's mouth dropped open for a moment, then his chin assumed a slightly superior tilt. 'I daresay you would. Do you have a particular favourite?'

Her forehead creased in thought. 'How can I have a

favourite when I've only seen drawings of them? Reverend White says *The Heroic Captive* is very fine, but I'd like to see the *Pietà*.' She applied herself once more to her task, handing them each a plate, then offering round a tray containing the neat slices of cake Mrs Leeman had sent in, adding unnecessarily, 'I've been reading a book about Michelangelo. It's very interesting.'

The reverend smiled at that. So did Daniel. He nodded when Daniel responded to her with a snippet of information about Michelangelo. Before too long Daniel dropped his patronizing tone and Siana her shyness, and there was an interesting conversation generated on the subject.

After her awkward start there was no false pride about Siana. Anything she didn't know she asked about, storing every detail in her remarkable memory. The three of them passed a pleasant and relaxed hour, chatting and laughing together.

When the clock chimed, Siana's eyes widened and consternation filled them. 'I must get home to help my ma . . . mother.'

Daniel rose. 'I'd like to talk some more. Allow me to escort you home.'

She gazed at the cake she'd forgotten to eat and sighed, saying straightforwardly, 'Thank you, but it would be better if you didn't. Someone might see us and tell my stepfather.'

'Would that matter very much?' Daniel quizzed.

She nodded and turned away from the young man. Her eyes engaged her employer's. 'Do you know anything about the marcher lords, sir?'

Surprise filled Richard. Where had she learned of such ancient people? 'They were staunch patriots and fierce defenders of the Welsh border. They were very powerful lords indeed. I have a book on the subject somewhere. If you'd like to wait a moment, I'll find it for you.'

'I have to finish the one on Michelangelo first. Perhaps next week?'

He wanted to grin at her earnest expression. 'May one ask why you want to learn about the marcher lords?'

She gave an awkward little shrug that was altogether charming. 'My mother mentioned them, that's all. She believes we're descended from them.'

He recalled that her mother was Welsh-born. For a long time after she'd arrived in the district there had been whispers that Megan Lewis worshipped the old gods. But what those old gods were, nobody seemed to know when questioned, and Richard himself had seen no signs of paganism in her. She attended church, seemed sincere when she prayed and was respectful towards him.

'Until next time then.' He saw Siana glance again at the uneaten cake and knew she would be too proud to ask for it, however hungry she was. He placed a couple of slices in a napkin and handed it to her. 'I can't let you go without tasting the cake. Take home a slice for your mother, as well. I'm sure she will enjoy it.'

Her smile was that of a happy child as she left, carefully carrying the small parcel.

'What do you make of her, Daniel?' he asked when the door closed behind her.

'The girl's surprising when you get to know her,' he

said thoughtfully. 'She's quick-minded as well as a beauty. It's a wonder she hasn't been married off to some peasant to breed his brats. How old is she?'

'Seventeen, I believe. I was thinking of offering her a position.'

'As a maid?'

'She's already that. As my clerk to start with. She's good with her letters and figures and has a quick, enquiring mind. I could train her, so eventually she could teach at the parish school or take up an appointment as a governess. As her employer I would be given the opportunity to have some say in her future. I think she deserves to be offered more from life than would otherwise be available to girls of her class.'

'Can it be you're intrigued by her supposed connection to the marcher lords?'

Richard gave a faint smile. 'I have only just heard of it. That she's a lost princess is a little far-fetched, and the claim would not be provable after the passing of so many generations. However, if the thought gives her some sense of self-worth I'd be the first to encourage it.'

Daniel laughed. 'Always the philanthropist, sir. But my father might have something to say about you hiring a girl for the job. He might also question the morality of such an undertaking.'

'I cannot see how when the girl wouldn't reside here. After all, nobody questions my relationship with Mrs Leeman.'

'Who is old enough to be your mother.'

'And I'm old enough to be Siana's father. Perhaps I'd see fit to remind my esteemed cousin about his lack of taste in the man he chose to wed your mother. Tom Skinner is an oaf.'

'We both know he was chosen for his broad back and farming knowledge rather than any sensibilities he may possess. The marriage was forced on my mother in a fit of pique.'

'You're nearly twenty-one, Daniel. The understanding between Sir Edward and your mother was terminated a year ago. Your father has educated and supported you, and will continue doing so until you are able to earn a decent living for yourself. The farm could have been yours too, but since you chose not to accept it he was compelled to make the best arrangement he could for the working of it. And may I remind you, Elizabeth was not obliged to accept the man as a husband.'

'What else could she do? My father had ruined her reputation. She had very few means of her own for support and nowhere else to go.' He shrugged. 'My father knew I wasn't cut out to be a farmer. If he'd waited a year or so, I'd have been able to look after her myself. Or he could have married her himself. He owed her that after leading her to expect it for all those years.'

And you expected to be made his heir, Richard thought, knowing exactly how much Daniel's illegitimacy rankled in his mind. As far as Richard was concerned, Elizabeth Skinner had ruined her own reputation. She had entered into a sinful relationship of her own free will, knowing the man was already wed to another.

When Edward Forbes had become a widower, Elizabeth's expectations of marriage had been disappointed. Although he liked Daniel's mother, Richard considered it was perfectly reasonable for Squire Forbes to select a partner who was morally sound as well as young and healthy. He tried to get this through to Daniel without causing offence.

'The barren state of his marriage to his late wife troubled him greatly. He needs to wed suitably and produce an heir before it's too late.' Richard threw a friendly arm around the young man's shoulder as they headed towards the door. 'You mustn't become bitter, Daniel. The fact that Sir Edward has provided for you all these years clearly demonstrates he has your welfare at heart.'

Daniel's soft brown eyes hardened. 'As you say, sir, but your own good self is more father to me than he is. For your efforts you have not only my gratitude, but my undying affection.'

Daniel's words pleased Richard, for he had no children of his own. 'Good luck then, Daniel. As I am your cousin once removed, as well as being your godfather, you must allow me to help out in any way I can.'

Daniel grinned. 'For a start, you can ask me to tea again with your little clerk.'

'Intriguing, isn't she?' Richard remarked absently, for his mind was already formulating his Sunday sermon. 'If you come to church on Sunday, no doubt you'll see the child there, for your father insists that his workers and their families attend without fail.'

Child? Daniel chuckled as he walked away. If his godfather thought Siana resembled a child, his eyesight was surely fading.

3

Elizabeth Skinner, mother of Daniel, former mistress of Edward Forbes and wife to Tom Skinner, gazed at her sister-in-law and hoped her dislike didn't show in her expression.

She wished Hannah would go home. The less she had to do with the Skinners, the better she'd like it.

The dislike was mutual. Elizabeth's beauty made Hannah feel ugly and awkward. Elizabeth's skin was pale and unblemished, her eyes were like bluebells and her hair shone like the fur of a fox in the sunlight.

Hannah didn't recognize her feelings as part of the envy endemic to her nature. If her brother hadn't insisted she visit Elizabeth and report back every little thing the woman said and did, she wouldn't bother coming.

Sucking at her tea she swallowed noisily, smacking her lips in satisfaction and staring at her sister-in-law in silence. Feeling inadequate, Hannah didn't know quite what to say to her. Then her eyes darted to Elizabeth's arms and she smirked. 'Our Tom be right handy with his fists. You should put some witch hazel on them bruises. They'll heal quicker.'

26

Elizabeth didn't want them to heal. She wanted everyone in the district, especially Edward Forbes, to know what a bully Tom Skinner was.

Edward had lied to her when he'd promised her respectability. All those years she'd made herself available to him, whilst his wife fought a losing battle with the madness to which she'd finally succumbed. She'd had respectability in abundance until she'd met him and fallen in love. Elizabeth had borne Edward a fine son in that time, and never in her wildest dreams had she imagined that he'd evict her from the Dorchester house and marry her off to a crude peasant. The other alternative had been the whorehouse.

'That boy of yours thinks he's too good to dirty his hands by being a farmer,' Edward had said to her. 'He gets his grand ideas from you, Elizabeth. Croxley Farm must be worked and Daniel could have had the deeds. He insulted me. Refused them, by God! Now I'll only offer you a roof over your head for life and a strong man to work the farm in exchange for his education. Take it or leave it. You get nothing more from me.'

And to think she'd loved Edward Forbes. Elizabeth, the only daughter of a parson, had been employed as a teacher in a charity school when she'd first met the squire. He'd been so dashing, quickly stealing her heart, her maidenhood and her reputation. As a result, her family had disowned her.

Now, over twenty years later, Edward had discarded her too, his promise of undying love being empty. She'd married Tom Skinner because nobody would employ her. One day, she would accumulate the means to leave him – if she didn't kill him first! The only thing stopping her was the fact that Tom Skinner wasn't worth hanging for.

When Hannah cracked her empty cup back onto the saucer, Elizabeth winced. It was made of the finest Staffordshire bone china. She should have used something of lesser value, but some part of her refused to reduce herself to Hannah's level and she gained a perverse pleasure from watching the woman struggle with the basic niceties.

Sometimes she hated herself for feeling that way, telling herself that Hannah was only a product of her background. It was Edward Forbes who reaped the benefit from keeping these people poor and uneducated.

'A haystack were fired the other night,' Hannah said with an almost avid importance. 'Our Tom were over Winterborne way at the inn, and caught the man. Will Hastings it were . . . him from the bottom end of the village. Squire was right pleased with Tom for catching him, I can tell you.' She sniggered. 'Will said it wasn't him what done it. Said he'd been over to Winterborne to visit his mother. Said it were already burning when he went over to investigate.'

'Perhaps it was?'

'Well, he would say that, wouldn't he? Tom told the squire he saw Will light it from his lantern.'

Elizabeth's blue eyes narrowed in thought. So that's why Tom had smelled of smoke when he'd arrived home that night, and with coins jiggling in his pocket. Her memory provided her with an image of Will Hastings, a rather thin, but pleasant young man who'd just married and whose wife was expecting an infant. She couldn't imagine him doing something so criminal.

''Tis quite likely the squire will have Will hanged as an example.'

Elizabeth gasped. Surely Edward would not be so cruel, but deep down she knew he was. It was not wise to cross him too often. 'Will's only a young man. Who will look after his wife and child?'

'She'll go into the workhouse, like as not.' Hannah's mouth twisted into a sneer. 'That flirty-eyed cat were walking out with our Tom long before Will moved into the district. No doubt she'll live to rue turning him down.' Her glance touched on Elizabeth's bruises and her smile was malicious as she inadvertently provided Elizabeth with the motive for the accusation. 'Anyone who crosses our Tom does so at their peril.'

A shudder racked Elizabeth's body and she closed her eyes for a moment. Tom had taken a stick to her last night, then forced intimacy on her. Fortunately, he'd had too much drink in him to sustain the assault, eventually pushing her aside with a muffled curse and rolling across the bed to snore like the pig he was.

She remembered being sickened by his rank odour and staring down at his naked body, perspiring from his efforts but awesomely powerful and well muscled, and thinking: All I need do is fetch the carving knife from the kitchen drawer and drive it into his heart. Would that she'd had the courage.

Hannah was making preparations to go. Elizabeth noticed that the silver teaspoon had disappeared from her saucer. It had probably been slipped into Hannah's pocket, and would end up in the pawnbroker's shop on the next market day.

Thank God she'd had the sense to hide the jewellery Edward had given her over the years. Not that it amounted to much in the way of financial value. They were trinkets containing semi-precious stones, but set in gold or silver all the same.

There was also a small stash of coins put by, for Edward had always insisted she look her best for his visits and although her allowance hadn't been generous, it had been reasonable and he'd never asked for an accounting.

Prudently, she'd drawn all of her allowance each month, saving any excess in a bank account she'd opened in Poole. It had accumulated into a useful sum. The biggest blow had been losing the house in Dorchester – a house which had been her home for over twenty years and which now stood empty by all accounts. When she'd finally agreed to marry Tom, Edward had given them a sum of cash as a wedding present. Her dowry had kept Tom in drink for a month, she thought bitterly.

If Tom ever found out about her secret hoard he would thrash her. But he never would. Apart from herself, only Daniel knew where she kept it hidden.

The chair scraped across the floor when Hannah stood up, her hands easing her back. She was a tall, large-boned woman with dirty straw-coloured hair and blue eyes. The infant she carried was concealed by the folds of fat about her waist.

'Our Tom said you had an old skirt I could cut up to make clothes for the babby.'

He must mean the garment he'd ripped from her body last night, Elizabeth thought, a delicate cotton gown with puffed sleeves and a scalloped and embroidered collar and hem.

'You fancies yourself to be a real lady in this, don't yer?' he'd spat in her face. 'But you're a whore underneath, same as all the other whores. You opens your legs to any man who pays yer enough. Well, just remember, you're mine to do what I likes to, when I likes and if I likes.'

Even if the gown could be repaired, Elizabeth knew she'd never wear it again now he'd defiled it.

She fetched it from the bedroom and, bundling it up, thrust it into Hannah's arms. Hannah's work-worn finger stroked the delicate material for a moment. Her expression was almost wistful. 'It must be nice to afford such things.'

She wouldn't be able to afford any more after the ones she already owned fell to pieces. 'You're not too old to bear a child yourself. Could be you'll give our Tom a babby soon, then he won't be so hard on you. He'd be right proud to have a son of his own.'

Elizabeth shrugged, saying more bitterly than she'd intended, 'I'd rather die than give birth to a child of his.'

A wave of animosity filled the room. 'If my brother be good enough to take on another man's leavings, he be good enough to father a brat of your'n. If I know our Tom, he'll keep at you until he puts one inside you. Just you be careful he don't get himself one by another woman and turn you out, Mrs Hoity-toity.'

'As far as I'm concerned, he can get himself one by lying in a sty with a sow,' Elizabeth hissed. 'I have ways and means to prevent such mishaps.' She had been taking her own precautions to avoid pregnancy, making sure that anything Tom Skinner tried to plant inside her didn't take root.

When the door slammed behind her sister-in-law, she sighed with relief.

'I didn't think she'd ever leave,' Daniel said from behind her.

She turned, smiling ruefully at the sight of her son, who'd left the warmth of the kitchen to conceal himself in the parlour when Hannah had approached the farmhouse.

'Neither did I. I'll be glad when she has her infant to keep her occupied. The less I see of the Skinners, the better I'll like it.'

A smile slid across Daniel's face. 'I met her stepsister yesterday—'

She kissed him. 'If you dare mention the name of another of that family, I'll slap you. As far as I'm concerned, they're all vermin.'

'This one only became one of them through marriage. She's seventeen, has eyes the colour of pine needles and hair as dark as midnight. Her name is Siana. The reverend said her family name is Lewis, and it's possible she's descended from the marcher lords.'

'Half of Wales claims descent from the marcher lords.' Noting the expression on his face, Elizabeth frowned. 'Where did you meet this girl, Daniel?'

'At my godfather's house. She works there as a skivvy and he's teaching her. She's such an amazing girl, so quick-minded. Richard said that although she'd only

32

learned some basic letters at her mother's knee, she was able to read fluently in four months. Imagine . . . she's reading a book on Michelangelo at the moment.'

'Imagine,' Elizabeth said drily. 'I wager the girl has good looks in abundance as well as being clever. You must be careful of your nature, Daniel. You're swayed too easily by a pretty face.'

His eyes took on a reproachful look. 'You'd like her, Mother, really. She maintains a conversation well and has a thirst for knowledge. The reverend is going to offer her a job as his clerk, I believe. He thinks she could be helped out of the circle of poverty the estate workers fall into, and learn enough to better herself.'

Elizabeth's heart sank. With his dark brooding looks and trusting brown eyes, her son had always attracted women. But she'd never seen him so taken by one, and this Siana creature had certainly made a strong impression on him. She knew that one day he'd marry, but she hoped he wasn't going to ruin his chances in life by bedding some ignorant little peasant girl who was out to use *him* to better herself.

Then she realized she was being unfair in her bitterness, by judging the girl before she'd met her. 'You sound as though you have some regard for her,' she said lightly.

Amazement flitted across his face, and then he grinned. 'Good Lord, do I? What a strange notion.'

'Don't forget we intend to set up house together. You cannot impose on your godfather's generosity for ever.'

'I must stay with the reverend until I've established myself as a lawyer, for I'm not welcome to stay here. Besides which, he's a useful man to know.'

33

'Which reminds me, Daniel . . .' and she told him about Will Hastings's arrest, relaying her fears that there might be spite involved in the accusation. 'Perhaps you could ask Richard White to investigate and plead with your father on Will's behalf.'

'I can try, but the landowners are sick to death of the constant rebellion.'

'What can they expect when men are forced to labour from dawn till dusk for a nine-shilling pittance, especially when they have wives and children to feed?'

Daniel looked at her with some surprise. 'Since when did you take up the cause of the poor?'

'Since I joined them,' she said bitterly. 'There's nothing like living with one of the lower classes to excuse the results of poverty. Do you think they smell because they're dirty? No, it's because they can't afford soap to wash with. Have you seen the open gutters in the village? They stink because the cesspits and pig-pens overflow and leak into them. Edward doesn't bother to maintain the cottages. When it rains, water seeps into the dwellings and takes the waste with it. Children are dying of starvation, of disease and neglect. Take a look at the faces of the women and children. They're too tired to cry and their eyes are dull with despair. Can you wonder if the men rebel?'

Daniel shrugged. 'I can understand only too well, but I've chosen the law as a profession, so I cannot condone lawlessness. Neither of us is in a position to help them, but I'll ask Richard to put in a word for Will.'

Neither of them had heard Tom approach, and Elizabeth wondered how much he'd overheard when he sneered from the doorway, 'Won't do him no good. Will were taken before the local magistrate this morning. He was committed to the assizes, tried to escape and was shot to death.'

Elizabeth's cry of distress went unnoticed while Daniel demanded to know, 'Who defended him?'

'Don't know nuthin about that, not being learned like you, and all. Squire brought the charges, though. Reckon that were enough to convict him without me having to be there.' Tom hooked his foot around a chair, dragging it towards him. Clods of mud from his boots scattered the floor. He straddled the seat and folded his beefy arms along the back rest, gazing at Daniel with unblinking dislike. 'Might have got away with transportation if he hadn't proved himself guilty by trying to run.'

Daniel stared defiantly back at him. 'It was only his word against yours.'

'Are you calling me a liar then, boy?'

'You wouldn't have needed to ask if I was.'

Elizabeth's hand went to her mouth. Although he was standing his ground, Daniel was nowhere near a match for Tom and she feared for him. Her husband's physical power was backed up with a rat-like cunning.

Tom's mouth stretched in a grin as he took out his knife and ran his thumb along the edge. 'You want to watch your lip, or someone might cut off your tongue.'

'Not if you want to keep this farm. It belongs to my father.'

'Your papa won't stop me. I knows too much about his dirty little schemes.'

Elizabeth gave a low moan.

'Shuddup and fetch me something to eat, woman.'

As Elizabeth scurried to do Tom's bidding, Daniel frowned. 'I'd prefer it if you treated my mother with a little more respect.'

'Would you now?' Tom nodded. 'I can see that, you being the whore's only bastard, and all. Got ideas above your station, you two have. I was talking to the squire just now. Sir, I sez, that by-blow of your'n needs a good thump around the ear, if you asks me. Guess what he sez?'

'Mind your own damned business?'

'Hah bloody hah. No. He looks down that great nose of his all haughty like. "As you're his stepfather I'll expect you to provide him with one, Skinner," sez he.'

Without further warning, Tom's hand lashed out, sending Daniel crashing back into the door.

Startled, Elizabeth screamed.

'I thought I told you to shuddup, woman. Fetch me something to eat. As for you, boy, you git outta here before I loses me temper with you.'

'Go,' Elizabeth urged when Daniel hesitated, 'I'll be all right.'

'Course you will, princess, just as long as you does what you're told.'

When the door closed behind Daniel, Tom turned to gaze at her. 'I ran into Hannah on the way. She tells me you're too proud to carry a son of mine, that you said I should lay with a sow in a sty if I want one.'

Elizabeth said nothing, just slammed a plate containing raw onion, a wedge of cheese and a loaf of crusty bread in front of him. His teeth sank into the onion, sending juice trickling down his chin. It was unnerving the way he watched her, his eyes unblinking as he crammed in cheese and bread, then washed it down with gulps of ale.

He belched, then stood up and stretched, his muscles bulging. As she turned to clear the table, his hand closed around her neck and he shoved her towards the door.

'A sow, is it?' he muttered, and pulled her back against him, shoving his pelvis hard against her buttocks so she could feel his gross arousal. His other arm came round her, his fingers kneading and pinching. 'A sow's got better than these little teats.'

Suddenly it dawned on her what he was about to do. Sickened by his crudeness she began to struggle as he half-pushed, half-dragged her towards the sty. The pigs hunched into a corner and squealed nervously when he dragged her inside.

Throwing her face-down across the trough, he dropped his trousers, laughed and, dragging her skirt up to her waist, proceeded to finish the act he'd started the night before. Every thrust brought a grunt from him, and every grunt a gust of onion breath, so she felt nauseated as well as violated. By the time he gave his final grunt, she felt completely humiliated. Dragging her upright, he grinned at her and said, 'By Christ, you're a skinny-arsed sow.' Then he threw her face-down again, leaving her bruised and sore, retching into the stinking mud as he strode off.

The chores finished, and with Daisy supported on her back in a shawl, Siana strode across one of the many hills of the Purbecks. She had come further than she intended, at least two miles, and was on a rise not far from the sea. To her left, the rocks named Old Harry were visible. Just within range of her vision, and to her right, was Corfe Castle, where King Edward the martyr had been murdered. The Roundheads had later reduced it to ruins whilst fighting the royalists.

Between the two hills were some ridges, where the remains of a Roman wall offered shelter from the wind. There, she set the burden of her sister down to play. She'd been told the ridges and tumbled stones in the area were part of the defences built by the Romans when they'd conquered Britain.

Here, perhaps, the soldiers had lived together, talking of wives and children left behind. Some would have died here, never to see their families again. Their bodies would have nourished the tough heathland grasses until their bones had become one with the chalky hills.

The day was warm and Siana would have liked to idle for an hour or so, but she didn't have time. Time enough perhaps to escape for a short while into a book. She could read the remaining chapter or two whilst she rested before heading back.

Carefully she removed a book from inside her bodice. Within seconds, she was absorbed in the pages.

Daniel came across her there. He was out walking the hills as he often did. The sea glittered silver, the light stretching into a glaring horizon where a bank of purple-edged clouds was piling up. There would be a storm before morning. Although summer had lingered, the wind over the water cooled the body and Daniel was seeking shelter, a place where he could sit and think.

A child's giggle drew his attention as he topped the ridge. Below him in the hollow, Siana sat, her back against a boulder, her glance firmly on the pages of a book resting on her knees.

The child was a pale, thin little thing, her laughter a delightful sound as her hand tried to close around a butterfly dancing over the golden dandelion heads. He experienced a moment of wonder that the child could laugh. What was the future for children like her, her tattered garments revealing her abject poverty? If she survived her short childhood, she'd only be handed over to a peasant labourer to bear his children year after year.

Daniel frowned, wondering who the child belonged to. Surely not Siana?

As he thought her name, she glanced up. Her hand came up to shade her eyes and they looked straight into his. She didn't appear surprised, almost as if she'd been expecting his arrival and had sensed him there. She closed the book in her lap and waited for him to join her, smiling as he scrambled down the slope.

'People don't usually come here. They think it's a haunted place,' she said.

'And is it?'

'Sometimes the wind sounds like voices. I dug up a Roman coin here once. My hand closed around it and I could feel the ghost of the man who'd last held it, as if he was inside my heart and head.'

'Did he say anything to you?'

'He felt homesick.' Her smile was tentative, as if she couldn't make up her mind if he was teasing her or not. 'My stepbrother took the coin from me.'

Without being invited, he sat beside her. The sun-warmed stones provided a comforting rest for his back. Flower scents were trapped in the humid air of the dell.

'Daisy, you can't eat that,' she said, and leaned forward to remove a clod of earth from the child's mouth. A kiss was placed on the child's face to compensate, an apologetic glance came his way as she stated the obvious. 'I have come too far and my sister's hungry.'

Daniel had the feeling it was a permanent state. He took an apple from his pocket, splitting it in half with a twist of his wrists. He offered both halves to her. 'It's not much, but better than eating dirt.'

Colour crept into her face. 'We don't usually eat dirt and I wasn't begging for food, Mr Ayres. I'll take some apple for Daisy, though.'

'I didn't imagine you were begging. It would please me if you'd take it all. It's only an apple and I ate its twin just a few minutes ago.'

He thought she was about to refuse. Then the child saw the fruit and began to grizzle, waving her hands in the air, her fingers fluttering and insistent like those of a pianist in the middle of a concerto. Siana took the pieces, glanced shyly at him and said quietly, 'Thank you, Mr Ayres.'

'You might prefer to address me as Daniel when we're alone,' he said, and took the book from her lap, smiling when he saw the subject matter. He'd forgotten about the artist. 'This is serious reading for a girl of your age. Why Michelangelo?'

'I feel the need to learn about people of the past, of other lands. It reminds me there is more to life than what the eyes see.'

'In what way?'

'Well . . .' She stared into space for the moment it took for her mind to formulate her answer. 'The more I think about people like Michelangelo, the more I wonder. First, the man himself. What did he look like? Was he married? How many children did he have? How long did it take him to paint a picture or carve his statues? Then you start wondering about his country. What were the houses like, the clothes . . . the landscape? It seems to come alive then, and there's an urge to go there and see for yourself.' Her voice trailed off. 'Not that someone like me ever could, and I wouldn't even know how to get there. It's nice to be able to read about it though.'

'Ah . . . you're a historian.'

Her head slanted to one side and her green eyes glinted. 'Do you seek to mock me for trying to educate myself, as you did when we had tea together?'

He flushed. 'Will you accept my apologies?'

'If they're sincere.'

'They are.'

Her face cleared and she smiled as she reached out to lightly touch the bruise on his face. Her voice had a husky undertone, like nutmeg sprinkled on honey. 'You've had an accident.'

'It's nothing,' he mumbled, reliving the humiliation of the moment her stepbrother had hit him. He couldn't tell her about that.

There was a sudden rumble of thunder in the distance and she rose to her feet, her arms reaching down for her sister in the same movement. By the time

Daniel struggled upright, Daisy was secured in a sling fashioned from her shawl, her skinny legs splayed either side of Siana's hip. Outlined against the melting sky, Saina's pose was womanly and natural. 'Return the book to the rector, please, Daniel. I've finished it.'

He was loath to part with her company. 'Would you like me to test you on the contents, see how much you've learned from it?'

She slid the uneaten portion of the apple into her pocket, shook her head and said, 'I must get home before the storm breaks. My mother needs me at home.' Then she was gone, her hair a torment of darkness in the wind. A pair of scuffed and stained boots stuck out from under the frayed hem of her faded skirt as she strode away. They were men's boots, too large for such slim ankles to support. Daniel suddenly felt sad for her circumstances.

He was tempted to go after her, but didn't. Instead, he climbed to the top of the ridge and stood there, watching her walk over the hill.

She had a natural grace. Her back was upright despite her burden, her hips had a rhythmic swinging motion that owed nothing to artifice. Much to his chagrin, she didn't look back once.

Daniel had enough arrogance to know his dark looks had attracted women from an early age, but he'd never thought he'd be drawn to a girl who didn't seem aware of his attraction. It was a humbling experience.

He told himself she was the wrong girl for him and, despite the circumstances of his birth, his social inferior. When he wed, his bride needed to be a woman with the means to help him establish his business.

She appeared to sink into the crest of the next hill, growing smaller and smaller as though she belonged to the earth and it was sucking her into its depths. It was an illusion, he knew, a trick of the light as she made her way down the other side, but at the very last minute he imagined she turned and waved to him.

He experienced delight that she'd spared him a moment of her attention, then a stray thought quirked into his mind. Perhaps he'd seen only what he'd wanted to see. Damn it, Siana was an attractive girl. It was only natural that he'd be attracted to her.

He shook his head to clear his mind, bewildered by the road his thoughts were taking. They had only just met, yet she intrigued him with her enigmatic ways. He shivered as he gazed around him. Had she really felt the presence of a ghost of a soldier stranded far from home?

He shook his head in disbelief. He must take heed of his mother's advice and not encourage the girl. From now on he must make every effort to try to avoid Siana Skinner.

4

The slice of barley bread was stale. Siana scraped dripping across the surface before handing it to Josh. 'Here,' she said, remembering the apple and pulling it from her pocket. 'It's gone a bit brown but it'll have to do.'

It wasn't half enough food for a growing lad. Josh wolfed it down, then licked his forefinger and harvested the crumbs from his shirt.

Her brother was small for a twelve-year-old. Born before his time, he'd barely survived his first year of life. A thatch of mousy hair flopped onto his forehead when he propped his chin on his hands. He gazed at their mother now through guarded blue eyes.

'Will Hastings's missus was turned out of her cottage today. She was crying fit to bust. They accused her Will of burning a haystack, but it ain't true. They shot him dead for nothing.'

'Whatever it is you think you know, I advise you keep your mouth shut about it,' Megan said. 'It's too late to save him now.'

'They said our Tom seen him do it. He's a bleddy liar.'

'Best you don't let him hear you say that.' The thundery weather had set the milk on the turn. Siana handed Josh a chipped jug. 'Run over to Croxley Farm and see if they've got any milk to spare so I can sop Daisy's bread in it before I settle her down to bed.'

'Our Tom would rather feed it to his pigs than give it to us.'

'If you're quick he'll still be at the boozer. Take this ha'penny to offer, it's all I've got. Mind you, don't offer it unless you have to. That fancy wife of his might give you some from the kindness of her heart if you minds your manners. I heard she ain't so bad, even though she won't give us the time of day in church on Sunday.'

'Not her. She has to do what Tom tells her else she gets a good hiding.' Josh grinned. 'No need to spend a ha'penny, anyways. That cow of hers will give me a good squirt or two without kicking up a fuss. She's a right obliging old moo.'

Siana exchanged a grin with her mother after Megan shouted out after him, 'Be careful Tom doesn't catch you at it, then.' There was no real warning behind her words. Josh's light-fingered ways drew a blind eye when a wild rabbit or a fish occasionally appeared in the larder. He had more lives than a cat, and more cheek than a monkey on a hurdy-gurdy.

'Why don't you sit down, Ma? I'll see to the rest of the chores.'

Megan stood in the doorway, her glance on the clouds purpling the sky. There was an air of sadness about her. 'I dreamed of your father this afternoon. He was searching for me. Smoke came from his eye sockets

45

and his tongue spat fire. You have the sight, daughter. Tell me what it means.'

Her words made Siana fearful. 'It's the weather, Ma. It was only a dream.' Siana took the opportunity to ask her mother again, 'Tell me of him, Ma. I have the right to know.'

'Perhaps it's time I did.' Her mother sounded weary. 'Gruffydd Evans is his name. He was a Methodist preacher by profession, and a man who cast a long shadow.'

Siana sucked in a deep, shocked breath.

Megan gave a faint smile. 'Now you know, daughter. He took what he wanted, then left me bleeding on the ground and walked away without giving me a second glance.'

Tears came to Siana's eye. 'Oh, Ma.'

Her mother's voice choked on a sob. 'The only good thing to come of it was you, my girl.'

Siana slid a comforting arm around her mother. 'Hush, Ma. You're tired and melancholy and the weather's getting you down.'

Her mother's hand folded over hers. 'Listen, Siana mine. The babby is dead inside me, I knows it. Good thing too, because we can't afford another mouth to feed. I'm worn out from carrying children and tired of praying for their eternal souls.'

'Stop it, Ma.'

'You're not a Skinner. If anything happens to me when this one's born, you get out quick. Take Daisy with you. Josh'll be all right, he's a lad.'

'You're talking nonsense.' Spooked by a low rumble

46

of thunder, Siana shivered. 'Where would I go without money?'

'You've got your piece saved with the reverend. Ask him for a reference, then you can get away from the district and go to the city. He might know someone who's able to offer you employment. When you marry, don't settle for a poor man. Find someone who has a bit behind him and can look after you both.'

Knowing what her mother's life was like, Siana wasn't sure that she wanted to marry anyone.

'The biggest mistake I made was to take up with Bill Skinner. He and Tom are two of a kind. Bill's no better than Tom, touching you every chance he gets. It ain't no accident, though he makes it seem so. Promise me you'll go.'

'I promise,' Siana said, mostly because her mother's voice had become agitated and she wanted to calm her.

As she kissed her cheek, she shuddered at the thought of her stepfather, who came home drunk every night and beat her mother at the slightest provocation. She'd learned to avoid his groping hands most of the time, but if anything should ever happen to her mother . . .

Neither of the women saw Bill Skinner sidle away from the window. As he sometimes did when his boss was away at market, Bill had taken the opportunity to sneak home early. As was his habit, he'd concealed himself to listen and watch.

Sometimes, he'd been rewarded. Once he'd followed Siana to the stream and watched her strip the clothes from her ripe young body to reveal her breasts with their hard, thrusting nubs. She was a virgin still. He'd made sure she remained that way, discouraging any lad who'd dared to call on her with a good thrashing. Oh yes, he'd made sure Siana wasn't bothered.

Today, though, he'd heard something entirely unexpected. He was angered by the deception of the two women. That treacherous wife of his would pay for it later, but not Siana. He had plans for her, and he didn't intend to mark that sweet young body of hers . . . not when it was going to earn him some money.

But first, he had to pay someone a little visit. Without a coin in his pocket a man didn't feel like a man. If all went well, tonight he might be able to manage a drop of the good stuff. Although a grin split his face from one ear to the other at the thought, his eyes displayed his humiliation. They glowed with the mean, simmering rage of a mad dog.

Richard White had finished his dinner and was relaxing with a glass of brandy when Bill Skinner requested permission to see him. Mrs Leeman's disdain clearly showed in her face when she disturbed him in the study, where he'd been pondering the merits of gas lighting.

'Bill Skinner is here, sir. He wishes to see you.'

'Did he say what about?'

'Oh yes. sir.' And her sniff conveyed the disapproving eloquence of her thoughts on the matter. 'He says he's come to pick up young Siana's wages.'

'Show him into the kitchen, Mrs Leeman, I'll talk to him there,' Richard said, dismayed on Siana's behalf. This would be a setback for the girl. After Mrs Leeman had gone, he opened the bureau and took out his account book, giving a cursory glance at one of the columns. Smiling to himself, he counted out an amount of coins.

Bill Skinner was standing near the back door, cap in hand. Mrs Leeman hadn't invited him to sit. She stood on the other side of a large scrubbed table, staring at the man, arms folded across her chest and a rolling pin clenched in her hand. Richard smiled slightly at that.

The kitchen was warm, the cast-iron cooker gleamed with lead blacking and the brass rails and handles gleamed proudly. Siana was a conscientious worker. A kettle sang on the hob, sending steam spurting out through the spout. On the table, candles guttered, the flames twisting and bending with the draughts coming through the chinks in the door and windows.

Mrs Leeman's chair was set by the fire and occupied by her tabby cat, who gazed at him momentarily through slitted eyes, then went back to sleep. A basket next to the chair contained her sewing.

'Good evening, Mr Skinner,' Richard said. 'How may I help you?'

Bill Skinner pulled an ingratiating smile onto his face. 'I've come to collect the bit of cash my daughter put aside, sir. My wife's been taken poorly and I needs to get her some medicine and such.'

'I see. Does Siana know you're here?'

The man's eyes sharpened. 'Begging your pardon, sir, but I don't need the girl's permission. I'm her father, see.'

Mrs Leeman's hands went to her hips. 'Everybody knows you're no such thing, Bill Skinner.'

'Stepfather then. Same thing, ain't it?' Skinner

turned to him, indignation in his eyes. 'I've brought that girl up since she was a newborn babby. Married her mother too, and from the goodness of my heart, 'cause I didn't have to, what with her being a bit free with her favours, and all.' His voice took on a self-pitying whine that set Richard's teeth on edge. 'Gave them both a home all these years with every shilling I've earned going to keep a roof over the girl's head and food in her belly. Now it's her turn to help the family. She wouldn't want her mother to suffer, now, would she?'

'Indeed, she would not. In fact, I believe she's been giving half of her wage every week towards keeping the family.'

'Has she now,' Bill said quietly, 'that's right good of her.'

Realizing his mistake, Richard hastily opened the book, exposing the column of neat figures. 'Now, how much did you say she had?'

The man's eyes darted to the figures on the page and his forehead furrowed. 'Now, let me see. She's been working here for . . . ?' Skinner gazed at him, his eyes sly. 'How many weeks be it, I forget?'

When Richard didn't offer him an answer he noisily cleared his throat. 'I forget 'zactly how much she said she had put aside. I reckon four shillings might cover it.'

Richard looked dubious. 'Mmmm . . .'

'Three, then, I think I remember her saying it was,' said Skinner hastily.

Getting him to take less would mean lying, so Richard took some coins from his pocket and placed them on the table. 'I'll need a receipt for that, so it's all above board. Mrs Leeman, I'd be obliged if you'd be good enough to fetch me my writing implements, then perhaps you would witness the transaction.'

A few moments later, Bill Skinner laboriously made his mark at the bottom of the page and slipped the money in his pocket. He glanced up, his eyes hardening. 'I reckon I'll be picking up Siana's wages myself from now on, sir. We'll be needing them with the new babby coming, and all. And if she's to work for you, we'll have to agree on a set amount. That way both of us will know 'zactly where we stand.'

Richard's heart sank. He might have saved Siana a few shillings this time without lying, but from now on she'd be lucky if she saw a penny for her efforts.

Much later that evening, Bill Skinner left the inn with another man. They shook hands, then parted company, the second man mounting his horse and heading in the opposite direction.

Bill looked up at the sky, grinning drunkenly. The storm was almost upon them. The roiling black clouds were outlined with flashes of brilliant light – light which stripped darkness from the land to reveal a stark, bleached landscape. It wasn't raining yet, but the trees were a frenzy of flaying twigs stripped of leaves. The grass bent low, cowed by the relentless fury of the wind. The air roared with its might and power.

None of this bothered Bill. His belly contained enough rum to warm him against the toughest storm. Far from being sleepy, his brain was sharpened by the drink – it had magnified the grievance he'd nurtured all evening, and the blast of fresh air had cleared his head, which had now come up with the solution.

'Deceivers,' he mumbled, 'I'll show the ungrateful cows,' and he headed for home. His smock flattened against his stocky body at the front and billowed out behind him, so he resembled an avenging angel flying on the wind as he left the village and headed onto the lane, which wound up the hill. It was wilder up there, the air smelled of salt and it started to rain. Soon, the drizzle turned to fat drops, then became icy, slanting needles that penetrated his clothes. He began to curse as depression threatened to overtake the warm glow the rum had given him.

Stopping in the shelter of a tree he tipped the remaining liquid down his gullet. His innards absorbed the fiery alcohol and sent it pulsing through every vein in his body.

As he flung the bottle from him, he felt his power surging back. He scratched himself between the legs, then grinned and shifted himself to one side for comfort. By heck he was ready for it tonight. He'd give it to her good, that would teach her to deceive him. He might even give it to Siana – it were about time she had a man, and it was about time he profited from keeping her all these years.

Then he remembered. 'No, not her,' he muttered. 'I've made arrangements for that maiden. If all goes well, there'll be a nice fat fee for me. Sod scrubbing the reverend's floors. She can make more money lying on her back for the gentry.'

Lightning flashed, revealing eyes red and rum-maddened. In the distance he saw a light flickering. A candle, by God! The extravagance of it. Did the silly cow think he was made of money? Ignoring the roaring storm he began to run, his feet squelching through the mud.

The Skinner cottage was bigger than the thatched cottages of the village. A roughly erected two-storey dwelling of red brick topped by grey slates, the crumbling mortar was kept intact by the stranglehold the ivy had on the walls.

The top storey consisted of two windowless rooms. In one slept Siana, Josh and Daisy. A straw mattress served as a bed for the three of them, their bodies huddling together under a ragged blanket for warmth in the winter months.

The second room usually served for Megan and her husband, through of late Megan had found it too difficult to climb the ladder and squeeze though the small square loft opening. She slept as best she could downstairs, usually on the kitchen table. It kept her off the packed dirt floor which absorbed the rain trickling under the door and over the step on wet days.

Siana had shared a dish of weak tea with her mother, who seemed dispirited and listless. Bill Skinner's dinner was in the cast-iron pot hanging over the glowing ashes. Shreds of bacon floated in the thin potato broth. The broth would serve as Bill's breakfast as well, and had been more than Megan and her daughter had eaten.

Siana kissed her mother goodnight and climbed the ladder. Josh was snoring. Keeping her clothes on for the warmth they offered, she drew Daisy into her arms and was soon fast asleep.

Downstairs, Megan waited for her husband to come

home. The wind sent smoke puffing down the chimney, making her cough. A feeling of unease was strong in her. Weather like this brought out her Welshness. She wondered what her family was doing now and an image of Grandmother Lewis flashed into her mind. If she was still alive, she'd be nearing eighty.

Megan's hands went to her stomach, to the dead infant inside. There was nothing for the babby in this world but misery, so it was best off out of it. A wave of depression flooded over her. Throwing her apron over her face she began to rock backwards and forwards, weeping bitter tears of despair.

A sudden gust of wind sent the door crashing back against the wall and the flame flying from the candle. A shower of sparks was coughed out from the grate, turning the plunge into darkness into a swirling, fiery hell.

Before Megan could gather her wits together, something crashed against the side of her head sending her sideways to the floor. Then Bill was into her, fists pummelling at her face, his boots thumping into her body. Blood spurted from her nose as the bone broke. It filled her mouth and lodged in her throat, making her gag. She managed to turn on her side and draw her knees up.

'You lying Welsh whore,' he yelled and his stick came whistling down across her back. She managed to draw in some air and scream. He'd never been quite so vicious before.

'Been keeping money from me, have you? That bastard of your'n been working for the reverend, has she? Well, from now on her wages come straight to me, but she won't be there much longer, I'll warrant. In fact,

I shouldn't be at all surprised if she ends up as some old man's darling.'

His foot thudded into her side and there was the snap of a rib. She moaned, gasping out, 'Stop, Bill. You've hurt me real bad.'

The fire had flared up. In the red brightness she saw him drop his trousers. Not that, not now! She hurt inside something awful. 'Please, Bill, no. I need a doctor.'

He took no notice, pushing her onto her back and shoving himself into her. Something inside her gave and she screamed with the agony of it. At the same time a pain lanced through her pelvis. Over his shoulder she saw flames licking at the ragged curtain that divided the kitchen from the main living area. Oh God, the sparks had set it alight. The cottage would go up like a bonfire! They were all going to burn. *Bill Skinner was going to burn.*

An unholy glee filled her and she began to laugh, until she remembered her children. 'Wake up, everyone, for God's sake!' she screamed out over her pain. 'Get out, the cottage is alight.'

Bill clamped a hand over her mouth and nose, cutting off her air. He was breathing loudly and grunting now. She could feel liquid spurting between her thighs, her waters had broken, but this was thicker. Blood?

Her senses began to swim. She was done for, but she had to save her children, and she wasn't going to leave Siana to the mercy of this swine. Groping around, within reach of her fingers she found the flat iron she'd been using earlier.

Curling her hand around the handle and using the

last remains of her strength, she brought it up over her head and let it fall. Bill Skinner's skull made a sound like an egg being cracked.

For a moment he stared at her, whispering before the light left his eyes, 'Aw, what the hell did you do that for, Megan, after I took you in, and all?'

'Oh God!' She shuddered and pushed him aside. Turning onto her hands and knees, she crawled painfully towards the loft ladder, leaving a trail of blood behind her.

Smoke woke Siana, searing her throat, her nostrils, her eyes and setting off a hacking cough. Through the cracks in the floorboards, smoke trickled and a devilish red light danced and flickered below.

She shook a reluctant Josh awake and, grabbing up her baby sister, crawled over to the ladder, the only way down. Beneath her, the walls were a conflagration of leaping red shadows, but thank God, the way out was still clear.

Her heart leapt into her throat when she saw her mother huddled beneath the ladder like a bundle of discarded rags. She was still – too still.

'Don't waste any time,' she shouted at Josh and, wrapping Daisy in the blanket, shoved her into his arms. 'Take your sister down and get out as fast as you can. Head for the oak tree and wait there. I'll try to get our ma outside.'

Her mother was heavier than she looked. Flames licked around them as Siana pulled at her. Suddenly there was a whooshing noise and the floor above them exploded into flame. Sparks showered around them. The air was so hot it seared her lungs as she dragged her mother across the floor. Megan was coming out of her stupor now, making small whimpering noises.

About to pull her backwards over the step and out through the door, Siana noticed Bill Skinner. He was lying on his back, one arm outflung. His eyes seemed to be staring through her. Steam rose from his head. Her brain registered the sight of the flat iron embedded in his skull, the congealing blood glistening around it. His legs were on fire.

Oh God! He was dead. Her mother had killed him! What if they hanged her for murder? She had to get rid of the evidence. Although she knew she couldn't afford the time, she dashed across to where he lay, picked up the flat iron and threw it as far away from him as it would go. His hair suddenly burst into flames, singeing her hands. His eyes shrivelled in their sockets and his mouth twisted with the heat. Air hissed demonically from it, catching fire as it did so.

She screamed and jumped backwards, unnerved by the sight. Using all her strength, Siana shoved her hands under her mother's armpits and began to pull. Josh joined her, taking their mother's legs under his arms as they lifted her and stumbled away from the cottage towards the oak tree, where Daisy, discovering herself abandoned and alone in a world of uncomfortable wetness, cold and noise, had set up a sobbing cry.

They'd just cleared the cottage grounds when the whole place exploded into a ball of flame behind them.

Neither looked back as they staggered over the rough, tussocky ground with their burden. They laid their mother gently under the tree, where a frightened

Daisy was still screaming for somebody to comfort her. There, they huddled together, stunned, staring at the burning cottage where Bill Skinner's body was now roasting like a pig on a spit at the spring fair.

'Bloody hell,' Josh whispered, his voice high with panic and shock. 'What are we going to do now?'

'Nothing until morning, then we'll see what can be rescued.'

Beside them, her mother gave a low, animal groan. Siana bent over her. 'It's all right, our ma. We're safe.'

'The babby's coming,' Megan whispered. 'I'm bleeding real bad and I need help.'

Siana handed the pacified Daisy over to her brother to nurse, and bent over her mother. 'I'll help you, Ma. It won't be the first time.' But somehow, she knew without being told, it would be the last time.

Two men spilled out of the inn, laughing at the storm which now raged around them.

Rudd Ponsonby gazed at the faint red glow beyond the hill. 'Sky's a bit red over yonder.'

'Another haystack, I shouldn't wonder.'

'Can't remember any stacks over that way, only Bill Skinner's place.'

'He went off with a right skin full. I pity his poor missus. He's a mean bastard when he's had a few and he was cussing her fit to bust,' the other said gloomily. 'Once, he killed his dog. Kicked the bleedin' guts out of it when it pissed on his foot.'

There was silence for a moment, then came the suggestion, 'It could be a lightning strike, I suppose. I remember

Bert's tree getting hit once. Sliced it clean down the middle. Missed his roof by a whisker when it come down.'

'That there blaze is too big for a tree.' The acrid smell of smoke was borne faintly to them on the wind. 'Fetch their Tom out, see what he makes of it.'

'He left a while back. Reckoned the widow woman he married needed his company. He was grinning when he sez it, so I reckon it be the other way round. I wouldn't go nowhere if my missus looked like her. She's a dainty little piece, that one.'

'And no respectable widow woman, either, so they say. Her boy is the spitting image of the squire. Rumour says she was his fancy woman.'

'Widow, wife or whore, they'm all the same in the dark,' and the pair burst into raucous laughter.

'Well, I'm going home, Rudd. Coming?'

'Nah,' Rudd said thoughtfully. 'That fire looks too big for a haystack. I might go over to have a look-see.'

'Might as well come with yer, then. I'll fetch some of the others.'

By the time the men organized themselves into a group and set out, the fire had died down considerably, the flames having consumed the rotten timbers of the Skinners' cottage swiftly. Sparks and smoke were being blown about by the wind, the smell of wet ash stung their nostrils.

'Jesus,' one of the men whispered as lightning illuminated the scene, 'I wonder if anyone survived?'

'I thought I seen something move under the oak tree,' someone shouted out.

The something was a young woman, her eyes glazed over with grief and shock, rocking the body of her mother back and forth. Megan Skinner was dead. Under her shawl, pressed against her heart, lay the baby boy she'd just given birth to. He was dead too, his face shrivelled up like a little old man. Fast asleep and huddled under a ragged blanket the men found the two younger children.

'Where's your father?' Rudd shouted above the banshee howl of the wind.

Her voice had a dead sound to it. 'He's in the house.'

'Someone had better run over and tell their Tom, then.'

A couple of them shuffled their feet. None of them had liked Bill Skinner, but the son was worse. They didn't trust him, not with the way he toadied up to the squire. Look what had happened to poor Will Hastings, a man who didn't have the heart to pull the wings off a fly, let alone put a torch to a haystack.

'Morning will do, I reckon. Reverend White will know what to do. What'll we do with the young uns? Can't leave them here, can we?'

'I'll take them home to Abbie for the night,' Rudd said. 'She'll squeeze them in somewhere. Tom or Hannah will have to take them in tomorrow, the poor little buggers.'

The girl looked up then. 'I'm not leaving my mother.'

'She's gone, dearie. The weather won't worry her none.'

'Do you think I don't know that?' she said fiercely. 'Take my brother and sister to shelter, but I'm staying here with my ma until morning.'

'You can't, love, not by yourself. It ain't right.'

'I'm staying,' she said fiercely. 'She's my mother, not some piece of rubbish to be left under a tree and forgotten.'

A man stepped from out of the darkness and looked around at the concerned faces of the others. 'My name is Daniel Ayres. It's only a few hours until dawn and the rain seems to have stopped. Siana is a friend of mine. You don't have to worry, I'll stay and look after her. Perhaps you'd call on my godfather, Reverend White, and inform him of my whereabouts.'

Rudd knew a moment of relief. 'Thank you, sir. I will that.' Problem solved, he tucked Daisy under his coat and headed back towards the village with Josh in tow.

When the villagers were gone, Daniel removed the shawl from Megan and placed it around Siana's head and shoulders. He then shrouded the woman and her infant tightly in the ragged blanket and placed them on the other side of the thick tree trunk.

He took off his topcoat and, wrapping it around the shivering Siana, pulled her close. 'There, there, I'll look after you,' he whispered.

She began to cry, giving great, gut-wrenching sobs which tore at his heart. Finally, when the sobs died down, she slept, her sooty, tear-streaked face pressed against his chest.

The pile of red ashes illuminated her face as Daniel kept his vigil over her. An occasional gust of wind sent sparks flying.

Ashes to ashes, he thought soberly when dawn traced a grey finger along the horizon to reveal the destruction. He shivered at the sight. Was this all that was left of a man's life, a pile of smouldering rubble that had become his funeral pyre?

He looked down at the woman in his arms, oblivious to her grief in sleep. But when she woke, what would become of her in the days to come?

5

Megan would have wanted to be amongst her dead infants, but to save the expense of digging two graves, she and her stillborn son were buried with her husband.

Not that there was much left of Bill Skinner. The fierce fire had burned most of the meat off him, leaving just blackened bones. His remains included the skull, which was cracked open at one side.

Francis Matheson, the examining doctor, gazed thoughtfully at the wound.

'Beam fell on him, I expect,' the undertaker muttered.

Francis grunted. A beam would have crushed the skull. A sharp-edged blow had caused this injury. Something like an axe. He didn't bother to argue, though. He had an appointment to keep and couldn't be bothered with the paperwork that reporting his suspicions would entail. Having examined the woman's body and noting her injuries, he suspected the man had deserved what he'd got.

But who had inflicted the blow was another question. Surely not that sweet young woman up at the rectory, smoke-blackened and shocked. And certainly not the younger boy. He looked too frail to even lift an axe.

Bill Skinner's remains were too gruesome to investigate further and he wasn't about to subject the girl to examination by a magistrate. He nodded to the undertaker and the remains were thrown on top of Megan in the roughly fashioned coffin.

When the ashes of the cottage were sifted through, Hannah managed to salvage a few household items. They included the cast-iron stew pot and the flat iron.

'Needs a good clean,' she muttered, rubbing at the iron with her sleeve. 'There's something sticky burned to the side.'

Before she left, she managed to catch several chickens. They squawked in alarm as she shoved them into a sack. A couple of fleet-footed young hens fled into the long grass and hid.

Tom carried off the scythe, the sharpening-stone and anything else that looked as though it might be useful to him.

Back and forth they went, sifting through the ashes like a couple of scavenging crows picking meat from a carcass.

Neither of them seemed particularly upset by their father's death.

Nothing was said about the younger children until after the burial service, when Richard White managed to confront the pair before they left. 'What arrangements have you made for the care of your siblings?'

Tom and Hannah glanced blankly at each other. 'I reckon I can take Josh in,' Tom murmured eventually. 'He's old enough to do a man's work and earn his keep.'

Hannah said shrilly, 'I'm not having that brat, Daisy. I'll have enough to do with my own babby.'

Siana's arms tightened around her sister. 'Daisy's my responsibility now. My mother wanted me to care for her.'

Josh sidled closer to her. 'I want to stay with you too. I don't want to work for Tom.'

Richard White frowned at them all. 'I can offer Siana employment and provide her with bed and board as well, but I can't be responsible for brothers and sisters.'

The undertaker stepped forward. 'Who's going to pay for the burial?'

Hannah's hands went to her hips. 'Not me. Megan Skinner was no kin of mine.'

'Nor mine,' Tom echoed, turning away.

'But your father was,' Richard argued. 'Are you forgetting he was buried too?'

'There was nothing but a few bones left of him, and that didn't take up much space in the coffin. If you want paying for him, you can dig them up again.'

Siana's chin lifted. 'I'll pay for the burial myself.'

Tom turned to her, his eyes sharp. 'What with? Any money left in that cottage was my father's. It belongs to me and Hannah.'

Behind them, the undertaker's horse pawed at the ground. It was late afternoon and the air had a damp chill to it. It had been the cheapest of funerals, a rough wooden box loaded onto the back of a cart.

The few people prepared to pay their respects to the departed had already left, their energy tuned to fight their own battle for survival. To dwell on mortality was uncomfortable. Besides, the ground had to be prepared and sown for next year's wheat, potatoes and swedes. Mangold-wurzels had to be picked, lime and manure spread for root vegetables.

Siana stared Tom straight in the eye. 'If you think your father had any savings you can go and rake through the ashes for it. I've earned a wage from my job at the rectory and Reverend White's put a few shillings aside for me.'

'First I've heard of any job. A real sly missy, you are. I bet the old man didn't know you was earning a shilling or two.'

'Because he would have spent it on ale. Half of it went to Ma to buy food. If it hadn't, we'd have starved to death.'

'Who's a bloody liar then?' Tom sent Richard an unfriendly glance. 'If you asks me it ain't Christian for a man of the cloth to keep an honestly earned shilling aside when a family is scratching for something to eat.'

Richard opened his mouth, then shut it again, deciding to be charitable. No need to add to Siana's troubles by telling her nearly half of her savings were gone. He exchanged a significant look with the under-taker. The parish would pay for the burial if he couldn't get it out of Tom or Hannah Skinner.

Daisy wriggled in Siana's arms. 'Horsey,' she muttered, pointing one wet finger towards the animal.

A cold wind tugged at Siana's skirt and she drew the shawl tighter around her shoulders. It was an old shawl, thickly woven and hand-spun from raw wool to keep out both the cold and the wet. It had been her mother's for as long as she could remember. With it wrapped around her shoulders, she felt close to her, which was comforting.

With Daisy wriggling in her arms and Josh pressing against her side, Siana felt overwhelmed by the responsibility of it all. If she didn't accept the reverend's offer, where would they sleep tonight? And what they would they eat? Despite her promise to her mother, she had to be practical.

Josh would be an added responsibility, she realized. She gazed at him apologetically. 'You'll have to work for Tom and live at the farm until I've got time to sort things out. Later on we might be able to combine our wages and rent a cottage in the next village. I'll pay for Daisy to be farmed out each day and we'll manage.'

'Promise?'

The desperation in his eyes made her feel guilty. When winter was over they could go on the road. There was always fruit to pick or charring to do and they could sleep in the fields like the gypsies. Tears pricked her eyes. 'Of course I promise. But I've got to work, and I must find a place for Daisy to stay meanwhile. I can't look after her as well.'

'I suppose I could take Daisy for a bit,' Hannah offered, unable to keep the avarice from showing in her expression. 'With you working at the rectory full time and all, you can pay a bit towards her keep. And I'd need a couple of shillings in advance because I'll have to buy her a change of clothes and extra milk and eggs.'

'You'll get extra eggs from the chickens you took from the cottage.' Unconsciously, Siana's arms tightened about Daisy. She had no choice really. Once she was settled, she'd think about finding somewhere else for Daisy to stay.

Richard dropped a couple of coins into Hannah's hand. 'That's taken care of, then.' He smiled genially.

'Come along. Hand the child over to Mrs Collins, there's a good girl.'

Daisy started to cry as soon as she left her arms. Siana thought her heart would break when she looked back. Josh had turned to stare accusingly at her. He stumbled when Tom cuffed him around the back of the head to hurry him along. Daisy's wails gradually faded as they got further apart, but Siana was filled with a sense of abandonment. Tears welled up in her eyes. 'I promised my mother I'd look after Daisy.'

'And so you shall, my dear. One day you'll marry a nice young man and your sister will live with you again. Just you wait and see.'

It was just words to comfort her, she knew, but she had to be content with them. If she allowed herself to believe them to be untrue, she'd fall deeper into despair.

Siana grieved for her mother, and missed her brother and sister. Knowing the nature of Hannah and Tom as she did, she worried constantly about the welfare of the children. Yet she knew she must remain employed to support herself and her sister, and it was her preoccupation with her job that kept her sane.

Much of her work concerned keeping the reverend's household accounts. All expenditure was entered in a ledger. She worked slowly, using a pencil first to make sure her sums and handwriting were neat and correct. Then, dipping the nib of the pen into the ornate silver inkwell, she'd laboriously trace over her pencilled marks. She was extra careful the nib wasn't too full in case it left an ugly blot.

Every week she added up the columns. Reverend White made her do this in her head, then he checked her figures on a small brass abacus encased in a wooden frame.

'You're wondering why I won't let you use this,' he said one day when she was wondering exactly that. 'It's because your brain needs constant mental stimulation if you're to learn.'

But after a week or two he trusted her skills enough to leave the books unchecked.

The work was totally absorbing and kept her mind from the horror of her mother's death. After the book work there was the housework to help Mrs Leeman with, or her studying to do.

She had been given the use of the library. In the evening she retreated to her small room under the eaves with a book, where she read voraciously. The light from the candle stumps Mrs Leeman allowed her to use up lasted until their wicks drowned in pools of molten wax.

Daniel came and went, giving her a pleasant smile each time they ran into each other, which wasn't often. He went out each morning, riding into Poole, where he worked. He didn't return home until after dark.

Sometimes she heard him telling the reverend about people he was doing important legal work for. She was awed by his cleverness.

'Daniel,' she said shyly one day, for there was something she'd been thinking about a lot of late. 'There's something of a legal nature I would like to ask you.'

He waited, his head to one side, a half smile playing around his mouth. 'What is it, Siana? Surely you don't intend studying to be a lawyer too.'

'It's about my name.'

His brow furrowed. 'What of it?'

'I was wondering . . . I've always been known as Skinner, but my mother wasn't married to Bill Skinner when I was born and he wasn't my father.'

'And you want to know what her name was before her marriage?'

'Oh, I know what it was. It was Megan Lewis.'

'I see. So what's the problem?'

'Do I have to call myself Skinner or can I use my mother's name?'

'It depends what you were registered as. If you were registered as Siana Lewis, then you can quite safely use the name.'

Her teeth dug into her bottom lip. 'I don't know what name I was registered under, or if I was registered at all. You see, I was born in a cow byre.'

A teasing light filled his eyes. 'And you think the cows might have forgotten to inform the parish? Perhaps you're registered as Siana the calf. Hmmm . . . is that a pair of horns I detect under that most unflattering cap?'

She laughed despite herself, the first time she'd done so since her mother's death. 'Stop teasing. Is it very difficult to find out if I was registered?'

'It's easy, and you don't need the help of a lawyer. Your name should be recorded in the parish register where you were born.'

'That was here.'

'Then my godfather can tell you.' He leaned against the wall. At ease and smiling down at her, he asked, 'How are you coping with things?'

'I love working here but I miss my sister and brother. Daisy doesn't smile any more, and Josh looks so tired and miserable when I see him in church. His hands are covered in sores where the blisters are infected.'

Daniel's face closed up a little and he straightened up. 'It's hard to act and work like a man when you're still a child. Josh's hands are bound to toughen up in time.' He reached out and gently touched her cheek. 'Tom Skinner is a hard taskmaster. No wonder you want to change your name. Siana Lewis is such a pretty name. It suits you well.'

He smiled when a blush rose to her cheeks.

It wasn't only Daniel who thought Siana good to look at.

Sir Edward Forbes had noticed her. In fact, he'd often observed her beauty in church. Set amongst the other village girls she was an exotic flower.

The church today was crowded. Although their wedding wasn't until spring, Isabelle was visiting, putting in an appearance for the peasants like a queen with her subjects.

It seemed as if most of the district's population was crowded in there to witness her appearance. The church smelled ripely of sweat and field muck; good, country smells he was used to.

But Isabelle was playing the lady with great affectation. Beside him, his bride-to-be held a lavender-scented handkerchief to her nose. She murmured something to her chaperone, a maiden aunt of extremely comfortable proportions, who gave a soft, high-pitched titter.

Isabelle Prosser was twenty-five, the only child of a Poole cloth merchant, who'd once been an unsuccessful tenant farmer over Salisbury way. Her mother was dead.

Isabelle's looks were indifferent, her thick, straight eyebrows drawing attention to her pale blue eyes, which were her best feature. The dark blue gown she wore was decorated with huge puff sleeves and a three-tier lace collar. Her large bonnet of pleated silk was topped with curling ostrich plumes. Tied under her chin with a huge bow, the whole structure seemed designed to support her short neck, plump cheeks and chin.

A beauty she wasn't, but Edward considered he'd chosen well. She was set to inherit a fortune, which, although he didn't need it, he might as well have. The generous hips he detected under her skirt were ideal for bearing him sons. She was almost as plump as her aunt Caroline, but that didn't matter as long as she fulfilled her function and bred for him.

In his early fifties, Edward didn't consider love to be of any importance now. He'd loved his wife Patricia with passion, Elizabeth Skinner with marginally less, when she was young. Elizabeth had learned to please him and her sensuality had kept him by her side for years. Lately, however, her constant manipulations on behalf of her bastard son had annoyed him and he'd ended the relationship.

He did what he could for Daniel, of course, even inviting him to dine with him at regular intervals. But he needed a legitimate heir, one who would acquire the skills to manage the land attached to the estate. He slowly shook his head. Damned fool woman, turning the boy into a lawyer. Daniel hadn't the instinct. He was too lazy by nature, always taking the easiest option. If the boy ever came into money, he would waste it on the fine living he craved, which was why Edward needed a legitimate heir for the estate.

Just then there was a stir at the back of the church. He turned his head in time to see Elizabeth enter. Damn her, did she have to draw attention to herself by making a late appearance? He frowned when she caught his glance over the heads of the congregation, then suddenly his heart jumped. There was a livid bruise on her face.

'Damn Tom Skinner,' he growled, and resolved to have a word with his tenant about Elizabeth.

Isabelle placed a gloved hand on his arm. Her eyes were cold and her mouth was set in a rigid line. The chill in her voice was not reassuring, 'Edward, you're not paying attention to the sermon.'

Richard was rambling on about the wealthy helping the poor. I help by providing them with jobs so they can feed their families, Edward thought bleakly; what more do they want? The lazy swine did nothing but grumble. It was time he and the landowners cracked down harder on the peasants. If the trades organizations were allowed to get a grip, the farm labourers would begin to think they were as good as their masters. Then they'd never get any work out of them.

He watched Richard smile at the Skinner girl. The reverend had given her a job, he knew. She was clean and tidy now, wearing a modest gown of drab brown. A woollen shawl was drawn around her shoulders. He wasn't the only one looking at her. Half the men in the place had their lustful thoughts written on their faces did they but know it – even her own stepbrother.

Previously, Edward had instructed his estate steward to

sound out the girl's stepfather about coming to an arrangement over her. Although the fellow had been agreeable, the man had died before the plan had borne fruit.

His eyes narrowed now as he wondered if she was still intact. His glance touched on the gentle swell of her breasts, then went to her eyes. He was reassured to see that the innocence in them wasn't feigned, but the girl wouldn't remain that way for much longer. She had no protector. All it would take was for her to drop her guard one day.

Tom Skinner came to mind again. Hmmm! The man had been useful to him in the past. Skinner would do anything to get ahead. He'd reported his own father once for sleeping on the job. Edward had made sure a day's pay was docked.

Perhaps he'd sound Skinner out about the girl, see what could be done. No doubt Richard would object, but not for long because his own living depended on Edward's largesse, which could be withdrawn at any time.

In the meantime he might just pay Richard a call, and he'd choose his time with care.

Siana felt nervous as she showed the squire into the drawing room. She dropped a curtsy as he seated himself

'Reverend White has taken Mrs Leeman to market, but they should be back soon. Would you like some tea while you're waiting, sir?'

'A glass of sherry if I may, my dear.' The squire smiled kindly at her. 'Aren't you the Skinner girl?'

She was taken aback, but slightly flattered by the query. 'I'm Siana Lewis, sir. My mother was Megan Skinner but I've taken her maiden name now.'

'Ah yes.' He cleared his throat. 'Such a tragedy. How are you managing, my dear?'

'Well enough, thank you, sir. The reverend is kind. I keep his books and he's teaching me my lessons, as well.'

Edward's eyebrow rose a fraction. Was he now? This was better than he'd hoped for. Not only was she well spoken, but the girl was teachable. 'Tell me, what are you studying?'

She smiled, charmed by his interest. At least he hadn't laughed at her. 'History and geography. I intend to be a teacher or a governess one day.' Her smiled faltered, for she remembered her promise to her mother. 'That's if I can find a post with a wage enough to support my baby sister. By the time I'm trained, my young brother will be old enough to help financially and we'll rent a cottage together.'

'I see.' The squire patted her hand. 'You have no intention of getting wed, then?'

'Oh, no, sir.'

He chuckled. 'A pretty girl like you?' he teased. 'There must be something wrong with the local lads if they're not queuing up to court you.'

Siana blushed as she moved to the sideboard to pour him a drink. There were two decanters and they looked exactly the same. She gazed from one to the other, perplexed. 'I don't know which is the sherry,' she confessed.

'The paler one. The other is a rather indifferent brandy.' He joined her at the buffet as she picked up the sherry, leaning over her shoulder. 'It belongs in the smaller glass, my dear.' He took the decanter from her hands and poured two glasses.

She wanted to move away, but he had her trapped there. Not that he was touching her, but she was certainly aware of his warmth. He held the second glass to her lips. 'Try a little sip, Siana Lewis.'

She didn't have time to protest when the glass was tipped. She was forced to swallow the liquid before it ran down her chin. It was sweet and slightly sticky, coating her tongue. She tried not to gasp when a worm of warmth trickled down inside her chest.

His eyes were the same colour as the sherry. 'Enjoyable?'

'Yes . . . thank you, sir. Now I must get on with my work.'

His eyes were filled with amusement. 'Relax, Siana. Join me in another drink.'

Siana thought she heard the faint click of a latch. Though it could be the kettle cooling on the hob, or the bridle on the squire's horse as it tossed its head, she decided.

His mount was a splendid mare, her coat quivering and polished to the high gloss usually found on the fruit of the chestnut tree. Muscles rippled under her skin and a plumed tail sprang from her powerful hindquarters. As the horse gave a little whicker and stamped her hoof, the squire's head cocked to one side in a listening attitude.

Firmly, she said, 'It sounds as though the reverend has returned. Sir, would you stand aside, please. I have work to do.'

He chuckled, staring at her for a moment, his eyes hooded over in thought. Then he grazed the back of his fingers down her face and whispered. 'You should be dressed in satin, silk and lace, and those pretty little hands should be covered in rings. I could set you up in a fine house with servants. What d'you say to that, girl?'

Siana was no fool. Her childhood had made her aware of the ways of men. She'd learned to cope with the stares, the seemingly accidental touching, the pinching, the innuendo and the blatant suggestions.

But those were the crude ways of farm labourers, not those of a man who smelled of soap, who dressed immaculately in the finest cloth and displayed a gentleman's manners.

Edward's approach flattered her. Edward Forbes was an attractive man, lacking the middle-aged corpulence most gentlemen of his age had acquired. His hair was an abundance of dark and silver streaks, his eyes were a warm tawny brown, reminding her of a lion she'd seen pictured in a book. He'd made it clear what he was about, and he was willing to give something in return for his pleasure.

Ahead of Siana was a life very much like her mother's had been if she wasn't careful. She hated herself for momentarily being tempted. It wasn't the thought of comfort, though it would be wonderful not to wake up and wonder where the next crust was coming from. But she had to think of Daisy and Josh. The responsibility of her siblings was a heavy burden to carry, but carry it she would. She'd promised her mother.

'Sir, I do not find you physically repulsive, but I promised my mother I would uphold certain standards. I've never craved silk or satin and I'm content where I am.'

The squire inclined his head and stood aside. 'You're certainly a sensible girl, Siana. Tell me your price and rest assured, I'll pay it.'

Colour rose to her cheeks as her anger mounted. 'Nothing you could offer would compensate me for the insult. I'm well aware of your past, for Elizabeth Skinner is married to my stepbrother, and your son Daniel resides in this house. I was in church last week when you introduced your bride to the district. What manner of man desires so many women? Not a good one, I'll be bound.'

'One who appreciates true beauty.' His eyes held hers for a long moment. 'A wicked man who knows how to please a woman in many ways.'

'You're not getting any younger,' she said brutally, 'you will need your energy to keep your young wife pleased.'

He shrugged. 'Isabelle will not need to be pleased. She is there to provide heirs for the estate, and will bear my name and title. You would be kept for my true pleasure.'

A little shudder ran through her, and it wasn't altogether unpleasant. Rattled by the sudden discovery of her sensuality, she gained the understanding that she wasn't going to be as in control of certain feelings as she'd expected to be.

She didn't know quite what to do, so she tore her eyes from his and whispered, 'I am as good as Isabelle. Let her be used for your pleasure whilst I provide you with—' She bit her tongue and her eyes widened at what she'd been about to say. 'Excuse me, sir,' she stammered, and, pushing past him, bolted from the room.

The squire smiled to himself as the door closed behind her. Up close, he was pleased with the girl's looks. Her manner was disconcerting, however, the deference shown to him by most of the workers' families was lacking – *almost as if she considered herself an equal.*

He didn't know quite what to make of her twisted logic, but somehow knew he wasn't as offended by it as he could have been. She was not bold, but she hadn't shied away from certain matters or reacted in too simpering a manner either. Innocent though the girl undoubtedly was, she was also aware of the ways of the world.

Dammit! Siana Lewis intrigued him mightily. He put the glass on the tray and picked up his hat. He would seek out Tom Skinner, he thought, striding down the hall towards the front door. He was a wily fellow who could be counted on to come up with a solution for a coin or two.

He tossed a penny to the lad who'd been minding his horse. The mare quivered as his strong thighs spread across her back. Ever the capricious beast, but the best hunter he'd ever known, she crabbed sideways, her iron-shod hooves fashioning an intricate dance on the hard-packed ground. He leaned forward, fondling her mane, gentling her. 'Steady, my beauty.'

He could feel the eyes of the girl watching him, but the lace curtains of the rectory hid the watcher well. Beautiful, mysterious eyes she had, her long lashes as dark as midnight.

She had not found him repulsive, she'd said, but then, women never did.

He smiled, raising his crop to his hat in farewell before spurring the horse forward.

He'd decided to have Siana Lewis, whatever the cost to himself.

And once Edward Forbes had decided on something, nothing was allowed to stand in his way.

6

The following Sunday, after the church service, the squire's steward paid Tom a visit.

The pair disappeared into the parlour, and when Tom shouted out for some refreshment, Elizabeth took them in a tray of tea and a fresh batch of scones.

Although they'd met on many occasions over the past twenty years, and his eyes engaged hers in a moment of recognition, Jed Hawkins nodded impersonally to her. He was the squire's man through and through.

She would have lingered outside the door to listen, but the floorboards creaked and she knew Tom would have an ear cocked for her to move away. Hawkins's visit would provide her with an opportunity to do something about Josh though. Shovelling some bread into her apron pocket, Elizabeth warmed a dish of broth, filled a jug with water and hurried out to the barn.

'Quickly,' she said to Josh and, loosening the bonds around his wrists, spooned the soup into his mouth. He swallowed it down eagerly, nearly choking on the bread. In her haste, half of the water went down his front.

She gazed at his bruises, knowing she could do nothing to help. Tom had beaten him black and blue for sneaking into the kitchen and helping himself to some bread and cheese during the night. The lad would stay tied up in the barn tonight to teach him a lesson.

'I'm going to have to tighten your bonds again. I'll make them a bit looser.'

Josh nodded. His eyes were large and wounded. He was just a child, reminding her of Daniel at that age. He'd never have been punished so severely for stealing food.

'I'm sorry, that's all I can do to help,' she whispered, fearful she'd be caught. 'I have to get back before his visitor leaves. Don't tell Tom I was out here.'

'Thanks, missus, but I'd die rather than get you in bad with our Tom. He ain't fit to lick the muck from your boots.'

She touched his face in sympathy. Such a thin little lad, but he was unexpectedly resilient, and brave. And to think she'd expected to dislike all the Skinners.

The child Hannah was caring for was a delight. Not that the care consisted of much. Daisy had become dirty and thin, her body was covered in sores from infected flea bites, her nose constantly ran and her hair was matted and filthy.

Hannah complained bitterly about her, and about the infant she carried. It was due to be born very soon, and Elizabeth wondered what would happen to Daisy then. The woman was a sloven. She didn't have the wit to care for one child, let alone two.

She ran back to the house, grabbing up a couple of

logs on the way and arriving just as the steward was preparing to leave. Tom stared suspiciously at her flushed face. 'Where've you been?'

'To the woodpile, the fire was low,' she said, breathless from running.

His gaze darted to the two logs in her arms and he seemed satisfied with her answer.

She didn't ask him what the steward had wanted because she knew that was what he wanted her to do. She'd learned that passive disobedience was much more satisfying than open defiance. Tom flared up at the least provocation, but although he might have a certain cunning, he didn't have the intelligence of sound reasoning, being more comfortable using his fists to settle an argument.

Elizabeth had never been subject to physical abuse before she'd married Tom. His unpredictable violence had her living on her nerves. She sensed in him a core of irrationality barely held in check. One thing she knew, she couldn't take much more of it. But then, she didn't quite know how to make an escape, either.

She flinched when he thumped on the table with his fist. 'Squire thinks I'm hurting you, Lizzie. Whatever gave him that idea?'

'He's got eyes in his head,' she muttered.

His hand folded around her bodice and he yanked her to her feet. 'If I thought you'd been telling him tales—'

'I haven't seen him, except in church, and then you've always been with me.' But he'd planted a seed in her mind now. Edward obviously cared enough to

81

dislike her being hurt. If she appealed directly to him surely he would listen.

'What about that boy of your'n? Has he been sneaking around here whilst I'm away?'

'No, Tom. I promise,' she lied.

He smiled nastily at her. 'I'd better not catch him at it, then. And from now on I'll only hit you where it don't show.' And he punched her in the stomach.

Elizabeth fell to the floor, drew her knees up and began to retch.

Tom stared down at her and laughed. 'And in case you're wondering if Sir Edward bloody Forbes is still interested in you, the old goat wants a younger bit of pie. He's after Siana.'

Shock filled Elizabeth's mind, then as the pain receded, she thought that the girl could do worse than take Edward Forbes as a lover. She could marry someone like Tom Skinner.

She remembered the tentative smile Siana had offered her in church, as if she'd wanted to make friends. Apart from the girl's beauty, there had been something achingly vulnerable about her. Siana had an indefinable quality that Elizabeth, whose status had excluded the friendship of other women, had been instantly drawn to. No wonder Daniel liked her.

It would be nice to have another woman to talk to, she mused, her own need surprising her. But she hadn't responded to the smile, remaining aloof and withdrawn into herself. She'd never been accepted when she belonged exclusively to Edward. Now she belonged to Tom, she might as well not exist.

She dashed away the tears gathering in the corners of her eyes. She would not give in to self-pity.

'The squire had come to an arrangement with my old man before he died, ' Tom was saying. 'I've always thought Siana would be a right juicy little tart. But he'll have to come up with a better offer, else I'll break her in myself.'

'She's not an object to be bought and sold.'

'He bought you, didn't he? And after he had you, I got offered the leftovers. It can work two ways, that can.'

Siana was lovely, with a fresh innocence about her. Men were corrupters with an appetite for the innocent. *Better Edward than Tom Skinner, though.* Elizabeth couldn't keep the disgust from her face as she spat, 'I think you're vile.'

'Not as vile as I could be.' He slid the belt from his waist, folded it in half and slapped it experimentally against his hand. Scrambling across the floor, Elizabeth hunched into a corner between the dresser and the wall, making herself as small as possible. The first stroke landed across her shoulders.

In the barn, Josh struggled against his bonds when Elizabeth began to scream.

Daniel couldn't remember the exact moment he'd fallen in love, but the realization had grown swiftly over the last month. Like a mushroom growing in a dew-soaked field, suddenly it was ready for picking, and urgent, before the sun sucked the moisture from the tender skin.

Love had come too soon, long before he was ready to accept it. But his initial anger had gradually become disbelief, then happiness as he accepted the emotion as a true one. His heart pounded when Siana was near and he was newly born, an infant in the face of this powerful, surging emotion.

He took to reading poetry, finding himself staring into space when his attention should have been on his work. He'd discovered he intensely disliked the profession he'd trained for. He felt trapped, cooped up in a stuffy room from morning until night, and he hated writing the dryly worded copies of the court reports, as required by his employer.

Perhaps he should have been a farmer after all. But no, he wasn't cut out for that either. A steward perhaps? After all, his father wasn't a farmer. The squire just ran the estate with the help of his steward. If he'd been born on the right side of the blanket, Daniel knew he'd be learning to rule the estate in the same way that his father did.

He tried to swallow his resentment. Edward Forbes had been as real a father to him when he was young, as he was remote now. The man had been kind, and interested in his education. Daniel had hero-worshipped him.

Learning he was second class had wounded Daniel. He'd been about twelve at the time, his life all mapped out for him. He'd been expected to learn the way of the land and it was made clear that the deeds to Croxley Farm would eventually be his.

But all he craved was the regard of the man he loved. His need to catch his father's attention and prove himself better than his expectations had sent Daniel on a different path of learning.

The resulting argument had driven home to Daniel his true status. The squire had all the power, and he was powerless. They were polite with each other now, two gentlemen meeting on a social level, their kinship and his bastardy never mentioned . . . though Edward Forbes sometimes asked politely after his mother. Not that he'd be interested in her ill-treatment. She'd been discarded in favour of Isabelle, who would provide the estate with sons and heirs.

Croxley Farm was a prize in itself, the cream of the land on the estate. Daniel hadn't recognized its potential then. He bitterly regretted allowing his pride to turn it down, especially since doing so had placed his mother in an untenable position.

But it was too late for her. Much as he wanted to, Daniel couldn't afford a wife on his salary at present, especially one with no dowry and a brother and sister to support.

He took the problem to his godfather, setting it before him after the Sunday service.

'Don't think I hadn't noticed your regard for Siana. Normally, I'd be delighted, for Siana would make you an excellent wife who'd be content with the small comfort your living would provide. But she's young, Daniel. She has a strong sense of duty towards her siblings. She'll not desert them.'

'I cannot support them all at the moment, but neither can I go on avoiding her without saying something. Tell me, what should I do?'

Richard smiled. 'Given time, you will be able to offer Siana a home. In the meantime, perhaps you could make it easier on yourself and procure lodgings in Poole. I know of a respectable widow who takes in boarders. She has a clean, comfortable house, with stable room for your horse. I could go and see her tomorrow if you're agreeable.'

It sounded like an ideal solution to Daniel. Then he thought, what if she gives her heart to another? Or worse, her innocence. He gazed at Richard. 'What if Siana does not care enough for me to wait?'

'Then you'll have to live your life without her. You must put the proposition before her, as I did with my own sweet wife. My dearest Jane waited several years for me.'

'Several years!' The thought of waiting that long for Siana seemed a lifetime to Daniel.

He spent the week deciding what to say and how to say it, then with everything straight in his head drew her aside after the church service and begged her to walk with him.

She was wearing a new skirt and bodice in pale grey serge, one she'd been making under Mrs Leeman's tutelage. It was decorated with a lace collar made by Mrs Leeman, and buttons embroidered to look like pink roses. Mrs Leeman had given her a bonnet, to which were added pink ribbons. She was a little self-conscious today, smoothing at the material and making sure her skirts were settled properly.

She'd been preoccupied for the past week and her eyes were anxious. 'Josh wasn't in church. Do you think he could be ill?'

'I'm slipping over to visit my mother later. I'll make enquiries on your behalf.'

'Thank you, Daniel,' she said gratefully. 'Daisy didn't smile at me today, either. I think she's forgotten me. Now Hannah's been delivered of her baby, I worry about my baby sister. I promised my mother on her deathbed that I'd look after her.'

'You're doing the best you can, Siana. I just wish I was in a position to look after you all.'

She gave him a shy, sideways glance. 'Do you, Daniel?'

Everything he'd rehearsed in his mind fled. 'You must know how much I care for you.'

The lane they trod was empty of people, except Mrs Leeman hurrying along in front to get back to her warm kitchen and the leg of lamb roasting in the oven. The hedges were winter-bare now, the long thorny twigs decorated with clusters of blood-bright berries.

When Siana remained silent, he came to a stop and turned her to face him. 'You do know, don't you?'

'Yes,' she whispered. 'I think I feel the same way.'

'Then I want you to wait for me. I'm moving into lodgings in town. In a few years I should be able to support both you and your brother and sister. Then we can wed.'

She gazed up at him, her eyes shining. The adoration in them wasn't hard to take. 'Oh, Daniel. It will give me something to hope for in the future.'

Gently, he took her face in his hands and kissed her forehead. About to take advantage of her sweet mouth, he heard a horse approaching. 'My godfather knows, but we must keep this a secret from everyone else,' he said hastily.

They sprang apart when the clip-clop of a horse's hooves came from behind them, each moving to opposite sides of the lane to make room for the rider to pass. But he didn't, instead, the horse slowed and was reined to a halt.

The squire tipped his hat to Siana and smiled. 'Miss Lewis.'

'Sir.' Eyes cast down, she stood there, not knowing what else to do.

'You look very pretty today.'

Her face turned pink and she became agitated. 'Excuse me, sir . . . Daniel. I must catch Mrs Leeman up.'

The squire dismounted. 'Well met, Daniel. Running into you saves me coming up to the rectory.'

'Sir.' Daniel waited, his eyes narrowed, watching his father watch Siana as she hurried off. He could almost read his lecherous thoughts and was disgusted by him.

The squire tapped his crop against his boot. 'Don't you find it odd that a peasant family can turn out a girl like her?'

'In what way?'

'Not only is she a fetching little piece, she has a good mind. Richard White is very taken with her.'

Daniel stared at him. 'What are you suggesting, sir?'

'I'm suggesting nothing, lad. Richard is the soul of propriety. Don't be so damned touchy.' He flung a friendly arm across Daniel's shoulder and they began to walk together along the lane. 'I've been talking to Robert Cruikshank about you. He's pleased with your progress and he's decided to review your salary.'

Daniel was pleased. 'Thank you, sir. I need the money.'

'Yes, I noticed you're looking a little threadbare. I'll leave word with my tailor. He can fit you out with a new suit of clothes at my expense.'

'Thank you, sir.'

'Think nothing of it, lad. You only have to ask.' His father withdrew his arm and, remounting, stared down at him, his eyes thoughtful. Gruffly, he said. 'For your own sake, don't encourage that girl, Daniel. Messing with female servants is a bad policy, especially when they get a loaf in the oven. Have you bedded the wench, yet?'

'Certainly not,' he stammered, taken aback. 'I wouldn't dream of—'

'Good, make sure you don't. I have other plans for you, and they don't include some opportunist little country bumpkin with children to support. You can do better than that for yourself.'

His father touched his riding crop against his hat, wheeled the chestnut around and cantered away without a backward glance.

The slur cast on Siana caused colour to mount to Daniel's face. He wanted to call his father back, ask him to explain his last remark. But at the moment he was in no position to. He relied too much on his father's largesse.

Moodily he kicked at a tuft of grass, wishing life was a bit simpler.

Dusk was falling when Daniel met his mother in the meadow behind the farmhouse. After he gave her a hug she glanced back at the house with its watchful windows. 'He's sleeping off his dinner, I can't stay long.'

She looked tired, he thought, the dark rings under

her eyes mirroring her tension. There in her body too, her stance suggested she was constantly on her guard. But there was a resilience about her she didn't have before, a resoluteness of expression, as if somehow she'd gained strength from her experiences.

He gently touched her face. 'How is he treating you now, Mother?'

'Tolerably. I'm learning to handle him. It's best if he's allowed to think he's the one in charge.' She called to the mule who ambled over to investigate the carrot she held out. Slipping a halter over its head, she fondled its ears.

'You seem stronger somehow, Mother.'

'I am. It's hard work being a farmer's wife. The exercise has given me strength, I think. I've discovered I'm quite good at milking the cow, plucking and drawing the chickens and handling the animals.' There was no self-pity in her voice, just a certain dryness. 'Especially the swine. I feel very proud of myself.'

'Siana's worried about Josh.'

A wry smile touched her lips. 'Tom keeps him locked up in the barn when he's not got him working. But he's warm enough, I make sure of that. Tell Siana he's had a bit of a cough lately. But he's on the mend. I swear, that boy's got nine lives. Tom's going to the farmers' meeting in Wareham next Wednesday. She's welcome to come and see her brother then, if she can get an hour or so off. The morning is best.'

His mother kept looking back towards the house. Secure behind the trunk of a hawthorn tree, Daniel had no qualms about being observed. Quickly, he gave her his news, omitting his arrangement with Siana. But he couldn't help mentioning her beauty, her goodness and her quick mind.

When he was about to leave, his mother said, 'Why don't you take Siana and the money I saved, and get away from here?'

'Does what I feel for her show?' he said with some alarm.

Elizabeth smiled. 'Only to your mother, who knows and loves you better than anyone. I saw her in church and can understand. But are you sure of your feelings? A girl so young and pretty is bound to attract men.'

'As to that,' Daniel shrugged, 'how do I know what's real and what isn't? When I'm with her it just feels different to anything I've ever known.'

'Tell me more about her.'

So Daniel did, telling his mother about the way Siana's eyes shone when she was happy, the way her head cocked to one side when she was listening and all the other little pleasures he found in watching her.

When he ran out of words, she kissed his cheek. 'Ask her to come on Wednesday. I want to meet her. Take the money,' she said again. 'Be happy with her if you are certain, Daniel.'

He was tempted, but the capital was such a small amount. Certainly not enough to set him up in business and secure decent accommodation. Better to do as Richard suggested and wait until his prospects improved. Perhaps a legacy would come his way? Not that he wanted his father to die, but the squire was getting on in years. If he died within the next year or so,

Daniel could well inherit. He frowned slightly as doubt crept in. Would Siana cope as lady of the manor? No, his godfather was right. It was best not to rush into anything yet in case it was a passing fancy. Whilst he remained unwed, his options were still open.

'No, Mother. I can't afford to keep us all. When I can, we'll go together. You, me, Siana, Josh and Daisy.'

'Then, at least take that little amber ring of mine for her to wear. Have her name inscribed inside, so she has something tangible to hold on to. It's important for a woman to have a love token if she is to wait.'

'Thank you, Mother, I will.'

'*Lizzie!*'

'Coming, you oaf,' she breathed, then, without her looking up from the mule, her mouth twitched into a smile. 'This is Jasper. I tell him all my secrets and he keeps them.'

'Nice to meet you, Jasper,' Daniel said, tears coming to his eyes because he could do nothing to help ease her problems. God knew, he had enough of his own.

Jasper's ears pricked forward and he stared at Daniel through large, sad eyes. There were whip marks on his haunches. His mother's fingers touched lightly against them. 'Poor Jasper, he tries to bite his master sometimes. I've been rubbing salve on his wounds, the stuff I used to put on your grazed knees when you were a child.'

Daniel had the urge to comfort her, but didn't dare in case he was seen from the house.

Her eyes flicked up to his. 'It was nice to see you, my love. God willing, I'll be here again next week.' She gave a gentle tug on the halter, clicked her tongue and began to stroll towards the stable, the mule ambling along behind her, munching on the carrot.

Daniel stayed where he was for a while. He saw Tom Skinner come out into the yard. After glancing up the slope he waited until his wife had taken the mule into the barn.

When she went to the house, she walked past him, her skirt held against her body and with her head held high. She was the essence of dignity.

Tom loosened his pants to urinate against a wall, then took another, careful look around the place before following her in. He slammed the door behind him.

Daniel walked off into the darkness, grim-faced. He knew he'd never forgive his father for what he'd done to his mother. She deserved better than Tom Skinner.

Edward Forbes had reached the same conclusion. Hands steepled under his chin, he gazed into the flickering fire-light and pondered on the problem of Elizabeth and her son.

'*My* son,' he whispered, unable to keep the smile from creeping around his mouth. If only Daniel's birth had been legitimized by marriage.

But it wasn't, and the offspring of Isabelle would inherit the estate. He frowned at the thought of Isabelle. Her lack of wit irritated him and he wondered if he'd been a bit hasty. Would she release him from the engagement she wondered. No, she was not the type to be cast aside lightly. Although she was civil to him, there was no warmth in her. She was young, but lacking the enthusiasm and fun of youth, as though a dowager was trapped inside her skin.

There was also a strident note evident when she addressed people she considered beneath her. Damn it, he didn't even like her!

He'd acted from temper and in haste at the time he'd offered for her. Now, given the choice between Isabelle and Elizabeth, he realized he'd chosen unwisely. He shook his head, not wanting to think about the way he'd foisted his former mistress on to Skinner. He no longer loved Elizabeth but he missed her and she was now lost to him. The delectable and intriguing Siana Lewis was within his grasp, though.

He frowned as he remembered the way the boy had looked at her. Puppy love, he told himself, yet that could quite easily grow into something more. First a smile, then a kiss, then the instincts took over. Daniel was a man and the Lewis girl was no fool. It was obvious she wanted more from life than her mother had. He'd be doing his son a favour by parting the pair before it went any further.

The only solution was to make provision for Daniel in his will, just in case he died intestate. Then he'd get Daniel out of the way and move fast on Siana Lewis.

Damn that Tom Skinner! He was a greedy swine and it was obvious that Edward would have to pay his price for the girl.

But he wouldn't hand over a penny piece until he had Siana Lewis in his bed and discovered for himself that she was still intact.

It was Wednesday. Josh's task was harvesting the swedes still remaining in the ground. The air was cold, the sky a sheet of drifting grey drizzle. Slippery with mud, the ground oozed over his boots.

Alongside him, sacks protecting their heads and shoulders, Siana and Elizabeth bent their backs to the same task. The three of them worked with a grim concentration. Daniel had put in a word for her with the reverend, and Siana had been granted a whole day off from the rectory. She'd never worked harder in her life.

At noon, Elizabeth straightened, her blistered hands going to her aching back. 'This shouldn't take us much longer.'

Eventually, the cart piled high with swedes, the patient Jasper strained to drag his burden back to the barn. After rubbing the mud from the mule's body with straw, Josh secured him in his stall, where he munched contentedly on some hay.

Half an hour later, the three of them were cleaned up and sitting in the warmth of the farmhouse kitchen with a bowl of thick broth and a wedge of crusty bread in front of them. Josh wolfed his down with the hunger of youth, then attacked another bowl with slightly less urgency. When he'd finished, he fell asleep, his head cushioned on his folded arms.

'So much for my visit,' Siana said, exchanging a rueful smile with Elizabeth.

The older woman cast a pitying eye over Josh. 'Poor lad. Tom works him too hard, and he snatches a moment of sleep when he can. He'll wake in a little while.'

Siana gently ruffled her brother's hair. 'Thank you for looking after him.'

'I can only do a little.'

Siana touched the woman's hand. 'I'm grateful for what you can do. One day I hope to be in a position to support both him and my sister, Daisy.'

'May that day come soon, for I'm frightened Josh might not survive. The lad is small for his age, and malnourished. Tom beats him. He also works him into exhaustion and keeps him tied up like a dog.'

Fear sent Siana's heart leaping into her throat.

Elizabeth's hand curled around hers in a comforting gesture. Across the table their glances met. 'Tom is a man without conscience and Hannah is lacking in mothering skills. Make a home for Josh and Daisy as soon as possible.'

'I . . . I'll try.'

Over the course of the day, Elizabeth's instincts about Siana had been proved correct, and they'd become friends. 'Daniel has told me you care for one another.'

Siana lowered her eyes. 'You must think me unworthy of him.'

'No, my dear. I want my son to be happy and if he finds happiness with you, I'll be contented.' She wanted to warn Siana against Edward Forbes, but she didn't know how to approach the subject. Still, she tried, picking her words with some delicacy. 'The time might come where you're forced to chose between Daniel and the welfare of your family.'

Siana's chin lifted a fraction. 'That would be no choice, for I promised—'

A rap at the door made them all jump before she could finish. Josh woke and jerked upright, his eyes wide with fear.

'Hannah,' Elizabeth whispered as the door opened.

'So this is what goes on when our Tom's away,' Hannah said, her gaze going from one to the other. 'He'll be interested to know our uppity stepsister visits his wife. No doubt he'll think it be real friendly like, but he'll wonder why.'

Siana's glance went to the child in Hannah's arms. 'I came to visit Josh.'

'Josh has work to do. I knows for a fact he had swedes to dig up today.'

'It's done. I helped him with it so he could spend some time with me. Where's our Daisy?'

Hannah shrugged. 'Last time I see'd her she was asleep.'

'You've left her alone? She's only a baby.'

'Won't be for long, will it?'

Hands on hips, Siana stared at her. 'I pay you to look after her.'

'Can't say the shilling doesn't come in handy, but then looking after the brat is a lot of work. In fact, I'm thinking two shilling might buy better care for her.' Hannah smiled. 'Yes, from now on it's two shilling or you can get someone else to wipe her nose and listen to her whinging.'

Josh came to lay his face against Siana's shoulder for comfort.

'How can you be so mean?' Elizabeth said coldly to her. 'You know Siana doesn't earn much, and Daisy is your sister, as well.'

'Well, listen to missus bloody snout-in-the-air,' Hannah said with a gloating smile. 'One word from me about what's goin' on here and Tom will strangle you, and with his bare hands, and all.'

Elizabeth smiled. 'And one word from me about the silver teaspoons you've been stealing to sell to the pawnbroker, and not only will your man lose his job on the farm, you'll never be welcome here again. It'll be the workhouse for the pair of you.'

Hannah paled. 'You wicked, lying shrew. I never did no such thing.'

'No doubt the pawnbroker will vouch for your honesty, then.' Elizabeth opened the door. 'Now, you go home and fetch Daisy back here, so Siana can see her. And make it quick. You can leave your baby with me. He won't come to any harm.'

'Cor,' Josh said, smiling cheekily when Hannah marched off. 'You didn't 'alf tell her.'

'And I enjoyed every minute of it.'

The three of them gazed at each other and laughed.

Hannah's baby woke up at the sound. He gazed unseeingly around him from pale blue eyes. He was a pale little thing with chubby cheeks and a wisp of gingery hair. He smelled of urine and vomit.

Siana gazed down at him, thinking what a sweet, innocent-looking little boy he was under his dirt. 'He looks like a Skinner. I wonder what his name is.'

'George, after the previous king,' Elizabeth said, trying to repress a smile. 'Hannah said he passed by her in a coach when she was small, and threw her a farthing.'

Josh grinned. 'It was probably the bishop. He be known for his stingy nature.'

They began to laugh.

But Siana wasn't laughing when she laid eyes on Daisy. Her sister was lice-infested, and was covered in bruises and weeping sores. She was too thin, her bones sharp under the covering of her skin. Dulled eyes gazed at her without recognition . . . or hope, come to that, Siana thought as she whispered, 'What have you done to her?'

'Nothing. I ain't done nothing.'

'That's obvious,' Elizabeth snapped. 'The child doesn't look as though she's had a bath or anything to eat for the last month and she's been ill-treated judging from those bruises.'

Hannah whined, 'It weren't my fault. I can't help it if she don't eat. And she's learning to walk now and she keeps falling over. There's somethin' wrong with her.'

Daisy had difficulty eating the milk sops Elizabeth prepared for her. She slept afterwards, as quiet as a mouse, cuddled against Siana's chest, her thumb in her mouth.

Siana hugged Daisy tight against her, guiltily remembering her promise to her mother. Whatever the consequences, Daisy was going with her when she returned to the rectory. She would never allow her out of her sight again.

7

'Glory be. I don't know what the reverend will say to this.'

Siana gazed helplessly at Mrs Leeman. 'It doesn't matter what he says. If he won't let me keep Daisy here, I shall have to leave.'

'But where would you go, my dear?'

'I don't know.' To Siana's consternation she burst into tears. 'Look at the state she's in, Mrs Leeman. How could I leave her with Hannah any longer?'

The housekeeper's face softened. 'Reverend White is a good man. I'm sure he won't turn her away when he sees her.'

He didn't, but he wasn't pleased. 'The child can stay until somewhere suitable is found. Hmmm, I don't like the look of her, though, she seems a little too lethargic.' His nose wrinkled. 'Is that rag all she has to wear?'

'Yes, sir.'

'I'll go over to Abbie Ponsonby's to see if she's got any spare clothes her children have outgrown to spare.'

'I don't want anyone's charity,' Siana protested, wrapping her shawl around Daisy.

Hc was annoyed by her answer. 'You're presuming on mine, and you have no choice. Your sister is dirty as well as ill and we can't leave her wrapped in a filthy rag. She needs to be bathed, fed and kept warm. If you have no money, you must accept what's offered and be grateful for it. The alternative is the workhouse.'

'I'm sorry, sir,' she said humbly.

'Come girl,' he smiled kindly, 'I'm sorry I spoke harshly to you. The condition she's in is not your fault and you did right to bring her here. I'll fetch Dr Matheson whilst you're cleaning her up. Once the child has recovered, I'll see if I can find a decent home for her.'

Which didn't sound like a good arrangement at all to Siana. She kept her mouth shut though, for she had no one else to turn to, unless . . . there were always her Welsh relatives, weren't there? But her mother had been driven from the village, never to return. They wouldn't welcome Megan's children back into the fold.

As it was, matters were taken out of her hands.

'She must be taken to the infirmary in the morning,' Francis Matheson announced, gazing over her head to direct his remarks to Reverend White. 'The child has pneumonia and will need nursing care if she's to survive. I suspect she also has intestinal worms. The standard of hygiene amongst the peasant class is appalling.'

So would yours be if you had to live under the same conditions, Siana thought resentfully, trying not to glare at this upstart with his air of arrogance and his blunt manner. She knew she'd never forgive Hannah for her neglect.

Later, wrapped in a flannel sheet, Daisy lay between

them on the kitchen table without moving. She'd subjected herself to the doctor's rigorous examination without a protest, and without interest.

'I'll be going to Poole tomorrow so I'll bring Siana with the child myself,' Richard murmured. 'We must try to find someone to care for Daisy afterwards.'

Siana gave a cry of despair. 'I must look after her myself.'

The doctor flicked her a look, his grey eyes astute and piercing. He made a humming sound in his throat. 'I take it this is a charity case?'

'Sir Edward has set a sum of money aside for such cases,' Richard advised him.

'And what would these people do without it?' The doctor's second look was a little more speculative. 'There are some suspicious-looking sores on the child's body. Perhaps we should satisfy ourselves that the child's mother is clean before we take the child in. Some diseases, especially those caused by licentious living, can be passed on by tainted blood. They often cause madness in later life.'

Siana flushed scarlet as she realized what he was suggesting. 'It will be impossible to examine Daisy's mother, Dr Matheson. She is dead and buried. But let me assure you, she had neither the time nor the energy to be licentious. The sores you refer to are due to urine scalding, I believe. They've become infected through neglect by her carer and the application of salve will soon relieve them if she's kept clean and dry.'

'Ah,' he said, looking slightly taken aback. 'Ah . . . yes, indeed, you seem to have some knowledge about the proper care of the young.'

102

'I may be a *peasant*, but I'm able to understand what you're saying. Also, I'd prefer it if you discussed arrangements made for my sister with me. I'm her guardian, not Reverend White, who employs me.'

The doctor stared at her for a moment – a long moment fraught with tension. Gradually, his eyes softened. 'My apologies if I was too abrupt. I had forgotten your circumstances. Am I to understand you're the eldest of Megan Skinner's children who survived that cottage fire?'

'Yes, sir.'

'There was some question in my mind about the manner of your stepfather's death at the time. Perhaps you could satisfy my curiosity.'

'I'll try, sir.'

The doctor steepled his hands together. 'It appeared to me that Bill Skinner had been hit on the head. Did you see an axe anywhere?'

Siana twitched with alarm as she remembered the flat iron. 'No, sir, I didn't see an axe,' she said truthfully. 'It was usually kept in the woodpile. Tom Skinner came for his father's tools, so he probably took the axe with him. You should ask him.'

He seemed satisfied by her answer for he only stared at her for a moment longer before following Richard into his study for a sherry.

'What was all that about?' Richard asked him, trying to keep his tone civil. Already annoyed by having his evening disrupted, he was now forced to entertain a younger man of vague religious belief, a man he found to be slightly self-opinionated and socially uncomfortable.

'Oh, nothing. It's just that the stepfather had a

suspicious hole in his skull.' He shrugged. 'I expect the undertaker was right and a beam fell on him.'

'Surely you don't imagine Siana had a hand in his death.'

'I'm sure she didn't!' Francis Matheson took the sherry offered to him and sipped it with a sigh of satisfaction, grateful for the warmth in his belly. The majority of his patients could offer him nothing, and he had another call to make before he could eat the meal his housekeeper had prepared for him and prop his feet up in front of the fire. 'I was thinking more along the lines of her mother.'

'For what reason?'

'Megan Skinner had been badly beaten. In fact, she had several broken bones. Unless I'm very much mistaken, there were signs that she'd been raped when she was in the process of giving birth.'

Richard stared at him, finding the conversation indelicate. 'The woman was married. It could hardly have been rape.'

'Perhaps not in the eyes of the law. But what would you call such an act under the circumstances? From what I can gather, her husband had consumed nearly a whole bottle of rum that night. He must have flamed up like a Christmas pudding. I'd like to know where he got the means to pay for it.'

Richard shuddered as his conscience gave him a nudge. But he told himself it wasn't his responsibility. Skinner was entitled to his stepdaughter's money while she lived under his roof. Was it his fault the man had got drunk on it and set about his wife?

'Who can account for the priorities of the lower classes? Perhaps I'll sermonize on the evils of drink next Sunday.'

'You do that, Reverend,' Francis said drily. 'They might sit up and take notice, and Megan Skinner might rise from her grave and applaud.'

Richard gave a shaky laugh as he tried to bring the unpleasant conversation to a close. 'I'd suggest your reasoning is flawed, Dr Matheson. With all those broken bones you mentioned, Megan Skinner would hardly have had the strength to fetch an axe, brain her husband then put it back in the woodpile before collapsing – and all this with the cottage on fire and herself about to give birth to a child.'

'We don't know that it was put back in the woodpile.' The doctor shrugged. 'I learned whilst I was at Cambridge that a man of logic can always reason things away to his satisfaction and mental comfort. It's not totally beyond belief, but I agree it sounds unlikely. However, it doesn't really matter, because even if Megan Skinner did manage it, no doubt her husband deserved it.'

'Thou shalt not kill,' Richard reminded him gently, for he didn't want to become embroiled in an argument.

A snort of laughter came from the doctor. 'Thou kills if thou is desperate enough. When you doctor these people you discover just how desperate they can get, and notice how easily their lot could be improved. A sermon doesn't fill a hole in an empty belly and drink dulls the pain of it.'

Richard didn't offer him a second glass of sherry. In

fact, if Francis Matheson hadn't been the cousin of his bishop, he wouldn't have offered him the first glass as he suspected him of being, at best, an agnostic – if not a complete atheist! Richard plucked the empty glass from the man's fingers and placed it on the tray, at a loss for what to say next. 'I have to prepare for evening prayers, so I'll say goodnight to you, Doctor,' he mumbled eventually.

'Fire and brimstone,' Matheson advised as he picked up his hat. 'That's what they understand. Fill their bellies with warmth and their minds with the fear of everlasting hellfire. Hope is a thin gruel these days, and if there's trouble simmering in the cooking pot, the travelling preachers will set it to the boil, you mark my words.'

Richard's mouth pursed slightly. 'I have no patience with the rantings of Methodist ministers.'

'Neither have I, but you've got to admire the way they preach. I've heard that one of their finest is travelling the country right now. You might drop in to observe his performance when he reaches Cheverton Chase.' Matheson jammed his hat on his head and strode out into the cold night, a tall and imposing figure, bristling with muscular energy. Before he mounted his horse he said, 'Good evening to you, sir. I'll expect the child in the morning if your God of goodness doesn't see fit to harvest her soul during the night.'

Richard sighed with relief when he shut the door behind him.

Siana had never been to Poole before. If she hadn't been so worried about Daisy, who'd developed a fever during the night, she'd have enjoyed the journey through the frosted fields.

The sight of prickly, green holly bushes laden with bright red berries reminded her that Christmas was almost upon them. But the thought of not being able to share it with her mother and siblings, however poor their fare had been in the past, filled her with melancholy.

The infirmary was attached to the workhouse. They were taken to a room of stark, whitewashed stone, which was filled with iron beds topped with thin mattresses. The beds contained emaciated figures, some sitting on the side, thin legs dangling, clutching at the edges for support.

It was not a place of rest. Hampered by the pain and stiffness of rheumatism, many of them groaned each time they moved. Some hacked their lives away in paroxysms of coughing whilst others, seemingly in the last stages of dropsy, gasped to fill their labouring lungs with the breath needed to stay alive one more minute, another hour or a day. There were no other children there.

It was bitterly cold. The damp and reluctant beech logs burning in the grate sent out only an insignificant amount of heat.

'Put the child in the corner bed,' a woman in a white apron and cap said a little wearily. 'Dr Matheson will be along shortly.'

An hour later he arrived, rubbing his hands briskly together to bring some warmth into them. 'Good, I see she made it through the night, then?' Gently he laid the back of his hand across Daisy's forehead. 'She's fevered and should go into crisis during the next twenty-four hours. I'll dose her on opium and treacle to help her through it, but don't expect too much.'

A sound of flatulence came from the woman in the next bed. The reverend held a handkerchief under his nose, saying hastily, 'Come, Siana, we must go. I'll remember Daisy in my prayers tonight.'

The tiny whimpering noise Daisy made sounded like a protest. Siana cuddled the child against her, smoothing her hair back from her forehead. She had the feeling she wouldn't see her sister again if she left her now. She gazed at the doctor, tears gathering in her eyes. 'Can't I stay? I can look after her, and perhaps help with the other patients too. I promise I'll be no trouble. I'll sleep on the floor next to her bed.'

Behind her, the reverend made an impatient clicking noise with his tongue. 'There's nothing you can do for Daisy now, Siana. Her life is in God's hands.'

Stubbornly, she said, 'But He allows men to train as doctors, so He must have intended them to do His work for Him. No doubt His holy spirit flows into Dr Matheson's hands to heal through them.'

And she looked so innocent and plausible! Francis smiled to himself, admiring the ingenuity of this young woman's reasoning and the flummoxed look on the reverend's face. Her use of flattery towards himself was duly noted, as was the fact she knew he wasn't fooled by it. However, he was quite content to indulge in a moment of comfortable idolatry and as it was obvious she was determined to get her own way with the reverend, he added his support.

'You can share the bed with your sister. No doubt the

matron in charge will welcome your help feeding the
infirm. As for God, I'd be honoured if He decides to
assist me in healing His flock.'

Siana slanted him a quick glance. Despite the
circumstances, he could have sworn he saw a gleam of
mischief in her eyes. The young woman was no fool.

Reverend White appeared out of countenance. 'But
my books—'

'Surely you can spare her for a day or two, Reverend
White? If this child was your sister would you leave her
to face dea— er, this battle by herself? The patient has
recently suffered the loss of her parents. Having her
sister near will be a comfort to her. It might even help
her to fight the disease.'

Noticing the doctor's slip of the tongue, and his
attempt to cover it up, Siana was grateful for his
sensitivity. Clearly, he expected Daisy to die. She took
the little pouch from inside her skirt and removed the
silver cross her mother had given her, placing it on
Daisy's pillow. 'Of course he can spare me.'

Reminded forcibly of his calling by the appearance
of the silver cross, the reverend prayed for humility to
overcome his arrogance as he made a dignified retreat.
It was a long time coming. Deep down he had a feeling
that the girl had made a fool out of him.

Disgruntled, he decided to call on Daniel and invite
him to lunch before he returned home. He admitted to
himself that he was having second thoughts about the
relationship between the two. Siana had displayed more
strength and stubbornness than he liked to see in a
woman, especially a woman beholden to him.

Still, now Daniel no longer lived at home, the pair might grow apart. He wouldn't interfere, of course, but neither would he do anything to directly encourage them. Should the matter crop up in conversation, he would counsel Daniel to caution.

That decided, as he hurried to his godson's place of employment, he told himself he need not mention Siana's presence at the hospital to Daniel.

He found Daniel seated at a desk, his head bowed over a court report he was copying. He had a good hand, but didn't look as though he was enjoying the task, Richard thought. The boredom on his face cleared, however, when he looked up.

'Sir,' he exclaimed. 'I had no idea you were coming to Poole today.'

'Neither did I. Can you be spared for lunch?'

He could, and was. The pair found a corner table in a popular dining hall attached to an inn overlooking the harbour. There they chatted through a hearty meal of steak and kidney pie, which was accompanied by several dishes of vegetables. This was followed by boiled suet pudding covered in a hot fruit conserve, which floated in sea of sweet, yellow custard.

They spooned the pudding into their mouths, then, replete, smoked aromatic cigars brought to them by their host as they sipped dark, fragrant coffee served in white china cups.

'Just the thing for a cold winter's day,' Richard declared, his belief in himself restored by the liberal application of inner comfort. It would fortify him on the icy journey home.

Daniel smiled. 'I doubt if I'll want to eat for a week after this, but my father has invited me to dine with him at the manor after church on Sunday. He said he has something to discuss with me. Do you have any idea what it is?'

Richard gently belched behind his hand. 'I'm afraid not. The squire doesn't take me into his confidence.'

There was no uncomfortable gluttony for Siana. The workhouse kitchen provided a stolid fare of coarse bread to dip into a thick pea soup. This had the addition of onion for flavour.

It was brought in in a pail, which was carried by a young woman heavy with child – a woman Siana recognized.

Leaving Daisy, who was now in a laudanum-induced sleep, Siana crossed to where the woman stood. 'Aren't you, Peggy, Will Hastings's widow?'

The woman avoided her eyes. 'That I am.'

'I'm Siana Lewis.'

Resentful eyes met hers. 'I knows who you be. Tom Skinner's sister.'

'No, I'm not his sister. He was my stepbrother.'

Her expression grew a little friendlier. 'Well, I'd disown him too if he was my stepbrother. He's a bad lot.' She shrugged. 'I heard tell that Bill Skinner and your mother died.'

'Yes . . .'

'In here, then, are you? It's not too bad a place if you don't mind sleeping on straw and picking oakum most of the day. At least you get to eat.'

111

'My sister's been taken ill. I'm just helping out,' Siana explained. She started filling the bowls and distributing them to the sick, stopping to help feed them where necessary. The sound of lapping tongues filled the air, as if the place were full of hungry dogs.

Peggy's glance went to the small, still form on the bed. 'You'd better eat your sister's share. She doesn't need it. Dying, isn't she?'

'No,' Siana said vehemently, 'I promised my mother I'd look after her.'

Peggy shrugged. 'How? Times is hard. Nobody wants to hire a woman with a child to look after. Best if she dies now.'

'I'll manage somehow,' Siana said fiercely. 'I'm employed by Reverend White and he's been good to me. He might let Daisy stay.'

'I wouldn't bank on it. Men says one thing when they really means another.' Peggy's glance was speculative. 'Still, with your looks . . .? The vicar's a widower, isn't he?'

Shock hit Siana. 'He's a lot older than me,' and she softly giggled as the ludicrous thought took root. 'He doesn't give women a second glance.'

Peggy stared at her. 'You could try and make him give you a second glance.'

'Don't be silly. He doesn't attract me in the least, besides . . .' She bit down on her tongue, remembering her relationship with Daniel was supposed to be kept a secret. 'I'd rather wait until I love somebody.'

Bitterly, Peggy said, 'It didn't do me much good. My Will didn't do it, you know.'

'Didn't do what?'

'Set fire to that bleddy haystack. It were your Tom.'

'Tom?'

'I walked out with him once or twice.' She shuddered. 'He couldn't keep it inside his trousers. Tried to force hisself on me when I refused. Luckily, my dad came along and knocked him senseless with his cane. I finished with Tom after that, started going out with Will.'

Siana stared at her, horrified. 'How do you know Tom set fire to the haystack?'

'I just knows. He swore he'd get even with me. What do you think he was doing over Winterborne way? He knew my Will had gone visiting and was lying in wait for him. When he saw him coming, he set the haystack alight. Will didn't own no lantern. He's a mean cuss, your Tom.'

'I know.' Siana sighed in despair, remembering the way Josh was being treated by him. 'Can't your dad help you out?'

Peggy sighed. 'Stomach flux took him off last winter. I'm all alone now. I don't know what I'm going to do once winter's over. I'll apply for a discharge and head off to London, I reckon. I might be able to find some fancy needlework in one of the shops if the babby dies.'

'When's it due?'

'Any day now.' She placed her hands over her rounded stomach and smiled. 'He doesn't 'alf kick hard. I don't really want him to die. He's the only thing left of my Will. I don't know how we're going to manage, though.'

Siana didn't know how she was going to manage

113

either. But she intended to make a home for her brother and sister and give them everything they needed. If that meant marrying someone like the Reverend White, then she'd do it. It wouldn't, though, because she'd find a way of coping until Daniel was ready.

Her resolve was forgotten when Daisy took a turn for the worse. As her sister thrashed and whimpered in a fevered convulsion, the woman in charge sent for the doctor.

'She can't stand much more,' he said, and Siana could have sworn there were tears in his eyes.

The little silver cross glinted in the candlelight. Siana felt very humble as her hand closed around it. *Please spare Daisy's life.*

The cross in her hand grew warm and a cool breeze tugged at her skirt. The candle flickered. 'Have faith in God,' Reverend White always said. But something else pulled at her, something as old and wise as the earth. One had to trust one's own instincts. The doctor was only a man and, although he was doing his best, it was not the right treatment for Daisy.

'Opium is wrong. We must cool my sister with water and her convulsions will stop.'

'Are you mad, girl? She'll die from the chill of it.'

'She will die from convulsions caused by the fever if she's left. So she has nothing to lose. We must wet the sheets.'

'I will not countenance such treatment.'

'I'm not asking you to, Doctor.'

'For God's sake,' he muttered, 'what nonsense is this? Am I to follow the advice of a mere girl? The child has

114

pneumonia. She's dying, and you are suffering from extreme idiocy.'

'No,' Siana said flatly. 'The fever is making Daisy convulse and the laudanum takes away her will to fight the disease. If we can cool her down it might save her life.'

'An old wives' tale, yet there's a train of thought within the profession that you couldn't possibly know about.' He stared almost angrily at her for a few moments. 'You do realize the probability of your sister surviving is remote? The laudanum will make her death easier to bear.'

'I know, but my sister is not being given a choice, so I must make it for her.'

He hesitated for a moment longer, then he sighed and nodded to the attendant. 'Do as she says. I'll take the child through to the consulting room and she can tend her there.'

It was a long night. The tepid water brought goose-bumps up on Daisy's body. The bed shook with the force of her trembling as she tossed and turned. When her fever increased and the heat from her body dried the sheets, Siana saturated them again. She bathed Daisy's head and trickled teaspoons of water into her mouth.

Daisy slept in fitful bursts. She shrieked and moaned, called out for her mama. Her teeth ground together as she tried to push the cold sheets from her body, then set up a clacking chatter as she shivered for long periods of time. Towards morning, she stopped resisting the treatment and fell into an exhausted sleep. I'm losing her, Siana thought.

She laid her hand against the child's stomach,

finding her to be icy cold and clammy. The child was almost dead.

'Don't leave me, my darling Daisy,' she whispered. 'I promise I will never send you away from me again.'

Wrapping her mother's shawl around Daisy's body, she drew her close, and began to sing the lullaby her mother used to sing to her.

'Baby of mine, the sun has gone and the shadows creep in like a mouse. But safe in my arms I'll keep you from harm till the morning light blesses our house . . .' Exhausted, Siana closed her eyes for a moment . . .

'Well, I'll be damned, she was right,' Francis said softly.

His patient was awake. Sucking her thumb, her other hand was entangled in a length of her sister's dark hair. A pair of solemn blue eyes regarded him.

Siana was perched precariously on a stool. The upper half of her body was supported by her folded arms but she was lying sideways and in danger of slipping to the floor.

'So you made it?' he whispered.

Siana stirred slightly at the sound of his voice, then jerked awake when the child gave an alarmed cry. Her sideways motion was restrained by the arm he extended to stop her.

For a moment she stared wildly at him, then straightened herself and turned towards her burden. Her eyes widened with disbelief as she stated the obvious. 'She's still alive.'

'Aye,' he said, and smiled. 'You're not going to go all weak female on me, are you?'

'Certainly not,' she laughed.

'Good, because she's not out of danger yet.'

Her smile faded. 'What must I do?'

'She must be watched carefully for the next few days and given plenty of fluids. When she's strong enough, she must be purged of intestinal worms. Then her body must be built up with good, nourishing food. Can you supply all that?'

'I'll have to throw myself on the goodness of Reverend White.'

'And if he isn't as good as his calling suggests he should be?'

Her chin lifted slightly. 'I'll do what I have to do to survive. I've told Daisy she will never be sent away from me again. I promised my mother I would care for her and I didn't. Now I must.' She kissed the matted hair on top of the child's head and her voice began to wobble. 'I've nearly lost her once. I won't let it happen again.'

May luck shine on you, then, Francis thought soberly. He'd seen many young women slide into a life of degradation under better circumstances than this one faced.

She had no home. And although she was employed, he'd wager the good Reverend White would find some excuse to turn them out before too long. In Francis's experience, the man rarely practised what he preached.

You're certainly going to need every bit of help you can get, he thought.

8

The first Daniel knew of Siana being in Poole was when he saw her gazing at ladies' hats on display in a milliner's window. Her eyes were wide with wonder as her breath steamed a round patch of mist on the windows.

She looked tired, he thought, and he wondered what her business was in Poole. He experienced a moment of dismay. Surely she wasn't about to visit him in his place of work? Just then, someone came out of the shop and spoke sharply to her. And no wonder. She looked like a beggar in her scruffy boots. Her skirt appeared to have been slept in.

About to catch her up and greet her, he saw his employer coming across the road. He drew back into the shadow of a doorway until he'd passed by. Daniel was ashamed of his action, but he knew his association with a peasant girl like Siana would attract speculation.

By the time it was safe to move, Siana had lengthened her stride. He quickened his pace and caught up with her just as she was turning into the gates of the workhouse.

'Siana,' he called out, 'wait!'

'Daniel?' A smile lit up her face as she turned to gaze

at him. Nervously, she tried to smooth her crumpled skirt. 'I just came out for some air.'

He glanced at the building, then back at her. 'What are you doing here?'

Weariness crept back into her expression. 'Daisy is in the infirmary. The reverend brought us here a couple of days ago.'

His mouth tightened. Why hadn't his godfather mentioned it when they'd lunched together? 'How is she?'

'Over the crisis and improving. Dr Matheson has been so kind. He's allowed me to stay with her. He said she'll be able to leave in a few days.' She shrugged. 'I might have to stay here though.'

'In the workhouse? But why?'

She explained her dilemma.

'I'm sure the reverend will allow Daisy to stay. I'll have a word with him.'

'Thank you, Daniel.'

Drawing her behind the tall pillar which supported the gate, he gently kissed her cheek, smiling as he watched her blush. He daren't kiss her mouth for it would affect his bodily comfort, but he couldn't wait until he could make her his own. The male urge was running rampant in him and he wondered briefly whether he could persuade her to stray in that direction.

But no. Daniel had come to the conclusion that despite her humble birth, Siana Lewis was not a girl who'd give her favours lightly to a man.

'I've got something for you.' He drew the amber ring from his waistcoat pocket and slid it onto her finger. 'It belonged to my mother and I've had it engraved with your name. It will remind you of what we mean to each other, even when we're apart.'

Tears sprang to her eyes, making them glisten darkly. Her eyelashes quivered as she gazed at the stone, glowing like liquid gold in the silver setting. 'It's so pretty, like leaves in autumn. I shall treasure it, always.'

'As I'll treasure you always.' His arms came around her, his chin rested on her head. 'I wish we could be together now, but we can't.'

The sound of footsteps sent them leaping apart as the doctor rounded the corner. He gazed from one to the other, his eyes narrowing. 'Ah, if it isn't Daniel Ayres.' He held out a hand. 'I'd heard you'd finished your studies. I didn't know you and Siana were acquainted.'

'Why shouldn't we be?' Daniel blustered. 'She works for my godfather.'

'Ah yes . . . the good reverend.' His tone suggested he thought exactly the opposite.

'I came to enquire after Daisy.'

'The child's doing quite nicely, thanks to her sister's care . . . and your godfather's entreaties to the almighty, of course. Like most of the unfortunates round here, she needs a solid roof over her head and a constant supply of nourishing food in her belly.' The doctor doffed his hat. 'Don't keep the girl too long else she'll miss out on her midday meal. There's precious little of it to go round as it is.'

'I was just returning to work,' Daniel muttered, made suddenly aware of his uncomfortably full stomach. 'Good day to you, Miss Lewis. I'm pleased to hear your sister is improving.' And he was gone, striding off towards the town centre.

'An attractive, but singularly shallow young man,' Dr Matheson remarked. 'He means well but he blows with the wind. Don't let him turn your head, my dear.'

But Dr Matheson didn't know Daniel as well as she did. Daniel was fine and good, a gentleman in every way, despite his birth. But still there was unease in her. How could Daniel love her when she was so beneath him? And why had he moved away? She saw so little of him now, and being apart made her doubt, as if her feelings towards him were false.

But when they were together, everything seemed real. Siana smiled as her fingers closed over the amber ring.

On Sunday, Daniel was relieved to discover that Isabelle Prosser had returned to her own home to prepare for her wedding to his father. He liked these man-to-man sessions with his father. They were comfortably familiar and usually had something in them that was to his benefit.

'It's to be a grander affair than I expected,' his father said gloomily after a splendid dinner consisting of several courses.

They had retired to his father's private sitting room, decorated with mellow wood panelling and redolent of polish. A matching pair of coach dogs rose from their position in front of the fire when they entered, baring their teeth and snarling softly in their throats until they recognized the intruder.

A manservant placed a humidor of cigars and a tray

containing a decanter of brandy and glasses on a low table, within reach of the squire's elbow. He bowed slightly and retired.

'No doubt I shall be paraded like a prize bull at a show for all her friends when the time comes.'

Daniel, well fed and relaxed, accepted a snifter of brandy and chuckled. He selected a cigar with a connoisseur's nose, for he enjoyed the finer things in life and liked to appear knowledgeable about them. His father looked on with approval and soon the pair were enjoying each other's companionship in a haze of aromatic smoke.

'Damn women. They enjoy making a fuss over weddings,' Edward grumbled.

'Yes, I suppose they do.' Daniel, who had been hoping to be acknowledged with a wedding invitation, was wondering whether there had been an oversight. He debated bringing the matter up.

He discounted the idea. He enjoyed being in this big house in the exclusive company of his father and would do nothing to spoil the evening. An opportunity might arise later.

'You may have been wondering why I invited you tonight,' Edward murmured, smiling expansively at him.

Daniel had been wondering no such thing. He considered these rare dinners with his father to be a right rather than a special event, even if they were few and far between. However, he wasn't required to give an answer as his father continued talking.

'I've been thinking, my boy. A young man like you should see something of the world before he settles down.'

Daniel's heart lurched. 'What are you proposing, sir?'

His father's eyes came up to his, as mellow as wine. 'The grand tour of Europe. Take a year out from your profession. It will give you a chance to make useful contacts and educate yourself in the ways of the world. At my expense, of course.'

Edward chuckled when Daniel inhaled too much smoke and nearly choked on it.

'You might even meet a rich widow.'

Daniel's mouth opened, then shut again when his father winked. 'Not necessarily with marriage in mind, of course. I daresay there's not much I can teach you about that side of life, eh!'

Daniel laughed. It was best not to mention Siana to his father. A year was not very long, after all, and she would wait for him. A girl in her position wouldn't receive a better offer. The chance of going abroad took his breath away, and to think it had just fallen into his lap.

'Can you be ready to depart in two weeks?'

'Two weeks?' he stammered. No wonder he hadn't received an invitation to the wedding. 'So soon?'

Edward gazed at him steadily over his glass. 'Why yes, Daniel. Your passage is booked and the ship will not wait. You don't have a problem with that, do you?'

'Why no, sir. It's come as a complete surprise, that's all.'

'A pleasant one, I trust.' His father rose and threw a friendly arm around his shoulders, subjecting him to a brief squeeze before letting him go. 'Stay the night and we'll discuss further details over breakfast. Hell! Why don't you move in as my guest for the next couple of weeks? Then I can make sure you're kitted out properly.'

Overwhelmed by his generosity, Daniel smiled. This was beyond his wildest dreams. 'Won't that be an imposition?'

'I'll be glad of your company. Females are all very well in their place, but sometimes they talk such damned fluff and nonsense. One can relax in the company of men.'

'Thank you very much, sir,' Daniel said, feeling very manly and so much in his father's confidence that he mentioned Siana several times over the course of the next ten minutes.

'One can't help feeling you think a lot of the girl,' Edward said lazily.

'I've never met anyone like her before. She is so brave, and clever.' Slightly befuddled with the brandy, Daniel lost all caution as he smiled broadly and announced, 'We have a secret understanding.'

Edward slowly exhaled. 'Is that wise, Daniel?'

'No, it's not wise, but she has responsibilities. She needs me.'

'Ah, I see. You know, sometimes the protective instinct in the male can be mistaken for something else. A clever woman will take advantage of it.'

Which planted another seed of doubt in Daniel's mind and, although Edward changed the subject, the doubt remained.

For an hour or so, they talked of politics and the state of the nation which, according to his father, was in a bad way. 'You cannot live indefinitely beyond your means, remember that, Daniel. Plan your life so there is money put aside. When it's time to wed, find a woman modest in every way except for her means.'

'What about love, sir?'

'Ah . . . love.' He was smiling now. 'Love makes you vulnerable. Never let love get in the way of good business sense. Women often misread your intentions and demand more than a man is prepared, or able, to give them.'

And Daniel knew Edward was referring to his mother.

'The moral of this, of course, is to promise nothing to a woman until you have sown all your wild oats and are completely sure of what you want from life.' Edward threw his cigar stump into the ashes then stood and rang for the manservant. 'Show Mr Ayres to the guest room, Harrison. I'll expect his every need to be met whilst he's here.'

The manservant smiled slightly. 'Yes, sir. I'm quite sure they will be.'

'Goodnight, Daniel. I hope you'll enjoy the comfort of the bedroom I've had prepared for you.'

Daniel was surprised to find the room he'd been allocated already occupied. The girl was young and slender, with long dark hair, soulful brown eyes and a full-lipped mouth. Seated cross-legged on the bed she smiled as he gazed at her. She looked totally innocent until she arched her back like an elegant cat, giving him a glimpse of dark shadow where her chemise had ridden up.

His crotch began to tighten and he sucked in a breath.

Stepping from the bed, the girl walked barefoot towards him. When she reached him she fell to her knees and loosened the flaps on his trousers. The rouge on her mouth formed a ruby oval as she cupped him in her hands and leaned forward. Her hair fell in a curtain of dark perfumed ripples as it tumbled over her face. Her tongue was warm and moist.

A few moments later in complete and absolute ecstasy, he whispered, 'Christ!'

He spent the next two weeks in the company of his father during the day. His nights were occupied by the delicious and dusky-skinned Jasmine. He hurriedly visited his godfather, and said goodbye to his mother. About to board the ship that was to take him to the continent, he remembered Siana Lewis and scribbled her a note, which he handed to his father.

Edward approached Reverend Richard White shortly before Daisy was due to be discharged from hospital.

'I need your advice, Richard,' he said. 'I have a letter for Siana Lewis from Daniel. The boy didn't have time to deliver it himself.'

Richard expressed surprise. 'He was here to say goodbye yesterday. Why didn't he leave it with me then?'

The squire shrugged. 'He's been busy. You know how hectic the social life of young men is. He didn't write it until last night. But I wanted to consult with you about his relationship with Siana Lewis. I don't really want the relationship to continue.'

'I've been thinking along those lines myself lately. I thought this trip might allow him to get over his infatuation with her.'

'It would, Richard. But she's a fetching little thing, and a year isn't long, especially if the girl is here to come back to. Daniel is not unskilled in the art of seduction. I wouldn't be surprised if she hadn't succumbed to him already. She's of an age.' He shrugged. 'But I've been listening to gossip and perhaps I'm doing the girl an injustice. Just because the mother had a reputation, it doesn't mean the daughter has inherited the same low standard of morals.'

Richard's eyes sharpened. 'Daniel surely hasn't indicated that she lacks virtue? I had the impression their regard for each other was pure.'

'I'm not suggesting it isn't. It's just idle talk.'

'Dear God!' Richard appeared quite agitated. 'I couldn't keep a girl of bad reputation under my roof. If the bishop got to hear of it, he'd take me to task.'

'Quite. Then there's the young sister to take into consideration. An infant would be a totally disruptive element in your household.'

'Yes, it had occurred to me that it might be wise to let her go.'

'You mustn't worry about it, Richard. I'll deal with the problem. The workhouse is under my governorship. It will be easier if you just write a note to the girl to that effect. I'll make sure she gets it.'

Richard sighed as he moved to the writing desk. 'Such a pity. She's a bright little thing and I thought eventually to lift her from her poverty.'

'You're too good, Richard. I'll do what I can for the family, of course. The father was one of my workers, after all.'

Richard wrote a note of dismissal to Siana, wishing her well in the future. He added a reference praising her work and enclosed a few shillings, the sum total of her wages and her small amount of savings. He sent Mrs Leeman upstairs to pack the girl's goods. Mrs Leeman's reproachful look filled him with guilt, but she said nothing.

Richard decided he would go over to the church later and pray for the girl's soul. The Lord in his wisdom would look after her. As an afterthought, he added an extra three shillings to the bundle, replacing the money which her stepfather had drawn before his death. His generous gesture eased the burden of his guilt.

'I'll send her chattels over to the workhouse in the morning.'

Edward eyed the small bundle. 'Have it tied to my saddle. I'll take them with me.'

They shared another glass of sherry as they discussed the Tolpuddle troublemakers.

'We simply cannot allow farm labourers to set up unions in the district. They call it bargaining strength, I call it an attempt to blackmail the landowners,' Edward growled. 'James Frampton is gathering evidence which will convict the five labourers concerned.'

Richard murmured, 'Squire Frampton is diligent in his pursuit of the miscreants.'

'They'll be going to trial at the Dorchester Assizes next month. I see no problem in getting a conviction. The judge is Baron Williams and the jury foreman is tipped to be William Ponsonby who, as you know, is the brother-in-law of the Home Secretary.'

'A worthy jury, I hear,' Richard said piously. 'Being magistrates, most of them have the experience to deal with the unusual charge. Are you expecting trouble?'

'Most certainly. Personally, I'd be inclined to hang

them all. But they have many supporters, so to avoid further unrest I imagine they'll be sentenced to transportation. It will get them out of the way whilst the hubbub dies down. They'll soon be forgotten.'

He changed the subject. 'By the way, Richard, I was talking to the bishop the other day. I'm thinking of suggesting an increase in the living for this parish.' As Edward prepared to leave, he picked up his son's letter to Siana Lewis. 'Your advice, Richard. Should I deliver it or not?'

Richard made the decision expected of him. Plucking it from Edward's fingers, he smiled and dropped the letter into the fire.

Edward was smiling too when he left. He tucked Richard's note to Siana in the pocket of his greatcoat and turned his horse towards Croxley Farm. It was time to finalize the contract with Tom Skinner.

Elizabeth was upstairs when she heard the hoof beats.

There was a little rush of blood to her face when she glanced out of the window to see Edward coming along the lane. Removing her apron, she tidied her hair, pinched some colour into her cheeks and sprinkled a little rose-water onto her neck and wrists.

She didn't hurry when he knocked at the door, just moved sedately down the stairs.

She affected surprise when she opened the door. 'Edward, how lovely to see you.'

He shuffled from one foot to the other. 'I came to see your husband.'

'Of course, but he's gone to the market.' She stood

aside. 'You look cold. Can I offer you some refreshment? I'd like to take this opportunity to talk to you about Daniel now Tom is absent. Some things need to be kept private between us.'

He stooped his head slightly as he entered. 'I can't stay for long.'

'Let me take your hat and coat.' She deposited the garments on a chair and smiled at him. Dear God! She'd forgotten how handsome he was. She'd thought Tom's brutality had deadened any such feelings in her, but despite all that had happened, the sight of Edward filled her loins with a familiar and unwelcome lust.

'Come into the drawing room. The fire's lit and it's warmer in there.'

He followed her in, his glance sweeping over her from head to toe. 'You look thinner, but it suits you,' he said, reaching out to gently cup her face. 'Is your husband still treating you badly?'

Elizabeth shrugged and turned her cheek in a brief caress against his palm. 'He knows no other way. He's learned to place the bruises where they don't show. But let's not talk of that. I wanted to thank you for what you did for Daniel. He's always wanted to go abroad.'

He inclined his head. 'I needed to do something for him. I'm thinking of investing a settlement for him before Isabelle provides me with an heir. It will mature when he reaches the age of twenty-five. That will keep the damned fortune-hunters away until he's learned some sense.'

Her heart sank when he mentioned his forthcoming marriage. 'Would you like a brandy?'

'Not if it's the rot-gut sold by the inn.'

'It's not. I brought this with me from your house in Dorchester.'

He gave a short bark of laughter. 'You dare to offer me a glass of brandy from a bottle you stole from me? I could have you thrown in jail, woman.'

'I stole a dozen bottles and I'm already in jail.' She gave a little groan as she rose from her chair.

His eyes hooded over. 'What ails you?'

'Nothing.'

In an instant he was by her side. 'You should know by now. When I ask a question, I expect a truthful answer. Let me see what he's done to you.'

When she shook her head, his fingers went to the buttons on her bodice. She shivered as he began to expose her breasts, stilling his hands when he uncovered a bruise.

'Damn that barbarian,' he muttered, 'I'll take a whip to his back.' She trembled when he caressed the mark. 'What did he use? His fists?'

'And his belt. The metal cut me.'

Edward's eyes came up to hers, full of fiery rage. 'I want to see all of it, Elizabeth. Every mark and every bruise.'

She bit back on her tears. Removing her bodice she allowed him to draw it from her arms. She then loosened her skirt. Stepping out of the garment she placed it across a chair. She stood there in her warm cotton chemise and stockings.

'Drop the chemise.'

'Edward,' she protested.

'Drop it!'

He loosened the ties himself and sucked in a breath when it pooled around her ankles. She felt no shame in

131

her nakedness. Edward had often seen her thus. The bruises and welts were livid against her skin. 'I'll kill Tom Skinner,' he breathed.

'I'm his wife. He has the right to do as he pleases with me,' she said dully.

'Like hell he does,' Edward growled. 'Do you have any salve?'

'There's some witch hazel in the kitchen.'

He fetched it. Holding the liquid in his cupped palm to warm it at first, he gradually applied it to her contusions.

His ministrations were soothing and she gave a little murmur of appreciation. Gradually his breathing began to grow heavier. When he had finished, he pulled her back against him, his erection pressing hard and urgent against the cleft of her buttocks.

'I'd forgotten how exquisite your body was, Elizabeth. You cannot throw me out in this state. I beg you, allow me some ease.'

She smiled. Edward had never begged for anything in his life. She was as aroused as he was now. He turned her round, his palms circling her breasts. His eyes were heavy with passion. 'How long have we got?'

It had been a long time since they'd made love. When they'd been together, her attraction for him had faded towards the end of the relationship. Now it was back with a vengeance, it seemed. She would have laughed at his need for her if she hadn't been inflicted by need herself. It had been a long time since anyone had treated her so tenderly.

They wouldn't be disturbed. She'd helped Josh complete his chores earlier that day and had given him some time off. 'Tom won't be back until after dark,' she replied. But it would serve him right if he came home earlier and found them together, she thought. It would be a delicious revenge.

He groaned as he hoisted her in his arms and headed for the stairs. He took her on the marital bed she shared unwillingly with her husband, filling her with the potent power of his need and making her cry out with each slow and ecstatic surrender.

It was nearly dark when his passion was finally expended. Edward began to wonder if he'd made a mistake in discarding Elizabeth.

Then he remembered the youthful and unsullied charms of Siana Lewis. She was the one he had to have. Pleased with the reaffirmation of his manly prowess, for he'd been jaded of late, Edward narrowed his eyes as he recognized in his craving something of the herd bull in him. He looked forward to being the one to storm the Lewis girl's defences and accept the surrender of her innocence, before someone else did.

On the way out he nearly tripped over a lad in the yard. He was thin and pale with large eyes. He gave a cheeky smile as he pulled his forelock. 'If it be Tom Skinner you're after seeing, he'll be at the inn, sir – as he is every market day at this time.'

Edward stared at him for a moment – a moment filled with awareness. A smile touched his mouth. Tossing the lad a coin, he mounted his horse and rode off into the gloom.

It was with a clear conscience that Edward ran Tom Skinner to earth at the inn. He felt like a man who'd given Tom a rare and precious gift, only to have that gift abused. The man was an oaf. There was no reason why Edward couldn't enjoy Elizabeth still, if and when he needed to. If necessary he'd take her back.

However, he had need of Tom at the moment. He needed him to help Siana Lewis realize the lie of the land. He wanted the girl to be grateful to him, and to come to his arms willingly, like Elizabeth had. This afternoon had taught him he was a man in his prime. Elizabeth being another man's wife simply added a dangerous and exciting edge to the relationship.

Love was a game. A game he intended to win. He intended to enjoy both Elizabeth and Siana, as well as get a child or two on Isabelle when they wed.

Although Elizabeth's injuries were uppermost in his mind, he knew he couldn't charge Tom Skinner with them and remain anonymous as her lover. Eventually he'd find a way to repay Tom for his treatment of her, though.

The hour was early and the few people in the room became quiet when he entered. He accepted an ale from the barman, then, buying a round of drinks, drew Tom Skinner to one side.

Despite his resolve to the contrary, money changed hands. It was more money than Edward had expected to pay for Tom Skinner's services, but he was assured the girl was untouched. Tom could expect the second half of the payment only if the goods proved undamaged.

Oblivious to the manipulation surrounding her, Siana was light of heart. Daisy had improved considerably and she was to be discharged from the infirmary the following day.

She wondered if Daniel had talked to the reverend yet about allowing her sister to live under his roof. Daisy didn't eat much and in return Siana was willing to accept less pay for her work there. In fact, the reverend had been so good to her in the past, she knew she'd work for just bread and board if it meant Daisy had a home with her.

Her hopes were dashed, however, when the woman in charge of the ward handed her a sealed package. There was a note inside.

Dear Miss Lewis,
Circumstances render me unable to maintain the continuance of your employment.
Enclosed is the sum of money due to you, which includes wages and the amount withheld by me in credit on your behalf. Your chattels have been deposited at the infirmary gatehouse.
Further contact will be neither expected, nor encouraged.
Yours faithfully,
Reverend Richard White

Totally unprepared, Siana stared at the note. Oh God! She'd lost her job. She couldn't believe Richard White would do this to her. He was a Christian.

But then, the man who'd fathered her had supposedly been a Christian, too.

She re-read the note in case she'd missed something. No, here was her money wrapped in another piece of paper and sealed with red wax. What was she to do now? She twisted the amber ring on her finger. Daniel, she must see Daniel! He'd sort this out. She just had time to catch him before he finished work.

Leaving Daisy asleep, she told the woman in charge she was going out, then hurried to Daniel's place of work. The afternoon was growing old. Shadows stole like thieves into the alleyways, making them appear sinister places.

Pulling her shawl tightly around her, Siana kept watch over the lawyers' office. A man came out, followed by another. As dusk crept in, a light began to shine in a window. Then it was extinguished. A man emerged, pulled the door shut behind him and inserted a key in the lock.

Siana scurried forward. If she didn't hurry the workhouse gate would be locked against her. 'Excuse me, sir. Is Mr Daniel Ayres still inside?'

The man turned. His glance travelled over her and dismissed her. Loftily, he said, 'Mr Ayres is no longer employed here.'

Bewildered, she stared at him. 'Not work for you . . . but, I thought . . .'

'Thought what?' He stared down his nose at her. 'Mr Ayres wouldn't concern himself with the likes of you. He's gone abroad for a year, I believe. If you've got yourself into trouble it's no more than you deserve. Now be off with you, girl, else I'll call the authorities and have you charged with making a nuisance of yourself.'

She stumbled away, ashen-faced and bewildered. Daniel had gone abroad? Why hadn't he told her he was going? She gazed at the amber ring on her finger, gently rubbing it in search of reassurance. Perhaps he'd been too busy. He wouldn't have given her this ring if he hadn't cared.

Dr Matheson had dropped in at the infirmary whilst she was absent.

'You can take Daisy home tomorrow,' the woman in charge said, at which news Siana promptly burst into tears.

'What is it?' the woman said kindly.

'We have nowhere to go. I must talk to the doctor. Perhaps he'll be able to help me.'

'The doctor is visiting his family for a day or two. Dr Bede will be taking over his duties for the time being.'

'I see. Then perhaps there will be room for me at the workhouse.'

The woman's eyes slid sideways. 'The workhouse is already overcrowded. Squire Forbes is calling an emergency meeting of the board, and no more people are being accepted at present. There's a couple of inhabitants suffering from consumption as well as an outbreak of measles. You'd be better off somewhere else if you can find a place.'

But where? With Richard White no longer an option and Daniel unavailable to help, that left only her stepbrother and stepsister, neither of whom would willingly give her a home.

Not that she wanted to live with either of them, but she had Daisy to think of.

She shuddered at the thought. She'd rather sleep in a hedge.

9

It was cold and wet the next morning as Siana left the workhouse with Daisy on one hip and her bundle of clothes on the other. Feeling desperate, she gazed up and down the street and grappled with the problem of which direction to take to the nowhere she had in mind.

She was surprised when Tom Skinner came along with the mule and cart. He jerked a thumb at the cart. 'Get yerself in.'

She drew back a step or two, undecided.

'Please yourself what you do, but Daisy's my sister and she comes with me,' he snarled. Leaping from the cart, he snatched their sister from her arms, climbed up on the buckboard and set the cart in motion.

Siana had to run to catch him up and was in danger of being run over when she trod in a pothole and sprawled face down in the mud. Tom laughed as he drew to a halt. Her knees and elbows skinned and sore, Siana scrambled up on the cart and hugged Daisy close, wrapping her in some sacking to shield her from the driving rain. Shortly, the child fell asleep.

Tom drove the mule at a fast trot out of town. They

were nearing the boundary of Croxley Farm when the rain became a deluge. Tom pulled off the road and drove up a lane into the grounds of a tumbledown cottage.

Suspicious, she turned to him. 'Why are we stopping?'

'She's fair pissin' down,' he grumbled. 'We'll wait until she's finished.'

There was barely enough roof left to find a dry spot in the cottage. Siana moved as far away from Tom as possible. Placing the sleeping Daisy on the floor, she wrapped her in their mother's shawl before easing the clothes bundle from her shoulder, intending to place Daisy on it for comfort.

Two strides brought Tom towards her. He snatched the bundle from her and upended the contents on the ground. Finding nothing of value, he snarled, 'Where's the money what Reverend bloody White gave you?'

She clutched her arms about her body protectively. 'I don't know what you're talking about, Tom.'

'Don't you now.' He came closer, so he was standing directly in front of her. 'Then you'd better remember, and quick smart.' His hair was a greasy slick across his forehead, his eyes bloodshot. A dewdrop trembled on the end of his nose. She shrank away from him.

A meaty hand reached out and took hold of her hair, the other one ripped open her bodice. There, in the cleft between her breasts, was her small cache of coins.

'No,' she cried out as he pocketed them. 'I need that to buy food for Daisy.'

He stared for a long moment at the swell of her breasts, mumbling, 'What else have you got that I don't know about?'

'Nothing.'

His tongue ran over his lips and he muttered. 'I'll just make sure of that meself, I reckon.' A foot behind the ankle sent her crashing to the floor. Then Tom was kneeling astride her stomach. 'Them's a nice pair of titties you've got, Siana Lewis.' His hands cupped around them and jiggled them up and down. Suddenly, he squeezed them, with just enough pressure to make her cry out in pain.

Something pressed against her stomach, and she knew exactly what it was. He put his hand over her mouth and laughed. 'Now see what you'm done, you Taffy trollop? Given me a man-sized itch. I might make you provide the remedy for that before I goes back to my loving wife.'

Siana tried to bite his hand. Loosening his grip on her mouth, he whipped his palm back and forth across her face until she felt dizzy and sick. Blood salted her tongue and seeped from her mouth.

Moving to kneel by her side, he threw her skirt up over her head. 'Now, you'm be nice and quiet while I searches you. Then 'e won't come to no harm.'

He was rough, pinching the flesh of her stomach, legs and buttocks, then moving his hand between her legs. She squeezed them tightly together. The laugh he gave contained a breathless quality as he gripped the soft flesh of her thighs and forced them apart.

His fingers groped inside her and he began to slide them up and down. She smacked his hand away. 'Stop it, Tom. I'll have you arrested for rape.'

'Now, don't you go putting no ideas of them sort in

my head. I'm just giving you a bit of enjoyment, is all. See how wet and nice you are, and all. Just panting to have a man inside you like a she-cat on heat, ain't you?'

He stood up and jerked her to her feet, forcing her hand against the hard swelling in his groin. 'See what I've growed in my trousers especially for you. But it's not going to be rape, for you'll still be intact. Now, on your knees and give your brother a loving kiss.'

She gazed at him in horror for a moment, then, realizing what he was about, shook her head and pleaded, 'Let me go, Tom.'

But his eyes were flint hard as he tangled his hands in her hair and applied pressure to try to push her to her knees. She resisted.

Twisting, she bit down on his arm and received a numbing blow to the head for her trouble. Dizzily, she remembered her mother whispering something to her. In desperation she jerked her knee up. The result couldn't have been more dramatic. Tom gave a long-drawn-out howl, clutched his crotch and collapsed to the ground, doubled up in agony.

Siana didn't bother to gather her clothes together. Snatching up Daisy, she ran outside, jumped on the cart and, depositing her sister in the back, set the mule in motion.

The hedges and fields seemed to blur together, making her feel nauseated. She'd just made it to the junction where lane met lane when her way was blocked by the squire's carriage. His horses squealed with fright and pawed at the air when she appeared.

Curses coloured the air.

Desperately she jerked the rein sideways. The cart slid, one wheel ending up in the ditch. Pitched from the buckboard, she landed in the mud, one arm stretched out to break her fall. The mule panicked and dragged the cart forward. A wheel ran over her arm. There was a sharp crack and pain nearly overwhelmed her. She groaned as the screaming Daisy landed on top of her.

Lying sideways as she was, Siana could see the carriage, dark and slick with rain. There was a series of clear visions. Water bouncing off the carriage roof and running in rivulets down the side. A door opening. The figure who emerged was top-hatted. Black boots appeared, highly polished. Legs in narrow grey trousers under a flowing black topcoat strolled towards her.

Mud began to fill her nostrils. Daisy's screaming went on and on. She put her uninjured arm around her sister, drawing her close. 'There, there, my little Daisy. You've had a bad time of it, haven't you?'

Daisy's screams became whimpering sobs. She snuggled her face against Siana's neck for comfort. Siana didn't think she could stand the pain much longer. The sky began to dim. *I must be fair mazed*, she thought. But no, it was the squire standing over her, blocking out the daylight.

A silver-tipped cane drew debris away from her face, allowing her to breathe. 'Are you all right, my dear?'

How booming his voice was, but how kind and concerned his expression. Her heart wrenched as she was forcibly reminded of Daniel.

'Thank goodness it's you,' she whispered, for had it been Tom she'd have been done for. 'I've lost my job.

There was no room at the workhouse for us and Tom Skinner attacked me. He stole all my wages and tried to . . . tried to—' Finding it too hard to say, she choked the words back. 'I think my arm is injured.'

He clicked his tongue in concern a couple of times. 'Don't worry, my dear, I'll look after you,' he said kindly, but his eyes were filled with a terrible anger. His polished boots sank up to the ankle in mud before her eyes, his immaculate trouser bottoms soaked up the water as he bent over her. He didn't seem to notice as he called out, 'Coachman, come and help me get the young lady out of here.'

'And Daisy,' she whispered. 'Promise you won't let Tom Skinner take her. He's evil.'

'I'm beginning to believe he might be,' the squire said tightly, as everything faded from her view.

Francis Matheson was surprised when Edward Forbes sent a messenger with an urgent request to come quickly.

'Be good for your aunt and uncle,' he said to Pansy and Maryse, the two daughters from his marriage. The pair had arrived a year apart, and greatly resembled their deceased mother. So innocent and lovely, at the age of twelve and thirteen years they already showed signs of the beauty that was to be theirs.

It was hard bringing up daughters alone and they benefited greatly from these extended visits with his brother and sister-in-law, though he missed them greatly when they were there.

Prudence made no bones about the fact that she would have liked to discover a daughter or two amongst her clutch of five sons and she said the visits gave the boys an excuse to practise their manners. Prudence made sure piano practice was strictly enforced; the art of embroidery was also strictly applied and patiently endured, except for the odd exchange of glances, giggles and perhaps an intake of breath when a finger prick drew blood.

Lessons were a daily routine. The girls, in the company of their cousins, were tutored in the schoolroom upstairs, where Francis and his five elder siblings had been schooled.

Pansy, in particular, was quick-minded, showing a leaning towards maths and the sciences. Maryse was a dreamer, preferring poetry and artistic pursuits.

The male influence on the pair was all too apparent. Pansy climbed trees like a monkey, earning the admiration of her cousins as they egged her on to even greater heights. Maryse was a little more sedate, but thought nothing of giving her boisterous cousins a clout around the ear when she considered it was warranted.

Now they hugged him tight, two girls so beautifully delicate in face and form they made his heart ache. 'I'll miss you,' he said gruffly.

Prudence circled an arm around each girl's waist and drew them away as he mounted his horse. 'You should wed again, Francis,' she said quietly. 'They need a mother.'

But where would he find a woman suitable to act as wife and mother? He wasn't exactly the most sociable of men. At the beck and call of his patients, he was constantly short-tempered through lack of sleep. He was not wealthy compared to his brothers, although his income from doctoring was adequate. It could be more than adequate if he ignored the plight of the poor and homeless. But how could he leave them to suffer when he compared their lot with the opulence of their masters?

A wife? He grinned at the thought. The woman would have to be a saint to live with him and he didn't attract saintly women.

He glanced back at the house, solid stone in its parkland setting. Here he'd grown up, the last of six aristocratic sons. His eldest brother had inherited the title of earl. Of the ones in between there was a magistrate, an admiral, a scientist and a former army officer. William Matheson had taken up land in Van Diemen's Land. He was urging Francis to join him.

The colony needs good doctors, especially those who possess surgical skills, William wrote. *I guarantee you would acquire wealth and reputation in no time.*

The thought of making a fresh start in a new land was appealing. But Prudence was right. He needed a mother for his daughters first, for he couldn't practise his profession as well as make sure they were adequately cared for. However, so far he'd had neither the time to spare nor the inclination to woo a woman.

It was late when he reached the manor. Edward Forbes was in his study.

'What is it, Edward? You don't look sick to me.'

'I'm not. It's Siana Lewis.'

His eyes sharpened. 'What of her?'

'She's in one of the upstairs chambers. Her arm seems to be broken and she has other injuries. She's in a great deal of pain.'

'Couldn't Dr Bede have seen to it?'

'He's a pill-pusher, not a surgeon. Besides, he's a gossip.'

Francis stared at him. 'What makes you think she needs a surgeon?'

Edward picked up the decanter. He seemed to be avoiding his eyes. The colour left his face as he murmured vaguely, 'Someone has set about her. There was a child with her. The Lewis girl won't let her out of her sight.'

'It must be Daisy.' Francis's eyes narrowed. Edward was hiding something. 'You said someone had set about her. Was it you?'

'Don't be ridiculous, man,' Edward said, testily enough for Francis to believe him.

'How did she end up here?'

'The mule she was handling took fright. It threw her into the ditch in front of my carriage over by the old cottage on the far border of Croxley Farm. Dangerous animals, mules.'

Francis wasn't satisfied by the answer. Why hadn't Edward taken her straight to the infirmary instead of going to the trouble of sending for him?

'I see. She was driving a cart, you say?'

'Must I keep repeating myself? It was the mule and cart belonging to Tom Skinner.'

'Has the man been detained for questioning?'

'Not yet.'

'Why didn't you take the girl to the infirmary?'

Edward shrugged. His reluctance to answer was so evident Francis gave him a warning look.

'I closed it to the admittance of further patients.

146

There was danger of an outbreak of an infectious disease.'

'There's always danger of an outbreak of something. Who diagnosed this infectious disease?'

When Edward didn't answer, Francis grunted. 'I sense you have a personal involvement in this affair, Edward. I'll want to know what it is after I've seen the patient, and I mean to have the truth.'

'Damn it, Francis. I didn't mean this to happen. I wouldn't cause her to be hurt deliberately.'

'And I'll make sure you damned well don't hurt her,' Francis said curtly. He took a moment to wonder at the anger coursing through him, eventually dismissing it as nothing more than professional compassion.

Siana had been settled in a guest chamber. She lay in the sumptuous four-poster bed, her body swamped by a voluminous nightgown. Her hair was tangled darkly over the pillow. Daisy was asleep, her thumb in her mouth. The child was curled protectively in Siana's good arm.

He experienced a moment of contentment at seeing them thus. This was a worthy, caring girl, who hadn't deserved what she'd been through. But what exactly had she been through, besides the breaking of an arm, now crudely splinted and supported on a pillow?

He slid Daisy to one side. Siana gave a distressed whimper when he probed the swollen flesh for the break in the bone. He made an apologetic sound deep in his throat.

When Siana opened her eyes, for a moment there was abject fear in them as she shrank against the pillow.

Recognizing the doctor, however, she relaxed and managed a wry smile. 'I'm sorry.'

'Hell, you've got nothing to be sorry for,' he said. 'But I need to examine you. Do I have your permission?'

The maid was a sensible-looking woman. He beckoned her forward when Siana nodded. 'Can you arrange the sheets so the patient's body can be decently examined?'

When the woman nodded Francis turned aside until she coughed to attract his attention. The gown had been unbuttoned down the front. Of average height, Siana Lewis was long-legged and slender, but her body was firm and shapely. His blood boiled when he saw her skinned knees and elbows and the array of bruises. The maid uncovered Siana little by little, keeping private her feminine part. One of her breasts displayed a bite mark.

He resisted the urge to touch the wound, giving it a perfunctory glance before it was covered up again. Although he knew the perpetrator of the beating, he needed to hear it from her own lips. 'Who did this to you?'

A shudder ran through her as she whispered, 'Tom Skinner. He was waiting for me outside the infirmary.'

The man was an animal. Francis tried to keep the growing anger from his voice as he said roughly, 'Did he violate you in any other way?'

Shame filled her eyes before the lids were lowered over them. For a moment he held his breath, then he smiled with relief when she gave an imperceptible shake of her head.

Francis retreated behind an impersonal manner.

'You'll be pleased to hear the fracture is a simple one. The bone will knit cleanly once it's splinted properly. As for your other injuries, you're young and healthy, the grazed skin will heal before too long and some arnica will relieve the pain of the bruising.'

The light went from her eyes as she said flatly, 'I have no arnica. I have nothing. Tom stole my wages.'

Daisy woke to gaze at him through eyes as blue as summer. Recognizing him as someone who'd been kind to her, the child smiled trustingly at him and went to sleep again. He remembered his own girls being innocent and tender little doves like this one. She was underweight for her age. It was unfair she should grow up in abject poverty.

Although he'd grown up in a wealthy home, since doctoring had become his business, Francis had learned to despise the landowners for their greed, and the wealth which was earned at the expense of his patients. It was heartbreaking to watch human beings die from diseases which could be prevented by good nourishment and decent living conditions. He decided to tackle Edward about the sewerage in the village whilst he was here. There had been an outbreak of typhus.

He frowned as he went about his work. Edward was not a philanthropist to take an idle interest in an impoverished girl like Siana. He would have a motive. Francis had a good idea what that motive was and began to examine the facts. Odd that Richard White had dispensed with her services, just as Daniel Ayres had been sent abroad. That time he'd seen Siana with Daniel they'd seemed closer than mere acquaintances.

He took another look at her, calculating her worth through the eyes of a man instead of a doctor. Shining dark green eyes, fine, proud features and hair of lustrous ebony adorned a face of singular and slightly exotic beauty. He remembered the way she walked, graceful and unconsciously upright, her chin held high. She was long-strided for a female, the sway of her hips womanly.

His eyes grew dark as his body reacted. He'd trained himself to ignore the effect the female body had on a man and drew in a deep breath. The thought of Edward using her was upsetting.

Edward had always been the sensualist. Now he'd discarded Elizabeth Skinner, he would have a hankering for someone new. Damn you to hell, Edward Forbes, he thought. Why can't you be content with the peevish Isabelle?

Siana placed her free hand tentatively over his when he finished the splint. It was a strong, capable hand, the nails dirty and ragged. He should have drawn his own away, refused the contact. He left it there. 'I was refused a place in the workhouse. There's an epidemic, I believe.'

He said nothing, but his blood boiled as Edward's scheming became clear.

She removed her hand, drew Daisy against her and gave a resigned sigh. 'I don't want to stay here, but I have nowhere else to go.'

'Don't think of that now. The squire's not all that bad.' Edward had better display a monk-like restraint towards this girl, though, he thought darkly.

'He ordered Will Hastings's arrest. Now the man is dead.'

There was no disputing the truth of that, though Francis liked it not. 'The squire acted within the law.'

'There was no proof,' she said. 'Tom Skinner held a grudge against Will over Peggy. It was his word against Will's.'

He remembered the Hastings widow. She was an honest and capable woman. He nodded. 'I'll visit Tom Skinner and get your wages back for you.'

Fear filled her eyes. 'Be careful, Dr Matheson. He has an unpredictable temper. I don't want you to be hurt.'

He smiled at that, folding his hand around hers and squeezing it for a moment. 'What makes you think I'm unable to handle myself? Now, get some rest, my dear.'

Her eyes were turbulent and anxious, and she seemed on the verge of tears. 'If you see Josh would you let him know where I am? I don't want him to think I've disappeared with Daisy and left him to fend for himself.'

Francis nodded, his heart too full to speak. He would do something for this girl. He didn't know what yet, but he'd think of something.

Francis was probably the only man in the district who would dare lay down the law to Edward Forbes. Much of his confidence was due to his breeding, which was a cut above most. He was blunt when he had to be, his ironic manner causing discomfort to many. He was also good at his profession. But, finding himself constantly disappointed by his fellow human beings, he'd learned to discourage attempts at close friendship.

Francis considered the squire to have a likeable manner, although his character was not of the most admirable type. He was hard-working enough, but not particularly honest. Still, he was clever enough to manipulate others into serving his own ends. Edward was driven by self-interest, and he kept an exceptionally fine cellar.

The drawing room was lit with a glow. Firelight lent a sheen to the timber panelling, as if it had been polished with gold dust. Holding a glass of brandy to his nose Francis inhaled the bouquet appreciatively. 'I understand a gang of smugglers was apprehended last month.'

Edward smiled slightly. 'There has been some activity of late. Contraband has been turning up in the markets. How's the girl?'

'She'll mend.' His eyes came up to Edward in a frank and direct gaze. 'What's your involvement with her?'

'I have no involvement, as yet. Actually, I was thinking of setting her up in the Dorchester house. She could do worse.'

'Am I to understand you persuaded Richard White to dismiss her, and asked Tom Skinner to beat her up because of your desire for novelty? Why didn't you just ask her?'

'I did. She refused.' A sullen expression touched his face. 'I didn't think Skinner would go as far as he did.'

'You have conveniently bad eyesight if you haven't noticed the bruises on Elizabeth Skinner.'

Edward winced. 'I misjudged the man. Now they're wed, it's too late.'

'Skinner will kill somebody one day. I'm taking a personal interest in this girl, Edward. If you violate her in any way, I'll personally strangle you.'

'Oh, don't be so damned stuffy, Francis. I'm not a rapist and I won't keep her here against her will. In fact, she can't stay here long. Isabelle might get to hear of it and take it amiss. I've noticed my fiancée is inclined towards suspicion.'

'As well she might be.' Francis finished his brandy and set the glass down. 'It'll serve you right if she turns out to be a shrew. You don't have to wed the girl, Edward. You already have a son.'

'Unfortunately, he's illegiti—'

Francis cut him off, saying drily, 'I'm going over to Croxley Farm to retrieve the money Skinner stole from Miss Lewis. She's too frightened of him to press charges. In your capacity as magistrate, I'd appreciate it if you came along to read him the riot act. It's no more than you deserve.'

Edward's eyes filled with chagrin and his lips pursed. Francis grinned humourlessly at him when he reluctantly nodded.

Skinny legs pulled up to his chin, Josh buried his face in his knees and covered his ears with his hands. It didn't block out the sound. Elizabeth was giving long-drawn-out sobs to wrench at his heart.

At least the screaming had stopped – for the time being. Josh rocked back and forth, keening to himself, hating his brother.

Tom had returned in a foul mood. He'd taken a lash to the mule, which had blood- flecked foam around its mouth and slashes across its flank. The door had not long slammed behind Tom when he'd loudly cursed. A dish had shattered, as if his brother had hurled it against a wall. Then Elizabeth had begun to scream. It had gone on a long time.

In the stall beside him, the mule shifted nervously in the straw. Josh spoke soothingly to his companion. 'He's a devil, is our Tom. One of these days I'll be big enough to take him on, then he can watch out.'

He flinched as another scream rent the air, 'Don't, Tom. No!' followed by a roar of rage from Tom.

Josh jerked upright and listened. The mad bastard would kill her if he didn't stop him. He had to draw Tom off so Elizabeth could get away from him. She'd shown him a hidey hole they could use if need be. One of the oak trees in the woods had a hollow trunk big enough to hold two. There was a blanket kept there in case of emergency. The entrance was concealed by an evergreen shrub.

Picking up a stick, he opened the gate to the mule's stall in case Tom decided to take it out on the poor creature, then headed for the house at a run. He peered through the window. Elizabeth was cowering against the wall. Blood oozed from her nose and her eyes were swollen.

Tom was standing over her, a knife in his hand. Eyes maddened, he swayed back and forth, glaring at her.

He'd have to be quick. His heart beating fit to bust, Josh picked up a wooden pail and swung it at the window. Glass shattered into the room. Tom turned towards him.

'You bullying pig's arsehole!' Josh shouted.

He was on the run before Tom opened the door. Racing into the barn, he pushed aside a loose plank and scrambled through. He doubled back just as Tom entered the barn at a run, and headed for the house.

'Quick,' he said to Elizabeth as he reached the cottage, and snatched up her shawl. As they fled across the meadow towards the copse, the mule started to squeal and hee-haw. At the back of his brain Josh registered the mule was angry rather than hurt. The beast's hooves stomped the floor a couple of times and there was a couple of dull thuds, as if it had kicked Tom.

Looking back, Josh saw a shadow stagger towards the pigsty. It made contact with the rail and pitched over the top. As the pigs set up a cacophony of squeals, Josh managed a shaky grin. 'Best place for him, I reckon.'

Elizabeth was staggering when they reached the woods. He put an arm around her for support. Lad and woman slowed down and, making their way to the hollow oak, scrambled inside. Panting, they sank to their knees in the dark, pulled the blanket over them and held each other tight.

It was silent, blissfully silent and dark in the womb of the oak tree. Nothing could hurt them here. In the bare canopy above, an owl softly hooted.

Back at Croxley Farm it was also silent. The pigs had settled down now, except for the satisfied grunts pigs make when they're tucking into a meal.

There was the sharp sound of a bone crunching, then a scream rent the air.

10

'Oh, my God!' Francis whispered.

Skinner was lying half across the doorstep in a pool of blood, making a gurgling noise.

Edward took one look at him and his face drained of colour. Clapping a handkerchief over his mouth he turned away. Francis could hear him gagging as he knelt beside the filthy and bloodied figure.

Francis didn't blame him. Skinner was covered in pig's ordure and the tip of his nose was missing. Shards of bone glistened amongst the shreds of one calf. The right leg would have to be amputated if he was to be given a chance to live. Even so, if the shock didn't kill him, infection from the wound would more than likely finish him off.

For a moment Francis wondered if the man was worth the effort. He was tempted to let Skinner die – this bully who ill-treated women and children without compunction. But Francis had also taken the Hippocratic oath, swearing to preserve life. That noble cause had to take precedence over his natural repugnance and reluctance to treat such a creature.

'Sorry, my stomach is usually stronger than that,' Edward muttered a few moments later. 'Is there anything I can do to help?'

'You can help lift him onto the kitchen table. I need to clean him up and examine him properly.'

At least Edward wasn't too fastidious to get his hands dirty. Whilst Francis removed the man's clothes Edward went so far as to strip down to his shirt sleeves. Filling a bowl full of water he slopped the dirt from Skinner's body with a sopping towel. He repeated the process with soap, rinsing it off in clean water. As bloody water scummed into pools on the floor, he fetched some sheets from a cupboard to dry the man's powerful body.

'I used to be an army officer so I'm not totally useless,' he said, managing a wry smile when Francis gazed at him in surprise. 'You're going to have to remove the leg, aren't you?'

Francis nodded. 'A lower limb amputation is a fairly simple procedure. He's unconscious at the moment, partly from drink by the smell of his breath. If he comes round he could be fighting mad. I might need you to hold him down. D'you feel up to it?'

'No,' Edward said shortly, then he grinned. 'But I'll make sure he's securely tied down to start with. I'll fetch your doctoring bag from your horse.'

Francis was examining his patient when Edward came back. He pointed out further injuries to him. On Skinner's head, a livid swelling was revealed. 'He'll be concussed from that, but I think his skull was thick enough to absorb the blow without serious damage to the brain.' Another wound on his chest bore the clear outline of a hoof print. There was a second set on his back.

'Stubborn brutes, mules,' Edward muttered. 'They never forget ill-treatment, and always repay a wrong when given the chance.'

Blood seeped from the twin holes on Skinner's face. 'If he survives the amputation, all I can do is clean the nose up and hope it heals. It looks as if he got the worst of this particular fight. See if his wife is around, would you? She might need attention, and could be able to throw some light on what occurred here.'

'It's obvious. The man is insane. After Skinner attacked Siana Lewis, he got drunk on the money he stole from her, then came back here and started on Elizabeth. There was a fight and she ran away. When he went looking for her, the mule kicked him. My guess is he was dazed and wandered into the sty, where the pigs got at him. There will be marks in the mud. I'll look at the situation in the morning.'

Francis gave him a steady look. 'No need for charges to be laid, then?'

'Of course not. The evidence is clear. I don't know why you're bothering to doctor him. It will be a blessing for everyone if he dies.'

'No doubt it will be convenient for some, hmmm? Elizabeth deserved better than this, Edward.'

Edward didn't need reminding. He glowered at Francis, then went off to search the house and the barn whilst the doctor prepared for his task. The barn was empty except for a black and white cow, and a mule which flattened its ears at the sight of him.

'It's old right, old boy,' he soothed, noting the bloody stripes on its flank. 'But it'll be the knacker's yard for you. Nobody will want you when word gets around, and if Skinner recovers, he'll flog you to death.'

When he went back to the house he gazed thoughtfully at the smashed plates and overturned chairs. He remembered the state of Siana Lewis. 'I hope Elizabeth isn't injured.'

Strolling to the door he gazed across the paddock to the line of trees, darker shadows against the dark sky. He would come back before dawn, search for her if she wasn't back.

There was a faint glow, signalling the moon's intent to travel up behind them. He cupped his hands around his mouth, 'Elizabeth! Don't be afraid. It's me, Edward.'

'She'll be all right. My guess is, she'll have Josh with her.'

Edward turned to gaze at the doctor. 'Josh?'

'The young Skinner lad. I've heard the pair look out for each other.' Francis handed over some strips of sheets he'd torn up. 'Tie Skinner down good and tight, will you?'

Guilt tore through Edward's guts and he couldn't meet the doctor's eyes as he hastened to do his bidding. He watched uneasily as Francis set out his instruments. Two keen-bladed knives, a saw, tweezers, needle and surgical thread. He pointed to a strange-looking apparatus of straps with a plate and screw attachment. 'What's that thing?'

'A screw tourniquet. It compresses the wound and helps prevent bleeding.'

The operation was messy. Edward tried not to look,

but the sound of the saw on bone set his teeth on edge and made him feel squeamish. Blood dripped through the loosely joined planks on the table top.

Thankfully, Skinner remained quiet, except for giving a low, animal groan now and again. Francis grunted with the effort, brow glistening with perspiration. Edward paled a little when the doctor picked up a knife and began to neaten the flap of skin left over. Turning his face away, Edward gulped back his nausea and guiltily wondered where Elizabeth was.

Afterwards, he helped to lift Skinner onto the cart. 'I'll stay here and clean up,' he said to Francis. 'I can't leave the place in this state for Elizabeth to find.' Fetching a pail, he headed for the pump.

Snug in the tree-trunk hideaway, Elizabeth cuddled the sleeping Josh close and cried with quiet despair as she felt his bones sharp against her flesh. Josh was a child, and Tom had him working like a man. *It wasn't fair! It wasn't fair!*

Tom had degraded her, stripped her of her pride. She couldn't take much more of his treatment. Her affection for Josh was the one shining core left of her spirit. The boy had become important to her. They supported each other with an exchanged look, a touch or a smile. She had to get them away from here before Tom killed them both.

Carefully, she reached upwards, feeling for the ledge – for the bag. It was a frivolous thing of pink satin embroidered with fine golden thread and hanging from a ribbon. She remembered the gown she'd worn it with.

It had been Edward's favourite, the bodice exposing her neck and shoulders, its three-tiered skirt scalloped and embroidered at the edges.

She smiled. How spoiled she'd been then, how in love – *and how naive to imagine Edward would wed her.* Though the contents of the bag felt satisfyingly plump when she squeezed it, she knew the money wouldn't last long. But there was a deposit box in her name with a bank in Poole, too. It contained cash. Not even Daniel knew about that one.

She might be able to find work to support them both if she moved to Poole. She could pass herself off as a widow and Josh as her son. But how could they leave the district without detection?

She held her breath as the shrub outside the tree began to rustle. The noise wasn't repeated. Aware of every single ache in her body when she quietly exhaled, she had not the room to make herself more comfortable. But before long her eyelids began to droop, her head fell to her chest and sleep came to claim her for a few oblivious hours.

Elizabeth was stiff and cold when she awoke. Alarm pricked her. Josh was nowhere to be seen. Crawling from the hole, she painfully stood. It was a chill, damp morning. Visible through the tree canopy, the sky displayed a jaundiced tinge. Wood smoke lingered in the air.

'Josh,' she called out quietly.

Josh was nearing the barn. A quick glance around the door showed the cart and mule gone from the building. Wheel and hoof marks led out of the muddy yard. His brother seemed to have already set out for the day.

Still, Josh was cautious. Shivering with cold and tension, he crept across to the back door. Once there, he thought better of going straight in and moved to the window, standing on tiptoe to peer over the sill. All seemed as usual. A kettle steamed on the fire. The mess of broken china had been cleaned up.

Everything looked so normal it was suspicious. Tom would never have cleaned up the mess. Had Hannah been called in? If so, where was she? Josh hated his half-sister only marginally less than he hated Tom.

Josh satisfied himself the downstairs rooms were uninhabited before noiselessly letting himself in. The kitchen was pleasantly warm, the wood-burning stove giving out a steady heat. He snatched up the remains of a loaf of bread and some cheese, breaking hunks off to stuff inside his pocket. He drank deeply from a jug of milk.

It struck him as odd that the table seemed to have been recently scrubbed. It was still damp. So was the floor. The place smelled odd, too, a mixture of the scrubbing soap Elizabeth used, plus an odour of animal guts and blood? As if someone had recently butchered and drawn a carcass.

The parlour door was ajar. The room was clearly empty. He sidled upstairs, using the sides of the steps so they wouldn't creak and give him away. Both of the front bedrooms were empty. Once again the doors were ajar. The door to the third bedroom over the kitchen was pushed back almost against the wall. All the room contained was an iron bed with a straw mattress and a dresser. No place to hide there.

The cow was bellowing in the barn. She needed milking. The surplus would be fed to the pigs. It was something he'd do after he'd told Elizabeth it was safe to come back down. The emptiness of the house made him relax his guard.

Feeling confident now, Josh bounded downstairs. Swigging the remains of the jug of milk on the way through, he closed the kitchen door behind him.

As he raced through the yard, his ears registered the thud of a hoof on the floor of the barn, the snicker of a horse. Used to such noises, Josh didn't realize the significance of it as he sped over the paddock towards the trees, shouting to Elizabeth that it was safe to come out.

Back at Croxley Farm, Edward had stepped out from behind the bedroom door and crossed to the window. As he watched Elizabeth emerge from the trees, a smile crept across his face. He should never have let her go.

Elizabeth was in her bedroom gathering a few clothes together when Edward appeared at the doorway.

'You needn't hurry. Tom Skinner is in the infirmary.'

Her eyes widened and her hand flew to her chest. She stumbled away from him, falling against the dresser with a frightened squeak. A candle in a brass holder crashed to the floor. 'I thought you were Tom.'

He began to burn with rage when he saw the condition she was in, sorry he'd startled her.

The next moment the lad slipped past him. He was a skinny little thing, his eyes large in a face so gaunt it made him look old. A wicked-looking carving knife was clutched in his hand, though he quivered from head to foot with the fright he felt.

'Make one move towards her, mister, and I'll stick you right through the gizzards.'

'It's all right, Josh,' she said, her hand going to his arm. 'This is Squire Forbes. He won't hurt me.'

Josh stared suspiciously at him. 'Aye, we met before.'

The child was obviously terrified, yet he was trying hard to be a man. Edward gave him an easy smile. 'You have much courage, lad. You must be Josh Skinner. Your sister, Siana, spoke of you.'

'Siana.' His eyes clouded over. 'She didn't come on Wednesday like she usually does.'

'Daisy was in the infirmary at Poole. Your sister stayed with her until she recovered.'

Elizabeth put an arm around Josh and kissed the top of his head. 'Go and milk the cow and feed the pigs, Josh. I'll be all right. I'll cook us some ham and eggs for breakfast whilst you're doing that.'

When he clattered off down the stairs, Edward gazed at her. 'Your husband is badly injured. It's doubtful whether he'll survive. I'm going to tell his sister and her husband to look after the livestock for the time being.'

Although Elizabeth paled, her expression was one of relief.

'I was about to leave him. I have a little money put aside. I thought I might go to Poole perhaps. I could start a business. A little school, teaching the daughters of merchants deportment and manners so they can improve their chance of making a good marriage. Or I could open a shop. Sell hats, gloves and fans.'

'I'd be willing to offer you a loan. Damn it, I've missed you, Elizabeth.'

Elizabeth's heart began to race, then faltered when he said; 'I didn't want to tell you in front of the boy, but Tom Skinner has half killed Siana Lewis. She's at Cheverton Manor at the moment.'

'Cheverton Manor?' Even Elizabeth had never been invited there.

'It's a temporary arrangement. There's a charming residence outside Poole I've just bought. I thought to move her there in a day or two. It sits on a rise in substantial grounds and has a meadow and stable attached. You can move in as well, look after her. It's secluded, but affords a fine view of the harbour from the back.'

'And the house in Dorchester?'

He heaved an aggrieved sigh. 'Isabelle's aunt and a pack of King Charles spaniels will occupy it shortly.'

Elizabeth stared at him. 'What is Siana to you? You must know she's engaged to be married to Daniel.'

His eyes hooded slightly, his manner became offhand. 'Why, yes, of course. Daniel told me. Why else would I take the girl in?'

Her suspicions were somewhat dispelled by his forthright manner.

'I need you to make out a list of what the girl and her sister need in the way of clothing. They have only the clothes they stand up in. You do understand there's nothing untoward in this, don't you?'

She knew him too well to believe his motives were entirely altruistic. 'Of course I understand, Edward.'

'Then you'll come to the manor and look after the girl? She can be your first pupil and should pose quite a challenge. God knows, she has rough edges enough, but I believe she is a quick learner. Between us, we will turn her into a fitting bride for our son.'

At least Elizabeth would have a safe roof over her head there. If Tom recovered he would not dare come after her whilst she was under Edward's protection. But she'd not leave without Josh. 'Josh must come too.'

Edward inclined his head. 'I've taken a liking to the lad and intend to offer him employment.'

'You must not work him too hard. He's taken too much abuse and is physically exhausted. He must live with me and his sisters until he's strong.'

'Anything you want, my dearest.' He opened his arms to her. 'Now, come here and allow me to comfort you.'

Her eyes hardened. 'I don't need your comfort, Edward. You need mine. I will not come to you on the same terms as before. I've learned that men cannot be trusted, especially those in a position of power. From now on, I refuse to be at your beck and call, and you will remunerate me for my services to Miss Lewis.'

Taken aback, he muttered, 'I will reinstate your allowance.'

'I would prefer it to be increased, for now I have the responsibility of others to consider. Namely, a young girl who will one day become my daughter.'

'*Elizabeth . . . Elizabeth*, we are doing this for Daniel,' he cried out softly, for he understood all too well the meaning behind her words. 'I deserve to be punished, but I know you still care for me. Your reluctance will only serve to fuel my ardour, especially after our last delightful encounter in this very room.' And I'm not a fool to give all and have nothing in return, he thought.

Elizabeth blushed when she remembered how weak she'd been. Sucking in a deep breath, she set the memory aside. 'I will pay rent for the house and have a tenancy agreement. Then you will not be able to evict me on a whim as you did last time. Those are my terms.'

'Anything else?' he said with a certain amount of humility, for she'd done more than just prick his conscience during this encounter. She was set to punish him further and he did not blame her for that. But she would bend to his will without too much persuasion, and ultimately, she would do as he pleased.

Elizabeth considered she might have pushed him far enough. 'I cannot think of anything more at the moment.'

'Good.' He'd drawn away now, hiding the wound she'd dealt his pride behind a barrier of aloofness. 'I'll take my leave now and will instruct my lawyer to draw up a tenancy agreement.' He gave her a reproachful look. 'The house in Poole is furnished, but if there's anything you wish to take from here . . .?'

She wanted nothing Tom Skinner had touched. 'Just my clothes, and . . . the mule.'

His eyebrows arched in surprise. 'That damned mule kicked your husband half to death. He's old. I was going to send him to the knackery.'

'He reacted because Tom beat him so.' Her hands went to her hips. 'He will be company for Daniel's horse. Jasper comes with us, otherwise I'll refuse to come.'

She would toss aside everything he'd offered for the sake of a flea-bitten mule? There was no logic to women. 'All right, damn it! We'll pick up the beast from the infirmary. But if that brute so much as bares its teeth at you, I'll mount its head in the trophy room.'

She smiled then and, crossing to where he stood, kissed the crossness from his cheek. 'Be careful, Edward. You are showing me your soft side.'

How wonderfully she flattered him, appealing to the male in him with an instinct as old as Eve's. He slid his arms around her waist. There was an earthy smell about her, reminding him of mushrooms and damp leaves. A cobweb bound the silky strands of her hair together and her bodice was stained. The stain displeased him. It reminded him he'd given her to a man who'd sought to ruin her.

He kissed her forehead and turned towards the stairs. 'I will send the carriage for you later in the morning then. Be ready, you'd best be out of here before the new tenant moves in.'

That same evening Hannah moved in to Croxley Farm. Feeling awed by her surroundings she crept through the rooms, touching the fabric of the bedcovers. The mattress was made of feathers. She sank into it, rolling back and forth. 'It be a bed fit for a queen. I'll be right comfy in it,' she whispered to her son.

She opened all the cupboards and drawers and, finding a torn taffeta gown and a pair of neatly darned silk gloves, she pulled them on, leaving the bodice open because it didn't quite cover her. 'I likes these pretty things,' she crooned, pulling the gloves up to her elbow and parading around the room.

George's watery blue eyes gazed dully at her. He had infected flea bites on his face and mucus coated his nose. He started to grizzle.

Irritated by his continual whining, she carried him through to the smaller room and, dumping him on the bed, shut the door and went downstairs.

The kitchen was still warm. Stoking up the ashes of the fire, she made herself a cup of tea, using Elizabeth's best china. Dainty little things they were. They made her feel like a right toff. She didn't wonder where Elizabeth had gone. Knowing her brother Tom, he'd either thrown her out, or killed her and buried her in the woods.

Either way, Hannah didn't care. She hoped Tom died so she could stay here for ever. She and Ben might be a bit slow in the head, but he was a nice-looking man and a right good worker with her behind him. A pity he was so randy with it, like a dog after a bitch. She wasn't having any of it, though.

She pulled a chair up to the fire, propped up her heels on the guard and listened to George cry as the heat warmed the back of her legs. Bleddy, noisy brat. He should have learned not to cry, by now. If he didn't shut his mouth soon she'd give him a good crack. After a while he stopped crying, like she knew he would. Face flushed and drowsy from the heat, her head began to nod. As she relaxed, her skirts gradually slipped up her thighs.

Her husband came across her like that. Transfixed, Ben Collins stood and stared at her bosoms, hanging like ripe melons from the bodice. Wasn't often he got to see them. Her thighs were all dimpled and quivering. She looked like gentry in that dress, just like the squire's intended. His tongue flicked out and he licked the dryness from his lips as he thought of Isabelle. She reminded him of a farm girl he'd once loved. A warm handful or two, that one had been. He'd nearly had her once.

He grinned to himself. Moving closer, he watched Hannah's chest rise and fall as she snored. She hadn't let him touch her since the baby was born. Tentatively, he placed his hands over each quivering mound. The skin felt soft and silky. 'Eh, them be a real nice pair of titties,' he whispered, and his stem lengthened until it was fit to burst out of its skin. He loosened his trousers so he sprang proud and free.

Suddenly, Hannah's eyes opened and awareness came into them. 'You dirty beggar,' she yelled, slapping his hands away. 'Didn't I tell you that you ain't planting no more of your brats in me? Now get out and feed them pigs. They be setting up such a ruckus I can't think.'

His trousers fell around his ankles and he scrambled to pull them up as she reached for a cast-iron skillet. He tripped and fell flat on his face. When the skillet descended on his bare backside he let out a howl.

Upstairs, baby George jerked awake, peed into his already soaked linens and began to scream as the acid attacked the flaming rawness of his skin. Irritated beyond measure, Hannah headed for the stairs.

Siana was propped up against the pillows. She'd never known such comfort. The room was wonderfully warm.

The linens were soft and smelled as if they were filled with fresh air and sunshine. Dosed with laudanum she felt lethargic, but although the opiate had dulled the pain in her arm it could not dull the pain in her heart. She felt like crying, even though she was surrounded by such luxury.

A cheerful maid who announced herself as Rosie had brought her sister in earlier, bathed, and dressed in a warm smock over a flannel dress. Daisy's blonde curls were tied with a blue ribbon to match her eyes. Her legs were encased in warm woollen leggings, her feet slipped into shoes of soft black leather tied with a ribbon.

Oblivious to her new grandeur, Daisy smiled happily at her as she brandished a rag doll in the air. 'Pretty dolly.'

Siana kissed her sister. If only her mother could see her dressed like this. She'd be so proud of her. 'It's you who looks like a pretty dolly.'

'She's a dear little miss,' the maid said. 'And no trouble. She cleaned up every morsel set in front of her. Cook was real pleased.'

The poor couldn't afford to be picky, Siana thought.

'The master sent the housekeeper out to buy some clothes for her.' She giggled. 'Some carry on with the old hen, though. "Something serviceable, no doubt," Mrs Pawley says to him, her lips pursed with disapproval at all the comings and goings.'

'Shall Rosie tell you what the squire says to her?'

Siana nodded.

Rosie giggled again and looked down her nose in a passable imitation of the squire.

171

' "My dear Mrs Pawley," says he, handing her a list. "You will buy everything written on that paper, and you will also purchase a pretty gown for the girl to wear on Sundays." '

' "Waste of money on that Skinner riff-raff," Mrs Pawley says, giving a sniff and being all hoity-toity on account of the fact she used to work for the late squire.

' "The child can't be blamed for her birth any more than you can help having a wart on the end of your nose," squire said back to her, pretty sharpish, like. "If you intend to insult my guests, you can pack your bags and clear orf." The old hag soon changed her manner, I can tell you.'

Fondly, she gazed down at Daisy. 'So here she be. You'm be all sweet and lovely now, don't you, my bonny one?'

Daisy jiggled up and down and held out her arms to the maid.

'Master says she's to sleep in the nursery tonight so you can get some rest.' Rosie slowly shook her head when Siana murmured a protest. 'Now don't you fret none, missy. Squire has put Daisy in my charge and I'll be up there with her. It's going to be a real treat not to hear Mrs Pawley snoring in the next room, I can tell you.'

Rosie stood up when someone tapped at the door. 'That'll be your tea, I expect. Light meals, the doctor has ordered. Now, make sure you eat it all up or cook will be after you.'

Apart from tea in a china pot, the meal consisted of thin slices of bread spread with creamy butter. There was a glass dish filled with gooseberry conserve and a slice of cake. Siana had never tasted such a delicious meal.

After Rosie and Daisy left, Siana slept, oblivious to the thin-faced woman who'd entered to remove the tray.

Mrs Pawley gazed down at the battered figure and wondered what the world was coming to when the squire gave house room to such a low creature. She sniffed. Now the other one had turned up!

What Miss Isabelle would say when she found out didn't bear thinking about. And Mrs Pawley intended to make sure she *did* find out. Oh yes, she most certainly would. There was such goings-on in this house that would make the old squire turn in his grave, upright gentleman that he'd been.

The shadows had moved around by the time Siana woke. It was late afternoon. She gazed at the cherubs on the ceiling and for a moment wondered where she was. Then she remembered and groaned in despair. She couldn't stay here, but she had nowhere else to go.

There was a tap at the door. The knob turned and somebody peeped inside. A maid smiled at her and turned away. 'Miss is awake now. You can go in.'

The first through was a boy – a boy so gaunt Siana didn't recognize him at first. The boy was followed by Elizabeth. 'Siana, my dear. Look who is here to see you.'

'Josh! Oh God, look at you! You've grown so thin I hardly recognized you. Come and give me a hug.'

Josh tried to hold back a sob but didn't quite succeed,

though he struggled manfully to get a hold of himself. Siana held out her good arm to him and drew him into a hug. He cried a little, then stopped and said with quiet despair, 'Why did me mam have to die?'

With tears in her eyes, Siana gazed over his thin shoulders to engage the eyes of Elizabeth. 'I don't know what I'm going to do, but I can't stay here.'

Elizabeth drew up a chair. 'You won't have to, my dear. Let me tell you what has happened and what is arranged. It will give us both some breathing space.'

Later, when Josh had composed himself and was occupied with examining every ornament and painting in the room, Siana said quietly to Elizabeth, 'Did you know Daniel was going abroad?'

'Not until just before his departure.'

'Where has he gone, Elizabeth? Why didn't he tell me he was going?'

Looking shocked, Elizabeth stared at her. 'Why, Daniel is in Italy, I believe, though he'll be travelling to many countries over the next year. I'm surprised he didn't tell you, but you were occupied with your sister at the time, and the trip did come up rather suddenly.'

The explanation was only just credible. Siana was wounded by Daniel's lack of regard for her feelings, especially since he had confessed to loving her.

At the end of the year, perhaps Daniel would decide they were not suited after all. She gazed at the amber ring and anger flared in her. Then again, perhaps she would decide that for herself.

11

Poole! Siana hadn't appreciated her surroundings during her previous visit, when Daisy was in the infirmary. Now she gazed at the bustling crowds with awe. They had left the quay behind and were negotiating the narrow main street.

Snuggled up to one side of her, Daisy had been rocked to sleep by the motion of the carriage. Opposite her, Elizabeth was an upright figure in blue velvet trimmed with grey fur.

Straightening her back and shoulders to match her mentor's, and clad in the serviceable brown skirt and bodice the squire's housekeeper had brought her, Siana wondered if she'd ever be as elegant.

Certainly not in the alternative garments the woman had purchased, a severe black skirt and bodice made of scratchy fabric, the seams of which chafed her armpits. Still, she was grateful to be decently covered and warm. Her new boots pinched a little, but in time they would shape themselves to her feet, if the opposite didn't happen first. The clothes would last her for many seasons if she looked after them.

175

She caught the squire looking at her. His amber eyes were slightly teasing. He gave a faint smile when she self-consciously pulled her mother's shawl tighter around her shoulders.

He turned to Elizabeth. 'Can you imagine what the redoubtable Mrs Pawley was thinking of when she bought the garment Miss Lewis is wearing?'

Elizabeth bestowed a small smile on him. 'I'd prefer not to. Her choice of style and fabric is an abomination.'

'You must make sure she has something more attractive to wear, and get rid of those clod-hopper boots.'

'They will do,' Siana mumbled, her face reddening. 'You have been more than kind as it is.'

The squire smiled. 'They will *not* do, my dear. If we are to make a lady out of you, you must dress the part.'

Siana couldn't forget the squire's proposition to her at Reverend White's house. But since then he hadn't been overly familiar with her, so she could only conclude he'd been the worse for drink. 'Why would you want to do that, sir?'

'Because Richard White saw something in you and it amuses me to help you rise above your class,' he said lightly.

'And Daisy and Josh?'

'Josh is a bright lad, and a survivor. He will serve me loyally.' He gazed at Daisy and smiled. 'As for the child, she reminds me of my daughter. Charlotte was about that age when she died from diphtheria. Her mother, Patricia, became ill from grieving.'

When his eyes came up to hers Siana saw the glint of

tears. A lump grew in her throat. Her sympathy reached out to him. The squire must have truly loved his wife. 'I'm sorry she suffered.'

'Patricia had eyes a little like yours, but a lighter green. Hers were as mischievous as spring before she became ill. Yours are as enigmatic as the depths of the forest, but your soul touches on the surface, as hers did. Sometimes, I can sense your mood.'

Closing her eyes for a moment Siana experienced the still depths of his sadness. There might as well have been nobody else in the carriage when she exchanged a smile with him. 'Is she always with you?'

The squire nodded.

Elizabeth leaned forward, breaking the contact between them. She placed a hand over the squire's and frowned slightly. 'You must try to put Patricia's death behind you, Edward.'

He squeezed her hand and let it go. 'Of course I must, Elizabeth. There's nothing quite so boring as a melancholy man.' Leaning back against the corner, he gazed out of the window.

Melancholy or not, Siana thought the squire anything but boring. She saw him smile faintly when Josh's laugh rang out.

Josh was seated with the coachman, a huge grin on his face. He felt like a proper toff in his warm clothes and new boots, his cap pulled down over his ears.

Unused to the motion of this mode of travel, his knuckles gripped the bucking seat rail as he gazed below him to where the shining rumps and powerfully muscled backs of two black horses undulated with each stride.

'By God, the wind whistles up here, all right,' he said to John, the coach driver.

The coachman's nose was pinched and red-tipped from the cold. 'You'll get used to it when you start work proper, my lad.'

Josh drew himself up. 'I haven't said I'm going to work for the squire yet. Besides, I'm ready to start work now.'

'Not according to the doctor, you ain't. He wants you stuffed like a Christmas goose first.' John shot him a sideways glance. 'Can't say I blames him either. You're as thin as a sparrow's whistle.'

'My sister said she'll soon fatten me up now.'

John slid him a grin. 'A bonny girl, your sister.'

'Better'n most of the girls around here, 'cept for Elizabeth, of course.' A smile illuminated his gaunt face. 'She be a real fine lady.'

'The squire can sure pick 'em, but that there lady be old enough to be your mother, so don't you go making any sheep's eyes at her, now. Not unless you want to be laughed at. She'll be an old lady long afore you be ready to sow your wild oats, young un.'

When Josh's face flamed red, the coachman chuckled.

They were moving along a quiet road with a backwater at one side and houses set back in splendid gardens at the other. The tide was out, leaving the sea bed exposed as a pungent ripple of mud flats. A few people were carrying pails or baskets. They poked at the mud with sticks, or dug with shovels, piling up the mud in cones. Sharp-eyed seagulls wheeled and screamed overhead, swooping now and then to pluck up a wriggling worm or a stranded fish.

'What be they digging for?' Josh asked.

'Cockles and crabs to sell on the quayside, I reckon,' John murmured.

Josh took note of it. He'd had his fill of poverty and had experienced the life of a labourer under a bad master like his brother. He'd seen how a toff like the squire lived, too. Josh didn't like his family being beholden to the squire. He suspected he'd be a bad man to cross if the fate of Will Hastings was anything to go by. But Siana was doing the best she could for them and he'd go along with it for now. Eventually, though, he intended to be his own master. If there was a means of making extra money in this town, he wanted to know of it.

The carriage took a couple of left turns into a quiet, leafy street, presently drawing to a halt outside a pair of painted iron gates.

A blustery, salted wind came across the mud flats. Ragged clouds chased each other across the sky. The horses' coats steamed a little and their tails flicked from side to side, sending pungent dung smells up to their passengers. One of the animals turned its head to look at him, its soft brown eyes patient and unconcerned, its mane blowing to one side. It stamped its hoof on the dirt and snickered quietly to itself.

'Here we be,' John said. 'Hop down and open the gate. When we reaches the house, you can unhitch that mean ol' mule from the back, then take him to the stables. Give him a nice rub down and a feed to make him feel at home. Let what happened to your brother be a lesson to you, young Josh. Remember: if you looks after your beasts of burden, they'll allus look after you.'

'What about the other nags?'

179

'Don't you worry none about them. They be my responsibility.'

The house took Siana's breath away. It was two storeys high with attics above, and built solidly of stone. The arched windows had an air of secretiveness about them.

Rosie, who'd been appointed their housekeeper and sent on ahead to ready the house, appeared round the corner, her cheeks apple-red from the wind and a beaming smile of welcome on her face. Her large white apron billowed in the breeze.

'Lordy me, if March hasn't arrived early to blow the cobwebs away,' she said, and taking a key from her pocket, handed it to the squire.

Siana followed the squire and Elizabeth up to the panelled oak door. Ceremoniously, he inserted a key in the lock. 'Rosie wouldn't have had time to clean all this by herself so it might be a little dusty inside,' he said apologetically. 'As soon as you're settled in, I'll hire a maid of all work to help Rosie.'

'I can help her,' Siana said, remembering a little wistfully the joy of polishing the Reverend White's wooden banister. 'It will save you money.'

The squire lifted an eyebrow at her words and exchanged an amused smile with Elizabeth. Embarrassed, and not quite knowing what she'd said wrong, Siana blinked as they advanced into the dimness. She stood uncertainly in the hall, watching John and Rosie carry in the luggage, wondering if she should offer to help. She wasn't quite sure what her status was.

Daisy woke up, stuck her thumb in her mouth and

gazed wonderingly about her. Don't get too used to it, Siana thought. We might be on the street again next week.

'I've put Mrs Skinner in the large room at the front,' Rosie said to John. 'Miss Lewis is in one of the smaller rooms overlooking the back garden. You can put her bags there.' Rosie turned and smiled at her. 'It has a door to the adjoining room where Daisy can sleep. You and she be far enough away from the other rooms not to disturb anyone's sleep.'

About to enquire where Josh would sleep, Siana managed to stop herself. She and Elizabeth would decide for themselves once the squire had gone.

But Edward didn't leave for two weeks. Instead, he moved into one of the guest rooms. Within days he'd hired a couple of servants, young women who were willing to do anything from laundering to acting as ladies' maid.

It was obvious Elizabeth enjoyed the squire's company. Siana had never seen her so happy or animated. Her eyes shone and her cheeks carried a becoming flush.

Siana had to admit, the squire had a great deal of charm. Gradually she relaxed in his company, allowing herself to be drawn into the conversations and shyly contributing with the limited knowledge she had when asked a question. She plucked up the courage to call him Edward when requested, stuttering it out at his bidding and blushing pinkly all the while. He and Elizabeth laughed at her reticence.

Neither of them drew her attention to her mis-pronunciation of words as Reverend White had. By paying diligent attention to the way her companions spoke, by imitation and by practising when she was alone, for she wanted to improve herself, Siana began to refine her country dialect.

'I'm pleased to notice you are modest, and not in the least opinionated,' Edward said to her one day.

'Indeed, why would I be opinionated when I grew up in a house where female opinion was not worth the air it cost to express it?'

'And your modesty?' he asked, sounding interested. 'You are not forward like most country maids.'

Which reminded her that she'd rebuffed his advances. Realizing he had not approached her in that regard again, she coloured a little as she gazed at the amber ring on her finger and tried to remember Daniel's kiss on her forehead. It was hard to recall, as if it had faded from her memory.

She thought of the lack of privacy she'd grown up with, and the crudely suggestive stares of Tom Skinner. Once she'd been bathing in the stream and had noticed her stepfather watching her from behind a tree. Unconsciously, she pulled her mother's shawl closer about her shoulders and shuddered. It was best not to be noticed.

As if she could read her mind, Elizabeth placed a comforting hand over hers and changed the subject. 'I have discovered a dancing academy in town and have determined you will learn to dance when your arm is not quite so painful.'

Edward smiled. 'A good idea, every young lady should be able to dance. We will invite some guests to supper to celebrate her eighteenth birthday. I will hire a pianist and a fiddler and Siana will be the belle of the evening.'

Her birthday was only six weeks away. Horrified at the thought, Siana's eyes widened. 'I will not know what to say or how to act.'

A slight frown creased his brow and he placed a hand on Elizabeth's shoulder, gently massaging the base of her neck with his forefinger. Watching them, Siana wondered what it felt like to receive such a gentle and intimate caress.

Her face heated as he noticed her gaze. As his finger continued to gently circle, he smiled slightly, his eyes half hooded, almost somnolent. His voice was a low growl. 'My dearest girl, Elizabeth will make sure you are ready. Won't you, my dear?'

Elizabeth's hand came up to cover his. 'Of course I will, Edward.'

'I'll be leaving here in the morning,' he said casually, and yawned behind his hand. 'I have an early start, so if you ladies will allow it, I'll retire early.'

Perspiration had pearled between Siana's breasts. She felt strangely light-headed and her skin tingled. She hoped she wasn't sickening for something.

Not long afterwards, Elizabeth announced her intention to retire too. Not wanting to sit around by herself, Siana thought she'd go to her bed, as well.

One of the new maids had lit the lamp in her room. She checked on Daisy, who was fast asleep, cuddling her favourite rag doll. As she gazed down at her sister, a lump grew in her throat. Daisy had survived because of Edward's largesse. God help her if they ever had to go hungry again.

Tentatively, for she found it difficult to demand help, she rang for one of the maids to help her get ready for bed. The girl did what was necessary, then brushed out her hair and bobbed a curtsy. 'Will that be all, miss?'

'That's all, thank you,' Siana mumbled and climbed into bed with the book she was reading about the marcher lords – an early present from Edward for her eighteenth birthday. It was the first book she'd ever owned and she reverently touched the brown leather binding before allowing her finger to trace over the title.

She turned to the inscription inside.

To Miss Siana Lewis in celebration of her 18th birthday on 12 April 1834, a gift from her obedient servant, Sir Edward Forbes, Bt.

He had lovely handwriting, she thought as her fingertip lightly slid around the curving loops of his name.

Her obedient servant? She giggled at the thought. How grand it sounded. If only her mother could see her now.

She opened the marked pages and read until the words jumbled and danced in front of her eyes. Only then did she turn down the lamp and snuggle under the covers, her mind full of the strange, savage people who'd guarded the Welsh borderlands. Her finger touched against a pulse in her wrist. Had her mother told the truth? Did their blood really run in her veins?

The house was as quiet as a church, with just an occasional creak from the floorboards or the click of metal cooling in the grate as the fire died. From outside came the sigh and rustle of the trees. They were friendly sounds she'd grown used to. Grand though Cheverton Manor was, she decided she liked this house better. Being smaller, it had a more welcoming, homely feel to it.

Nearly asleep, Siana was jolted awake by a muted cry. Heart thudding, she listened intently until all she could hear was the loud hiss of silence pressing against her ears. The cry was not repeated and she relaxed. It must have been an owl.

Edward must have risen early, for the sound of his carriage departing woke her the next morning. She sprang out of bed and rushed to the window in time to see Josh close the gate behind them.

Siana saw very little of Josh after that. She cornered Rosie one day. 'Where's Josh sleeping?'

'He has a loft over the stables, miss. He said he prefers to sleep there rather than in the house. He comes inside for his breakfast and dinner though, as hungry as a horse. Hollow legs, that there lad's got. Just like my brother had when he was Josh's age.'

Josh was nowhere to be found. 'Who knows what he gets up to?' Rosie said. 'He goes off somewhere when his work's done.'

Siana, satisfied that Josh's quarters were snug and warm and his belly was kept full, concluded that Josh was old enough to make his own decisions regarding his comfort.

The house felt oddly empty and unsettled without Edward. Siana pondered the relationship existing between Elizabeth and Edward. Sometimes she caught herself wishing Edward would call off his marriage to Isabelle. When Tom died, he could wed Elizabeth instead.

One day when they were eating breakfast, Elizabeth looked up from her plate and said, 'Edward has offered to lend me the capital to start my business. It's a fine morning. Now our bruises are healed and we do not look such frights, I'm going to consult an agent about finding suitable premises for my Ladies' Accessories salon.' She eyed Siana's brown dress. 'Edward has also charged me with fitting you out more suitably, so if you have nothing better to do, you can accompany me. We shall look at some material and patterns. Rosie can mind Daisy.'

Siana didn't quite know what to say, so she mumbled, 'The squire has been kind to me.'

Elizabeth was in the middle of spreading honey on her bread. She paused for a moment, her head tilted to one side. Her eyes were sad as the golden drops of sticky liquid gathered at the end of the spoon. 'Sometimes his kindness takes hostages.'

Siana didn't understand what she meant. 'He loves you, I think,' she dared to say.

Elizabeth's fine blue eyes were turned her way. 'Edward's love is unpredictable.' The globule of honey lengthened into a string that stretched slowly downward. It spread into a miniature golden sun on the edge of the plate. Elizabeth laughed a little unsteadily. 'Yet for all its danger, the pull of it is hard to resist, as if one is a bee being drawn to the source of the honey.'

Leaving her seat, Siana impulsively kissed her cheek. 'Perhaps he will not marry Isabelle, after all.'

'You have a romantic soul.' Elizabeth smiled and gently patted her cheek, adroitly changing the subject when Rosie came in with a tray of tea. 'I wonder what

186

that awful housekeeper was thinking of when she bought you that gown. It must be the ugliest garment in the world.'

'It most certainly is not; the black one is. This one is the second ugliest.'

'She's a black-hearted old hag is Mrs Pawley,' Rosie grumbled almost to herself. 'She can jump on her broomstick and fly off into the night for all I care.'

They both began to laugh then, gazing at each other with pleasure, were joined by some inexplicable bond of togetherness.

Mrs Pawley had taken advantage of her master's absence to visit her sister in Dorchester. The two women hunched over a pot of tea and ate a chunk of fruit cake stolen from the manor pantry, spreading it with black-berry conserve from the same source.

The room they were sitting in was mean and dark. It smelled of mice droppings and stale urine.

Agnes Pawley, older than her sister, bent, crone-like and dressed in black, gently felt her bodice then picked some crumbs from it. She ate them one by one, sucking them through the gaps in her almost toothless mouth. She gave a sigh of satisfaction. 'A nice bit of cake that, our Ethel. Won't it be missed?'

The housekeeper shrugged. 'If it is, no one will suspect me. I've bin there too long.' She leaned forward, dropping her voice as she began to gossip with her sister. 'You'll never guess what's bin going on up at the manor lately.'

Agnes leaned forward too, her eyes milky, her face

avid for any news that might involve the manor. A good titbit of gossip in the right ears would see the pennies cascade into her begging cup.

Ethel Pawley could hardly contain herself; squeezing her thin thighs together, her voice hissed triumphantly from her mouth like a blast through a tin whistle. 'There were two of them damned strumpets in the house last month. As bold as brass, they were. That Siana Lewis was one of them, all bruised up and with her arm broken. She had an infant held in her good arm. About a year old it were, and looking like her who up and died on him all them years ago. Squire fussed over them both like he owned them. Wouldn't be surprised if the kid ain't his, neither, and the mother no more than seventeen. It's not decent.'

'Never,' Agnes breathed, her dim eyes gleaming.

'Guess who he gets in to look after her? Go on, guess.'

Agnes shook her head.

'His other harlot, the one he foisted onto the girl's stepbrother. She looked as beat up as the girl. Next thing they was all bundled into the carriage and taken away. I overheard the squire tell Elizabeth Skinner that he had bought them a house in Poole to live in. What d'you make of those goings-on, then?'

'There'll be a fine old dandy when that sweetheart of his gets to hear of it, that's what I think.'

'D'you think she will get to hear of it then, our Agnes?'

Agnes gave a sly chuckle. 'Wouldn't be at all surprised. You could allus tell 'er yerself.'

Ethel's mouth became a spidery pout. 'Of course I

could, dearie, but we wouldn't want it to get back to the squire's ears, now, would we? It would lose me my job, then where would we be?' Sliding her hand into her pocket, Ethel brought out a coin and handed it over to her sister. It was immediately snatched from her hand and slipped into her sister's pocket.

Ethel smiled a little when Agnes said, 'I reckon she might learn of it, at that. Word of mouth is a funny thing. A hint here, a hint there . . . but not yet a while. She be in London right now, being fitted for her trousseau. I heard she's got so fat they had to put a panel of material in her wedding gown to let it out.'

Ethel sniggered. 'Squire likes them a bit on the lean side. She looks a bit like his late wife, does the Lewis girl. A real lady, she was. He doted on her. A pity she went mad. He had to lock her in her room in the end. It's still locked. Nobody's bin allowed in there since she died, not even to clean it. Sometimes he goes in there and stays there all day.'

Edward inserted the key in the lock and turned it. The door had begun to squeak, he noticed.

Closing it behind him, he sat in the pink-brocade armchair by the cold, ash-filled grate and listened to the sounds of the departed. The room was hushed and whispery, smelling faintly of lavender.

Over on the dresser a bowl of water had evaporated, leaving a series of faint brown rings, like tide marks on a sea wall. Dust coated the furniture, the curtains were drawn across, the blue velvet faded now from a couple of summers of neglect. The bed was unmade, the covers thrown back.

The last time he'd seen Patricia she'd been lying there, dead and cold. Her hands crossed on her chest, her hair fanned loose and free on the pillow. Adjoining, was the room of their child, empty for more years than he liked to think about. His darling baby girl had been cruelly choked by an illness that had started as a simple sore throat.

'I'm sorry, I'm sorry,' he whispered. 'But I was left behind to live with it, and for the first time since, I feel totally alive.'

Rising from the chair, he strode to the window and jerked the curtains aside. Light streamed through the window, dust motes danced. He sneezed and gazed up at the portrait over the fireplace, handkerchief held to his mouth.

Patricia stared back at him, her painted smile wryly amused. Her hair was black, her eyes green and brilliant. Her skin was painted in delicate brushstrokes of peach tints on almond silk. Shadows cleaved between perfect breasts peaking under a bodice of pale green satin. Diamonds shone on her fingers and in her ears.

Patricia had not aged well. Her mouth had pulled down at the corners with snarling discontent, her eyes had developed a vacant, staring meanness to them. She had scarred herself constantly, scratching at her breasts and stomach until she bled.

He could almost see the rise and fall of her chest as she breathed. Almost feel her warmth. Almost . . . but not quite.

He closed his eyes in anguish. She'd fought him when he'd held the pillow over her face, but not for long.

A heart attack, Dr Bede had put it down to. Edward gave a faint smile. Thank God for Bede's incompetence. Francis would have spotted his guilt in an instant.

Funny how the peasant girl had picked up on his sadness in the carriage. 'Is she always with you?' Siana had asked.

Of course she was. Every minute of every day. A man couldn't easily shed his guilt over a woman he'd murdered, however much she'd needed to be put out of her misery.

He smiled one last smile at Patricia's painted face. 'You do understand, don't you, Patricia? I did it for your own good and mine too. I needed my freedom. Now I'm in love again. No matter how unsuitable the match seems, she will provide me with heirs.'

'I miss my dear Charlotte every day. We never did talk of her death, did we? You were so self-absorbed. You didn't give a thought for anyone else's grief but yours and refused me the right to have another child.'

The expression on the woman's face in the portrait didn't change.

'The servants will come in here and talk about you – about me. They will handle your clothes and gossip. They'll try to imagine what you were like. No doubt Mrs Pawley will tell them.'

'The poor mistress was insane from grief, she'll say. Lord, how that woman likes to gossip.'

He shrugged and managed an apologetic smile. 'You must go now. From my house, my life and my heart. I'll leave the door open this time, so you can get out. Goodbye, Patricia. Look after our beautiful girl until we meet again in heaven.'

Blowing her a kiss, he turned on his heel and left, leaving the door wide open behind him.

Going to the drawing room, he poured himself a stiff brandy and gazed out into the windswept garden. It was late afternoon, the light gloomy. He sat for a while, sipping at his drink and thinking his thoughts, growing increasingly mellow. Eventually, he reached a conclusion that both startled and pleased him.

Spring had already started to lay a bloom over the land, he noted. Soon, the earth would blossom. He smiled, feeling himself blossom. A great weight seemed to have dropped from his shoulders.

Summoning the housekeeper to the drawing room, he stared at the funny little black-garbed woman, recalling her from his childhood. She was as thin as a stick, dried up. He wasn't sure that he liked her, but it didn't matter. Her function was to make sure his house was kept clean and she did it well.

The house was large, it needed children to fill it. Several children. He thought of Isabelle, flat on her back, her legs spread wide, her bosoms flattened against her chest like two round pillows.

He chuckled as he shook his head to dispel the image.

'I want the rooms of my deceased wife cleared out,' he said. 'The furniture, ornaments and pictures can be taken to the attic. The personal items must be burned, clothing, furnishings, toiletries, toys . . . everything.'

'Yes, sir,' Mrs Pawley said, her eyes beginning to gleam.

'Be aware,' Edward said gently, 'I'm familiar with every item remaining there. Should any of them turn up in the market place, I will hold you personally responsible.'

192

12

The Dorchester Assizes. March, 1834

'The object of all legal punishment is not altogether with the view of operating on the offenders themselves, it is also for the sake of offering an example and a warning.'

Judge Baron Williams exchanged a brief glance with William Ponsonby MP, foreman of the Grand Jury, and brother-in-law to the Home Secretary, Lord Melbourne. Then he allowed his glance to rest on the remainder of the jury – on the representation of magistrates. Morally sound, upright men, every one of them. With the wealth of legal expertise present, there was no doubt in his mind that they'd reach the right conclusion.

Rapping his gavel to demand attention, the judge then ordered, 'Bring in the prisoners. Let the trial commence.'

Josh had got rid of his cockles early that day, the crowds outside the assizes only too eager to sample his cooked shellfish. He could have sold three times as many. They'd fetched a nice price, too. Twice what the sailors paid him for them on the quay at Poole.

What with that and the shillings garnered from his cartage business, he was in possession of what seemed to him to be a small fortune, even though he'd had to spend much of his precious earnings by buying a small cart from a bankrupt baker the month before.

Josh was proud of his cart. JOSHUA SKINNER, COCKLES AND CARTAGE, POOLE, he'd painted on the side in large blue letters, after acquiring some marine paint on one of his night forays into town. The writing was a bit uneven, but still, it got the message across. As an afterthought he'd added, SMALL GOODS ONLY, because neither he nor Jasper would have had the strength for large or heavy loads, even if the cart had had the room, especially over a long distance.

Business was brisk. At the rate he was going, he knew he'd soon be his own man rather than be obliged to take up the employment offered by the squire. His brother Tom had been in the squire's pay, and look what it had got him. A whole heap of trouble. Everyone had hated Tom Skinner when he was able. Now he was down-and-out he didn't have a friend in the world.

In fact, people were waiting for him to die, but the bugger was too mean to let go of life. Instead, he took up a bed in the infirmary and gazed through hate-filled eyes at everyone who went near him. Josh had heard that Tom snuffled like a pig through his chewed nose and his skin was covered in boils from the pig shit he'd wallowed in, especially the stump of his leg. It had poisoned his blood, the doc had been overheard saying. Josh couldn't think of a better fate for Tom.

He whistled happily to himself as he gave Jasper a

194

feed of oats. 'Now don't you go to sleep on the way home, after that,' he warned, and one of Jasper's ears swivelled back to listen. 'You can have a bit of a rest while I go in the bank when we gets home. All right?'

He reckoned it was about time he opened a bank account. But not in Dorchester. Oh no! If Tom happened to recover and got wind of it, the thieving bastard would soon have it off him. Josh had already decided. He'd use the same bank in Poole as Elizabeth used.

Turning the cart around, he walked Jasper through the milling crowds.

'Oi! Josh lad,' somebody shouted. 'Wait up.'

Josh turned, grinning at Pete Barrow who, with cap pulled down over his eyes, came sauntering out of a laneway.

'What can I do for you then, Pete?'

'Be you going back to Poole?'

'Sure, but if you want something delivering it'll cost you sixpence a piece.'

Pete lowered his voice. 'There's a couple of parcels of trout to go to the fishmonger. Make it thruppence and there might be a regular run in it.'

Josh laughed. 'D'you take me for a fool? Risky business, trout. I reckon word must be out and they be keeping an eye on your usual runner. A tanner apiece. That's my cut.'

Pete thought for a moment, then nodded. 'Fair enough. Wait for me at the clearing down by the stream.'

'Not for too long, I gotta get back to Poole. Got some business to conduct,' he said importantly. 'I be going to open meself a bank account.'

'Going up in the world then, are you?' Pete grinned. 'Well good luck, young un, that's all I can say,' and he melted back into the crowds and was gone.

The clearing was deserted. Josh ate a pennyworth of meat pie whilst he waited, appreciating the rich gravy. It sat nicely in his stomach. He wished he'd bought two portions. 'By crikey, I gets hungry these days,' he said to Jasper. 'Seems to me that the more you get to eat the more you want.'

Soon Pete arrived. The man was out of breath as he threw two sacks onto the cart. Josh held out his hand and a shilling was pressed into it.

'Quickly, get going. I think someone followed me.'

Josh was on the road inside a few minutes. Jasper went at a fast trot for half a mile, then Josh slowed the mule's pace to something less tiring. They had a fair lick to go and he didn't want to wear the old boy out. Rounding a bend, he came upon Hannah, her infant squalling in a sling on her hip, a basket in the other arm.

He was tempted to pass by her without a word, but when she moved into the middle of the road he had no choice but to stop.

'I'm fair worn out. Give us a lift to the turn off, our Josh.'

Taking her basket from her, he jerked his thumb at the back of the cart, saying ungraciously, 'Hop up, then.'

George stared at him for a moment, his eyes blue and watery. Mucus ran from his nose.

The poor little bugger, Josh thought, and smiled at him. George burst into tears and Hannah smacked his arm. 'For God's sake shut up, else you'll get a good hiding next,' she shouted.

'Leave the kid alone,' Josh said fiercely.

'And who d'you think you be to tell me what to do with me own child?'

'The person who owns this cart, that's who. If you lay one finger on George in front of me you can bloody well get down and walk home.'

Hannah's eyebrows rose. 'Since when did you own a cart? I know where you got that murdering mule from, and good riddance to him. But how d'you get the money to buy this rig. Steal it?'

'By working for meself, that's how.'

'Working for yerself? Glory be, Josh Skinner, you allus was a sharp un. You'll be riding in a carriage next, and too good to speak to the likes of us.' Her eyes took on a sly slant. ' I thought mebbe Siana gave you the money now she's bedded down with the squire.'

'What d'you mean, bedded down with the squire?'

'You know 'zackly what I mean. The whole village is talking. They say the squire's allus been a stallion, and now he has two mares in his stable. Tom is right pissed off about it, I can tell you. I wouldn't like to be in Elizabeth's shoes if he recovers.'

Josh's face flamed as the shock of what she'd said sank in. Surely his sister wouldn't allow the squire to take liberties. Course she wouldn't. Not Siana. 'May God strike you dead for your wicked lies. Our Siana's not like that.'

The motion of the cart had sent George off to sleep. Hannah settled him down comfortably on the sacks before saying almost charitably, 'Siana mightn't have had any choice, since she's bin lumbered with you and Daisy to look after. She's gotta find some means of feeding you, ain't she? The squire don't give nothing for nothing.'

'I won't hear a word more of your wickedness.'

'It's only what everyone else is saying. Besides, I reckon her being the squire's fancy piece would be better'n marrying a farm labourer and worrying about where the next meal's coming from all the time, like I have to.' She shrugged. 'Though if'n our Tom dies we might get offered the tenancy of the farm.'

There was the sound of horses coming up behind them and a shout. Josh's heart began to beat very fast when the squire and his steward pulled up. He'd have to try to brazen it out.

Hannah's mouth fell open when Josh doffed his cap and said pleasantly, 'Good afternoon, sir.'

'Ah Josh, it's you.' The squire's eyes went to the wording on the rig. He seemed amused by it. 'Cockles and Cartage, is it?'

'Yes, sir. No offence, sir, but I be my own man now.'

The squire's smile broadened. 'So, the Forbes Cartage Company is to have competition.'

'No, sir. I only be local, and small goods at that. I'm not venturing afar, like London. Jasper be too old for heavy loads. Besides, I don't know how to get to London.'

The squire chuckled at that. 'Perhaps I can throw a bit of business your way then. Bainbridge and Son is looking for someone reliable to deliver small parcels to

198

homes hereabouts. I can put in a word for you, if you like.'

'Thank you, sir,' and Josh prayed the poached trout he was carrying wouldn't queer his chances.

The squire's eyes went to Hannah. 'It's Mrs Collins, isn't it?'

'That be my name, sir – her whose husband be looking after Croxley Farm.'

The squire's lips twitched. 'Quite so. And what do you carry in the basket, Mrs Collins?'

'Flour and sugar, sir.'

'Take a look, would you, Jed,' the squire said.

Hannah's expression was self-righteous when Jed Hawkins dismounted to search through the basket. He glanced at the baby sleeping on its bed of rough sacks. His nose wrinkled as he remounted the horse. 'It's as she said, sir.'

'Have you seen anyone on the road for the last mile or so, Josh?'

'No, sir.'

The squire nodded, seemingly satisfied. 'On your way, then, lad.'

'Bloody cheek. Who do they think they is?' Hannah muttered indignantly when the pair had cantered off the way they had come and were safely out of earshot.

The premises were obviously perfect for Elizabeth. Standing in a fine position in the high street, the shop boasted two large windows in which to display goods.

Elizabeth signed the lease on the spot and dismissed the agent. After he left she turned and said, 'I thought to use the room at the back for the display and sale of under apparel and night wear. I hear pantelettes are becoming popular and I have it in mind to make ladies look prettier altogether, with silk and lace instead of plain linen and cambric.'

'But why bother when nobody can see them?'

Elizabeth smiled at Siana. 'When a woman takes the care to appear feminine, it pleases her . . . husband. Some gentlemen enjoy silk, lace and perfume on a woman. Display is important to them. What a woman keeps hidden both intrigues and attracts them. They might like a woman to be demure in public, but they enjoy it if she's provocative and responsive in the privacy of the bedroom.'

Siana blushed as she remembered Elizabeth's relationship with the squire. Did she wear silk and lace for him? Not that she'd noticed anything untoward going on between the pair. The squire slept in his own room when he stayed overnight, and so did Elizabeth.

Perhaps there was nothing between them now Elizabeth was a married woman. Then Siana remembered his caressing finger. The end of her breasts hardened and began to tingle. For a moment she closed her eyes, enjoying the sensation.

There was a sense of guilt when she opened them again, as if she'd done something shameful. 'Have you heard from Daniel lately?' she quickly asked her companion.

'My son is not much of a correspondent.' Elizabeth turned away, obviously reluctant to talk of anything other than her plans for the shop. 'For the sake of privacy I thought to curtain off the entrance to the other room. Red velvet perhaps, with a gold tassel so it could be tied back on occasion. What do you think of red? Would blue or green be a better choice, perhaps?'

'Pale pink and grey would be discreet as well as feminine,' Siana murmured.

'I hadn't considered pink and grey, but I do believe you're right. I saw some pretty pink-flowered wallpaper amongst the decorator's samples the other day.'

Siana looked around her, trying to imagine it all as Elizabeth described it in detail. Embossed wallpaper, plush covered chairs, mirrors on every wall. There would be lace screens behind the window displays to keep out prying eyes yet still allowing the light in. Linen screens would create an illusion of privacy, cocooning the clients whilst they were seated at a small table. An assistant would bring the goods for inspection.

'My assistants will not wear superior airs like those of Bainbridge and Son. They will be familiar with every piece of merchandise and treat the clients with respect, even if they only buy a piece of ribbon or lace.'

Elizabeth continued excitedly, 'There are some living quarters upstairs. As I'll be away much of the time selecting the latest merchandise from the London wholesalers, I thought to advertise for a young woman of honesty and good sense to manage the shop in my absence.'

Siana tried not to feel hurt. 'Then you were not thinking of asking me?'

'My dearest Siana, you would not be able to work here and look after Daisy and Josh adequately, as you promised your mother on her deathbed. Your job is managing the house we live in, and you must continue to educate and refine yourself in all ways. See how well you're dancing now? In two short weeks we'll celebrate your birthday.'

For what reason though? Dancing well would not supply her with employment in the future and she'd never be able to support herself if she didn't work. Being dependent on Elizabeth and the squire's kindness was beginning to rankle, but Siana didn't know what else to do. Even so, she'd been silly in thinking Elizabeth would deliberately set out to hurt her.

She smiled to show that no offence had been taken. 'There is someone I'd like to suggest for the position, and I'm sure Francis Matheson would give her a reference. Her name is Peggy Hastings.'

'Will Hastings's widow?' Elizabeth looked slightly shocked. 'I thought she was with child.'

'Josh told me the infant was stillborn.'

'Ah . . . such a pity.'

'Is it? When you don't know where the next meal is coming from, the loss of a child at birth might be a blessing – especially when there's a strong likelihood it might suffer and die from the effects of poverty, anyway.'

Elizabeth gave her a hug. 'Let's not quarrel over something we cannot change. Save your passion for a time when you're in the position to do something about it.'

'That will be never.'

'Sometimes fate leads us along a different path to what we'd expect.'

Siana smiled. 'You're right, Elizabeth. I never imagined I'd live in a fine house and eat every day. I never thought

I'd learn to dance and play the piano, however badly. And I imagine Peggy Hastings expects to pick oakum and dish out pea soup in the workhouse for the rest of her life.'

Elizabeth grimaced. 'I'll give some thought to the matter of Peggy Hastings whilst we order your wardrobe. God knows, she's suffered enough from the sounds of it.' She gave a faint smile. 'Better if Edward is kept in ignorance though.'

'But why?' Suddenly remembering why, Siana exchanged a glance of understanding with Elizabeth. Her mouth took on a wry twist. As she herself had received only kindness from the squire, it was hard to imagine him as a man whose cruel action had sent Will Hastings to his death.

Josh had arrived at the bank too late the night before. Now he stood and looked around him, a small, scruffy figure, his cap in his hand. His other hand he kept in his pocket, jiggling his coins to reassure himself he hadn't lost them.

He didn't know what to do or who to approach in this matter of business. From the richness of the polished wood, the ornate ceiling and shining brass rails, everything about the place seemed bent on intimidating him. Around him, tall figures moved confidently to the counter or stopped to chat to each other.

On the opposite side of the bank Francis Matheson watched the boy. The gaunt malnourished appearance had gone. He was pleased to see that Josh had gained some flesh, and colour had crept into his cheeks. What on earth was he doing inside a bank though?

He was about to go across to him when one of the

clerks moved self-importantly to loom over the boy. 'You've got no business in here, lad. Off you go.'

'That's where you be wrong, mister. I've got seven shillings, and I wants to open a bank account.'

'Oh yes, and how did you come by that? Not honestly, I'll be bound. Be off with you, you young varmint, else I'll send for the constable.'

'Don't you be calling me no thief unless you can prove it. I worked for this money, mister,' Josh said flatly. 'One day I'm going to be rich, then the likes of you can kiss my arse.'

Somebody chuckled.

Finding it hard not to laugh himself, Francis strolled forward as the clerk took a grip of Josh's collar. 'Josh, how nice to see you again. You've come in to open your account, have you? I'll be quite happy to stand as your referee.'

Josh shrugged out of the suddenly loosened hand. He shot a triumphant glare at the clerk, who bowed and melted back behind his desk. Josh grinned broadly at Francis. 'Thanks, Doc, but I reckon they don't want me as a customer.'

'Nonsense.' Francis lifted his hand and beckoned to an older man. 'Mr Denning is the head clerk, Josh. Perhaps you would see to this young friend of mine personally, Mr Denning.'

'Certainly, Doctor. Please take a seat, sir, whilst I take your details.'

Alarm filled Josh's eyes. 'What be them? I don't think I've got any details.'

Francis chuckled when Denning leaned forward, his

eyes twinkling. 'Your details are your name and address, young man. Also the name and nature of your business and the name and address of your referee. Can you sign your name?'

'Yes, sir. My sister showed me how. And I can read a bit, as long as they be simple words, like. Reading comes in right handy at times, it do.'

'I'm sure it does,' Denning said gravely. 'How much did you want to deposit?'

Deposit? Well, Josh knew what that was. Posh talk for what cows left behind in the fields. Least, that's what Elizabeth had called them once. But he didn't think the bank wanted a cow pat.

'Your money,' Francis whispered in his ear.

Josh withdrew his shillings from his pocket and lined them up on the desk. 'That be the deposit. Seven of them, see. I got half of them for selling cockles, the other half for carting goods. And I've got a couple of regular runs now,' he bragged. 'One for *Bainbridge and Sons* on Fridays. I make more in two days doing that than my dad made in a week working for the squire.'

Mr Denning looked suitably impressed. 'And the other run?'

But Josh couldn't tell him he was going to cart the squire's trout for the fishmonger up the road to sell from under the counter. He turned bright red and mumbled, 'I haven't decided on that un yet.'

The form was filled in and duly signed and witnessed. They stood up to leave.

Mr Denning smiled and shook his hand. 'Thank you for your custom, Mr Skinner.'

Josh felt about ten feet tall when they left the bank. 'Mr Skinner? Mark me for a posh toff!' he said, and jerked a head at the mule and cart. 'Can I give you a ride anywhere, Doc?'

'No, thank you, Josh. I have my horse, and I'm off to take a look at your sister's arm. How have you been? Are you eating well?'

'Don't you worry about me none. Cook up at the house thinks I'm a goose that needs fattening for Christmas.' He patted his stomach and grinned hugely. 'Shouldn't be surprised if I split open one of these fine days.'

Francis smiled at the lad and shook his head. He had no need to examine Josh. The Skinners were a tough lot.

He was thoughtful as he mounted his horse. Tom Skinner was dying the hard way. Francis could do nothing for him but to make sure he was comfortable. Eventually, Tom would succumb to the poisons circulating in his body. If he hadn't despised Tom for the damage he'd inflicted on the two women and the child, he could almost have admired his endurance.

He kicked his horse into a canter, suddenly looking forward to seeing Siana. The bone in her arm should be set by now. He just hoped she and Elizabeth were at home.

Siana ran to the window when she heard the horse coming up the short carriageway. She smiled and waved. 'It's Dr Matheson.'

'Were you expecting someone else, then?' Elizabeth said.

'I thought it might have been Edward.'

'If it had been, he would have been cross with you. A lady doesn't rush to the window every time she hears a horse. She waits until the caller is announced, then decides whether she can receive him or not. If she cannot, he will leave his card.'

'But of course we will receive Dr Matheson. He's our friend.'

'But what if we were entertaining another friend at the time? It might be inconvenient to see him.'

'How could it be when he's come such a long way to visit us?' Siana seated herself when the maid entered, arranging the skirt of her new gown. It was a pretty gown of ruby silk that they'd purchased that very morning. The cape collar was edged with lace, her feet encased in flat pumps decorated with silk roses to match the one she wore in her hair. She tapped her feet self-consciously on the floor before slipping her splinted arm into a silk scarf fashioned into a sling and saying to the maid, 'Show Dr Matheson in and bring him some refreshment.'

'Yes, miss.'

Elizabeth said sharply to the maid, 'Ask Dr Matheson to kindly wait for a few minutes, then show him in.'

Siana blushed when the maid had gone and Elizabeth gave her a stern look. 'Do not be so eager. It gives men the wrong idea.'

'He's a doctor. He's here to examine my arm.'

'He's also a widower, which makes him susceptible to encouragement.'

'He's from an aristocratic family,' Siana argued,

exasperated by Elizabeth's attitude. 'He's hardly likely to be interested in a peasant girl.'

'You will remain a peasant girl only as long as you continue to act like one. And there are different degrees of interest, depending on the impression a woman gives out. Francis Matheson is, first and foremost, a man. You must conduct yourself with more decorum, lest he form the impression that you're interested in him.'

'How can I be when I'm promised to Daniel?' Siana gazed soberly at the amber ring, which appeared to have lost some of its glow. It seemed a long time ago that he'd slipped it on her finger. Had they been fair to each other by binding themselves to a promise on such short acquaintance? She twisted it around her finger. Why hadn't Daniel written to her about Italy and the art treasures he'd seen?

The door opened and the maid announced the doctor.

Francis inclined his head to Elizabeth. 'Mrs Skinner,' he said, 'you look well.'

'Thank you, I am.'

Siana wriggled impatiently on her chair whilst Francis and Elizabeth engaged themselves in a brief conversation about the weather. She held her breath when he at last turned her way, and was gratified when his eyes widened. 'Can this vision be Miss Siana Lewis?'

'It certainly can,' she said, her mouth stretching into a wide smile. She found it almost impossible to behave like a lady with Francis, when his smile was so friendly and his eyes so filled with mischief. 'I hope you've come to tell me my arm is mended. It certainly feels better. And I have been using it without too much bother.'

'I will go and order refreshment,' Elizabeth said. 'You will stay for a while, won't you, Dr Matheson?'

'Only if the pair of you will call me Francis.'

'I'll certainly call you Francis,' Siana said, after Elizabeth graciously inclined her head and left the room. 'It's a saint's name, so you must be a faith healer.'

He glanced up at her, subjecting her to a dark scowl. His frown didn't quite reach his eyes though, as he pulled up a chair and proceeded to unwrap her bandaging. As he bent down to his task, she gazed at his dark head of hair. It was threaded with fine strands of grey.

'You're too young to have grey hair,' she said softly.

'I'm thirty-five. Almost halfway through my life. The grey hair is caused by patients who believe I perform miracles instead of using practical doctoring skills.'

She giggled at his fierce voice and wriggled her fingers under his nose. 'But see, you have repaired my arm quite beautifully. However, I shall withdraw your saintly halo and replace it with horns if that will please you.'

He chuckled as he probed the length of her forearm with his fingers. Finally he professed himself satisfied with his handiwork. 'The arm is healed. I will not need to visit you again.'

Disappointment filled her. 'But you will visit as a friend, yes? Otherwise I will have to break the other arm to entice you back. I will ask the squire to invite you to my birthday celebration.'

'He's already invited me.'

'And have you accepted?'

'Of course. We are friends now, are we not?'

209

'I sincerely hope so. Would you still like me as a friend if I hadn't changed and become a lady?'

'Why do you ask?' he said gently.

'Sometimes I feel as if I'm someone else completely. I didn't think fine clothes and manners would make such a difference.'

'It seems to have given you confidence, but the Siana I learned to like and respect is still the same person. Tell me, how is Daisy?'

She smiled. 'As bonny as a buttercup in spring. She is having a rest at the moment, but Rosie will bring her down when she wakes. She has the sweetest nature.'

'Then she must take after her sister,' he said with heavy gallantry.

Her smile faded a little and she briefly touched his cheek. 'You need not play drawing-room games with me, Francis. I don't want anything less than total honesty between us. It could damage our friendship, which I value highly.'

'Aye,' he said, and smiled. 'You have a good mind, so let's talk of other things. I ran into Josh on the way up here. He was opening a bank account. I provided him with a reference.'

Siana tried to hide her proud smile. 'He's determined to grow into a man beholden to no one but himself. He has even declined a room in the house, preferring to sleep in a loft over the stable.'

Francis knew Josh had once been a runner for men trying to organize themselves into labour unions. Those same men had been sentenced to seven years' transportation, a harsh penalty which left their wives and children to fend for themselves. But the unrest hadn't stopped. In fact, it had increased and was spreading. If Josh insisted on sleeping in the stable, it meant he was free to come and go at night.

In his profession Francis kept his ears open and his mouth shut. People weak from hunger and ill-treatment were liable to be bitter towards their employers. He didn't blame Josh for wanting to be his own man. The lad took risks, but he was astute and had already achieved more in his short lifetime than many. If he was careful and didn't get himself caught breaking the law, the boy would end up comfortably off.

'I wish I could do more for the poor of the district,' he said quietly.

'You can. I have asked Elizabeth to consider Peggy Hastings for a position in the establishment she is opening and suggested she ask you for a reference. I believe she is trustworthy.'

'I'm sure she would be grateful.'

'But can she read and write and do her sums?' Elizabeth asked him, sweeping into the room with two maids behind her, both carrying heavy trays.

'Oh aye. Peggy attended school in Wareham until she was fourteen, I believe. I've always found her to be honest, diligent in everything she does, and clean in her habits.'

'Well,' Elizabeth said, gazing from one to the other with a smile. 'Perhaps you wouldn't mind asking her to present herself at the shop to be interviewed next week, Francis. I'll be there every morning overseeing the outfitting of it.'

'I'll bring her in on Monday myself.'

'Thank you.' She poured tea into a cup and handed it to him, saying, 'I'd be grateful if you didn't mention the matter to Edward. Indirectly, he was responsible for her husband's death.'

Francis's hand jerked, the cup rattled violently in the saucer and liquid spilled onto his cuff. Elizabeth laughed and, seating herself on the footstool next to his knee, applied a napkin to the stained cuff. 'I'm so sorry, Francis, I didn't mean to startle you.'

Her eyes engaged his, blue and bright with suppressed laughter.

Francis gave a low chuckle. 'It's nothing. The stain will soon rinse out. Of course, the matter will remain confidential.'

'And the irony of the situation appeals to you, no doubt.'

'I find it hard to believe Edward will connect the two. The incident and its ramifications have already been put from his mind.'

'Which will make the situation the more amusing if he finds out.'

The pair's laughter seemed to exclude Siana.

Elizabeth is flirting with him, she thought, and Francis seems to be enjoying it. Quite suddenly, the bottom fell out of her stomach, leaving a void filled with a dismay she couldn't quite account for.

It wasn't until later that she appreciated the subtle lesson Elizabeth had taught her.

13

Isabelle Prosser was in a foul mood as she discontentedly surveyed the selection of confectionery the tearoom serving maid had brought.

Spreading a napkin over her lap, she pointed to the largest, a fondant-covered confection. 'Leave the tray,' she snapped, her eyes darting from one offering to another as the girl was about to withdraw. 'I may want another.'

And another and another, her aunt Caroline thought irritably. Isabelle had been a disagreeable companion of late. It wasn't as if the foolish girl was in love with Edward Forbes. In fact, she was in love only with herself.

Isabelle looked hideous in a purple gown with matching bonnet. Her plump neck and arms were a sickly contrast, as were the angry patches of red on her cheeks.

'It's a scandal,' she hissed, helping herself to another cake. 'How could he keep two mistresses? Everyone must be laughing at me.'

'But we do not know if it's true.'

'If it's public knowledge, it must be true. Nobody would deliberately spread such a vicious rumour if it were not. I knew Edward had a son by that woman. But now I hear he has a young daughter by the other. What's more, she is a low peasant.'

'As your mother was before she married your father and became the wife of a tenant farmer.'

Isabelle gazed sulkily at her. 'My father became a cloth merchant.'

'But only because he inherited his brother's business. Before that he was a tenant farmer, and you a farmer's daughter. If I hadn't insisted on finishing school for you, you would not possess the airs and graces you now have. As for your wealth, it is due to my eldest brother's industry.'

'Which you wish you had inherited instead of my father,' Isabelle said spitefully. 'And much good it's done me. The only offer so far is marriage to a man old enough to be my grandfather.'

'You should not look a gift horse in the mouth, my dear. The squire has position and looks. You should count it a privilege you are chosen to bear his heirs.'

'I am not looking forward to such events when I would prefer to be wanted for myself instead of my inheritance and breeding abilities. I know I'm not attractive. I will feel like a cow being put to the bull, and I suppose he will expect me to feel grateful for his attention.'

Caroline gasped at Isabelle's indelicacy.

'I will not turn a blind eye to his infidelity. And I will tell him so the next time we meet.'

'Be careful, Isabelle. He is not a man to tolerate another's interference in his private life.'

'His private life is now public knowledge. He has made me a laughing stock. Perhaps I will take a lover myself when we are wed. It would serve him right.'

Isabelle's secret fantasy came into her mind. It involved a peasant boy who had once worked for her father. She'd been overweight even then, but he'd thought her attractive. He had embraced her in the barn and, touching her budding breasts with reverence, had told her how pretty and soft they were. He'd put his private part in her hand and she'd felt it grow and harden when he'd declared he loved her. He'd been the only person to ever say that to her.

She had been fourteen at the time. She'd often imagined what would have happened if her father hadn't disturbed them, and when she thought of him now, she knew the outcome would have been pleasurable.

Her aunt shrugged as she watched the crumbs drop onto Isabelle's bodice. Was the girl really so stupid as to believe the squire would be faithful to her, even *after* they were married?

She gave a delicious little shiver. Edward Forbes was so handsome. No wonder he could attract women so easily and bend them to his will. The way he sat his horse, so strong and positive. His amber eyes, so penetrating they seemed to stare right into a woman's soul. He was the type to make any maiden's heart beat faster. She pressed her hand against her chest as her own maidenly heart fluttered in agitated response to her thoughts.

'I will find out where these trollops live,' Isabelle said, and her eyes were as vicious as those of an adder about to strike. 'And I will order them out of Edward's house. They will rue the day they laid claim to the man I regard as mine.'

Isabelle's mood seemed to take a sudden turn for the better. Helping herself to another sweet cake, she cut it into small squares, biting into them one after the other with her sharp, yellow teeth. When she'd eaten her fill she sat back, her plump hands folded over her bulging stomach, staring pointedly at her empty teacup with a smug smile on her face.

Her mouth pursed slightly, for the almond-flavoured square her niece had just devoured was her favourite, Caroline reached for the handle of the teapot. It was hard being the poor relation and she felt like emptying the contents over the girl's head.

Elizabeth was at the shop and Siana was playing with Daisy in the nursery room upstairs when she heard the carriage.

It was a boisterous day in late March. The peculiar, salt smell borne on the gusts of strong wind told her the tide was out, the mud exposed.

Josh would be down there, digging up his cockles. Her brother worked hard, but he enjoyed keeping himself busy, and enjoyed even more the money his efforts brought in. Not that he ever spent any of it. Straight into his bank account it went.

She had teased him for being a miser, one day.

'Mr Denning at the bank said I have to be careful with me money if I want to be wealthy. If I leave it in the account long enough, the bank adds some to it. It's called interest.'

'So you've decided never to buy anything for yourself?'

He had smiled cheerfully at her. 'That I haven't. I be saving up to buy meself a house, in case we ever hit hard times again.'

216

'Oh Josh,' she'd said, trying not to laugh at his grand plans. 'I'm so glad you're my brother. Whatever would I do without you?'

He had shrugged, gazing at her through anxious eyes. 'If you didn't have me and Daisy to care for, with your looks I reckon you'd be married to a prince by now.'

'I don't want to marry a prince. I would rather look after my family.'

His glance had slid around the room. Carefully, he'd said, 'What about the squire then?'

She had laughed out loud. 'Edward has been good to us. He's more Elizabeth's friend than mine. They have known each other a long time, and although I enjoy his company when he visits, he is Elizabeth's visitor. Besides, he intends to wed Isabelle Prosser shortly.'

Now a carriage had arrived, and Isabelle Prosser was being announced by Rosie.

Siana's heart sank. This could be no social call. 'Show her to the drawing room and tell her I'll join her in a few moments.'

A feeling of tension seemed to have entered the house with Isabelle. Whatever she was here for, Siana was sure it could mean only trouble. Nevertheless, she removed her apron and tidied her hair before going downstairs, Daisy held on her hip.

She smiled at her visitor as she entered, though in truth, she was rather taken aback by her appearance. Clashing hideously with the dark rose coloured velvet sofa she was seated on, Isabelle wore a gown of brown and yellow stripes and a matching bonnet trimmed with curving brown feathers. A huge brown bow was tied under her chin.

'Miss Prosser?' Siana said pleasantly. 'I'm so glad you called. May I offer you some refreshment?'

'You may offer, but I won't stoop to take refreshment with you,' Isabelle replied. 'I am here for one reason only. To tell you and the other whore who lives here to pack your things and get out of this house.'

'I . . . I beg your pardon?'

Isabelle was formidable when she rose, tall, broad and heavy. 'You heard me, girl. I want you and the other one out of this house. I will not share my husband with other women, as I intend to inform him.'

'You are mistaken if you think I—'

'Do you deny that the bastard in your arms is his?'

Siana's arms tightened protectively around Daisy. 'Daisy is no bastard. She's my sister, born to my late mother and stepfather. Would you kindly leave now, Miss Prosser? You're no longer welcome.'

'Not until you agree to move out.'

'I'll agree to nothing of the sort. I'm not a signatory to the lease of this house. Mrs Skinner is. I'm her guest.' She rang for Rosie, who appeared so swiftly Siana knew she'd been listening outside the door. 'Show Miss Prosser out, please, Rosie. If she doesn't leave willingly, call Mr Grantham in from the garden to eject her by force.'

'Lay one finger on my person and I'll make sure you're dismissed from the squire's service,' Isabelle hissed as her person flounced towards the door.

Siana left the room after her and headed for the stairs. 'Don't think you'll get away with this,' Isabelle shouted, noticing her escape. 'If Edward wants to get his hands on my fortune, he'll do what he's told.'

A few seconds later the door slammed behind her.

'Good riddance, you sack of rotten mangold-wurzels,' Rosie muttered. 'You looks like a giant bumble bee in that outfit.'

Siana was trembling violently now. She sank down onto the stair and gave in to the hysterical laughter bubbling inside her. Then the laughter abruptly changed to tears. Daisy stared at her, her eyes round and blue. Her bottom lip trembled and she started to cry in sympathy.

Rosie bounded up the stairs and took Daisy from her lap. 'Now don't you fret, Miss Siana. Squire will soon take the fancy out of that there Isabelle when he finds out what she's been about.'

'You mustn't tell him,' she cried out.

'Won't have to, will I? She's bound to tell someone else. Nothing is kept a secret for long around these parts, especially from the squire. Now, you go and have a rest and I'll bring you a nice drop of brandy from the squire's special bottle. Good for all things medicinal, it is. I sometimes have a drop meself when I'm feeling poorly, and sometimes when I'm not.'

So Siana, cosseted by Rosie and relaxed by the unaccustomed imbibing of alcohol, fell soundly asleep, the book about the marcher lords lying open on her stomach, where it had fallen.

Gruffydd was at Lord Llewellyn's court at Aber. He had not seen his father for a while, who was occupied with Gwenwynwyn's raids on the border. His sister had recently been born to Joanna, and though he despised the mother, he adored little Elen. How his father could have married King John's daughter was beyond his understanding. Making sure nobody observed him, Gruffydd leaned over the crib and tickled the child under the chin.

'You won't come to any harm whilst I live,' he murmured.

Young as she was, Elen felt his protection surround her and gave him a smile.

There was another tickle. 'Siana, wake up.'

Her great-grandmother came to stand over the crib. She was white-haired and old, but her eyes burned with the light of the soul. 'You must heed your husband.'

Siana came out of sleep, slightly bewildered. 'Who am I then?'

There was a chuckle from the chair. 'Don't you know?'

Turning her head to one side, Siana saw Edward seated in the chair, his long legs stretched out comfortably in front of him. He'd been reading a letter, which he now set aside. Between his forefinger and thumb, an ostrich feather twirled back and forth.

'I dreamed I was a child in a crib.'

Leaning forward, Edward plucked the book from her stomach and threw it to one side. 'You read too much. It over-stimulates the brain.' He picked up the brandy glass, sniffed it and raised an eyebrow. 'I hope you do not come to crave brandy. Women who are addicted to spirituous liquor can become tedious.'

She flushed as she sat up, feeling totally vexed. 'Indeed, that's the first time I have tasted it and I'm enamoured of neither the taste, nor the effect.'

220

His eyes were as bright as autumn berries. 'Then why did you drink it?'

What had Rosie said he called it? She smiled. 'It was for medicinal purposes.'

'Are you ill, or do you refer to the after-effects of the visit from Isabelle?'

'Yes . . . I mean no.' She could see from his annoyed expression that evasion was not the right path to take. She sighed. 'Yes, I confess. It was Isabelle who upset me. How did you get to hear of it so quickly?'

'I saw her carriage as I came through town and added two and two together. She was looking unbearably smug.'

Siana didn't know quite what to say. 'I'm sorry you were bothered by something so trivial.' About to swing her legs from the bed, she was surprised when Edward put his hand against her midriff and pushed her gently back down onto the pillow.

'Stay there and tell me about it.'

'Really, it was nothing.'

His mouth quirked into a wry smile. 'It was enough to drive you to drink and forget you were Siana Lewis when you emerged from the stupor the brandy induced.'

Annoyance filled her. 'You exaggerate. I was in no stupor, and I was dreaming of a story I'd just read in a book. If you continue with this inquisition, I will . . . Stop that!'

He was laughing now, tickling her under the chin with the feather. 'What will you do, Siana mine?'

She giggled at the amusement in his eyes. 'I'll strangle you with my bare hands for teasing me, that's what I'll do.'

His eyes suddenly sobered and he said in so low a voice that she could barely hear him, 'Would you wed me first?'

A breath was exhaled shakily from her own mouth and she seemed to lack the will to replace it with another. 'You should not jest about such matters.'

'Of course, I do not.' When he leaned over and kissed her on the mouth, she was unable to resist. It was pleasant, his kiss. It warmed the darkness inside her and the glow spread right down to her toes. But more – much more, was the strange, wild longing it planted inside her. She felt the danger of it and knew she'd be powerless before its onslaught.

She gazed into his eyes, almost hypnotic in their intensity, and reminded him, 'We're both promised to others. Myself to Daniel and you to Isabelle.'

'Are we? What if I have decided not to marry Isabelle after all?'

Stunned by the events of the morning, Siana heard herself say as if she was seriously considering such a preposterous idea, 'You will lose Isabelle's fortune.'

'I can do without it. After what's happened here today, I have come to the conclusion that the penalty of having Isabelle for a wife will be too high.' He slanted his head to one side and his eyes glittered. 'Rosie told me what happened.'

Siana shook her head slowly from side to side in denial. 'I told her not to.'

'It's I who employ the girl. She had no choice but to tell me when I asked her.' There was no softness in him now, just the fierce gaze of a man determined to have his own way.

Siana placed her hand on his arm. 'Please don't look at me like that, Edward. Your intensity is scaring me.'

His voice was as tender as the caress of his fingers against her cheek. 'Don't be frightened, my sweeting. I'd never hurt you.'

'What about Elizabeth?'

'Don't worry about Elizabeth. We have come to an arrangement.'

'But I'm not good enough for you,' she protested. 'There's already talk about us and my name is being dragged through the mud. However unjust the accusation, it will stick.'

'I've heard the talk.' He dismissed it with a shrug. 'What I'm offering you will lift you above such talk. Think of Daisy and Josh, too. They will be given a better start in life.''

He certainly knew how to manipulate her emotions. 'Your own class won't accept me. You'll be an outcast.'

'Damn them, they can all go to hell then,' he muttered, and rose to his feet. 'When will you give me your answer?'

'I must think about it.'

'I will not be kept dangled on a string like some trophy. I'm doing you an honour, girl. I could have you without marriage.'

'I'd rather starve,' she said, knowing that she wouldn't.

'I doubt it. I'll expect an answer by your birthday. Wed me or, to hell with it, I won't marry at all.'

'Why me?' she managed to murmur, and he gazed down at her, his expression vulnerable, his eyes strangely sad.

'Hasn't it occurred to you yet? I'm in love with you.'
He swept from the room almost angrily, leaving an
empty space still full of his presence.

Siana cried a little. For Edward, and for Elizabeth
who had loved him all her life. And for Daniel, a man
whose ring she wore on her finger, yet whom she could
hardly remember after a few short months apart. It was
odd how their parting had eroded her feelings towards
Daniel. Her own fickleness made her feel shallow.

A little while later she heard Edward ride away.

Collecting her thoughts together she rose from the
bed and sighed. She loved Edward in her own way, but
was it enough? Her glance fell on the letter he'd been
reading. It had slipped to the floor when he'd stood up.

Picking it up, she saw it was from Daniel. Dear God!
How could she forget him? How could she consider
betraying him, especially with his own father? What if
she married Edward and fell in love with Daniel all over
again when he came home?

Yet Daniel had removed himself from her life
without a word, and had made no effort to maintain
their relationship with correspondence.

The letter aroused her curiosity to an extent that she
could think of nothing else. Finally, she gave into temptation. With trembling hands she opened the missive.
Daniel's handwriting was a neat script of even strokes.

Dear Sir,

*Our party is leaving for Naples in the morning, where we
will spend some time as guests of Mr and Mrs Anderson and
their delightful daughters, Esmé and Julia. They have hired*

for the summer a villa which looks out over the bay.

You will be interested to know Mr Anderson owns a shipping company in Liverpool, and has distant connections to Lord Rotherhull through a second cousin.

Esmé is a delightful, graceful creature of twenty-four years, with hair the colour of gold and cornflower-blue eyes. She is wonderfully accomplished and has a sweet and lovable nature. Esmé is everything a woman should strive to be, and every man who comes in contact with her is instantly smitten. Julia, at fifteen, is tomboyish in her ways, and strong willed.

Dearest Father, I shall not forget the delightful time spent in your company before I left for Italy, and your generosity towards me.

Fondest regards,
Your son,
Daniel Ayres

Isabelle was halfway home when Edward waved her hired carriage to a halt.

She held her handkerchief to her nose. His horse was well lathered and the sweating, overheated flesh stank to high heaven.

Of course, she knew why he was here. She had passed him earlier, heading towards the house she'd just left. His anger was written all over his face now, and she experienced a moment of trepidation. She would not allow it to sway her, of course. He must get rid of those women if he wanted her.

She made it clear to him right away, holding up her hand imperiously for silence and not giving him a chance to put his case first. 'I will hear no argument, Edward.

Elizabeth Skinner and that other coarse creature must be got rid of, else I won't marry you.'

She was taken aback when he threw back his head and laughed. 'Good riddance to you then. Let the engagement be brought to an end, for I will not bow to your dictates. I'm on my way to see your father now. As for that coarse creature you refer to, you are not fit to clean the mud from her boots.'

Her mouth fell open a little and she stared at him, fish-eyed, when he leaned forward. 'You are an insult. How dare you, a woman who is little more than a peasant by birth herself, don your airs and graces and presume to tell me and my guests what they should and shouldn't do.'

'Edward,' she soothed, trying to placate him, for she suddenly saw the position of lady of the manor slipping through her fingers. 'I apologize if I angered you. Can you forgive me?'

Flatly, he informed her, 'Absolutely not. Your actions are unforgivable. I'm sorry I ever set eyes on you.'

He did not mean it. 'If you love me, you will forgive me.' She offered her cheek to him. 'See, I will allow you to kiss me before our wedding day.'

He recoiled slightly. 'Love you! What a preposterous notion! As for kissing you! A man would have to be blind to even be tempted.' He gazed down at her and said abruptly, 'One day you will bend your knee to Miss Siana Lewis.'

A flick of the whip and he was gone in a cloud of dust, leaving her staring after him, her jaw slack with shock and tears springing to her eyes. She should have listened to her aunt Caroline. She'd never get another chance.

The dressing down had caused her great embarrassment. She needed a pee, and she needed to collect her thoughts. Face burning, she descended from the carriage and said to the smirking carriage driver, 'I'm going into the woods for a short stroll. You can wait here until I return.'

No please or thank you, and his passenger still acting like she was Queen of the May, the driver thought. And she'd haggled him down in price, the mean cow. Ah well, at least he'd insisted she pay him half the fare in advance. He watched her waddle off. The squire hadn't half let her have it. Wait until he told his missus!

'Don't be long,' he called after her, 'I wants to get home in time for my dinner.'

Isabelle followed a small path until she came to a clearing. There she did what she had to, then sat on a fallen log, placed her head in her hands and bawled her eyes out.

After a while she became aware of someone watching her. She looked up, her face blotched, her eyes reddened and puffy, to see a man standing nearby. He was shabbily dressed, yet strong-bodied and handsome to look at.

'Miss Isabelle,' he said, 'who be upsetting you, then?'

She'd have known him anywhere. 'Ben Collins?' she exclaimed. 'You used to work for my father, Farmer Prosser. Remember?'

Ben stared at her ample breasts, covered in yellow satin. The palms of his hands itched. They were a right pretty pair. 'I remembers thee, miss. That I do. What makes thee so sad?'

She beckoned to him, bidding him sit on the log beside her. At the back of her mind was the need to get back at Edward for spurning her. Tears still spilling from her eyes, she laid her head on his shoulder. 'Put your arm around me, Ben. I'm so sad.'

'I be dirty, Miss Isabelle. Too dirty to touch a pretty little missy like you.'

She gazed up at him. 'You think I'm pretty?'

'The prettiest little girl in the county of Dorset. Allus was. Now, don't you be sad no more. Ben Collins will look after thee.'

He had strong muscular thighs under his corduroy trousers. 'Do you remember when my father caught us together in the barn? You said you loved me.'

Ben vaguely remembered touching her tits and getting a beating for it. He gazed around him at the still forest, then smiled boldly at her, noting the flush on her cheek. She was as ripe as a sow in season. 'I allus loved thee, Miss Isabelle.'

She shivered, remembering his caressing hands. His arms were strong, his palms callused. 'I don't mind your dirt,' she said slowly, and, taking his hands in hers, she placed his palms against her breasts and closed her eyes.

Ben couldn't believe his luck. Hannah wouldn't have none of him lately, and here was his old sweetheart just begging for it.

Soon, he had her mewing like a cat. He loved the feel of women's flesh, their smell and the noises they made. This one was a real nice handful, and she looked so pretty in that big yellow bonnet of hers. Like a daffodil in spring.

Lord, he was in a right ferment, his need rearing up to press hard against his belly. She was panting like a bitch in the sun! He loosened his trousers, tipped her on her back and straddled her, guiding his bulging stem through her resistance before she realized what they was about. He grinned widely. Lord, it were a fat little pudding of a comforter. It swallowed him up to the hilt. And he was getting her fine feathers all mucky.

A memory came into his head of her belonging to the squire. The man must be fair lacking in his manly ways for his lady to bother with the likes of himself.

When he tried to untie the bows under her chin, she shouted authoritatively. 'Leave it, you stupid fool.'

'Yes, your ladyship,' Ben said humbly, for he knew he was stupid.

Her eyes flew open for a moment, then she smiled and wriggled her belly beneath him so he slid more comfortably inside her. Set to explode, he grabbed a handful of each of her buttocks whilst he rode her hot and strong.

'That's my big bull,' she gasped out. 'Do you still love me?'

'You be my own true love,' he grunted in her ear. Isabelle forgot all about Edward as she took her delicious revenge for being spurned.

The carriage driver was becoming restless. It was getting late, and his wife was expecting him home before dark.

What if the woman had fallen and hurt herself? He

couldn't just drive off and leave her here. After dark there would be men abroad bent on mischief, and she might be harassed. The peasants were in a surly mood, the squire and his ilk, always unpopular, were more so after the trial of the Tolpuddle men and their sentence of seven years' transportation to the colony of New South Wales.

He sighed, deciding to have a quick look for her. If he couldn't find her, he'd drive on and report her disappearance to the authorities.

He didn't have to go far. Drawn by the soft squeals coming from the clearing, he grinned when he saw what was going on and returned to his vehicle.

She emerged a little later, her bonnet askew, her hair escaping from under it in long untidy strands of pale ginger. He saw the back of her gown was stained with earth and dead leaves as he helped her into the carriage.

'I hope you're feeling better after your walk, miss,' he said solicitously.

Her smile was one of satisfaction as she seated herself. 'Thank you, driver. I'd be obliged if you kept the exchange you observed between myself and the squire private. A little misunderstanding, that's all.'

He touched the brim of his hat with his whip. 'Rest assured. Old John can be the soul of discretion when called upon, *your ladyship.*'

She gave him a searching glance, then reddened. Later, she tipped him very generously indeed.

That evening, he and the missus had a good old laugh about the goings-on.

14

Sir Edward Forbes Bt requests the company of the Reverend Richard White at a social gathering to celebrate the 18th birthday of Miss Siana Lewis.

In view of the gossip about her, Richard was reluctant to attend. But he knew that the invitation, coming from Edward as it did, was more of a summons than a request. Richard was suffering from guilt over the affair. If he hadn't closed his door on Siana, she wouldn't have been in the predicament she now found herself in.

If he attended her birthday celebration, he could perhaps counsel the girl, point out that a life lived in sin would not win her a place in heaven. After all, what sort of example was she setting for Josh and Daisy?

He decided to go to the church and pray for her soul. She had fallen from the path of righteousness and he wanted to bring her back to the Lord. If need be, he could arrange for her sister and brother to be farmed out. The convent would take her in, and there she could live a life of penitence to save her soul.

The day was characteristic of early April. A gentle wind brought drifts of soft rain to fall across the land.

Chased by sunshine, every blade of grass and trembling leaf sparkled with rainbow colours.

Richard drew in a deep breath and lengthened his stride, nodding to Abbie Ponsonby as he passed by. A God-fearing woman, Abbie. Her brood of children were well cared for. He noticed her swelling stomach and gave a slight frown. He must talk to her husband about the need for abstinence after this one. After all, the woman was no longer young.

Abbie jerked her thumb towards the church. 'A stranger is waiting to see you, Reverend. I tells him where you lives but he sez he needs to pray.'

'A stranger, you say. Did he give a name?'

'No, sir, but his eyes looks all tortured and holy, as if Christ hisself had come down from his crucifix.' She shivered and her eyes grew round and large. 'I was fair mazed to look at him.'

'Thank you, Abbie,' Richard said, smiling at her flight of fancy. He was fairly positive Christ wouldn't go out of his way to visit him at his church. He was much too unimportant a man.

He hesitated when the square bell tower of the church came into view. The sun had caught a shower and created a rainbow arching over the top. But the image was dispelled almost immediately, and he hurried forward, unfurling his umbrella when drops of rain spattered against him.

The stranger was on his knees when the reverend entered, his arms raised towards the stained-glass window dedicated to the birth of the baby Jesus, which held pride of place over the altar.

232

The window had been donated by an ancestor of Edward Forbes. The Forbes family had provided almost everything for the church, including the font with its carved base and the silver chalice and crucifix. The altar cloth had been embroidered by Edward's first wife, Patricia, the tapestries by his mother and grandmother.

Edward himself had renewed the prayer and hymn books recently, and every one of them contained a dedication to that effect. In fact, the Forbes name appeared on nearly everything. The mortal remains of the Forbes family were buried in, under, and outside the church. Although he tried not to be uncharitable, sometimes Richard resented the fact that one family could have so much power.

The man's voice was deep. His words were spoken in a tongue Richard was unfamiliar with. Totally absorbed, the stranger didn't notice Richard's presence as his voice rose and fell in a resonant and lyrical cadence.

Long-bearded and gaunt, he finally brought his hands down to cover his face. His shoulders began to shake and Richard realized he was crying. For a moment he was embarrassed to witness such naked misery. Then he thought, the man is tortured, I must do what I can to help ease his troubled mind.

The man jerked around when he touched him on the shoulder. Richard forgot about the problem of Siana Lewis under the stranger's intense gaze. The eyes flared light blue and agonized in the haggard face, yet they burned with some sort of inner light.

'I am Richard White, rector of this parish. Can you tell me your name, sir?'

'Gruffydd Evans, servant of the Lord and despicable sinner. I have travelled the length and breadth of the land these last ten years seeking the truth.' He buried his head in his hands and rocked back and forth, whispering, 'I cannot go on without knowing.'

'Knowing what?' Richard asked him, relieved the fellow spoke English, though his accent branded him as a native of Wales.

'The truth, man. The truth.'

'How can I be of help, sir?'

The man stood up. His tall frame was thin and stooped, his coat threadbare and the sole of one of his boots yawned open. 'Come outside. My offence is such that I cannot utter my sin in the house of the Lord.'

'If it is money you need I can give you a little from the poor box.'

'Money?' He sounded bewildered. 'Take me not into temptation, for I am weak and sorely troubled and have taken a vow of poverty until my sin is atoned for.'

'Share a meal with me, then,' Richard said quietly. 'Even the poor and sorely troubled need bodily sustenance.'

Gruffydd Evans passed a shaking hand over his unkempt beard. 'Kind of you to offer, sir. A meal, is it? I can't remember the last time I ate a good meal. I can't remember it at all.'

So saying, he buckled at the knees and slid to the ground. His eyes rolled up in his head and he began to jerk and shake. Froth gathered at the sides of his mouth.

Richard ran quickly from the church and sent the first boy he came across scurrying for the doctor.

Then he fetched the grave digger. Between them, they loaded the unconscious Welshman onto his cart. At least the man had stopped jerking.

By the time Francis arrived at the rectory, his patient was resting against the pillows in Richard's guest bedroom. Conscious now, his eyes were unfocused and staring, his face pale.

Richard described the circumstances of his collapse.

'It sounds as if he suffers from the falling sickness,' Francis said. He smiled at the patient. 'How long have you been having these seizures?'

'Since the blind witch laid her curse on me. "Preacher man, you will travel the land seeking your kin," she said. "Until you find she whom you wronged and ask forgiveness, the Lord will wither your loins and visit his wrath upon you."'

'Nonsense, man,' Francis said briskly. 'What you suffer from is a common disorder of the brain. Let's have a look at the rest of you.'

The sparsely fleshed body didn't take long to examine. The man was tall and angular. Rib cage gaunt, stomach swollen, eyes protruding from his head, pelvic bones supporting wasted thighs and withered genitals – Francis had seen it all too often.

'He's suffering from malnutrition,' he said almost angrily to Richard. 'He will need food and rest to recover his health properly. I might be able to find room in the workhouse for him in a day or two.'

'No,' Richard said firmly, for the Lord had seen fit to deliver the sinner to his church and he felt a strange kinship and responsibility towards the Welsh preacher. 'I will care for him here.'

'He probably has worms as well. I'll leave you something to purge him with.'

'And the fits?'

Francis shrugged. 'Wait for the Lord to cure him, for I can't. Perhaps you could try prayer. What's the man's name?'

'Gruffydd Evans,' Richard said stiffly.

Francis thought for a moment. 'I've heard that name before, somewhere.'

'He's a Methodist preacher.'

'Ah, that must be why it's familiar. Fire and brimstone, and all that.'

'And Francis,' Richard said, frowning as the man headed for the door, 'the power of prayer is never really wasted. You should try it sometime.'

Francis turned. 'It didn't work on my wife.'

'Neither did your doctoring.'

The pair stared challengingly at each other for a few seconds, then Francis gave an ironic smile and inclined his head slightly. 'You're right,' he said and, turning on his heel, departed.

Tom Skinner gazed with loathing at the pea soup, but he swallowed every morsel. He had to get his strength back.

The bandages had been changed today. His stump had healed, but it was still sore and covered in boils which oozed pus. When it had healed properly he could have a wooden peg leg to get around on, the doctor had told him. But the man hadn't been able to look him in the eyes when he'd said it, so Tom knew he was expected to die.

He wasn't going to die yet, though. He'd heard the talk. The squire had taken Elizabeth back. Going into business, was she? And Peggy Hastings, who fetched and carried in the workhouse because she wasn't much good for nothing else except lying on her back, was all cock-a-hoop because she'd been offered employment by Elizabeth and today was her last day at the infirmary.

He watched her ladling out the soup, her breasts straining against her bodice with every movement of her arms. Look at her, he thought; a sympathetic word in one man's ear, a smile for another. Strumpet!

But she had no smile for him though. Her eyes were filled with loathing and fear. His mouth stretched in a smile. He'd told her long ago he'd get his own back for her kicking him aside, like he was dirt under her feet. He'd chosen his time well, doing for her man when the squire had had a bellyful of the goings-on in the district and was itching to mete out his own brand of justice. Squire had taken the crop to Will's back before he'd handed him over to the authorities.

Much good it had done Tom, though. The squire had taken Croxley Farm back from him – and he'd taken his woman back along with it. No matter that she were the squire's first. Elizabeth was married to him, Tom Skinner, all legal like. Damn it! She belonged to him. He had the right to her until he decided otherwise.

As soon as he got some strength back he would deal with his strumpet of a wife and her lover. The Welsh by-blow would get it next. The squire still owed him for her. From all accounts, the man had had his money's worth from her. She was like her mother. Whores, the pair of them!

Then there was Peggy Hastings. His eyes narrowed in on her. She'd refused him what she'd given willingly to another man. He would have her yet, when she least expected it. And he'd make her beg for mercy.

Her laughter died as she turned and saw him watching her. When he smiled at her, she shuddered and turned her head away.

Oh yes. If he was going to die, last thing he'd do was make those responsible pay for his misery.

Elizabeth was delighted with Peggy Hastings. The woman was polite, eager to learn and proved to have a flair for arranging the merchandise to display it advantageously.

She moved into the rooms above the shop without delay, and Elizabeth had decided to leave the supervision of the interior decorations in her hands whilst she took the coach up to London the following week.

Siana was troubling Elizabeth a little. The girl seemed preoccupied with something, but wouldn't be brought to confide in her.

She asked Josh, 'Have you any idea what's troubling your sister?'

Josh smiled. He was pleased with his present lot in life, his plans and his growing bank account. These days he thought of hardly anything but his future. By heck he was going to be someone. 'Nothin' as far as I knows. I reckon she be reading too many of them books. Gives

238

her ideas, they do. She's allus been inclined to being dreamy-headed.'

'Keep an eye on her when I go to London next week, would you?' Elizabeth said. 'If she's got a problem I'd like to know about it in case I can help.'

'I don't know why you be going up to London. There's nothing there that I can't get cheaper.' He looked around him and whispered, 'I know lots of seamen who goes to France and other places. Silks, satins, lace and ribbons. Music boxes, fancy furbelows and buttons, jewels, pots of scent and what-nots. You just let Josh know what you want and Josh'll get it for you.'

'That's smuggling, Josh.'

He grinned. 'It cuts out the middle-man, don't it? Gives you a bit more profit. Tell you what, Miss Lizzie. You go up to London to stock the shop. Then, when you opens, you give me a list and I'll see what can be done. Special things for special customers, see. Do it gradual, like. Slide a bit of this in here and a bit of that in there and nobody'll know any different. A small percentage for Josh for his trouble is all it'll cost you.'

'If the squire found out—'

'If he does, just ask him where his special tipple of brandy comes from.'

'Not Edward, surely!' Elizabeth exclaimed.

'Never is as never does,' Josh scoffed. 'I hear tell he's cast that Isabelle Prosser aside. And I hears she's taken up with our Hannah's man. By crikey, I'd like to be there when our Hannah finds out. A right vicious wench she be, when she's riled up. Them two is well matched if

239

you asks me. If it came to fisticuffs I could sell tickets on them.'

'Isabelle and Ben Collins?' It was such a preposterous notion Elizabeth began to laugh. 'Siana isn't the only one who's dreamy-headed lately. Get off with you, Josh Skinner.'

After he'd gone, Elizabeth's eyes narrowed. Had Edward really abandoned his plan of making Isabelle his wife?

Her heart began to thump as she wondered whether he'd had a change of heart about her.

But no. It was no good getting her hopes up. Just as she thought she'd been about to resume her relationship with Edward, he'd told her he'd decided it would be wiser not to mix business with pleasure.

'I feel I've more than discharged my obligations towards you by providing the capital for your business,' he had said. 'You indicated that this was what you desired most. I'm sure you'll make a great success of it.'

She'd given a heartfelt cry, of rage, of anguish, or relief. She knew not which. Mixed with the sadness of being cast aside a second time was the thought she would no longer be beholden to him.

He'd placed a hand over her mouth, cutting the cry short. 'Be quiet, you will raise the household.'

'What about Daniel?' she had said, in control of herself once again when he released her.

'Daniel's a man now, and must stand on his own two feet. It would be better if you untied him from your apron strings, Elizabeth.'

Slowly, she had said, 'You know I was willing to be

more to you, Edward. I was only trying to punish you by withdrawing my favours for a while.'

'I know, Elizabeth, just as I know we would have resumed the relationship if fate hadn't intervened. You must not think less of yourself, or of me, because of this. Something I cannot control has occurred.' He had taken her by the shoulders and gazed intently into her eyes. 'We have loved each other in our own way for many years, but now it's over. We will always be friends, I hope.'

Something he could not control? Had he become less than a man, perhaps, and was too ashamed to admit it to her? She couldn't imagine it. The last time they'd been together in that way he'd been almost insatiable.

Yet, if rumour was to be believed, he'd discarded Isabelle. Her heart now gave a jolt. Was Edward contemplating naming Daniel as his heir, after all?

In his latest letter Daniel had said he had come to an understanding with a girl he'd met in Italy. He'd asked her to break the news to Siana. So far she hadn't found the courage.

Francis Matheson couldn't think of an excuse to go out of his way to visit Siana Lewis – until, by chance, he found a perfect one.

He found her in the garden, chasing a giggling Daisy around the lawn. The infant was steady on her legs now, and her face gleamed pinkly. When the child saw him, she moved to Siana's side and hid behind her skirts, emerging with a shy smile when she recognized the doctor, to wave a podgy fist.

'I was visiting my brother and my two daughters and found it in the stables,' he said bringing the kitten from inside his coat and placing it in her arms. 'I thought Daisy might like to look after it.'

Siana gave a cry of delight and cuddled the kitten against her neck, caressing the tabby fur with her face. The expression in her eyes was soft as she slanted a glance up at him. 'He's so sweet. Thank you.'

Picking up Daisy he spun her around, gave her a kiss and set her back on her feet. Siana handed the child the kitten, admonishing, 'Be careful with him. He'll scratch if you hurt him.'

The child made soft cooing noises as she stroked its fur. The kitten mewed and purred contentedly. Seaweed perfumed the air and the gulls screamed in the distance as Francis and Siana gazed at each other, smiling. They were so comfortable with each other that for a moment the rest of the world seemed to fade away.

Then Siana said, 'I didn't know you had two daughters. What are their names?'

'Pansy and Maryse. They are twelve and thirteen years.'

She looked surprised. 'You must have been very young when they were born, then.'

'I have never regretted fathering them.'

'They're fortunate. I've never known my father.'

The wind tugged at her skirt. It was tinted pale green, like spring, with little sprigs of flowers printed all over it. Her bodice was dark green, like her eyes. Resting in the hollow of her throat was the little silver cross on a chain. He remembered it from the infirmary, lying on

242

Daisy's pillow. She wore no bonnet. Her hair was braided, coiling about her crown like a coronet of darkness. Wisps had come loose to blow about her face.

'Your wife . . . did you love her?' she asked.

It took a moment for Francis to look inward and remember the softness of her – the frailty. He shrugged, saying gruffly, 'Not at first, it was a marriage arranged for convenience. Catherine was older than me and brought a small dowry to the union. She was a gentle soul with many good qualities, and I came to love her.'

She smiled at him. 'A man like you would have done.'

His wife had depended on him and he'd failed her when she'd needed him most. Francis experienced a moment of anguish. 'I couldn't prevent Catherine from dying.'

'She died feeling loved. That must count for something.'

'It's no consolation to me.'

'It would have been for her. She left you a precious gift in her children.' She tucked her arm into his and drew him across to a seat of wrought iron, urging, 'Tell me about your girls.'

'Maryse is the elder, and the most like her mother in looks and ways, though both have brown curls and eyes. She is a gentle-natured child who is artistic in her ways.' He grinned slightly. 'Pansy is more confident. She is quite the peasant, at times. She climbs trees and thinks nothing of cuffing her male cousins around the ear, on occasion. In fact, her aunt despairs of ever turning her into a lady.'

She grinned wryly at him. 'It's not quite so hard as

you imagine for a peasant to be transformed into a lady. Peasant or peer, we are all the same under the skin. You should know that.'

It took a moment for him to realize his blunder and he stammered; 'I most humbly beg your pardon, Siana. No offence was intended.'

'I'm not offended. I know you didn't mean it in a personal way.'

'The fact that your background didn't occur to me must bear testament to your success.'

Her laugh had a slightly bitter ring to it. 'My rise in social status was not by choice. I'm the recipient of condescension due to the need of someone's conscience to be appeased. If I was ugly, the plight of Siana Lewis and her siblings would not have been given a second thought.'

Her comment proved to be wounding. 'Am I to be included in this harsh assessment of character?'

She touched the back of his hand gently with her finger. 'Be certain you are not, Francis. You give without demanding reward, and are the most truly unselfish man I've ever met.'

'You need not accept such condescension.'

'Need I not? I have Daisy to care for and have no choice. You have seen her near death from starvation. Now she is healthy. I cannot see her starve again. I had not thought to live on someone else's charity and give nothing in return, yet I cannot refuse it. Edward has been good to us and I like him.'

She knows only the side of him he chooses to show her, Francis thought. Edward would throw her out on the street without a second thought if she ceased to amuse him.

'Come and work for me,' he offered. 'There is room for Daisy and Josh.'

'Do you think I'm unaware of the talk that will create? Already my reputation is unjustifiably besmirched.'

'Then does it matter if the gossips talk some more?'

'Yes, it does.'

Despite her terse answer, he experienced a moment of relief. So, Siana was not involved with Edward Forbes to any serious extent. He had wondered. 'You've heard the talk, then?'

Her smile was sad. 'Scum always floats to the top.'

Rising in one graceful movement, she picked up the kitten and took the child by the hand. 'It's time for Daisy's rest. Come and take tea with me. I'm a bit melancholy today and will be glad of your company.'

'You're too young to be sad,' he said, taking Daisy's other hand.

Her smile was just a shade too brilliant. 'It will pass. I'm an ungrateful wretch who is bored with books, dancing and piano lessons. It all seems so aimless, when a few short weeks ago I was wondering where the next meal was coming from.'

'I thought you were researching your Welsh ancestry,' he said as they strolled towards the house with Daisy giggling and swinging between their hands every few steps.

'I have given it up. Besides, what would my Welsh ancestors care about me? My mother's family deserted her in her time of need and my father doesn't even know I exist. The women of her village hacked off her hair and drove her out while she was carrying me. I cannot understand how people are able to turn their backs on their own blood.'

'*Let those without sin cast the first stone?*'

'Exactly.'

When they entered the house Siana gave Daisy a kiss and handed her and the kitten over to the maid. She turned back to him with a slightly chastened expression.

He smiled at her, saying gently, 'There have always been degrees of hypocrisy and it's human nature to recognize it only in others. However much we strive to live by the rules set for us by others, most of us find it impossible to be perfect. We have learned to lie to ourselves in the most convincing way.'

Her expression was as uncertain as her sigh. 'You're right, Francis. You are always right.'

He chuckled and took her hands in his. 'Haven't I just told you that can't be the case? What has happened to unsettle you so?'

She opened her mouth as if to say something, then bit down on her bottom lip. 'Nothing has happened.'

She led him into the drawing room, which was furnished in soft creams and several shades of rose pink. Sun streamed through the windows. A vase filled with daffodils stood on the table, a piano in a corner.

'Can you play?'

'Elizabeth is teaching me in the evenings. She says I have an aptitude for music, but I keep hitting the wrong notes. I should practise more.'

'Play me something so I can judge for myself.'

For the first time she gave a spontaneous laugh. 'You will regret asking me, I think.'

There was a sheet of music on the stand. She seated herself and attacked the piece with the hesitation of a beginner. When she'd fumbled her way through it, she grinned widely at his pained expression. 'It is not so bad, considering I could not read a note of music a month ago. I think my singing is better, though.'

Francis joined her on the piano stool. 'Then I will play and you will sing.'

The piece was a simple lullaby. Her voice was sweet and full of longing. He turned when she choked on the words, surprised to see tears in her eyes.

'My mother used to sing that song to Daisy.'

He nodded and took a handkerchief from his pocket, touching it gently to her eyes. 'You miss her, don't you?'

'I feel lonely without her. I didn't realize it would be so hard to be responsible for my sister and brother.'

'Which is why I have paid Siana the honour of asking her to become my wife,' Edward said from the doorway, and crossed the room swiftly to lay a possessive hand on her shoulder.

Shocked, Francis scrambled to his feet. Edward was going to wed her! He gave her a formal little bow. 'You didn't say you were to marry Edward.'

'That's because she has not decided one way or the other yet.' Siana sat, her hands folded in her lap, held prisoner to her seat by that firm hand on her shoulder. Edward gazed down at her, 'Have you, my dear?'

She gave an imperceptible shake of her head.

Edward smiled at her. 'I heard you playing the piano as I came in. You've improved.'

Her eyes slanted up to his, then met his glance square

on. Her smile was one of a woman who'd just become aware of her desirability and was pleased by it. 'It wasn't me playing, it was Francis.'

'Then it must have been you singing like a nightingale.'

She blushed so sweetly from the praise that Francis felt betrayed by her. He looked at Edward and caught his breath. The man's feelings were almost incandescent. Edward Forbes was besotted with her.

Well, well, Francis thought wryly. Who was it preached to her about hypocrisy? Who must now acknowledge that this awful feeling inside him was envy?

Edward had seen the intent in him as soon as he'd entered. He'd sensed the danger of a challenge and made his prior claim to her clear right away.

Siana shrugged Edward's hand aside and rose as a maid came in with the tea tray. 'Fetch another cup for Sir Edward,' she said.

She didn't look at him directly for the rest of the afternoon. Watched by Edward, she played the hostess to perfection.

For Francis, the afternoon became an agony.

15

'You're turning down my proposal?' Edward couldn't believe it. 'I took you off the street and gave you and your sister a home. I cancelled my engagement to Isabelle for you.'

Which wasn't exactly the truth. He'd cancelled it because he found the damned girl repulsive and she'd meddled in his affairs. He'd done the right thing in casting Isabelle aside, he told himself. If the rumours were true and she had been desperate enough to take up with a rough labourer, he'd had a lucky escape. Now, here was this snip of a creature rejecting his honourable proposal of marriage. And what's this she was saying?

'I thought you acted from the goodness of your heart. I didn't expect to be constantly reminded of my obligation to you.'

'There's no goodness in my heart at this moment. You've wounded me to the core.'

Siana couldn't look at him as she twisted the small amber ring she wore around and around her finger. The ornament seemed vaguely familiar to him. Now where had he seen it before? 'I'm sorry, Edward. I've promised myself to Daniel.'

'Who has tossed you aside in favour of another,' he pointed out more brutally than he should have done. He suddenly recalled buying the trinket for Elizabeth and leaned forward to examine it more closely. It was a pretty thing, but inexpensive. 'Did he give you this ring?'

'Yes.' Stretching out her finger, her eyes softened as she admired the trinket. Remembering Daniel with fondness, no doubt. It incensed him, that look.

'The ring was a gift from me to Elizabeth. It's a poor secondhand token for a man to give to the woman he's supposed to love.'

There was a cat-like alertness to her eyes now. She struck with a pointed delicacy. 'Daniel had told me it belonged to his mother. A rich man gives a diamond when a poor man can give only his heart. Which has more value to the recipient?'

He hadn't expected her to turn his words back on him. Her quickness was slightly disconcerting. But then, he had not crossed swords with her before and he found it stimulating – as long as she did not take it too far.

'Daniel is a young man who gives his heart easily and forgets just as easily.'

'Because you choose to tell me so?' Her eyes were challenging as they came up to his. 'Daniel has not written to inform me that our understanding has come to an end. Until he does, I will honour the agreement I've made with him.'

Now he felt angry enough to hit her. 'Surely you must have been tempted to read the letter I left in your room?'

250

Her eyes narrowed, their greenness glittering from between her dark, feathery lashes. Her voice was too controlled. 'You left it there on purpose, then?'

She'd trapped him and he tried not to glare at her, because a thought had occurred to him and he was made suddenly aware of her lack of distress at losing Daniel.

He chuckled. 'Of course I left it on purpose. Well? Did you read it or not?'

She gave a thin, satisfied smile. 'You hold small opinion of me if you imagine I'd read private correspondence addressed to another.'

She was lying, he knew it. 'You're a woman. Admit it, you did read it.'

'I admit I'm a woman. I admit to nothing else.'

'You're a damned aggravating one,' he growled, enjoying her contrariness now he had her measure. 'What if you hear this from the lips of Daniel's own mother? Will you believe it then?'

She gave a faint smile. 'Are you telling me that Daniel lacks the courage to inform me himself?'

'Will you or won't you?' he roared.

She put her fist to her hips, peasant fashion, standing her ground. 'If you are about to burst a blood vessel because you cannot get your own way, perhaps I should call Francis back.'

Like hell she would! From his observation, the pair had been altogether too familiar, gazing at each other and laughing together when he'd come in. The surgeon was personable and twenty years younger than himself. What he'd felt for Siana had been clearly written on his countenance, and it wasn't just lust. Edward knew he must win Siana's heart quickly before she gave it to another. Once they were wed he would teach her to be biddable.

He fell to his knees and, taking her hands in his, turned them over and kissed each palm. 'I adore you and yet you are being deliberately cruel to me, Siana.'

She laughed, seemingly pleased by his flamboyant gesture. 'Get up, Edward. One of the servants might come in and see you.'

He stood to gaze down on her, wondering if he should kiss her. Her lips were soft, the bottom one sculpted to a perfect little natural pout in the middle. Laughter curved them as her eyes came up to meet his squarely. 'You may kiss me again, if you wish.'

He was disconcerted, but only for a moment. Taking her face in his hands, he gently caressed the side of her mouth with the balls of his thumbs until her eyes closed, the better to savour the sensation.

Her mouth trembled to the touch of his lips, parted under the pressure and accepted him. Her surrender was indicated by a little sigh – by the sweet, sucking pleasure of her warm mouth. He wanted more of her than this. Much more. He needed to crush her beneath him, to take her innocence and strip away the surface. He would awaken the raw sensuality he detected in her and she would enjoy every sweet assault on her body.

She gave a little shiver when he withdrew. Laying her hand against his chest, she took a step back, and with it a deep breath. The kiss had had an effect on her. 'Your relationship with Elizabeth. Have you informed her of your feelings towards me?'

Her acceptance of the situation with Elizabeth made him wonder if he hadn't been premature in ending the association. Hell, he couldn't insult Siana by expecting her to share him with another woman, however friendly they were. She would not have mentioned Elizabeth's name otherwise.

'My association with Elizabeth is one of friendship. I will inform her of my feelings for you when she returns from London.' He fished in his pocket, brought out a jewellery box and changed the subject. 'I have brought you a gift.'

She appeared awed when she opened it to find a simple circle of pearls, perfect in their purity, nestled on a bed of black velvet. Tears trembled on her lashes when she gazed up at him. 'Thank you, Edward. They're exquisite. Will you fasten them for me?'

He chose to forget Siana had not had the upbringing to know the significance of such a gift. That she'd accepted the pearls bound her more firmly to him in his mind. He placed them around her neck, a little pearl collar, fumbling with the clasp as she leaned her body slightly back into his. He kissed the top of her head, groaning a little as he pressed against her.

She turned, slanting him a look that was all innocence. 'What ails you, Edward?'

If this had been Elizabeth, she'd know exactly what ailed him – know exactly how to soothe his turbulent needs. He smiled ruefully and turned away, picking up his hat and cane to hold them casually in front of him. 'It's nothing, my love.'

Her fingers touched tentatively against his lips, understanding came into her eyes and she gave a faint smile. 'I will come to the door and see you off.'

'So you can tease me further by making me kiss you again?' he growled. 'I think not, my love.'

His words were the catalyst for a rosy blush that brought her palms whipping against her face to cover it. He chuckled as he strode off, confidence restored, choosing to forget the fact that Siana had still not accepted him.

Siana watched him go, her heart thudding with she knew not what. It was hard to believe this distinguished man had fallen to his knees and told her he adored her. She touched the pearls, cool and creamy against her skin.

'Marriage,' she whispered. Never again would she have to scrub pots, go without food, wear patched rags or shiver from cold in the winter. Her sister, brother and future children would never know poverty. Her bed would be her own.

But no! It would not. She would have to accommodate her husband. Perspiration gathered on her forehead. For a moment she felt a rush of excitement mixed with the fear of the unknown.

Her children would be Edward's children! She touched a finger to her lips, recalling the feel of his mouth against hers. It had been pleasant, that kiss. Beneath its gentleness, she'd discovered a restrained passion. Her body had responded to the power of it, pushing her in directions she hadn't dared to go. It had been hard to keep her distance from him.

Even now she could feel spring surging inside her. Her breasts were taut inside their skin, like buds about to burst, her moisture designed to trap instead of sustain.

Edward seemed to have sensed the exact moment when she'd become womanly in her desires, and had connected in some way to the very core of her.

But was it love? Was Edward who she wanted? He was certainly not the man from whom she'd expected to be offered marriage. Daniel was. Her smile faded and a tiny wound opened in her heart. Daniel had proved to be fickle. Her own heart had proved to be fickle. She must forget him, yet she'd rather hear from his own lips that he no longer loved her.

Francis came into her mind then. She had an enormous admiration and respect for him. He had a special place in her heart and she loved him for his compassion and his honesty.

She shook her head, bemused at the way her thoughts were going. Was she wicked-natured to crave the company and admiration of three men? Francis would always be her friend, and that's how they would stay. Nothing about the way he dealt with her had suggested anything more personal. He'd been in love with his wife and was still in love with her memory. Siana was pleased he had their two daughters to remember her by.

She shrugged. The fact that she didn't love Edward in the way she'd expected to feel love didn't really matter. How was love supposed to feel? She'd promised her mother she'd take care of Daisy, and what better way to do it? She'd be a fool to turn down Edward's proposal.

Edward was obliged to stop at a house in town, set discreetly in a back street, where he was relieved of his hat and cane by the manservant.

'Is Jasmine receiving visitors?'

'I will make enquiries, sir.'

A few minutes later he was led to an upstairs chamber, dimly illuminated by an oil lamp. Jasmine was reclining on the bed, her dark hair drawn into a golden ring. Her body was wrapped in a filmy gold cloth. She looked like an erotic painting when her almond eyes gleamed at him through painted-on defining lines.

He said nothing, just seated himself in the chair.

Jasmine began to writhe, then she contorted her body. First she folded herself this way, then that, keeping the cloth covering her all the while, so never a personal glimpse was afforded to her audience. She ended up on her stomach looking at him. Slowly, her legs came up and slid over her back, pulling her pelvis with it. She ended up folded in half, her chin resting on her arms, and looking at him from between her slightly spread legs. Her tongue flicked rapidly in and out of her mouth as the gold cloth gradually slipped sideways.

'As always, you are innovative, Jasmine,' he murmured as he threw some coins onto the bed. The girl slid to the floor and snaked sensuously across the rug to the chair.

He didn't need any more of the stimulation of her play-acting. Impatiently, he pulled her to her knees in front of him, leaned back into the cushions with a sigh and thought of another as Jasmine began to earn her pay.

They met in a clearing in the woods, several men sworn to secrecy, their lanterns held aloft.

'They says George Lovelace is ill and still in jail. The other five Tolpuddle men are in the prison hulks

Leviathan and *York,* which are lying off Portsmouth. Soon, they'll be shipped off to New South Wales.'

It was a cold night. The labourers shuffled from one foot to another and hugged their chests as the spokesman of the group stepped forward. 'We all know James Frampton got them on a trumped-up charge. Administering an unlawful oath be somethin' only sailors can be accused of, I were told.'

One or two of them spat on the ground, the rest began to mutter amongst themselves.

The man they'd come to meet, known only as Captain Swing, held up a hand. 'There's going to be a protest march in London next month. The labour unions will march on Whitehall to present a petition to Lord Melbourne himself. In the meantime, keep up the harassment, gentlemen. The landowners can't be allowed to get away with this.'

The man shook hands all round. 'I'll be gone then. Make sure the lad passes on the message.'

After Captain Swing headed for the road, the remaining men gathered together and passed around a stone jar of the local scrumpy cider. 'I don't know if we can trust Josh now his sister be the squire's woman,' one of them said.

'Wouldn't mind a little bit of that one, meself.'

Someone laughed. 'Nor me. As for young Josh, he be as trustworthy as they come. The lad has fingers in more pies than a horse has teeth. I hear tell he transported the squire's trout to Poole right under the man's nose.'

There was a gruff laugh. 'Talking of the squire, I hears you be doing his intended a favour, Ben.'

'Did you, then?' Ben reached out for the man. 'She bain't be his intended no more, so you keeps your dirty tongue to yourself or I'll rip it out by the roots. Anyone who insults Miss Isabelle insults Ben Collins hisself.' He thrust the man backwards and gazed belligerently around them. 'That goes for all of you.'

'Calm down, Ben, he didn't mean no harm,' the spokesman said. 'Now, let's plan the night's mischief.'

Half an hour later a haystack in the Cheverton Manor home meadow erupted into a conflagration. The red, flickering glow brought Edward jerking out of his downward slide into sleep. Where the hell were the watchmen he'd hired to guard his property?

He swung his legs out of bed and, still in nightshirt and cap, opened the door to his room and bawled out to rouse his servants before crossing to the window. He cursed. It was too late to save it . . . but they might be able to stop the fire spreading to the second rick if the wind didn't change direction.

Doors opened and shut, people whispered together. Edward already had his lantern lit and was pulling on his trousers when his personal servant arrived. 'Fetch Hawkins. Tell him to meet me in the hall, then send someone to rouse the rest of the men. Tell them to bring pitchforks,' he snapped, shrugging into a shirt and pulling a warm coat over the top.

'I've already done so, sir. Allow me to assist you into your boots.'

Edward loaded a pistol and shoved it into his waistband, just in case it was needed.

Booted up, he took the stairs to the lower level two at a time. Jed Hawkins was already there waiting for him, his nightshirt tucked into his trousers.

'Let's go, we have no time to waste,' Edward shouted at him. 'If you set eyes on those watchmen we hired, bring them to me immediately. I'm of a mind to give them a good flogging.'

But the two watchmen were already on the scene when they got there, ineffectually trying to beat out the flames with some branches pulled from a shrub.

Edward took one by the scruff of the neck and shouted, 'Where were you when this happened, man?'

'Where the stream widens into the pond, sir. We heard a whistle or two from over yonder and saw a gleam of light from a lantern. We reckoned someone were stealing your trout, sir, and went over to investigate.'

At least they'd been awake, if not alert. 'A diversion, obviously.'

The man looked apologetic. 'Most likely, sir, but we wasn't to know that. There were signs someone had been there recently. Fresh footprints in the mud. We intend to keep a better watch on that place in the future.'

So, his estate had been attacked from several quarters. The peasants were becoming over-confident and Edward resolved to make an example of the next miscreant he caught.

The house servants were swarming over the remaining stack now, inexpertly pitching forks full of hay about, grunting with the effort and shouting unnecessary instructions to one another. Had they been labourers they'd have done this task easily.

259

Sparks were shooting to the heavens now. Edward coughed as smoke drifted across to him. Damn! The breeze had turned.

He thought he heard his mare give a loud squeal, which set all the others in the stable to snorting, squealing and stamping. They were spooked by the smell of smoke, no doubt. He must send someone to settle them down, else they'd keep it up all night.

Before he could, an explosion of sparks caught the base of the second stack and it began to burn. 'Keep watch below you!' he shouted to the men clambering about the partially dismantled stack as he started beating at the flames with his jacket.

He'd just managed to smother the flames when another part of the stack caught alight, then another. The heated air seemed set to explode as bits of burning hay fell about them. Sweat poured from his body as he joined his servants in the futile battle to save the stack.

It was a while before Edward was ready to admit defeat. By that time the men were exhausted and he, like them, was nearly choked by the smoke. They stood around saying nothing as, dispirited by their failure, they watched the stack burn. Their soot-streaked faces and slumped shoulders showed their exhaustion as dawn crept over the horizon.

The noise from the stable hadn't yet abated. 'Give the men a tot of brandy when you get back to the house,' Edward said to Jed, then beckoned to the groom and the coachman. 'Let's go and settle the horses down.'

The scene that greeted Edward was unnerving. The coach horses, usually creatures of placid disposition,

260

rolled their eyes and stomped and whinnied. One shied away from the groom until it seemed to recognize its handler and calmed down, quivering as the groom breathed into its nose and spoke softly.

Edward stared at his mare, tears in his eyes. She was lying on her side, twitching and shivering. Her head turned towards him when she heard his voice and she tried to rise, squealing in agony as her front legs refused to take her weight.

'No, no, my beauty,' he soothed. 'Those legs will never support you again.'

Her fetlocks had been smashed with the knob end of a stout and ornately carved stick, the weapon tossed carelessly to one side. The haystack fire had provided a diversion for this cruelty to go ahead unhampered. It was not some spur of the moment thing. Tears trickled unheeded down Edward's cheeks.

'Shall I do the deed, sir?' the groom said quietly, the pistol he'd loaded at the ready.

Edward sucked in a deep breath and took it from his hand. 'No, I will.' He leaned forward, fondling the mare's velvety nose so she could breathe in his scent and know her master. He whispered words of love in her ear, calming her fears. 'I'll find the person who did this to you and I'll punish him,' he whispered and pulled the trigger.

The shot was loud in the confined space. It spooked the mare's stable mates and set them whinnying and rolling their eyes again.

Outside, rooks rose from the trees in the copse, circling in panic until the echo died away. The ruins of the haystacks smouldered and smoked, sending a pall of darkness to stain the pale, slate-coloured sky.

Presently Edward left the stable and strode towards the house, where he called his servants together. He showed them the carved stick. His expression was full of contempt, his eyes ruthless. 'Somebody used this to maim my horse. Anyone who provides me with the information to apprehend the man who owns it will be well rewarded.'

He didn't bother cleaning himself up. Riding a gelding and with Jed Hawkins in tow, he headed for the village. There, he called the village women together and speared the stick into the ground. He repeated what he'd said to his household.

The stick brought only blank stares. Needing revenge, he searched every cottage, kicking over washtubs and butter churns in a quest to find anything to connect someone with the deeds of the night before. The women muttered resentfully, but not loud enough for him to hear the words. They snatched their children to their hips and gazed at him tight-lipped when the tension communicated itself to them and they began to cry.

'Hear me,' he said, snatching up the evidence in preparation for leaving. 'When I find out who the troublemakers are, I'll personally flog them before I hand them over to the magistrate – whether they be man, woman or child.' He flipped a gold coin in the air. 'A guinea for any information.'

A round woman stepped forward, an army of children in tow. She dropped him a curtsy. 'I think I sees that stick afore now,' she said. 'It belongs to a stranger to these parts, a holy preacher man. He be ailing and be staying at the reverend's place, sir.'

'And who might you be?'

'Abbie Ponsonby, sir. My man, Rudd, be an overseer of your'n.'

Edward couldn't place the man, but nodded as he tossed her the gold piece. 'Ah . . . yes, of course. Thank you, Mrs Ponsonby. There will be more where that came from if he turns out to be the one I'm after.'

The village women were subjecting Abbie to resentful stares. She ignored them, and slipping the coin in her pocket waddled indoors, shepherding her children fussily before her like so many ducklings.

'Do you know her man?' Edward asked Hawkins as they rode away.

'A good worker and a God-fearing and conscientious man.'

'Should he be considered for the tenancy of Croxley Farm?'

'He was last time, but was passed over in favour of Tom Skinner.'

Edward didn't need reminding of his folly over that matter. 'I have it on good authority that Skinner isn't likely to recover, so let's consider Rudd Ponsonby again,' he said as he spurred his horse forward. 'With all those children to feed, he should be grateful for the opportunity to earn a decent living – and a grateful man is a loyal man.'

Richard White wasn't expecting visitors, so when Edward arrived in such a dishevelled state he was surprised to say the least.

'Good gracious!' he said when Mrs Leeman showed him in. 'You look as if you've been up all night. What on earth has been going on, Edward?'

Edward told him in as brief a manner as he could, then handed him the stick. 'I'm told this belongs to a guest in your house.'

'It's possible.' Richard looked at the carving on the stick, then took it to the window to examine it more closely in the light of day. He smiled. Two dragons chased each other around the top. Into the length of the stick was carved an intricate design of celtic crosses held inside garlands of laurel leaves and inscribed with the names of towns. 'Actually, it's more than possible. This is fine work.'

'No doubt, but somebody used it to cripple my horse last night.'

'Not my guest,' Richard said calmly and handed it back to him. 'Can I offer you some refreshment?'

'First, I would like to speak to your guest. After which, I have another matter to discuss with you.'

Richard had heard that the squire had thrown Isabelle Prosser aside, and supposed it was that he wanted to discuss. He couldn't say he was surprised. He'd thought the girl to be totally unsuitable for Edward and considered her slightly overbearing in manner.

Richard crossed to the bell pull and smiled when Mrs Leeman appeared. 'We're going to see the patient now. Why don't you prepare some refreshment and a slice of that delicious fruit tart you made yesterday? We will have it when we come down.'

Mrs Leeman bobbed a curtsy and returned to the kitchen.

264

A couple of minutes later Edward found himself gazing down on a gaunt figure lying in a narrow bed.

'This is Gruffydd Evans,' Richard said and leaned over the man. 'You have a visitor, Gruffydd. May I present Sir Edward Forbes. He has found your cane.'

A pair of piercing blue eyes were turned Edward's way. 'My heartfelt thanks, sir. That cane was years in the making and is the work of an abject penitent. It isn't finished yet, but it has brought me here and I know it's close to completion.' Half sitting up in bed, his eyes blazed with fire. 'The blind witch said the pagan girl, Megan Lewis, will come, and I will find peace when I am granted forgiveness.' He fell back on the pillows. His eyes stared at the ceiling and he began to talk, his voice rising and falling in a musical cadence that was quite mesmerizing.

'What the devil's wrong with him? What's he babbling about?' Edward said, taking a step back as goosebumps prickled his skin. 'Is he talking in tongues?'

Richard smiled at the thought that Edward would be so fanciful. 'His conscience troubles him and he's praying in his native language. This is not the man who crippled your horse, Edward. I swear he has not left this bed. That cane was taken from the church where it was left.'

They went back down to the drawing room. 'Now, what was the other matter you wanted to discuss?'

'Siana Lewis.'

A pained look came to Richard's face. 'The girl has fallen from grace as far as I'm concerned. Far be it from me to tell you your business, but I have to inform you that I consider your part in her downfall deplorable. I intend to talk to her and guide her back onto the right path.'

'The devil you will,' Edward drawled. 'Well, you're welcome to talk to her, of course. But Siana Lewis is still as pure as the driven snow. Until I make her my wife, she will remain that way.'

There was a gasp from outside the door and cups rattled on the tea tray. Then Mrs Leeman was inside, beaming all over her face as she set the tray on the table. 'Forgive me, but I couldn't help overhearing, sir. May I be bold enough to offer my congratulations. Such a lovely, considerate girl despite her upbringing. I'm so pleased, that I am.'

'Thank you, Mrs Leeman. I'm gratified by your approval. I'll make sure you receive an invitation to the wedding.'

The woman went off looking pink and delighted.

'Well?' he said to Richard, who was staring at him, dumbfounded. 'Don't you have anything to say for yourself?'

'She's Megan Skinner's daughter, born out of wedlock.'

Edward began to frown. 'Yes, that's something I'm aware of.'

Richard jerked a thumb at the ceiling. 'Gruffydd Evans is looking for Megan Lewis.'

'What of it?'

'Megan Skinner was a Lewis before her marriage.'

'The woman who died in the fire? He's probably a relative. Doesn't he know she's dead?'

'I haven't told him.' Richard gave an odd smile. 'The man is no relative to Megan Skinner, but he is to Siana Lewis. He fathered her.'

'What!'

'Gruffydd Evans fathered Siana Lewis and has spent all these years on a quest to find Megan and his lost daughter.'

Edward sat down rather heavily, then he began to chuckle.

Richard sighed. 'I can't see what's funny about the situation, Edward.'

'I can.' Edward leaned forward and gazed into Richard's eyes. 'I'm going to make that girl my wife, Richard.' His voice hardened slightly. 'In fact, I'm determined to find a way to achieve that aim as soon as possible and neither you nor that damned Welsh preacher upstairs will prevent me.'

Richard looked shocked. 'But why, when you could have your pick of women more suited to the position?'

'Why?' Edward's eyes were lit from within as a tender smile pushed at his lips. 'Now there's a question deserving of honesty. After myself, you shall be the first to know. I've fallen in love with her, of course.'

16

Edward found the perfect way to achieve his aim that very day.

Still furious, and willing to lay the punishment for the death of his mare on anyone, he was taking no chances as he doubled the watch. The road ran through his property, and every vehicle was to be searched, especially those coming from Wareham.

As dusk approached, he was rewarded when one of his vigilantes brought in a felon.

Edward's heart fell when he saw who it was. 'Oh Josh,' he said, shaking his head.

'I caught the varmint red-handed,' the watchman said. 'There were several trout in a sack on his cart.'

Josh stared him straight in the eye and lied. 'I found them on the road and was bringing them to you. A shame to waste them, I thought, when the squire could have them for supper.'

'Enough, Josh.' Edward's sadness and anger at being offered a falsehood by a lad he'd trusted – on top of being stolen from – knew no bounds. Shaking with a rage so fierce that he had to bunch one fist into the other to prevent himself from letting fly, he couldn't trust himself to deal with Josh now because he felt like killing him. 'Lock him in the cellar. I'll deal with him in the morning.'

'What about Jasper and my cart?' Josh shouted, struggling as he was dragged away.

'In the morning, burn the cart and make sure the mule goes to the knackery,' Edward instructed as he walked away.

'Don't kill Jasper,' Josh begged, wriggling desperately to free himself from the watchman's beefy fist. 'He's just a poor dumb creature who ain't done nothing wrong.'

The Lord giveth and the Lord taketh away, Edward thought irreverently when he reached the house. Going into his study, he reached for the brandy bottle.

Later, sprawled in his chair, shirt undone and his legs stretched out towards the fire, he felt his age nudging at him. Most men who'd reached his time of life had grandchildren. What did he have? The memory of a wife he'd killed out of love, the daughter they'd lost and a son born on the wrong side of the blanket who wanted more than he could give him.

Loneliness crowded in on him. He thought of Patricia and his daughter Charlotte, waiting in the churchyard for him to join them. How easy it would be. He picked up his pistol and cocking it, held the barrel against his temple. His finger exerted pressure on the trigger. One squeeze would be all it required. He could feel the regular beat of his pulse against the cold metal. He squeezed. Metal clicked loudly against metal. His heart quickened.

He laughed as he threw the weapon aside. 'Not yet, Patricia.'

What he needed was a purpose in life. He needed someone who would look up to him and bear children to warm his hearth. So that when his time came, he could die knowing the estate had gone to his legitimate heir. Daisy was a fine replacement for his little lost Charlotte, and Siana looked the type to carry boys.

'Siana Lewis.' He sighed. She was an exquisitely tender morsel with her green eyes and sable hair. Siana was gloriously alive. She was a girl of the land – not the frail, sad ghost of a city woman seeking the child she'd lost.

Siana filled his heart and mind. He didn't give a damn who her parents were. Yet, whilst every bit of him yearned for her, she made him wriggle like an eel on a hook. He'd even gone down on his knees to propose – and she'd told him he must wait.

He thought of her brother, Josh. Damned if he'd wait! His mind suddenly cleared of its melancholy fog and he laughed out loud. It was all so simple. He held the winning hand.

Ringing for a servant, he sent him with instructions to the stable lad, then took a lantern and sauntered down to the cellar. It was cold and damp down there, the height of the various water marks on the wall testament to the vagaries of the nearby stream, which sent its excess sneaking underground to flood the foundations of the manor after a deluge. Sometimes the flooding reached halfway up the cellar stairs.

The cellar was dry now, except for blackish-green

slicks of slime here and there, caused by the constant seepage. It smelled earthily of mould, not an unpleasant smell, Edward thought.

Bottles of wine and spirits were neatly racked above the water line. Rare, French brandy took up one wall. Edward grinned to himself. His grandfather had made most of his fortune by smuggling. Edward, as had his father before him, kept his grandfather's contribution for special occasions.

For himself, he loved the land and preferred the life of a gentleman farmer to that of an adventurer. His investments were widespread though, with property merely a small part of them. Sometimes, a stray crate of fine spirits found its way into his cellar. Half was laid down for the future, the other half kept for his own pleasure. Like a fine woman, good quality brandy should be savoured slowly, he thought. It should be smooth to the tongue, warming to the heart and possessed of a rare essence. It should be satisfying enough to leave a man craving for more, for both wine and women were addictive.

He found Josh curled atop a table with only a sack for warmth. He was sound asleep. Edward nudged him with his foot and watched him scramble upright, his eyes blinking against the light.

'Get out. You'll find your cart and mule waiting outside,' Edward said harshly. 'Tell your sister I'll be along to discuss this with her in the morning. I'll expect you to be there. If you're not, I'll have a warrant sworn out for your arrest.' And he sent him on his way with a boot in the rear that sent him sprawling on his face.

'Yes, sir,' Josh said after picking himself up from the ground. The lad sauntered off full of bravado, hands shoved in his pockets and whistling cockily to himself.

Edward watched him go, frowning ominously. If the lad thought he'd got away with it he'd find out differently in the morning.

Oh yes, young Josh, you certainly won't escape without punishment and afterwards you'll never dare steal from me again.

The next morning Siana waited nervously for Edward to put in an appearance.

She'd dressed in a blue gown covered in forget-me-nots and wore his gift of pearls in an attempt to appease him.

'Why did you do such a thing, Josh?'

Knowing he was losing money by hanging around waiting when he should be digging up cockles whilst the tide was out, Josh shrugged. 'It's no worse than what everyone else does. Even the squire does a bit of smuggling on the side.'

'He's our benefactor. If it wasn't for him we'd be in the workhouse.' Josh was growing out of his clothes again, she thought despairingly, noting the expanse of bare ankles above his boots. 'You'd better let me have those trousers so I can let the hems down.'

'You've already let them down. I'll hafta buy a new pair.' He looked gloomy at the thought of spending money for a moment, then he smiled. 'There's been a couple of funerals lately. The widows will be cleaning house. I'll be able to pick up a secondhand pair next time I go to market. Shouldn't cost me more than thruppence if I wait till the end of the day.'

'Get them on the big side, our Josh, then they'll last. I can always turn them up.'

'And you a lady of leisure, our Siana,' he mocked. 'Shame on you. Your fancy man will have a fit if he knows you're still acting like a peasant woman.'

His tone of voice brought her looking sharply at him. 'And what exactly do you mean by that?'

His lip curled slightly. 'D'you think I'm deaf as well as daft? Whilst you're acting the toff the whole district is talking about you and the squire.'

Dismay filled her heart. So Josh had heard the rumours. 'Whatever they're saying, it's lies.'

'Is it, Siana? I've got eyes in my head. The squire follows you around like a dog on a leash.'

'He wants me to marry him.'

'Christ! That I didn't expect.' Josh sat down heavily on the chair. 'My sister married to that old man. You're not telling me fibs, are you?'

'No. But I haven't agreed to his proposal yet.'

A grin chased across his face. 'No wonder he let me off then. Fancy being the lady of the manor, do you? Ma would turn in her grave.'

'I said I hadn't yet accepted his proposal, so don't you go telling anyone.'

'Not me. I'd never live it down.' Josh burst into gales of laughter.

But it died on his lips when a thunderous knocking came from the front door. A few seconds later, Rosie came in, her face pale. 'A message from the squire. Miss Siana. He wants everyone to assemble out front, except Miss Daisy and the nursemaid.'

Instinctively, Siana stood in front of Josh. 'Me as well?'

'Especially you, miss. He said to tell you to bring Josh out.'

She turned to gaze at her brother, fear in her eyes. 'It seems you have not been let off, after all. Shall I try and talk to him first?'

Josh attempted a smile. 'It might queer your pitch and you've got Daisy to think of.' He took in a tremulous breath. 'It won't be the first flogging I've had and I reckon he ain't going to kill me in front of witnesses.'

So saying, he marched off towards the door. Snatching up her skirts, Siana ran after him, catching him up at the front door. They went through it together.

There were two of them. Edward on an indifferent-looking horse she'd never seen him ride before, and his overseer, Jed Hawkins.

'Edward,' she said, hurrying forward. 'Please forgive Josh. He'll not do anything like that again. I promise.'

Edward's face was set in stern lines. 'Josh Skinner handled stolen goods for profit. On the first count of killing game without a certificate the fine is five pounds.'

There was a gasp from the servants and Josh muttered, 'I didn't take the damned fish or kill them.'

'For the second charge of trespassing on private property, the fine is two pounds, or five pounds if in the company of others. An additional sentence of transportation could be imposed if I decide to put the matter in the hands of the magistrate.'

Siana paled at the thought of Josh being sent away.

'And the alternative?' Josh asked him.

The squire slapped his riding crop into the palm of his hand. 'A beating here and now, witnessed by the people present. Then we will forget it. What say you, Josh? Will you take your punishment like a man?'

'No!' Siana burst out. 'I beg you, Edward. Please don't beat him.'

The amber eyes turned her way were ruthless. 'Be quiet, girl. This is between him and me. The lad must be taught not to steal from me.'

Josh shrugged. 'I'll take the beating. It can't be worse than our Tom used to give me.'

Not a word was spoken as Jed Hawkins tied Josh to the trunk of a tree. Josh twisted his head and gave his sister a faint, brave smile. His bottom lip was trembling and Siana couldn't see him as a man, only a terrified boy.

Edward was tall and powerful and, despite his abundance of silver hair, had the look of a man in his prime. He wore a dark coat and dark trousers tucked into black riding boots. They gave him a sinister air as he stood with legs slightly apart, slapping the crop gently against his thigh whilst Hawkins readied his victim.

The crack of the riding crop against her brother's back was sudden, and terrifyingly loud. Siana jumped when Josh gave a surprised yelp. Then she saw him close his eyes. His body tensed and his mouth clamped shut. He said not another word as the beating continued with ruthless efficiency.

Soon welts appeared and blood trickled.

Josh moaned softly in his throat.

Tears filled Siana's eyes. *Stop it, stop it*, she silently prayed.

275

The next stroke criss-crossed a welt. The moan was louder.

Edward was perspiring slightly. The crop rose and descended. Blood ran. Josh screamed.

As if she were sleepwalking Siana pushed between them, catching the next downward stroke at the junction of her neck and shoulder. The leather tip stung her just below the line of pearls. Her skin burned like fire as she turned to face Edward, her palms spread in supplication. Behind her, Josh was whimpering like an injured dog.

'I beg you to stop,' she whispered.

Edward's eyes were frightening, almost predatory, certainly calculating. She shivered as she suddenly realized what this was all about, knowing with absolute certainty that Edward would beat Josh to death unless she put a stop to it.

'If you want me to wed you, cease this punishment, Edward.'

He stared at her for a long moment, the darkness in his soul revealed to her. This man would always have his way. As her words sank in, the turbulence in his eyes cleared. He nodded. 'The first Sunday in May?'

She touched her fingers to the welt he'd raised across her neck. They came away sticky with blood. Her eyes were filled with disdain as she gazed at him, needing desperately to burst into tears. Whether it was from pain, shock, or the absolute helplessness of seeing her brother so cruelly beaten, she didn't know. But she knew she was loath to display such weakness in front of Edward, and felt such hate for him at that moment she wanted to kill him.

Jerking the pearl necklace from her throat, she

hurled it at him. The pearls, stained red from her blood, landed at his feet. He stared at them for a moment, then ground them into the earth under his heels.

Giving a faint smile, he threw the bloodied crop to one side. 'See to Josh,' he said to Hawkins and started towards her.

She couldn't trust herself to speak to him and turned to run towards the house. Dizzy from shock and pain, she felt the world begin to fade. Her knees crumpled and she staggered forward. The last thing she saw before she fainted was the concern in his eyes as he caught her.

'What kind of man are you?' she whispered, as soon as she came round. Edward was seated by her bed, a cloth soaked in witch hazel held against her neck. It was soothing.

'I'm sorry, my dearest Siana. I wouldn't have hurt you for the world.'

'Josh—'

'Will be all right in a few days. I didn't use excessive force.'

She struggled to her elbows. 'Am I supposed to feel grateful for that? He's just a small boy.'

His expression assumed a touch of hauteur. 'Had it been anyone but Josh I'd have shown them no mercy at all. He came along at the wrong time and I couldn't allow him to get away with stealing from me. Let me explain what happened.'

Shocked when he related the fate of his mare, she shuddered and the tears she'd been valiantly holding back began to trickle down her face.

He brushed the hair back from her face and smiled

down at her, his gaze openly adoring. He said in a voice so tender she could hardly believe the change in him, 'You will never regret agreeing to marry me.' Leaning forward, he kissed her with more passion than he'd previously displayed.

She hated herself for responding, for wanting such attention from him. When his mouth slid to kiss the swell of her breasts above her bodice, she trembled with pleasure. His thumbs brushed over the hardened nubs just once, leaving them tingling unbearably.

'Don't,' she entreated, for she couldn't trust herself to say no if he continued, when it was obvious his cruelty had aroused him.

He was breathing heavily as he drew away, his eyes slumbrous. 'It's all right, my dearest. I can wait until our wedding night. I've already discussed this with Richard and we'll start calling the banns the Sunday after next. I will announce our engagement at your birthday gathering.' A glass of brandy was held to her lips. 'Sip this, it will strengthen you.'

'Is this one of the bottles which came straight off the ship from France?'

He chuckled at that. 'Come, Siana, do not berate me for my peccadilloes. Another's sin is my birthright. That is something Josh will learn when he's achieved his dream of unlimited wealth – and he will, but not at my expense. Take a sip.'

The brandy warmed her, making her feel weak, so when he kissed her again, it felt as if he would possess her utterly.

'Come, tell me you love me,' he murmured.

A moment ago she'd hated him. Wonderingly, she touched his face. 'Yes . . . I love you, but sometimes I don't like you very much, Edward. How can that be?'

'You will like me better when you begin to know me.' He placed the glass on the table and straightened up.

'I'm sorry I ruined the pearls.'

'They're not ruined. They can be cleaned and restrung. They're unimportant. I'll buy you diamonds.'

'I don't want diamonds.' She reached out to entwine his fingers in hers. He kissed each knuckle and placed her hand back on her stomach. Whether by design or accident, he caressed her in a most personal manner, briefly kissing her mouth at the same time.

'You shall have them anyway,' he promised, his voice a soft caress against her ear.

She watched him go, everything inside her flaming with desire. Suddenly, she couldn't wait for their marriage to take place.

As April progressed, the landscape took on a bright new verdancy as the soft showers did their work. Oats, barley, carrots and clover were sown. Potatoes were planted and yard muck spread over the turnip fields to add a rich, ripe pungency to the air.

As the planting work commenced, the local trouble lessened. Word filtered down from London that the unionists' petition had been refused by the Home Secretary, Lord Melbourne.

The peasants went about their work, sullen-faced.

Ben Collins, responding to the demands of Isabelle's flesh, began to neglect Croxley Farm. Hannah did her best to keep the labourers working but the planting soon fell behind. She complained at great length to her husband, her remarks becoming ever more virulent until Ben could stand it no more and clouted her in the mouth, knocking out her front teeth.

'I've got a new woman, one who knows how to treat a man real nice,' he told her. 'I be going off to live with her.'

Incensed, because she'd chosen to ignore the rumours and felt like a fool, Hannah bundled George into a ragged sack and thrust him into his father's arms. 'Take your good-for-nothing son with you then, Ben Collins. He be stupid like you, and the bastard does nothing but eat, crap and bawl, anyway. See if the fat whore wants him too.'

To Hannah's surprise, Isabelle did.

When Isabelle first set eyes on the smelly little creature called George, she felt a moment of revulsion. But by the time she'd bathed him, fed him, tended his sores with salve and cuddled him all clean and warm against her, she was as besotted with George as she was with his father.

Young George felt the same about Isabelle. Here was a woman such as he'd never known, soft and loving. Being male, he instinctively responded to her attention and, smiling with contentment, he laid his claim.

Placing his hand on her breast he wooed her by softly murmuring, 'Ma,' and falling asleep on her shoulder.

Josh, resilient in his youth, recovered quickly from the beating. He hadn't been left with permanent physical marks.

The absence of scars left Siana feeling indebted to Edward for being as lenient as he'd said he'd been. She noticed Josh had lost his cocky manner and seemed more grown-up. Good food had now laid a healthy covering of flesh over his bones and his physical work had produced muscle.

Josh spent time looking for ways of making money, hoarding every penny he earned. He continued to transport the squire's trout, raising his fee to a level that made the risk worth while. He guessed the squire wouldn't search him again now he'd dealt him a beating.

Had Edward known it, the only lesson Josh had learned from the beating was to find a better place to stash the fish. He'd built a false floor into the cart.

Elizabeth returned from London a few days later. After spending more time in the capital than she'd first expected, she was bubbling over with news. 'It was such an exciting place to visit. I met several useful people and made some good friends amongst the wholesalers.'

Siana took her into the drawing room and spoke to her before she lost courage. 'I must tell you this straight away, Elizabeth. Edward has asked me to marry him and I have accepted.'

Elizabeth appeared shaken for a moment, then treated her to the serenest of smiles. 'My dearest Siana, I have noticed the regard Edward holds for you and have watched you grow to love him. You have my blessing.'

She made no mention of Daniel, which only served to confirm what Siana had read in the letter – that Daniel was involved with someone else.

'But I thought you might be upset.'

Elizabeth kissed her on both cheeks. 'I value your friendship too highly to allow this to come between us. We must forget the past, which is gone and cannot be undone. You must allow me to prepare you for your wedding day. Your gown will be my gift to you.'

'You are the most generous of women, Elizabeth. I love you dearly,' Siana told her, and her words came from the heart.

Elizabeth was inclined to believe Siana was right. She *was* the most generous of women, because right at that moment her heart was breaking into several thousand pieces. She'd sensed Edward's growing interest in Siana, but hadn't imagined he'd had marriage in mind. Still, if Edward and Siana loved one another, there was nothing she could do about it. She would have to accept this marriage and hope, for the sake of these two people she loved, that they'd succeed in finding happiness together.

As the night of her birthday drew near, Siana was beset with nerves. What if she failed Edward and his friends didn't accept her?

Her gown was fashioned from silk tinted the colour of hyacinths, with delicate, paler embroidery to discreetly emphasize the scalloped hems of the triple-tiered skirt. A matching lace collar dipped across the slope of her shoulders, the draped full sleeves ended at the elbow, where her evening gloves would begin. Her silk shoes were dyed a deeper shade to match the ribbon bow at her waist and the flowers Elizabeth was fixing to the crown of her head.

Elizabeth smiled at Siana's reflection. Her glossy dark hair had been parted in the middle and drawn up to the crown with just a few curls left to bunch at her ears. The strong blue of her gown was reflected on the surface of her eyes, lending them a dramatic and mysterious darkness. But there was a worried expression on her sweet, heart-shaped face.

'I wish I hadn't damaged the gift of pearls Edward gave me,' she said.

'Pearls would not suit this gown anyway.' Elizabeth smiled at her and proceeded to the door. 'Please try not to look so worried, my dear. The expression produces unpleasant lines on the face over time. I promise you, this will not be the ordeal you expect it to be.'

Panic raced through her. 'You're not leaving me to go downstairs by myself?'

'Of course not, but I must fetch my fan and, as hostess, must not neglect my guests.' Elizabeth smiled at someone outside the door. 'Siana is ready to see you now, Edward. I will expect you downstairs shortly.'

Edward looked distinguished in a black cutaway jacket, the contrasting revers matching his embroidered waistcoat. A frilled shirt and stirruped trousers completed his evening ensemble. His amber glance scrutinized her from head to foot. He smiled as he crossed to her side. 'You are exquisite.'

She let out as much breath as her tightly laced corset would allow. They were excruciatingly painful garments to wear, but Elizabeth said they must be endured to present a fashionable waistline.

Edward spanned her tortured waist with his hands,

bringing her closer without crushing her skirt. He teased her mouth with a tantalizing kiss. 'Happy birthday, my dearest love. Close your eyes, and don't open them until I instruct you to.'

She quivered with happiness when he clipped something to her ears, then placed a cold band around her forehead. He turned her round, whispering against her ear. 'Now you may open them.'

Diamonds sent out blue sparks as the facets caught the light. The headband dipped to a point just above the juncture of her brows, where a larger single diamond matched the drops quivering amongst the curls.

'Oh, Edward,' she breathed, her voice revealing the awe which threatened to overwhelm her, 'I don't deserve such a fine gift when I've been so mean towards you.'

Her reaction seem to please him. He kissed the back of her neck, sending shivers racing along her spine. He extended his arm to her. 'Your pleasure is mine, Siana. Shall we join our guests?'

Her eyes implored him. 'I'm nervous.'

He patted her hand. 'I know. Just remember, all you have learned so far has been leading towards this moment. After today, your life will change for the better.'

Better, she'd learned, was wearing corsets to change the figure to one that fashion dictated. It was laughter stifled behind a lace handkerchief lest its raucous sound offended another's ear. It was fanning one's face to keep at bay the perspiration a country girl took for granted. *Better* was saying one thing and meaning another.

She giggled softly as they reached the bottom of the

stairs. 'If thee really thinks I can be bettered when these poxy corsets be so bleddy tight, you be fair mazed, Edward Forbes.'

He slid her a grin. 'I be fair mazed right now, my sweet and innocent Dorset girl. And I expect to uncover a completely wicked creature inside that corset when we are wed. I hope you don't disappoint me.'

She was blushing furiously when they went into the drawing room. Edward's eyes were full of laughter as he clinked a spoon against a glass for silence.

'Ladies and sirs, with the permission of my hostess, Mrs Elizabeth Skinner, may I present Miss Siana Lewis to you. On the occasion of her eighteenth birthday, I'm delighted to inform you that Miss Lewis has just done me the honour of agreeing to become my wife. The banns will be first published on Sunday.'

There was a moment of complete silence, then someone said almost inaudibly, 'I'll be damned! I thought you said the girl was a clod-hopper.'

Siana caught Edward's eye and they both began to laugh.

Someone gave a cheer and their laughter was lost in the clapping, cheers and the plethora of congratulations and good wishes being aimed their way.

Francis managed to catch her eye. He raised his glass in a regretful salute before Edward attached her to his arm and took her on a round of introductions.

Already she was a triumph. Francis wished he could feel as happy about the marriage as Edward looked.

17

The people of the district had never seen such goings-on. First it had been the ungainly Isabelle, now the bastard peasant girl, Siana Lewis, who'd been brought up in the Skinner family.

Not only was the estate church crowded, but people lined the grounds waiting to get a view. One of their own to be elevated to the ranks of the aristocracy? It was unheard of. They wanted to see it with their own eyes. Most of them didn't much like the thought and were there to satisfy their curiosity rather than to wish the couple well.

They were not to be disappointed. The squire's carriage pulled up, the horses fretting, farting and snorting. They tossed their heads in lively fashion as their leathers creaked and jingled.

The villagers crowded forward, necks craning this way and that as the door was opened and the step lowered.

The first to descend was the squire, who assisted a woman out.

'It's Tom Skinner's missus,' someone said.

286

'Shame on her. It bain't be right, a married woman with her man lying on his deathbed, flaunting herself with another.'

'Who would want that swine for a husband, anyway? A pity she didn't cut his throat after she bashed him over the head.'

Elizabeth gave no indication she'd heard them, though her face paled at the unjust accusation.

The second woman to descend brought an awed gasp from the crowd. 'There's bonny, she be. Just like her ma when she came here.'

'I can't remember her ma being that clean and well dressed. That gown must've cost a pretty piece.'

' If Megan Skinner could see her now, she'd turn in her grave, poor soul. That girl didn't get the gown by grubbing for taters in the dirt, I'll be bound.'

'Good luck to thee, lass. You'll need it. You've sold your soul to the very devil, that you have,' someone said loudly.

And so it went on, with everyone making comment of some sort, and hardly any of it complimentary.

Siana flushed and was inclined to return to the safety of the carriage, but Edward took her arm in a firm grip. 'You will behave with dignity and take no notice of the talk.'

They proceeded into the church. Edward ushered them into the Forbes pew at the front then, seating himself next to Siana, patted her hand to comfort her. The coachman and Jed Hawkins took the seat behind, as if protecting their backs.

There was an atmosphere of discontent in the

church. Her face pale, Siana felt sick and apprehensive all through the service, as muttering and shuffling came from the back.

Richard White's voice droned on, his sermon seemingly never-ending. The second lesson was read and Richard glanced around the church.

The congregation stared back at him, expectant expressions on their faces.

'I publish the banns of marriage between Edward Forbes, widower of this parish, and Siana Lewis, spinster. If any of you know cause, or just impediment why these two persons should not be joined together in holy matrimony, ye are to declare it. This is the first time of asking.'

'What happened to Isabelle Pross—' a man shouted from the back, but the words were cut off when the sound of a struggle ensued.

Edward and Elizabeth stared straight ahead. Siana couldn't help turning her head a little, just in time to see one of the estate workers ejecting a labourer. She noticed other men in Edward's employ scattered throughout the congregation and began to feel better.

'Siana,' Edward reprimanded in a voice meant for her ears alone. She turned back, but not before she caught sight of Francis. She sent a smile in his direction and hoped he'd wait for her after the service so they could pass the time of day.

But when they emerged into the warm, spring sunshine he was gone, and her feelings were dampened by the slight. She'd expected Francis to be happy for the chance she'd been given to provide a secure future for herself and her siblings, but so far he hadn't even congratulated her.

At the reverend's house, Gruffydd Evans had been woken by the church bells.

'Sinner. You masqueraded as a holy man yet you stripped the innocence from a child of the gods. Only the child of the child can forgive you – and the time of the reckoning is near.'

Ignoring the sibilant voice hissing in his head, he slipped out of bed and stood at the window to pray before the cross casting its invincible shadow on the church wall.

'Lord, help me find Megan Lewis and the infant of my seed, spilled from the loins of this sinner into her womb. Let not the sins of the parents be visited on the child.'

He opened his eyes in time to see the congregation streaming from the church. A goodly crowd the reverend attracted. A good man altogether. He must ask him to pray with him. Surely God would listen to both of his humble servants petitioning on this matter.

Then he saw her, coming from the church on the arm of an older man. How pretty she looked in a gown and bonnet of pale green. And how young she still was. His withered loins stirred at the sight of her and he knew at once it was to remind him of his weakness.

Tears coursed down his cheeks. At last, his journey was over. Now he could go to his maker with his conscience purged. But he knew he must atone for his sin in public first, confess to the Lord in the church and ask for his soul to be taken into heaven.

He placed his hand against his heart, feeling the

erratic beat against his palm. Every beat was a pain, every pain a penance. Yet, soon, he would find peace.

His eyes clouded over and he fell to the floor. Froth filled his mouth, his teeth ground together and chattered in his jaw and he began to jerk uncontrollably.

Elizabeth had thrown all her energy into her shop, and right from the start she knew the venture would pay off.

Peggy Hastings had turned out to be clever and quick to learn. She used just the right amount of deference to encourage the clients to confide in her, and was discreet enough not to repeat their confidences. Soon, she and Elizabeth learned who was indulging in an affair with whom, and it was to those customers the more intimate and sensual apparel was sold.

Drawers had become very popular amongst those of social status. Cambric and percale were worn, and silk when bathing, or when wearing pantaloons under riding habits.

Elizabeth's creations were fashioned from the finest silk which clung to the body in a most sensuous manner, covering the more desirable aspects of the female body but emphasizing the forbidden fruit beneath in a most erotic manner. There were frothy red petticoats to wear under the demurest dress, stockings of silk with garters of flowers and ribbon. Parisian corsets and demi-corsets designed by Delacroix with padding to enhance the breast. Silks and satins, ribbon and lace, chemises of such delicacy that the female figure could be observed right through them when light caressed them from the right direction.

Then there was the perfume Josh supplied her with,

the tiny glass flagons of precious Parisian scent, bringing her, and him, vast profits. Soon, Elizabeth could not keep up with the demand and was thinking she might open another shop to sell only the most intimate apparel.

'I've heard the shop next door is becoming vacant,' Peggy said. 'If we could get that, we could put a door through, so the clients can have access to it without the embarrassment of being seen entering a shop devoted exclusively to intimate apparel.'

Elizabeth consulted Edward about it. He had arrived just before trading ceased, giving a faint smile when he glanced over her books. 'I hadn't realized there was such a trade in women's undergarments.'

'You have not seen them yet.' Elizabeth took him to the secluded back room and seated him in a cubicle whilst Peggy Hastings began to tidy everything away preparatory to closing. Soon, the table before him was displaying a range of the exotic undergarments. He picked up a chemise, allowing the material to pour through his fingers. It flowed like a fall of cool water bathed in moonlight. He examined the silk drawers, noting the flap crossing over the front and back to maintain an illusion of modesty.

He laughed, delighted by them. 'The cost of these titillations?'

The price was outrageous. It stunned him. Yet he knew it would be worth every penny he owned to see Siana wearing these on her wedding night. Right away he purchased the chemise, the drawers and a lace corset designed for pleasure rather than restraint. He added several pairs of finest silk stockings and ribbon garters.

'And the second shop, Edward?'

His frown remained as, uninvited, she added an expensive flagon of perfume.

Lightly, she said, calculating it into his bill, 'A little aphrodisiac, Edward. Although you don't need it, you will enjoy the effect it has on your senses.'

He laughed, flattered by the compliment to his virility. He wondered, for old time's sake, whether she was still attracted to him any more. She was still a beautiful woman. Regretfully, he shook his head. He could wait another week. With Siana to satisfy him then, he would not need anyone else.

Elizabeth gave the items to her assistant to package in a pink and grey box, which was embossed with the name of the shop in gold lettering. The packaging was obviously designed to draw attention to the establishment, but he was disinclined to carry something so feminine-looking himself.

He watched the assistant walk away, assessing her desirability out of habit, and frowning slightly at the flicker of animosity he'd surprised in her eyes. She was a handsome, capable-looking woman, in a nondescript way. Too tall for his taste. 'What's your employee's name?'

There was something slightly forced about Elizabeth's smile. 'Her name is Peggy Hastings. She's a widow.'

Edward couldn't recall seeing the woman before, and neither did he recognize her name.

She bobbed him a curtsy when she came back, keeping her eyes lowered. He handed the box to Elizabeth. 'Give them to Siana to wear under her wedding gown.'

Elizabeth had planned to make them a gift to Siana in any case, as part of her bridal outfit. Now Edward had seen them, he'd saved her the expense. She inclined her head. 'A good choice.'

'I'm nervous about this marriage, Elizabeth. Siana is so young and innocent.'

But she wouldn't remain innocent for much longer. The last thing Elizabeth wanted to talk about was Siana's youth. Much as she loved the girl, she knew she would be pleased when she was off her hands now. Siana could think of nothing but her own happiness at the moment, and not a thought was spared for Elizabeth's feelings. She found it hard to maintain her veneer of pleasure for Siana's good fortune when sometimes her jealousy threatened to overwhelm her.

'You have completely won her over, Edward, so I'm sure her youth will be a bonus,' she murmured. 'You have not advised me yet about the idea of a second shop?'

'With the initial sales figures you've just shown me, it cannot fail. I'll put in a word for you with the landlord and give you an advance for stock.'

'The interest?'

He thought for a moment, then smiled. 'If you can repay me within six months of opening, I will forgo interest. After that time any private financial arrangements between us must cease, and you must conduct further business through the bank.'

As they shook hands, their eyes joined in a moment of intimacy. His hand tightened around hers, his thumb caressed her palm for a moment. With the slightest encouragement from her he'd take delight in making love to her right here in the shop. Edward couldn't help himself. He was amoral. He'd enjoy the danger it would pose.

It would mean nothing to him, of course. Nothing but instant gratification of his immediate needs. It was Siana Lewis he loved. Whatever passed between them now, whatever the words spoken, Edward would walk away from her without regret and wed another on Sunday, Elizabeth thought.

She removed her hand from his, turning away as Peggy opened the shop door to admit a late client who was looking for a specific ribbon trimming for a hat.

'Perhaps you're right,' he said softly and, picking up his hat and cane, he departed.

On the dawn of her wedding day Siana was nervous.

Foremost in her mind was the thought that although she loved Edward, that love was based on little more than the enjoyment of his company and the heightened awareness of her senses when she was near him.

She'd never felt like this about his son. Her feelings for Daniel had been innocent compared to the wicked turbulence of body and mind she experienced towards his father.

Edward knew women. He'd set about his pursuit of her with the experience of a seasoned womanizer, using every weapon available to him in a manner so blatant that she'd overlooked his ruthlessness in the excitement of the chase. His wickedness appealed to her and she was slightly ashamed of her weakness.

Now she was nearly his – and at least she would have the respectability of marriage. No one could call her whore any longer.

She caressed the little silver cross at her throat, which

294

had escaped her stepbrother's near rape of her. Odd that such a nasty incident had brought herself and Edward together and had led to marriage. Though why Edward had been on that road at that time escaped her, for it led only to the shell of the cottage and, beyond, to Croxley Farm.

Perhaps he'd been going to see her stepbrother. She shuddered, trying not to think of Tom Skinner, but knowing that whilst he lived she would never feel really safe.

The cross grew warm to the touch. She would wear it on this her wedding day, she thought dreamily and an image grew in her mind.

Her mother danced in a meadow around a stone so old it was covered in green and yellow lichen. Her long, black hair flowed down her back and was wreathed in honeysuckle. She was singing, her voice high and full of joy.

A cloud passed over the sun. There was danger! Siana tried to call out to Megan to warn her, but her voice was strangled in her throat and all she could do was croak.

She saw him then, striding over the long grass, his face full of purpose, his body full of power.

Her mother saw him too. She stopped to stare at him.

'Pagan!' he screamed out. 'The Lord wants me to punish you.' And his eyes were burning . . . burning . . .

Megan began to run but the Lord's messenger caught up with her, wrapping his powerful arms around her and bearing her down into the long grass.

Megan began to cry out a name, 'Siana . . . Siana!'

Siana whimpered. It was not her name that Megan was calling out. It was the name of her great-grandmother, the woman whose name was inscribed on the cross.

'What is it, my dear, are you in pain?' Elizabeth said, coming up behind her and placing a cool hand on her shoulder.

Siana turned her face to the woman and smiled. 'It's wedding day nerves, that's all.'

'You're supposed to be resting,' Elizabeth scolded and, leading her back to the bed, tucked her under the covers.

'I'm much too excited to sleep.'

'My dear, on this occasion you will do exactly as I tell you. The day will be taxing and you will want to look your best.'

'I feel like a witch's cauldron with everything bubbling away inside.'

Elizabeth kissed her. 'Close your eyes and count the bubbles, make each one a pleasant wish and it will all come true.'

She watched the girl close her eyes and, in a little while, was rewarded with the sight and sound of deep and even breathing.

Tears filled Elizabeth's eyes. Siana was no longer the pinch-faced little creature she'd first met. She was glowing with health and possessed of such innocence, anticipation and beauty. Her hair was spread on the pillow like a dark cloud, her lashes rested on skin so translucent and fine the colour on her cheekbones was the merest tint of pink.

Edward would sit and watch her sleep from this day on. Edward would change her whilst he loved her, so in time all that was ethereal and fey in her would become earthbound.

She went through to the dressing room and began to lay out the girl's wedding finery. First the under-garments Edward had chosen for her. Virginal white, they were designed to incite the male into possession. Siana had not seen them yet.

Next the gown. It was a drift of pale lavender silk over layers of tulle petticoats. The gown was simple, the lace shawl neckline falling over narrow sleeves tapering to a puff at the wrist. The veil was a cascade of lilac silk drifting like mist from a tiara of white silk flowers worn high on the crown of her head. The same flowers decorated the hem of the veil as it spiralled to below the waist line.

Siana would look like a beautiful water sprite and, although Elizabeth had instructed Edward to wear a lilac waistcoat and stock, it was the only hint he would get of the vision to be presented to him at the church.

He had sent his carriage and an escort for them. It had arrived the night before. The coach gleamed. The escort and driver would wear full livery for the occasion, the horses would wear white plumes on their heads and halters of flowers would be placed around their necks before they reached the church.

Josh would escort his sister into the church. No longer a child but not yet a man, he would be uncomfortable in his suit of fine clothes and self-conscious in the role as he gave his sister to a man who'd flayed the skin from his back. He'd stood his ground over that, determined to act his part, as was his right. Siana had backed Josh against Edward's wishes – a decision in which the groom had indulged her.

Siana gave a sigh and turned over. A soft breeze billowed the curtains into the room and the air smelled of hawthorn blossom. It was a well-behaved day, appropriate for a wedding, Elizabeth thought as church bells began to peal in the distance.

Gruffydd Evans was feeling stronger and was allowed out of bed for short periods of time now.

Today, he had the strength to struggle into his clothes, now clean and repaired by the nimble fingers of the good Mrs Leeman. He pulled on the new boots supplied by Reverend White, then he removed them because they pinched his toes. He didn't need them anyway.

His long beard was white and clean, free of tangles because the housekeeper had given him a brush made of bristles to keep it groomed with. He also smelled clean, as though the sin had been washed from his body, if not his soul.

There had been much activity at the church for two days now. Women had gone in and out with buckets and cloths. Windows had been polished to a high shine. Armloads of flowers and garlands had been carried in.

The local squire was taking a bride for himself, it seemed.

Reverend White walked around muttering to himself as he practised the service of marriage, using different inflections until, to Gruffydd's ear, it sounded too perfect to be heartfelt. Mrs Leeman, wearing a wide smile, had asked him just ten minutes earlier if he thought her hat was becoming.

'It's a wonderful creation of a hat for the first Sunday

of May and, surely to goodness, God's creatures will smile on you,' he told her. And indeed, it was a wonderful hat, decorated as it was with a pair of humming birds, wings outstretched and nesting on a drift of dried white heather for luck.

Mrs Leeman smiled, dismissing his extravagant compliment, but pleased by it nevertheless. ''Tis only a simple hat. Someone will be along later to give you your dinner. Annie, it is. Her who helps out with the cleaning. Not that she's much good at it, mind, so I have to keep going over it after her. Not like young Siana Lewis. She was thorough.' The humming birds sprang about in agitation as she bobbed her head and said almost to herself, 'And to think she be marrying the squire now . . . fancy.'

Gruffydd's ears pricked up. A peasant marrying the gentry, is it? And one with a Welsh name. Siana Lewis, was it? Now, that was interesting. Very interesting indeed, he thought as he positioned himself behind the lace curtain.

Villagers were gathering outside the church now, the women with children on their hips, chattering and laughing. Carriages began to line the lane. Men strutted about, confident-looking in peacock clothes. Women swayed gracefully, their waists like stalks, their hats blooming into flowers atop their heads.

'Ah, the vanity of it all,' he whispered, watching Mrs Leeman march through them all, her humming birds bobbing iridescently as if they were trying to launch themselves into the air.

Gruffydd did so love a wedding, and this one seemed especially interesting. He went downstairs, his legs wobbling from the unaccustomed exercise. His cane took his weight as he let himself out and carefully moved towards the small door at the back of the church, enjoying the feel of the dirt and grass beneath his feet.

The gravestones glistened bone white in the sun. Dust to dust, ashes to ashes. He passed the grave of Megan and Bill Skinner and their newly born son, locked six feet under in a grisly embrace. The world was renewing itself, and that was how it should be, he thought, as he let himself into the church.

The eyes of Jesus gazed at him from the cross, accusing him.

The reverend was on his knees. 'May the sinners repent and find salvation in your house, Lord.'

Amen, Gruffydd thought as he slipped past him. Climbing a short set of stairs, he crawled under a curtain into the pulpit, where he sat on the floor and stared through the lacework of the carving.

The church began to fill up.

Siana was trembling as they approached the church. She felt different today, as if another person lived inside her skin.

'A right pair of toffs we be,' Josh said, making her smile.

Elizabeth, dressed in a soft cream ensemble, alighted first. After arranging the skirt of Siana's gown for the umpteenth time, she kissed her on the cheek and proceeded into the church, slipping into a back pew, where Daisy was seated with the maid, Rosie, in case her teething problems made her fretful.

Siana saw the usher inside the door signal to someone.

'You can always change your mind,' Josh said

quietly. 'I be making enough to keep us now if we was careful, I reckon.'

She gave him a quick hug. 'Don't talk daft, our Josh.'

'I reckon our mam would be right proud of you this day.'

'I reckon she would be proud of us both, Josh Skinner. You look like a dandy, that you do. A right handsome devil too. The girls will be after you like a flock of seagulls in a couple of years.'

'That'll make me feel a flaming twerp.' He ran a finger round his shirt collar, easing it away from his neck, then offered her his arm and said gruffly, 'Come on, girl, the sooner you be turned into Lady Forbes the sooner I can go home.'

There was a collective intake of breath as they proceeded down the aisle. Siana hoped her legs would carry her all the way to Edward, who stood in solitary splendour waiting for her.

The enormity and solemnity of this moment suddenly occurred to her and she hesitated, but Edward had such a tender smile on his lips that she was filled to the brim with courage. What he had told her had become reality. Not many men in his position would take a girl like her in marriage. He truly loved her, and she was humbled by the knowledge.

Then she was by his side, her hand safely clasped in his, and the words were being said that would bind them together as husband and wife.

'Dearly beloved, we are gathered together in the sight of God, and in the face of this congregation, to join this man and this woman in holy matrimony . . .'

Gruffydd gazed at the bride, entranced. She had flowers in her hair, like those Megan Lewis had worn. But this was not Megan Lewis. The girl was too young. This was Megan's child. This was the fruit of his loins – his sin.

But what was she doing, tying herself to a man old enough to be her father?

'I require you both, as ye will answer at the dreadful day of judgement when the secrets of all hearts shall be disclosed . . .'

Gruffydd whimpered as the pain in his chest came.

'. . . that if either of you knows any impediment why ye may not be joined in matrimony, ye do now confess it . . .'

The preacher rose, his arms raised high. His voice rang out. 'I confess before the Lord to the sin of fornication. I was tempted by the pagan woman and the result stands before the altar. All bear witness that Siana Lewis is my daughter. To atone for her mother's wantonness, she must remain pure in body and heart. I will not allow her to marry this man, who looks upon her with lust in his heart.'

There was not a sound as everyone gazed at him. Power came, first filling his chest and arms, then his whole body, with a pain so great it was hard not to gasp as he embraced it.

Peace and forgiveness came in a shining white light. He toppled forward.

From the very back of the church, Mrs Leeman cried out as Gruffydd Evans landed at Siana's feet. He was face down, his arms outstretched as if worshipping her. Had Siana but known it, the soles of his feet were sad-looking, dusty and callused from the miles they'd tramped to find her.

Giving a startled gasp, she was about to kneel to assist the man when Edward's hand closed under her elbow, preventing it. He turned to beckon to Francis.

Francis stepped forward, felt for the man's pulse and shook his head slowly from side to side. 'His heart is beating strongly enough. A seizure of some sort, brought on by the excitations of Reverend White's sermonizing, no doubt.'

Siana couldn't quite stifle a giggle at Francis's words.

'Have him removed,' Edward said calmly.

She whispered, 'He said he was my father?'

Edward frowned as two men stepped forward to carry the body away. 'The man was obviously deranged.'

Siana gazed at Richard White. 'Do you know what his name is?'

In his church, in front of the altar, before his God and his congregation, and especially before his benefactor, who was frowning ominously now, Richard White lied. 'He was but a poor wandering soul I gave sustenance to.'

Edward's brow cleared. 'Good man. Let us proceed with the ceremony, shall we?'

Richard cleared his throat.

'Wilt thou have this woman to thy wedded wife, to live together after God's ordinance in the holy estate of matrimony? Wilt thou love her, comfort her, honour, and keep her in sickness and in health; and, forsaking all other, keep thee only unto her, so long as ye both shall live?'

Edward answered firmly. 'I will.'

18

The last carriage had gone. Outside, the flares illumi-
nating the carriageway were sputtering out one by one.
The last guest had departed.

The reception had been beyond Siana's expectations, with dancing and food fit for a queen. Francis had
partnered her in a dance, but it was not the Francis
she'd always known. This was a stiff and formal man,
who wouldn't quite meet her eye and called her 'my
lady' in a mocking tone that made her aware of her
humble background. Above all else, that made her ache
with the wound of it, for she knew she'd somehow lost
his friendship.

Elizabeth had not attended the reception, neither had
Josh. They'd left her to her new life, cut her adrift in a sea
of strangers, there to float or to sink. During the evening
she'd maintained a confident façade she didn't feel, to
earn the approval of Edward, her husband. She'd felt the
weight of his eyes following her, watching her performance. His expression every time they exchanged a
glance signalled either his approval or his disapproval. It
had been a nerve-racking time.

Now she was waiting. Waiting for what? His pleasure? How did real ladies behave? Should she ring for a maid . . . did she even have one? Perhaps she should undress and get into bed? That thought alone made her blush. He might think that too forward. She would wait, she decided – wait for Edward to tell her what to do.

Siana was alone in a room of splendid proportions. Several candles were arranged in groups of softly-coloured glass holders. Their gentle glow reached out to all the corners of the room. The chamber was decorated in the softest of lilacs, the bed and window hangings were of embossed brocade threaded through with silver.

There was a large cupboard in which her gowns were already laid flat, in possession of the many sliding trays. They slept on their backs, elegant and empty. How pretty they were, though. How expensive. The cost of any one of them would have kept a labourer's family in food for several weeks.

The dressing table contained perfume and cosmetic creams. There were silver-backed brushes, a comb and hand mirror, already monogrammed with her new initials. Her new jewellery box, lacquered and inlaid with mother-of-pearl and decorated with ornate silver hinges, sat in solitary splendour. She flipped open the lid. Her diamond earrings and headband glittered coldly on a tray.

Her pearls were also there, cleaned and restrung, little incandescent moons. She picked them up, running their flawless perfection through her fingers. After that stupid, childish incident where she'd thrown them at Edward, they were still pure and unsullied. Like her.

Everything smelled new. The mattress awaited the imprint of her body, the pillows her head. The velvet on the chair was uncrushed. She sensed Elizabeth's hand in the furnishing of this room. Lilac had always been Elizabeth's favourite colour for her.

There was an atmosphere of sadness in the room, like a sigh of regret which had never been expended. It surrounded her, so that her skin absorbed it and it prickled just under the surface.

The silvered surface of the long mirror presented a bland reflection, another room captured inside. Siana moved towards it, gazing at her own reflection, pale and unsure. She seemed to be looking at someone else standing on the other side of the glass. She didn't know this girl in her splendid gown, only the peasant child looking out through her eyes.

She gazed at the ring on her finger, two golden hands clasped for ever in a circle. She spread her fingers wide. Her hands were soft, the calluses of yesterday gone.

Opening a trunk, she took out her night attire and laid the voluminous white cotton nightdress and nightcap carefully on the bed.

Someone chuckled. She turned to find Edward standing at the open door to the adjoining room. Barefoot, he was dressed only in his trousers and his shirt, open at the neck. He carried two glasses filled with champagne.

A few steps brought him to stand in front of her. He gazed silently at her for a moment, then handed her a glass. 'Your servant, Lady Forbes. Shall we drink a toast to a happy and fruitful marriage?'

The wine was delicious and she drank every drop. He'd hardly touched his when he set it down on a table. Cupping her face in his hands, he kissed her so gently she melted with the love she felt for him.

When he reached out to loosen the tiny buttons on her bodice, his lips brushed against her shoulders and he licked delicately at the rise of her breasts. Next the skirt and petticoat were discarded, his fingers sure on the fastenings when hers would have fumbled. He sucked in a deep breath and turned her round to face the mirror, his arms circling her from behind.

She gazed into the eyes of his reflection as he caressed her body, his fingertips sliding over the silk. Her heart was beating like a drum. The laces of her corset were loosened, the garment discarded. Her breasts sprang free, the nubs eager to harden and tingle against his palms.

Her breath shortened, becoming a little gasp of pleasure as his fingers slid inside the flap of her drawers to seek out the treasure they kept hidden. He smiled and gently bit her shoulder.

Siana hardly noticed when the drawers pooled around her ankles, when her chemise followed the drawers to reveal her in nothing but stockings and ribbon garters.

Behind her, Edward surged hard against the cleft in her buttocks. 'How beautiful you are naked, my petite one.' He pulled the combs from her hair and it tumbled to her waist in a gleaming dark torrent, releasing the perfume Elizabeth had touched against her scalp.

His hand moved against her, inside her, until she was slick and moist and her eyes were closed with the ecstasy

of it. Her knees were weak with wanting . . . wanting . . .
As they buckled he caught her up in his arms and carried
her to the bed, throwing the night-dress and bonnet aside.

'Hush,' he said when she was about to speak, as he
discarded his clothes and stood before her, proud in his
manhood. She reached out to caress her finger gently
against the silky skin.

He shuddered and fell to his knees. Cupping her feet
in his hands, his lips found the soles and he gently bit
each arch. As if a fuse had been lit, fire crackled up her
legs to explode into flame in her pelvis. She no longer
felt like being passive and gave a small gasp of pleasure
and impatience.

Tangling hands in his hair, she dragged his head up.
'I cannot accept all this pleasure and give nothing in
return. What must I do?'

'On this occasion, nothing, my darling. Just allow me
to savour your enjoyment of this night when you
become a woman.' Lowering his head again, he kissed
her stomach and thighs, and a moment later flicked his
tongue in a flurry of the most intimate of caresses.

Her pelvis arched and her spine contracted as
exquisite pleasure teased through her. Swiftly, he took
advantage of her helpless state to slide up her stomach
and pin her with his body.

Siana felt pain then. Everything in her was raw, and
aroused to the point of acceptance. She was helpless,
naked and throbbing, like a sacrifice spread out on an
altar waiting for the knife to plunge and skewer her. She
tensed, placing her hand against his chest to push him
away and bring her thighs together.

He made a short, angry sound in his throat. His arm came under one of her knees, lifting it so it wouldn't impede this first moment of his possession of her. She felt the power of his muscles as they bunched and tightened.

Her initial resistance was plundered by a firmly pressured thrust of possession that caused her to draw in a sharp breath. Then the disagreeable sensation was lost in wave upon wave of pleasure, until her mewing cries became a gasping surrender – until her senses were absorbed in the pummel and thrust of the urgency of his release.

They lay entwined for a short while, her face burrowed against his shoulder. Presently he lifted himself to one elbow and gazed at her. 'Did I hurt you, my sweeting?'

'Just a little . . . at first, but the pain was soon over.'

He nodded and smiled to himself, seemingly pleased by her admission.

She traced a finger over his lips, blushing as she admitted, 'I thought . . . that which occurred between us was enjoyable in the extreme.'

'I am not without finesse in such matters, but that was an introduction only, a quick meal to ease my hunger and to sharpen yours. There are many variations of making love, and from now on our intimacy will become a feast of pleasuring.'

Her body reacted positively to the thought. And later when they made love for the second time she found the long-drawn-out saturation of pleasure almost unbearable, so when she finally found release, she throbbed with the ecstatic relief of it.

She fell asleep almost at once in his arms. Edward gazed down at her, taking pleasure in the lips swollen from his kisses, her breasts pert and proud against his chest and the moist, inviting venus pressing against his thigh.

He wanted more of her, but he was no longer a young man and the effort of making love twice within the hour had taxed him. He also knew she would be tender in the morning. Still, he was pleased with his bride. She'd enjoyed the act of loving, unconsciously displaying a willingness to participate in his pleasure.

Sliding her tousled head carefully onto the pillow he eased himself out of her bed and fetched one of the candles closer to examine the sheet. Not that he doubted his judgement. He just wanted to confirm it. He smiled in satisfaction when he saw the small stain, and walked through the connecting door to his own room, leaving her to her dreams.

Siana was disoriented for a moment when she woke. Sun came through the curtains, causing moving shafts and triangles of intense light to burn against the wall.

Then she remembered and smiled, stretching her body like a cat in the sun until the energy in her muscles came alive.

She felt like running amongst the flowers on the hills. Leaping from her bed, she drew the curtains aside, then took a quick step back.

Her room occupied a corner of the house. Thick iron bars stretched from top to bottom of the window frame. Between them and below her, she could see the garden in front of the house. The flower beds were divided by ribbon hedges into an intricate knotted design. The carriageway formed a circle around the beds before meandering through yew trees and lilac bushes to a pair of huge iron gates.

A sudden melancholy filled her. From behind these barred windows escape was so near, yet so far. Behind her, somebody seemed to sigh. She spun around to see nothing but her own nakedness reflected in the depths of the mirror. Goosebumps climbed up her arms to tremble at the nape of her neck.

There was a knock at the door. Rosie called out as Siana snatched the cotton nightgown from the floor to pull it over her head, ''Tis me, Lady Forbes.'

Lady Forbes! What had happened to Miss Siana, she thought, as she scrambled back on the bed and pulled the covers up to her chin. 'Come in.'

Rosie carried in a jug of hot water. 'Master said to wake you at ten. You're to breakfast and bathe and be ready to accompany him to the horse sales. He said you're to wear that dark-green gown and matching bonnet.'

'Horse sales?'

Rosie pulled back the covers. 'Best hurry, my lady.'

It was then Siana saw the smear of blood on the sheets. 'Oh,' she said, feeling somewhat dismayed. 'My menses have arrived early.'

Rosie smiled as she whispered, 'It's not your menses. It's the bride's way of telling a man he's collected his due on his wedding night.'

'Collected his due?'

'It's your virginity, see. The sign informs your

husband that no man has had his pleasure of you afore him, if you see what I mean.'

Siana did see what she meant. Her face flamed as she clutched at the servant's wrist and said in a horrified voice, 'Promise you'll not tell anyone else, Rosie.'

'Don't you fret, my dear, I'll change the sheet right now and wash it myself.' And Siana didn't notice the woman's secret smile as she turned away.

Siana couldn't meet Edward's eye at first, though she could sense his intimate grin.

'It's a lovely morning,' she said awkwardly when they were alone and settled in the carriage.

'It is, and your blushes are very sweet.' He lifted her chin with his cane. 'Try to keep your back erect, your shoulders back and your chin slightly elevated, other-wise the gown will lose its shape.'

She wanted him to kiss her and smiled at the thought. 'Are you going to correct me in everything I do, Edward?'

'You were not brought up to this life so I shouldn't be at all surprised.'

She frowned.

'Your expression should remain pleasant, but serene. Always you must appear to be graceful and agreeable for your husband to look upon.'

Detecting a teasing note in his voice, she flicked her eyes up to the tawny warmth of his and giggled. 'How can I appear graceful when my thoughts are less than serene? You're being an ogre, Edward Forbes. Would it be seemly for me to kiss my husband good morning?'

He chuckled. 'On this occasion I'll allow it. Keep it chaste, though, otherwise I'll be obliged to make love to

312

you in the carriage whilst we're on a public highway. That would be most unseemly.'

'Especially if we were discovered.' She laughed as she flung herself onto his lap and covered his face with kisses.

It was a less than immaculate pair who descended from the carriage later. Siana shook the creases from her skirt and straightened her bonnet. 'Was that graceful enough for you?' she whispered in his ear.

He grinned. 'The whole exercise was totally disgraceful. You are a completely wicked woman.'

'Then a man whose ways are as dissolute as yours should serve me well.'

The horse market was a place of great excitement and colour. There were not many women around, but a great many men. Edward seemed to have brought her there to be admired, she realized. Indeed, there were acknowledgements from some she recognized as being guests at their wedding the day before. Many winked knowingly at Edward or patted him on the back while their covert glances at her made her blush, and Edward chuckle.

She began to feel like one of the horses on parade, except the men stopped short of discussing the strength of her fetlocks, the length of her tail or the width of her rump. In front of her, at least!

The glossy, black-coated horse Edward bought for himself could have done with a little schooling, Siana thought, as it flattened its ears and kicked out at the groom.

It was a large horse, recently gelded. The beast

seemed difficult and unpredictable in temperament, but sound of wind and fleet of foot. When Edward learned its pedigree was connected to the ancestry of the mare who'd been so cruelly maimed, that fact alone swayed him in its favour.

He turned to her. 'We must find a mount for you.'

'I've only ever ridden astride a donkey.'

'You must learn to ride like a lady.' He stopped in front of a pen containing three mares huddled together. He contemplated them in silence.

When Siana clicked her tongue, one of them turned to gaze languidly at her. The beast was thin, but she had melting brown eyes and dark eyelashes. Siana clicked again and held out a hand. The horse detached herself from the others and ambled over to investigate, her soft muzzle whuffling moistly into her palm. The fall of her tangled mane and tail was almost black. Siana smiled and rubbed the dull hair along the length of her nose. The mare closed her eyes in contentment.

'Can I have this one, Edward?'

'The dark bay?' He sounded surprised. 'She's out of condition. Are you sure you wouldn't prefer the grey? She's a much prettier horse.'

'This one likes me and she's affectionate.'

'A horse is not a pet.' He turned to the groom. 'Your opinion on the bay?'

'She's been neglected, but it wouldn't take long to bring her condition up, sir.' He consulted the paper handed to him by the agent. 'Irish blood stock. She looks to be a docile creature.' The horse was walked up and down to inspect her gait. Her ribs were too obvious

314

under her flesh, but she stepped daintily, her head held proud and her step high.

'A pretty gait,' Edward murmured to himself.

Siana hovered anxiously by the two men as the various parts of the bay's anatomy were discussed. The horse lifted her upper lip and bared her teeth obligingly at the touch of the groom's probing fingers.

Siana giggled at the sight and when Edward turned towards her she held her breath. She let it out when he smiled and nodded. 'She will do you.'

Siana slid her arms around the horse's neck and hugged her. 'We must think of a name for you then.'

'Her official name is Keara Aisling, meaning, dark dream,' the groom said.

'Keara it is, then.' Her eyes shining, Siana turned to Edward. She felt like hugging him as well.

He anticipated it for he reached out to caress her face, saying drily, 'You seem to have sprouted some horse-hair whiskers. I would suggest you resist cuddling animals until a more appropriate place and time.'

She slanted him a glance. 'Whatever you wish, Edward.'

Whilst Siana was at the horse sale with her husband, Hannah Collins was being turned out of Croxley Farm by Edward's steward.

'You ain't got no right to do this,' she shouted. 'The tenancy of this farm belongs to my brother, Tom Skinner. I be minding it until he gets his strength back.'

'Tom Skinner's almost dead meat and your man's deserted you,' Jed Hawkins said callously. 'The farm's going to rack and ruin and the squire wants you gone.

You have until the end of the week. If I come back and find you on the property after that I'll have you charged with trespass and thrown in the watch house.'

'It's the doing of that ungrateful wife of his,' Hannah whined to herself after he left. 'After all the kindness us Skinners showed her, taking her in and making her one of the family.'

She picked up a boning knife and went out to slaughter the pigs and chickens. The butcher would give her good money for the carcasses once they were trimmed – and no questions asked.

Two days later, Abbie Ponsonby saw Hannah move through the village with her bundle on her back, then she and her husband, Rudd, borrowed the undertaker's cart, loaded their worldly goods onto it and moved into the farm. None of the villagers lent her a hand. She was known to have the squire's ear now, and although they didn't begrudge her the good fortune, they resented the sly way she'd gone about getting it.

Croxley Farm had been left almost uninhabitable, Hannah had seen to that. She hadn't dared set fire to the place, though, as was her original inclination.

The kitchen was splattered with the dried blood and entrails from the slaughtered animals. A door left open had invited the blow flies inside, so maggots crawled on every surface. Chicken feathers were thrown about, mattresses stained, and every surface smeared with stinking substances into which the chicken feathers had stuck.

Abbie Ponsonby recoiled from the mess. Settling her family down in the barn in the charge of the oldest girl, she set pots and kettles to boil on an open fire and rolled up her sleeves.

Sensing the friendlier fate in store than that inflicted on the pigs, the milking cow ambled down from the edge of the forest, lowing painfully as its swollen and leaking udders swung from side to side. The children took turns emptying its burden into a pail, laughing at their good fortune. A cup full of the creamy liquid was handed out to each and the churn fetched from the wagon. The boys set the hens free from their wooden prison to forage for food.

Rudd was given his orders. He and his two eldest sons walked the fields and grubbed some taties and carrots from the earth. They were put to boil in a pot with an onion and some beef dripping for flavour.

Soon, the sound of scrubbing was heard. The laundry tub was put to good use as the mattresses were emptied of straw and the covers put to soak.

Later that night, Abbie Ponsonby gave birth to her ninth child, a boy. The infant slipped easily out of her like a lamb from a ewe. The family gathered round her in the barn, lanterns held aloft. They smiled at the infant, who bawled lustily back at his welcoming committee.

'He's a right bonny lad,' Rudd said, beaming proudly at all his bonny lads and lasses. 'What shall us call him, then?'

'He must be named after the squire,' Abbie said firmly. 'For the man must be honoured for giving our family a decent roof over us heads.'

Hannah slept behind a hedge that night. In the morning she set out for the infirmary. It was the first time she'd seen her brother since the accident. She shuddered at his scarred, pig-like face, at the smell rising from his stump.

His eyes gleamed malevolently from the ruins of his face.

'Squire has given the tenancy of Croxley Farm to the Ponsonbys,' she told him. 'It's Siana who did this to us. If she hadn't taken up with the squire he would have married that Isabelle. Then Ben wouldn't have left me. They took my little George with them as well. Turned him against his own ma, she has.' Self-pitying tears sprang to her eyes. 'I'm going to pay that blubber-cheeks back for what she's done, just see if I don't.'

Tom didn't know who she was talking about. It didn't really matter. He'd take his revenge on them all now he had Hannah to help him. What's more, he'd found a way of getting in and out of the infirmary at night. But he needed help, and if he didn't start taking his revenge soon, he never would. The doc had brought him a peg leg and crutch to practise on, but Tom knew there was nothing more the man could do for him. He could smell the rot forming in his own stump.

He beckoned his sister forward and snuffled, 'There's a few people I've got to settle a score with too. That wife of mine to start with. But we needs a horse and cart for I can't walk far.'

'Our Josh has got the mule from the farm, and a right fancy rig to go with it.'

'I ain't going near that damned mule unless it's to slit its poxy throat. Josh wouldn't let us have it anyway. There's plenty of work horses in the fields this warm weather. One should carry us both.'

'Josh is living with Elizabeth in Poole now, I hears.'

'That hoity-toity madam has set herself up in a fancy shop. Where she got the money from, that's what I want to know.'

And as Hannah let all the venom pour out of her, Tom sucked it into his brain to add to the cesspool of his own discontent.

Siana soon realized that, although Edward adored her, the majority of the staff treated her with an air of disdain. They were polite, so she could not complain to Edward about rudeness, but they were slow to obey any requests she made. Sometimes, they were ignored altogether. Refreshment ordered often didn't arrive or, when it did, it was so late the tea was lukewarm and the accompanying food stale.

The animosity stemmed from the housekeeper, Mrs Pawley, who seemed to regard her position in the household as inviolable, and went to great lengths to let Siana know it.

'I was personal maid to the squire's first wife,' she said one day. 'She was as well bred and as beautiful as the day was long. Sir Edward loved her truly. When their infant died she sickened from grief and eventually died herself. He kept her room as a shrine to her memory until recently. I'm surprised he put you in that room.'

'Why shouldn't he when I'm his wife?' she reminded the woman.

Ethel Pawley shrugged. 'There are those who say you remind him of her. I say, blood will out. Sometimes

319

I goes up to the attic to look at her portrait. There's a wide gulf between those born to a life of luxury and those who ape their betters.'

'I'm not aping anyone. I didn't even know the woman.'

'Sometimes I can feel Lady Patricia's presence, all sad and lonely. She was jealous of any woman the squire looked at twice. She had the madness in her. Be careful her ghost doesn't come creeping in to harm you when you be asleep.'

Remembering the bars on her windows, cold crept up Siana's spine at the malice in the woman's voice. 'Best you remember you're a servant, Mrs Pawley.'

'Oh, the squire won't get rid of me, *Lady Forbes*. I've bin here too long.'

'Edward,' she said to him the same evening. 'I don't feel comfortable with the bars on my windows. It feels like I'm in a prison cell. Can they be removed?'

He subjected her to an astute scrutiny. 'Have the servants been gossiping?'

'They resent me, I think.'

'Of course they resent you, but you must learn to handle them. Make an example of one if need be.' Picking up her hand, he turned it over to kiss the pulse at her wrist. She felt it leap against his mouth. 'You're being fanciful, Siana mine. The bars were put there to prevent Patricia from harming herself, not to keep her in. Had she not been ill, there would have been no need for them.'

'And we would not now be man and wife.'

'That's true, my dear. I would be in the unenviable position of being in love with you and not being able to do anything about it.' He pulled her onto his lap, gazing into her eyes in a way that suggested he could see into her very soul. 'Do you doubt that I adore you?'

She smiled. 'How can I doubt it when the inclination to prove it is so strong in you? You are a lion who has conquered me completely.'

He chuckled. 'It's flattering for a man of my age to be complimented on his prowess. You are a delight. Tonight, this lion will take his little cat into his lair and make her purr with pleasure. It will be a very different experience, I promise.'

And a very exciting one, as she found out later.

The housekeeper wasn't going to make things easy for Siana, mistress of the manor or not.

'She bain't be no lady, that's for sure,' Ethel told her sister Agnes. 'Not only do she be a peasant girl, she be a bastard and all, and not the virginal bride she was supposed to be. I took a look at the sheets the day after her wedding night. Not a trace of blood to be seen. She'd bin had afore, that one.'

A few days later Agnes was in her usual begging corner when she heard footsteps coming along the pavement and saw the blurred outline of a woman – a maid by the looks of her. 'I can tell thee the latest gossip from the manor for a ha'penny piece,' she crooned.

There was the clink of a coin in the cup.

A moment later the woman scoffed, 'Anyone could say that. How do I know it's not lies?'

'It'll cost you another ha'penny to find out.'

There was another clink.

''Tis like this,' the blind woman said, leaning forward and speaking confidentially so no one else got the benefit of the information without paying. 'My sister, Ethel Pawley, is head housekeeper at Cheverton Manor . . .'

When Rosie got back to the manor, she slipped into the steward's office and told him what she'd heard.

Jed Hawkins smiled. 'Thanks, Rosie. Make sure the mistress gets to hear of it.'

She held out her hand. 'That cost me a penny piece.'

'No doubt the squire will make sure you get a bonus in your wages as well. You're a loyal servant to him, Rosie, and he appreciates loyalty.'

'I happen to like the mistress as well. She loves the squire and I'm not having some bitter old crone plant doubts in his mind about her.'

'Oh, she won't do that. The squire ain't daft. He knows what's going on. He's been waiting for an opportunity for the lady of the house to show her mettle, and I reckon this will do it.'

Siana had just come back from a walk with Daisy when Rosie told her what was being said about her. Her lips tightened. *Take control,* her husband had said, *make an example of one of them.*

She sent the child up to the nursery with the maid to have her tea. 'Ask Mrs Pawley and the under-house-keeper to attend me at once,' she said to Rosie, her face flaming with anger and embarrassment.

She had a long wait. Finally, the two women arrived. Mrs Pawley gazed at her almost insolently. 'You wanted to see me, madam?'

'Yes, Pawley. It has been brought to my notice that

one of your relatives is selling information of a personal nature about me in the streets. The gossip is of a distasteful type that could only have come from you. Hand me your house keys please. You are dismissed from our service.'

Mrs Pawley paled and blustered as she unhooked the keys from her belt. 'All lies. We'll see what the squire has to say about this.'

'He'll be most displeased by your disloyalty. If I were you, I'd leave the grounds before he hears of it.'

She waited until Mrs Pawley left the room, then turned to the other woman. 'What's your name?'

'Maisie Roberts, my lady.'

'I'm displeased with the service you're being paid to provide. In fact, I find most of the domestic staff disrespectful and lazy.'

The woman dropped a hasty curtsy. 'I'm sorry, Lady Forbes. 'Twas Pawley. She made it hell for anyone who went against her, begging your pardon for my coarse language.'

Siana tried not to laugh as the woman bobbed from the knee again, nearly tripping over the edge of the rug in her haste. She handed Maisie Roberts the house keys. 'I expect the household to be run properly from now on, otherwise there will be further changes made. Do you understand, Maisie?'

'Yes, my lady.'

'You may leave, then. I'll expect refreshments in fifteen minutes.'

Ten minutes after the woman left, Edward sauntered in, saying casually, 'You look flushed, my love.'

She laughed at his transparency. 'Don't pretend you don't know I've been practising my Lady of the Manor role. I imagine Mrs Pawley confronted you like an agitated hen.'

'More like a whipped cur, my dear. Well done.'

Siana felt anxious now her temper had cooled, but she was willing to argue with him if need be. 'Tell me you did not allow that woman to stay. She has spread malicious gossip about me. About us.'

'It must be extremely malicious if your agitation is an indication. Pray, tell me what is it, my dearest,' he coaxed. 'Perhaps I can refute it by proclamation in the market place.'

'I would be mortified.' Noticing his grin, she began to laugh. 'Damn you, Edward!'

Crossing to where she stood he took her in his arms and kissed her until her senses spun. Softly, he said, 'You and I know it is all lies, my dearest.'

She blushed and slid her arms around his neck. He held her against him, his hands under her buttocks as they gazed into each other's eyes. Presently, he kissed her again.

Maisie knocked and, getting no answer, walked inside. Placing the tray on the nearest table she backed silently away. She was grinning as she hurried back to the kitchen with her own piece of gossip.

19

The trouble in the district continued, with livestock being maimed and outbuildings and haystacks torched. The landowners established a band of burly vigilantes. They rode abroad at night, scattering any gatherings or shouldering their way menacingly between the labourers in the taverns. They slapped dangerously solid truncheons against their palms and sometimes cracked the heads of those foolhardy enough to challenge them.

Lawbreakers were dealt with severely. The courts sentenced them to long periods of transportation.

In the penal colonies of New South Wales and Van Diemen's Land, those who were there of their own free will – worthy gentlemen for the most part – were granted large tracts of land. Referred to as the squatocracy, they welcomed the influx of free labour with open arms because they needed men to help clear their acres and create their estates.

The change to the three-field agricultural system in England had seen many farm labourers thrown out of work in the past. Some had drifted off to the cities, others starved to death or became criminals. Those still left employed in the rural industry were forced to accept low wages and bad conditions. The landowners had expected trouble to fester amongst them, and they hadn't been disappointed.

Edward set extra men to guard the grounds and they patrolled the perimeter wall of the manor at regular intervals. Siana was not allowed to go out without Edward, and when they did go abroad they were accompanied by several outriders.

Siana had expected Elizabeth to call on her, but when she brought it up with Edward he shook his head. 'My dear, of course she will not call. It would be beyond the bounds of propriety.'

'Then I must visit her.'

'That's not possible.'

'But why? She's my friend.'

His mouth tightened. 'It's a friendship you cannot now pursue. I will hear no more of it.'

Mutinously, she opened her mouth, then shut it again, realizing how much scandalous talk would be caused by her maintaining a friendship with Edward's former mistress.

Yet it was obviously within the bounds of propriety for Edward to visit Elizabeth. Sometimes he brought home gifts of intimate apparel for Siana to wear for his pleasure – garments that could have come only from Elizabeth's establishment. She loved the soft colours and sensuous materials, but still she thought she might like to select her own on occasion.

Siana was growing lonely with just Daisy for companionship. Although they had all attended their wedding, the wives of Edward's friends had chosen not to call on her. Neither did she receive invitations to call on them.

Edward had not mentioned the loss of his social life. Nevertheless, she felt she had failed him in some way and went to lay her face against his shoulder one day. 'I'm sorry I've been the cause of you losing friends, Edward.'

'It's not your fault. They're feeling a little awkward at the moment but they will soon come round.' He sighed as he twisted her face up to kiss her. 'I need to visit Croxley Farm today and talk to Rudd Ponsonby. I've heard Croxley was robbed of much of its livestock before the Collins woman left. I've sworn out a warrant for her arrest. Although you're connected to her through marriage, I won't be swayed from a prosecution on this occasion.'

Hannah to be arrested! Her stepsister would probably be transported to New South Wales. Siana thought about it for a moment and decided she didn't really care.

She laughed at Edward's gruff voice and kissed his cheek. 'You're anticipating an argument and I won't give you one.'

He chuckled. 'I must make a note of it in my journal, then.'

She gently bit his ear.

'Perhaps you'd like to come with me,' Edward was saying. 'The journey will provide you with some riding practice over a distance, and you can call on Richard whilst I conduct my business. Would you enjoy that?'

Siana could also visit her mother's grave. Then she

remembered the man who'd fallen from the pulpit in front of her – the man who'd claimed to be her father. He'd had a Welsh accent like her mother, she recalled. How very strange. Perhaps the reverend would have learned a little more about the man's background since.

'Yes . . .' she said slowly. 'I would very much like that.'

Her horse, Keara, was still a bit on the lean side, but the animal's coat gleamed now, and she was an easy horse to ride. Dressed in a black riding habit, Siana hooked her knee over the horn and waited for Edward to mount.

His horse was skittish, but obedient to his master's command. Siana had admired Edward's patience with the gelding as he'd worked to gain its initial trust and respect.

Watching the horse's muscles power under its shining black coat, she knew she would not like to ride him herself. Edward's thighs worked in unison with his mount's movements rather than against them. He was not reckless, yet still he courted danger.

She felt it surrounding him, like a taut and powerful aura. Unpredictable power was part of his nature, she thought in sudden surprise. He rarely told her what to do, but somehow his expectations always became hers. He controlled her without seeming to. She had known him to blatantly enforce his will on her only once, when he'd whipped Josh. When he'd used the punishment to force her into marriage she'd realized how ruthless his underlying nature was, now she acccepted it was part of him.

Since then he'd totally spoiled her – with gifts, jewels and loving. Their life had been harmonious, their unions were exciting and sensuous, and always at his command and, because of his unpredictability, they were often encounters of unusual intensity and variety. Yet, he'd never physically hurt her in any way.

She remembered then that he'd been responsible for Will Hastings's death. Would he have whipped Josh to death if she hadn't stopped him? She thought so. She shivered as his tawny glance met hers.

His slow, intimate smile took her breath away. His thoughts were obvious to her. If Jed Hawkins hadn't been bringing up the rear he'd have probably taken her into the forest and made love to her right there and then.

She grinned at him and he chuckled when she gently fluttered her eyelashes.

He kept his horse reined in next to hers for a while, obviously checking her progress. She automatically straightened her shoulders and tried to maintain a fluid and graceful motion with her own horse. Laughing, he edged his mount ahead.

Aware of the excitement building up inside her, she urged her own mount after him, faster and faster, so the trees became a blur on either side of them. He allowed her to catch him up. For a while they raced neck and neck, then his horse surged forward.

Keara had a good turn of speed, but Siana had not the riding expertise her husband had and her horse was no match for his new gelding. Gradually, she slowed to a canter. Jed caught her up and smiled. 'You're doing well with that horse. You made a good choice and are developing a good seat, considering the short time you've been riding.'

'My husband has a better one,' she said, breathing heavily from the exercise.

'Sir Edward was practically brought up on a horse, of course. His riding is superb.'

So is his love-making, she thought with a smile.

Edward was nowhere to be seen when they rounded the bend. It had rained during the night and, judging by the hoof prints in the damp earth, his horse had lengthened his stride.

They finally came upon him outside Richard's house. His gelding looked as though he had enjoyed the gallop. Edward lifted her down from Keara, pulling her close to kiss her mouth for all to see. 'Richard is expected back soon. His housekeeper will give you refreshment whilst you wait.'

Mrs Leeman was waiting at the door, her face lit up by a beaming smile.

Siana didn't want Mrs Leeman to treat her like a guest. Giving the woman a warm hug she said, 'I'm so happy to see you again. How well you look.'

She had barely finished her tea when a knock came at the door. Siana heard Francis's deep voice and went to greet him, a smile on her face. He was in the process of handing his hat to Mrs Leeman.

She watched him run his fingers through his hair, smiling at the familiar gesture, which although designed to tidy his unruly locks, usually had the opposite effect. A lump came into her throat when she realized how much she missed his company.

'Francis,' she whispered, 'why have you been avoiding me?'

He turned, his mouth wavering somewhere between a smile and a frown. 'Siana!'

Mrs Leeman bustled off towards the kitchen. 'I'll go and prepare some refreshment, Doctor, whilst you attend your patient.'

She seemed to be observing Francis through fresh eyes. He was younger than she remembered. Easily as tall as Edward, he seemed to dominate the room. Had his eyes always been such a clear and penetrating grey? Had he always carried such an aura of energy with him?

Her heart nearly burst with the affection she held for him. She felt like hugging him close but something about him told her not to. 'It's wonderful to see you again, Francis.'

He stepped towards her. Taking her hands in his, he gazed down at her. 'Marriage has brought a bloom to your skin. Are you happy?'

She nodded. 'What of you? You look tired.'

'I was up all night with a sick child. There's been an outbreak of typhoid in the district.'

'Poor, dear Francis. That explains why you haven't been to see me – and I cannot call on you.'

The light died from his eyes and he let go of her hands. 'Excuse me, Lady Forbes, I have work to do.'

'Francis,' she said, wounded by his manner. 'There is no need to be so stiff-mannered with me just because I'm married to Edward.'

'No, of course not. It was stupid of me.' He headed for the stairs. 'My patient is waiting.'

'Reverend White is sick? I thought he was out.'

He turned at the bottom, swivelling gracefully from the waist to stare at her for a moment or two. 'It's not Richard who's my patient. It's the Welsh preacher.' His voice took on a mocking tone. 'Surely you remember him, Siana?'

'How could I forget?' Startled, she put a detaining hand on his sleeve when he was about to mount the stairs. 'Edward said . . . I understood he had died?'

'You understood wrongly. The seizure he suffered has rendered him reluctant to move or speak, a departure from his usual volubility. I think his state is induced by excitations of the mind rather than bodily malaise. His heart is quite strong. Richard and Mrs Leeman are caring for him.'

She fingered the silver cross at her throat. 'He said he was my father.'

Francis nodded. 'There's something I want to show you.' He picked up a walking stick from the hall stand. It was carved with celtic crosses, within which were inscribed the names of different places. At the top, her mother's name was carved into the wood.

'This represents his journey to find his daughter. It starts in this Welsh village – you see – and covers the length and breadth of England. It ends here, in this very last space, in this village. This can be no coincidence. He needs to carve your name here.'

Cold crept up her body as she remembered her mother telling her that her father was a Welsh preacher. She sucked in a deep breath. 'What's this preacher's name?'

'Gruffydd Evans.'

She gave a little cry of anguish. 'My mother spoke of him to me. Take me up to see him, Francis.'

Halfway up the staircase she felt a little dizzy and gazed wordlessly at him. He put an arm round her and she leaned against his body to recover for a moment.

You should have married me.

His thought was so clear, for a moment Siana thought he'd spoken aloud. She gazed at him, astonished.

He gazed back, his expression naked with longing. 'Siana,' he said quietly, tasting her name on his tongue, 'you know, don't you?' The longing in his voice cut her heart into ribbons.

How can I love two men in different ways, and both at the same time, she thought as she nodded. Then his arms were round her and his mouth was pressed against hers in a caress of sublime tenderness. She responded, she couldn't help herself, taking his hunger into her and making it her own.

It was he who pulled away first, the expression on his face stricken. 'Now you know why I cannot come to see you.'

She nodded. 'And we must never speak of this . . . never show what we feel for each other, especially in public.'

A smile touched his mouth. 'Then you *do* feel the same.'

She gently touched his face. 'Edward is good to me. I cannot betray him.'

'My feelings for you are deeper than the mere carnal, my dear. I'll live content with the knowledge that my love is reciprocated, and will neither expect nor encourage you to be unfaithful to your husband.' He was smiling now. 'Let's go and introduce you to your father. It might do him some good to know you are here.'

Gruffydd Evans was lying flat on his back in a white nightshirt, his blue eyes wide open and seemingly studying a crack in the ceiling. He looked like an angel with his flowing white beard and gaunt, pale features.

Francis attended to his doctorly duties, then said into the preacher's ear, 'I have brought your daughter to see you, Gruffydd.'

There was no response.

Moving closer, Siana leaned into his line of vision. 'I am Siana Lewis. My mother was called Megan. Megan is the woman whose name is carved into your walking stick. She is the beginning. You need mine to carve in the space at the end.'

'Alpha and omega.' He chuckled, his long, gaunt body quivered slightly, his eyes focused until she became aware of the power surrounding him. A bony hand closed around her wrist. 'Forgive me my sin, daughter. Only then can I die in peace.'

'But I do not want you to die, not when I've just discovered you. Besides, only my mother can forgive you.'

Francis gave an approving nod at her words.

'Then send the pagan temptress to me at once.'

Anger came in a hot rush of blood through her veins. How dare he blame this on her mother! 'Megan lies in yonder churchyard. She has told me the circumstances of my birth. I see no reason to doubt that she was the victim, you the perpetrator. Lie there and feel sorry for yourself if you wish, sir. I hope my mother rises from her grave, seizes you by the scruff of the neck and gives you the thrashing you so richly deserve for ruining her life.'

'You should not treat a dying man so,' he muttered, in an altogether self-pitying and pathetic manner.

She gave a careless laugh. 'Dying! What makes you think that? Francis assures me that your heart is strong. It's your mind which is at fault. I think you've allowed melancholy to gain the upper hand and are wallowing in it like a hog up to its hams in muck.'

The preacher made a spluttering noise. 'I did not expect to discover a daughter so disrespectful.'

She laughed again, taking pleasure in goading him. 'Respect is something you'll have to earn, my dear papa. If you want to see me again you must learn to be a man instead of a hypocritical and arrogant worm.' She turned and stomped away from him before she slapped him.

Francis followed her down the stairs. He was almost choking on his laughter. 'That was a scene I would not have predicted in a thousand years.'

'Considering the manner of my mother's death, the matter is not one for levity,' she hurled at him. Picking up her skirts, she side-stepped the astonished-looking Mrs Leeman who'd come to investigate what all the fuss was about, thrust open the door and began to run towards the church.

Francis joined her a little later, when her temper had cooled and she was gazing with some perplexity at the headstone erected on her mother's grave. It was fashioned from expensive white marble. Mourned by her daughter,

Lady Edward Forbes. On the line underneath in smaller lettering was stated, and Joshua Skinner and Daisy Skinner. It gave her the impression that she had no name of her own now, and had been deliberately separated from her siblings by name and rank. There was an etching of a dove at the top, carrying a ribbon in its beak. Words unfamiliar to her were inscribed along its length.

'I was insensitive,' Francis said. 'I see too much death in my profession and didn't stop to think.'

'I know you didn't mean it, Francis. What does *requiescat in pace* mean?'

'It's Latin and means, rest in peace.'

Tears touched her eyes. 'My mother deserves to rest in peace, for she had precious little rest whilst she lived. Edward must have had the headstone placed here.' She smiled through her tears. 'He's such a good and loving husband.'

So why did she sound as though she was desperately trying to convince herself of the fact? She avoided the wound exposed in Francis's eyes by her careless remark and was relieved when she caught sight of Richard White coming towards them.

He kissed her on both cheeks, tucking her arm in his as they began to stroll back to the house. 'You look well, my dear.'

'And so do you, Reverend. What do you think, Francis?'

'The good Reverend looks positively resurrected now he has a mission in life. You'll be relieved to know your guest is recovering, Richard.'

Richard's warning look brought a bark of mirthless

laughter from Francis. 'You need battle your conscience no longer. I've taken it upon myself to inform Lady Forbes of the facts.'

'But Edward said—'

'You would do well to remember I'm not accountable for my actions to Edward. In this instance I've put the need of my patient first. I should warn you that it worked, his pride was punctured in the process. Although he may sulk for a while, the self-sacrificing rubbish he usually spouts should cease. But from time to time you might need to remind him he's not humble enough for true martyrdom.'

Siana giggled.

Richard opened his mouth, then thought better of it and shut it again.

Edward had concluded his business and was gazing out of the window at them as they came up the path together. His usual smile was lacking when they went inside and he greeted them a little gruffly, 'You've been gone a long time.'

'Have we? I hadn't noticed. I've been visiting my mother's grave. Thank you for the headstone, Edward. I'm touched by the gesture and the thought behind it.' She crossed to where he stood and kissed him on the cheek.

'You'll have to excuse me,' Francis said stiffly. 'I have other patients to see.'

'Siana has missed your company. You must join us for dinner some time.' Edward slid an arm around her waist and pulled her close, his voice as soft as cream against her ear. 'Mustn't he, my love?'

'Yes, he most certainly must. Perhaps the weekend after next? Can you bring your daughters, Francis? I'm longing to meet them.'

Edward looked sadly reflective for a moment. 'I'd forgotten your delightful children. Of course you must bring them. Daughters are very precious creatures and a father should seize every opportunity to be with them.'

'Then before you learn it from somebody else, Edward, Francis has made me aware that the man upstairs is my father.'

His eyes became flat and inpenetrable, his voice dangerously soft. 'Have you, by God! What prompted you to take the matter into your own hands, Francis?'

Francis picked up his hat. 'If Siana has a father, she deserves to know it.'

'Allow me to be the judge of what my wife does and doesn't deserve to know.'

'Edward? What are you saying? I have a mind of my own and would prefer to decide for myself.' Siana tried to pull away from him, but his hold on her was firm and if she struggled she'd make it too obvious.

The two men were staring at each other now, like a couple of duellists sizing each other up. *Damn, damn!*

Mrs Leeman came in with the tea and, noticing nothing amiss, proceeded to lay out cups and plates. There were several almond tartlets laid out on a plate. The strong smell of almonds seemed to surround her. At first it was pleasant, if strong, then suddenly it became entirely disagreeable and her stomach began to churn. Perspiration dewed her face as nausea attacked her. She was overcome by dizziness.

'Edward,' she murmured as the room began to dissolve.

She heard him swear as she slumped against him.

She came to with a sudden shock as a sharp smell cut into her senses. She was lying on the sofa, a pillow under her ankles. Edward and Francis were leaning over her. Francis was holding a vial of smelling salts to her nose.

Edward looked frantic. 'What's wrong with her?'

'Ugh!' Wrinkling her nose, she knocked the vial away and gasped in a deep breath of air to ease her stinging nostrils.

Francis had an exasperated look. 'Stand back, man, whilst I find out. In fact, you can leave the room until I've examined her – you stay, Mrs Leeman.'

'But Siana is my—' Edward began.

'Out!' Francis barked. 'My consultations are private unless I state differently.'

'It's nothing. I fainted, that's all,' she whispered, but Siana had her own suspicions of what had caused the faint and the beginnings of a smile glimmered on her lips.

Francis was impersonal in his examination of her. Siana wanted to snuggle her face into his palm when he laid it against her forehead. She was so aware of him, so responsive to his touch, she was surprised Mrs Leeman didn't notice. When Francis asked her a couple of personal questions, awareness came into his eyes and she knew she'd guessed right. She smiled with delight when he finally caught her eye, she couldn't help herself. He returned the smile a little ruefully before he stood up and instructed Mrs Leeman to show Edward in.

'What's wrong with her, man?' Edward shouted at him, almost frothing at the mouth with the indignity of being dismissed from the room in such a cursory manner.

Francis grinned when Siana giggled.

'Nothing serious, I assure you, Edward. In fact, she's a perfectly healthy girl who is suffering from a normal condition. It seems you are both to be congratulated. Siana is expecting an infant.' He closed his bag with a snap. 'I must away now.' He swept Mrs Leeman before him, leaving them to share a moment of privacy.

'Don't forget our dinner engagement or I'll be cross with you,' she called after him, and he turned and winked at her.

The incredulity in Edward's expression, especially when mixed with the remnants of his frown, was a delicious reward to savour. She'd never seen him so lacking in control of himself.

'My dear,' he murmured, 'not for one moment did I imagine . . .'

Slanting her eyes up at him, full of the knowledge that she had his complete attention, she murmured softly, 'How surprising, when you are wont to prove your potency at the most unpredictable and inconvenient of moments.'

Giving a chuckle, he fell to his knees and drew her so close she could feel his heart beating against her ear. 'You are my constant temptress. My dearest love, you have made me the happiest man alive.'

'I find that hard to believe when you were so grumpy and rude to Francis, just now.'

340

'I invited him to dinner, didn't I?' he said, and the remark was slightly truculent. 'The man presumes too much on his family connections.'

'He is a friend who has helped me in the past. I was delighted to see him again.'

'He's too familiar with you. You are a married woman who cannot have friends amongst the opposite sex. People will talk.'

'I believe you might be jealous of him?' she said, provoking him because now he knew she was carrying his child he would allow her to get away with it.

'Of course I'm jealous,' he admitted with a sigh. 'The man is twenty years younger than me. Besides, how dare he decide what's right and what's wrong for you, my wife?'

She pressed a kiss against the side of his mouth. 'You are my husband and I love you, Edward. But I won't allow you to run my life, either. The man upstairs is my father. You had no right to keep us apart. I'm annoyed that you conspired with Richard to keep it from me. I intend to tell Richard his attitude was unworthy of a minister.'

He chuckled and brought her face round to his. Eyes alight with amusement gazed into hers. 'Come, my heart, do not take me to task when we have such delightful news to share. I plead guilty only of trying to protect you.' His hand splayed against her lower abdomen and he smiled. 'The infant you carry inside you is my heir, Siana. You will say nothing to embarrass Richard White, a man of no means and whose living it's within my power to withdraw.'

Was there a threat behind his words?

'You will be protected and guided by me, whether you like it or not – and in any manner I decide is fitting.'

When she opened her mouth to argue, he simply brought his lips down to capture and possess hers. She responded to his attention with the surge of wilful excitement she always felt when he touched her, his claim to ownership adding piquancy.

She couldn't wait until they got back home so they could make love. Neither it seemed could he, for, halfway through the forest, he declared his lady too tired to ride any further and sent Jed on to bring back the carriage whilst they went a little way into the woods to rest.

There, in a clearing of dappled light, they spent an intense hour satisfying their hunger for each other. When Jed Hawkins returned, Siana was truly exhausted and extremely satiated, as if she'd eaten too much at the one time.

But when she'd closed her eyes, it had been Francis she'd called to mind, his grey eyes alight with ironic laughter, his dark hair tangled in her fingers and the strength of his younger, sturdier body conquering hers. As she allowed herself to be totally possessed, she recognized the fact that she could love two men at the same time and pledged her undying love to Francis, almost calling out his name in the throes of her passion.

Edward had never known Siana to be quite so abandoned and sensual. He was well satisfied by this peasant wife of his. When she became too swollen for him to comfortably make love to her, he decided he would not seek relief elsewhere, he would simply teach her other ways to pleasure him.

The surge of warm weather brought some ease to Tom Skinner's body, even whilst the poisons in his blood were slowly and surely going about their deadly task. His time in the infirmary had wasted some of the flesh from his body, so he was leaner, lighter and less muscular.

His nightly forays with Hannah, who'd moved into the deserted cottage on Croxley Farm and who met him after sunset at the back entrance to the infirmary, yielded a wealth of information. He had watched the comings and goings at the manor and knew to the exact minute when the guards patrolled.

The horse they borrowed was a sturdy beast, used to the plough. Each night before dawn, Tom was returned to his bed and the horse to its meadow, neither of them the worse for wear.

Hearing that the manor housekeeper had been dismissed, Tom sent Hannah to milk Ethel Pawley of information. She returned with a badly drawn diagram of the inside of the manor, each room and its function clearly marked.

'The old harridan weren't exactly friendly towards Siana,' Hannah said. 'I gets the feeling she'd be more'n happy to bring her down, in more ways than one.' She pulled a couple of keys on a ring from her pocket and dangled it provocatively from the end of her finger. 'A real turn up, Siana marryin' the squire, and all. Our dad must be turning in his grave knowing he worked his guts out to feed that little trollop. These, here, are the keys to their bedrooms.' She snatched it away when Tom made a grab. 'No you don't. This little lot cost me a fortune.'

'It were my pigs you sold.'

'Strictly speaking, they be the squire's, on account of you never paid him back for the loan in the first place.'

Tom shrugged. 'Keep the bleddy keys then. I was thinking, mebbe we could see what we can get from the place. Hardly anyone there but a couple of servants on Sunday, everyone else is in church. I hear there's a cove in Blandford that'll take the silver and jewels off our hands.'

Hannah smiled. 'Then we could go up to London to start a little business. We could live the high life, like that wife of your'n.'

Tom scowled at the thought of Elizabeth. He'd see to her. He'd stay alive just long enough to savour the satisfaction of choking the life out of her. London didn't interest him. He could die just as easily here.

Hannah was still on the practicalities of the robbery. 'We'll need a cart.'

'There's a hay cart kept around the back of the manor stable and I knows a back road we can use to get away.' He spat into the dirt.

So, on the last Sunday in June, the pair set out to take their revenge.

20

The dinner turned out to be an ordeal. Much to Siana's disappointment, Francis didn't bring his two daughters.

'My sister-in-law insists the children be in their beds by nine o'clock as they have to attend to their studies in the morning. I will bring them to church on Sunday and you can meet them then.'

For a moment she wondered if Francis's sister-in-law thought her not good enough to socialize with her nieces. Of course she did. The woman was a countess. If their positions were reversed, she'd probably think the same way, Siana conceded.

Francis looked handsome and distinguished in a high-buttoned embroidered waistcoat and winged collar. Their eyes locked in a moment of rapport.

For the evening she'd chosen a lavender gown covered in embroidered flowers, which showed off her bare shoulders. With it she wore drop earrings glittering with diamonds, and the headband which had been a gift from Edward. Her dark hair was swept up.

Francis's expression was openly admiring as he kissed her hand. 'May I compliment you on your appearance, Siana. Becoming a mother obviously suits you.'

Siana, so aware of him she ached, needed a moment alone with him when she could be herself, not some perfectly turned out hostess, stiff with manners. 'Come up and see Daisy before she's put to bed. I've told her you're visiting and she's looking forward to seeing you.'

Much to her chagrin, Edward came with them. Daisy's blue eyes lit up and her giggle when she saw Francis was matched only by her beaming smile when she saw Edward.

'Papa?' she said, holding out her arms to encompass them both.

Edward quickly swung her into his arms, claiming possession.

Francis chuckled. 'Daisy is fickle in her affection. She used to call me that.'

'She has the predatory instinct females have for placing their affection where it draws the most advantage,' Edward said silkily. He took a coin from his pocket and dangled it in front of Daisy's nose. 'Will you give Papa a hug for this?'

He laughed when Daisy obliged, allowing her to drop the coin into her money box. 'See, she sells herself to the highest bidder.'

Annoyed, Siana took her sister from his arms and, giving her a goodnight kiss, handed her over to the nursery maid. 'You are teaching her to be mercenary, Edward. I know you do this in fun but it's to her detriment. I don't like it.'

'Do you not, my love?' Edward's eyes glittered, but his tone remained mild. 'Then I'll cease the practice, for your every wish is my command. What do you think, Francis? If Siana were your wife, would you allow her to dictate terms to you?'

'Undoubtedly,' Francis said, his smile already strained.

Siana had seen men behaving brutally towards one another, both verbally and physically. Listening to the savagery that two men of intellect used to torture a friendship over the course of an evening was excruciatingly painful, especially when she loved them both and knew that she was the cause of the rift.

The atmosphere was fraught with tension. Her nerves were strung so tightly they seemed to vibrate with warning. She was frightened she'd say something wrong, do something wrong, or display her humble background so it could be remarked on by Edward.

So the evening proceeded. Edward was so exceedingly polite and distant she wanted to leap upon him and strangle him with her bare hands. Then he began to bring her into the discussion, starting each sentence with, 'Wouldn't you agree, Siana . . .' so she was forced to either argue or side with him. Invariably, she took the latter course because she thought he was waiting to pounce and pour scorn on her uninformed opinion.

Francis kept himself under control but his tongue grew increasingly barbed as his patience decreased. His eyes glittered with anger. Eventually, he took his leave, seemingly relieved to have got through the evening without losing his temper altogether.

'Oh, must you go?' Edward tossed at him carelessly. 'Siana and I were so enjoying your company, weren't we, my dearest?'

'It was lovely to see you,' she said, her voice thick because she felt miserable and angry at the same time and wanted to burst into tears.

Later, when Edward came through to her room she said, 'It was a horrible evening.'

He came up behind her at the dressing table. 'Really? I didn't notice anything untoward. But you really must learn not to take your husband to task in front of guests, my darling. Remember, Daisy would be in the workhouse if I had not taken her in.'

Tempted to remind him it was Francis who had saved the child's life, she managed to bite her tongue in time. 'Do not imagine I'm not grateful for that. If my conduct has given you cause for complaint please tell me now.'

His hands went to her shoulders, kneading at the tension in her muscles. His voice was a soft whisper against her ear as his hands circled her throat and gently tightened. 'You must *never* give me cause for complaint.'

She experienced a moment of fright, then, heart beating wildly, she pulled his hands down. 'Please do not do that, Edward.'

His arms circled her body, his tongue slid along her bare shoulders. 'Such pretty, translucent skin,' he murmured and gently nipped her, a ruse almost guaranteed to arouse her.

But for the first time since their marriage Siana didn't welcome his attention. 'I'm tired, Edward.'

'Too tired to accommodate your husband, my dear?'

'Yes,' she said, 'you are in a strange mood and . . . I don't feel *accommodating*.'

'Am I to take it you're vexed with me?' He laughed then, and taking her chin between his forefinger and thumb looked into her eyes for a moment. 'Then I will be quick so you can get some rest.' Pushing her backwards onto the bed, he threw her skirts up over her head, held her there with one hand and ripped her undergarments away.

There were no words of love, no lead up of loving caresses, just a terrible, insulting assault on her body that seemed to go on for ever as he thrust himself between her thighs. But there was no joy for him in this rape either, for his manliness failed him before conclusion.

Tears trickled down her cheeks as she remembered her mother being subjected to similar treatment at the hands of Bill Skinner. At least Edward hadn't beaten her too.

'See what you have done to me,' he shouted and, cursing horribly, he pulled himself out of her. His footsteps echoed across the floor. The door slammed. There was a click of a key in the lock, then another.

Rising from the bed she tried the doors. Both of them were locked! 'Edward?' she said against the panel. 'Don't be angry with me. I can't bear it.'

He didn't answer her.

She thought she heard someone give a soft chuckle and whisper his name against her ear. '*Edward.*' She whipped around to encounter nothing but flickering shadows.

It had been a female voice, sibilant and soft and came from she knew not where. Something moved in the shadows. Shivers raced up her spine and she told herself not to be silly, nothing moved, nothing spoke. It was the strange, fey sense she'd inherited from her great-grandmother. Her mother had told her not to be frightened of it.

Yet that same sense now spoke strongly to her of doom. She began to weep, then sob, eventually crying herself to sleep.

Later, Edward came to sit by her bedside. He was sorry he'd been angry with her, sorry he'd almost lost his control. Her chamber was cold. Odd, he thought, because the night was warm. The candle guttered and shadows leapt.

Patricia's bed had been in the same position. She'd been asleep when he'd put her out of her misery. He picked up a pillow. It had been so easy to cut off her air. A short struggle . . . *but she wasn't struggling now!*

'*What the hell am I doing!*' he muttered in alarm and dashed the pillow to the floor.

Siana hauled some air into her lungs but didn't wake. He kissed her tear-stained cheek. 'Forgive me, my sweeting.'

Her eyes fluttered open and she whispered something he couldn't quite catch. He sat by her side all night, watching the rise and fall of her breathing, loving her, this girl who was giving him so much – and hating himself for making her unhappy.

She woke early and gazed at him. Awareness came into her eyes, then pain. 'How long have you been there?'

'All night.' That he'd caused such an expression in her eyes distressed him. 'My darling, I love you too much,' he said.

'Edward.' His name trembled in the air, so soft and unsure it captivated him.

She smiled and held out her arms to him. When she took him first into the warmth of her arms, then into her bed and her body, the shadows of the room retreated and he was made a whole man again.

It was the last Sunday in June. Daisy was suffering from mild quinsy and had been left at home with the nursery maid.

The sermon had been over-long. Richard White was tediously pedantic in his oratory and Siana was pleased the service was over.

It was a warm day. The sun was high overhead as the carriage travelled through a lane of plane and oak trees which met overhead in a loosely woven ceiling of light and dark greens.

Siana slid her hand into Edward's. She'd learned he was a man who needed to know he was appreciated. He was also a man of exceedingly generous nature, and that appreciation was rewarded by an abundance of gifts and goodwill on his part. Although she never sought to capitalize on that, his nature did encourage her to respond to the goodness in him.

She'd decided she would not like to cross him, though. He carried with him a core of ruthlessness, the demonstration of which she'd witnessed more than once. Something took over his nature. It was as if good and bad worked independently inside him.

Today, he'd been in an expansive mood and had allowed her to visit her father for a short while after the

Sunday service. She had found Gruffydd Evans seated in an arbour, his nose buried in a book. When she had cleared her throat, he'd glanced up, startled. Tears had turned his blue eyes into a sea of emotion. Her father's appearance had improved, but the tortured expression in his eyes had been hard to bear.

'Daughter,' he'd said, his voice raw with pain, 'I did not expect you to consider me worthy of another thought. You look well in lavender, like bluebells in the woods.'

'Ah . . .you must have the soul of a poet.'

'I'm Welsh. The men of Wales are all poets.'

'One day I must visit the place of my birth. Perhaps my great-grandmother Lewis is still alive and would like to meet me.'

'Beware, girl. That one is a pagan priestess who placed her curse upon me.'

'The sight is a gift given to the few and used only for good, or so my mother said. My husband says a curse can only come true if the mind believes it and makes it real.'

'Your husband should learn some humility, lest the Lord find him lacking.'

Siana hadn't thought Edward would countenance such a scathing notion from the Lord.

'My husband is humble when the need arises. He is disapproving of our connection, but has permitted a short meeting between us today. We must make the most of it.'

Edward had been strolling in the garden with Richard White. She'd felt his glance seek her out and she had sent him a small, grateful smile before turning back to the preacher.

'Mrs Leeman tells me you are improving.'

'I'm growing stronger, it's true. My heart is still in turmoil, though. Yesterday, however, the reverend took me to pray at your mother's grave and I found a moment of peace.'

She had hesitated before tentatively asking, 'Has Dr Matheson been to see you? He was going to bring his daughters to meet me but was not in church today.'

'I understand he was called urgently to the bedside of a sinner in childbirth. The woman is suffering mightily for the sin of conception out of wedlock.'

'Sin!' She had struggled to contain a flare of anger as her hands strayed protectively to her belly. 'You think a child born of love is a sin?'

'This one was conceived in lust, I believe, for the woman has taken another woman's husband unto her loins and his seed into her womb.'

'What of the man's sin?'

'He will be punished, as are all men for their lusts.' He had fallen silent for a moment, then said in a low voice. 'Would you forgive me the sin against your mother, then?'

'How can I? You forced yourself upon her and only she can know what suffering it cost her. But whilst I condemn your behaviour, I cannot help but be glad you sinned. If you had not, then I would neither exist nor experience the happiness I now enjoy.'

'Such happiness cannot last, for the sins of the parents are visited on the child.' He had leaned forward, his eyes fired with the inner zeal of a true evangelist.

'Did you know your husband is a whore-monger who sups off the sweat and blood of others? Whilst you enjoy the food on his table and parade in your fine silks and conceit, you mock God, daughter. The people who work to feed your vanity die from disease and starvation caused by the conditions they live in.'

She had not wished to hear this harsh condemnation of the man who had taken her from that same poverty. Annoyed with him for pointing out the truth she chose to forget, she had snapped, 'I will hear no more of your bitter invective against my husband. Nor will I shoulder the sin on your conscience.' She had turned and hurried away, to the haven that was Edward, where she and her sister would never know hunger or want again.

Now, as the carriage headed back towards the manor and as Edward's hand tightened around hers and her mouth accepted his possessive caress, she tried not to think of the heartache and poverty of her upbringing. That she couldn't dispel the seed of doubt Gruffydd Evans had planted in her mind – that she might have sold her soul to the devil and her body to Edward, and the two just might be one and the same – troubled her.

Edward controlled her, true. But it was a pleasant prison, without bars and with no punishment or want. Her every wish was his command. The trouble was, his every command seemed to have become her wish.

She turned to gaze at the handsome profile with its classic nose, full-lipped mouth and haughty, tilted chin. He turned towards her. His tawny eyes met hers, confident and untroubled.

'What is it, my dearest?'

354

'What would you do if I ever disobeyed you, Edward?'

A moment of truth passed between them as he weighed up this small challenge from her; as he acknowledged something in himself and measured it in his response. It was a moment when she saw the darkness gather in his eyes. Then his expression was masked, and he shrugged. 'It would be advisable if you didn't, I think.'

When she gave a small shiver, he gave a slightly reflective smile and turned to gaze out of the window.

They arrived home to find chaos. Rooms had been ransacked, most of the silver was missing and Siana's jewellery case had been stolen.

'Daisy!' she cried out and raced pell-mell upstairs to the nursery.

Her sister was safe, being cuddled on the lap of the nursery maid. The child was rosy-cheeked with fever as she slept, her breath a husky rasp.

Thank God she is safe, was Siana's first thought. But was she? Giving her sister a considering glance, she reflected that she might need to send for Francis.

'The nursery maid heard nothing untoward, but the nursery is situated at the back of the house,' she reported to Edward.

'I'm aware of where it's situated,' he said, not bothering to hide his exasperation. She backed away from the sting of his reply, unable to hide the wound it caused her.

He gave her a searching glance, muttered an apology then gently touched her face and turned to stride off when the sound of muffled thumps and shouts were heard.

The two servants left behind were discovered sore-headed, hog-tied and secured in a closet. The thieves were long gone. The servants had seen or heard nothing prior to being cudgelled from behind. They received a severe tongue-lashing for their lack of vigilance from their incensed master, despite their sorry state.

When the rest of the servants arrived back from the church service, they were rounded up to go after the thieves. But when they reached the stables it was to find the horses had been driven off into the forest.

Edward soundly cursed everyone concerned. Only the steward, Jed Hawkins, had a horse and the coach-man was obliged to saddle up the carriage horses so the three of them could make a foray into the forest to retrieve the scattered stock.

Siana saw to the injured servants whilst they were gone, swathing their broken heads in bandages. When Edward returned, she hoped the sight of the bandages might divert his feelings towards compassion rather than anger.

Edward was somewhat mollified when he found the hay cart sunk to its axles in a boggy patch, the manor cart horse trapped between the shafts. The mare's hind legs were half buried. Her flanks strained and her forelegs tramped the muck as she tried to pull herself and the cart free of the sticky mud.

'Be still, my beauty,' the groom whispered to her. The animal immediately stood patiently, her tail flicking at the flies that swarmed to bother her.

'There's a good old girl, then. We'll soon have thee

out.' Between them, they dug around her buried hind legs with their hands and heaved and pushed the cart. Finally, they managed to get the gentle giant free. The animal emerged with a sucking noise and plodded forward a few paces. They were covered in mud when they finished

'Off thee goes now, back to the stable, old girl. I'll see to thee when I get back,' the groom said as he turned the cart around and sent the animal plodding back towards the manor.

Edward gazed at the footprints in the mud. 'One of them is a lad by the looks of these footprints.'

Jed was staring at them. 'That's odd.'

'What is?'

'The larger footprints.'

'What's odd about them, man?'

Jed Hawkins looked perplexed. 'It's only a left foot.'

Where the right footprints should be were neat, round holes filled with water. Edward's smile was not pleasant. He knew exactly who it was now. Hadn't he helped Francis remove that leg himself?

'The only person I know of with one leg is Tom Skinner. The smaller footprint must belong to his brother, Josh.'

'But I heard Tom Skinner is near to death.'

'Obviously he's not as sick as he pretends. Come, gentlemen, let's round up the horses, then we'll go and pay the patient a visit. And I want everything on the road stopped and searched until my property is found. The Skinners must be apprehended on sight. I'm determined to rid the district of that vermin if I die in the attempt.'

But Tom Skinner's bed was vacated and he was no longer in residence.

With the aid of Siana's mare, Tom and Hannah reached Blandford after night had fallen. It didn't take them long to complete their business transaction.

They headed for Poole. They used a twisting, round-about route, covering the eight or so miles over two nights, forced to hole up during the day and avoid the main roads. Once in the harbour town, they ignored the public inns, sleeping in a merchant's stable accessed from a dark laneway. The merchant himself was in London.

The same lad who stabled Siana's horse, fetched them a jug of ale and a meat pie apiece from the inn. The boy was deaf and dumb and had the look of an idiot. Yet he was well aware of the benefits of using the premises to run his own business when his master was absent.

Hannah fingered the diamond headband she wore around her neck. She hadn't sold it with the other stuff. Instead, she'd removed it from Siana's jewellery box to hang around her grubby neck. It was a pretty thing, the reflection of the stones shining against her fingers in the lantern light.

She was filled with envy at the thought of Siana having such nice things to wear. The headband would be her stake for when she reached London. She gazed at her brother, who was snoring like a stuck pig. She scowled. The greedy bastard hadn't given her a penny yet. He probably never would.

She crept across the floor and gently patted his

pockets. Suddenly his arm lashed out. His clenched fist caught her across the nose as she was back-handed across the stall.

'Try that again and I'll kill you,' he muttered and turned away from her.

Whimpering, Hannah cowered in a corner, nursing her swelling face and bruised eyes.

A false dawn was just breaking when she woke. Tom was still asleep. He looked like something from a nightmare. She shuddered.

The boy was nowhere to be seen. He'd left them bread and cheese and a jug of water. Tom had payed him in advance the night before.

Hannah ate her share, washing it down with the water. She took out the boning knife, gazing at its thin, sharp blade. Now for Ben Collins and the whore Isabelle. She knew where the fat cow lived. She could get it done before they woke, and Ben would hang for the deed.

Siana's horse gazed at her from the next stall, then bared her yellow teeth and snickered. 'Stupid beast. You look pretty, but you bain't good for nothin' but carting a toff on your back. Only she be no toff. That be a peasant's arse she puts on your bleddy back.'

Isabelle Prosser's fall from grace had caused her father a fit of apoplexy. He lay in his bed, unable to move, to speak or to care for himself.

Ben Collins, the man who had caused his downfall, looked after him like a baby. Eventually, Mr Prosser grew to like the genial giant who lived in sin with his daughter, and was shortly to father his first grandchild.

'Now, don't you fret none,' Ben said soothingly to him from time to time. 'I'll be you'm legs and arms.'

Aunt Caroline, who had nowhere else to go, lived in the servants' quarters upstairs. She avoided Isabelle, who treated her with disdain and would have thrown her out in the street if Ben hadn't forbidden it.

'There's plenty of room in this big old house,' Ben said to her. 'Now you leave the old girl be or I'll tan your backside till thee can't sit down for a week.'

And Isabelle knew he'd carry out his threat because he'd done it once before when she'd pushed him too hard.

Everyone loved young George who, in his turn, loved everyone. Like Ben, he was a simple soul who responded to the love he'd been denied early in life. Each member of the household competed for his attention so the child was petted and praised from all angles. The result was that he was growing up with a trusting and loving nature.

The household rubbed along with a certain contentment, as long as father and daughter and aunt and niece mostly ignored each other. Ben got along with them all. Isabelle grew fatter with contentment and Ben kept her happy and fulfilled whilst he fulfilled himself.

Soon, she'd have a child of her own to hold. She hoped to have a son like George. Isabelle didn't care what people said about her behind her back. She'd never really wanted to marry a man above her station. She loved Ben and wanted the house filled with their children.

She'd bought Ben a closet full of smart clothes to

wear and called herself Mrs Collins, insisting her staff refer to Ben as Mr Collins. And although Ben didn't have to work, she drove him to the warehouse early each morning so he could help to shift the goods from the stockroom to the shelves, whilst she checked over the books further down the road at the shop.

Most of the cloth for the business came straight from the cotton and woollen mills in Lancashire, great bolts of it conveyed by canal boat and wagon. Isabelle had heard that there were steam engines pulling carriages along rails in the industrialized north of the country, now. She couldn't imagine such a sight, and would like to see it for herself, one day.

The business stocked drabbet for the peasants' smocks, kerseymere for gentlemens' outfitters, and a range of cotton dimity and cambric, as well as flannels and the black bombazine needed for mourning dress. There were also fine silks, taffetas and brocades on the shelves.

Apart from the warehouse, which sold fabrics to dressmakers and gentlemen's outfitters, there was the shop, opened by Isabelle's father. It was to provide herself with an occupation, she knew, but she'd made a success of it, and intended to expand it eventually, selling the locally made lace buttons, and other accessories necessary to trim gowns. Now her father was incapacitated, the running of the business had fallen on her shoulders. Isabelle enjoyed it and, although Ben was not too bright, he could lift and carry and liked making himself useful.

Nothing much ever went missing from the shop. Isabelle knew every item that came in and went out, and was meticulous in accounting for it all. The cost of anything missing was deducted from the wages of her staff, which caused them to watch each other like hawks and report any stealing to her.

This morning, Isabelle had just dropped Ben off at the warehouse and set off down the hill when Hannah came charging out of a laneway and stood in front of her, waving her arms.

'What d'you want, you ugly witch?' Isabelle snarled.

About to rein in the horse, Isabelle saw the knife in Hannah's hand. Her heart began to thud wildly. Hannah wanted her man back, no doubt. Well, she wasn't going to get him, or the poor little lad she'd neglected. Isabelle intended to keep them both and was not about to debate the issue.

She quickly glanced around her at the deserted street, then urged the horse forward. The animal tried to stop when it saw the woman but the weight of the cart on the slope kept up the momentum and pushed it forward.

Although Hannah tried to jump out of the way at the last moment, she lost her footing and went tumbling to the ground. There was a wet crunch as the carriage wheel ran over her.

The fatal moment was so quick and so quiet. The horse was quivering as Isabelle brought it to a stop. She took a moment to soothe it, then glanced back at the still figure lying in the road – at the dark, wet stain seeping from under the head. Hannah couldn't possibly have survived that.

Dawn was a pale yellow glare over the roofs of the houses now, the chimney pots sinister in contrast. The shop fronts either side of her were still dark, their windows blind, deaf and mute. Yet she felt the force of unseen eyes on her, as if she was being watched.

She shook off the feeling as fanciful.

Isabelle hesitated for a moment. Her brain presented her with several scenarios. With no witnesses, it couldn't be proved she was involved in the *accident*. And nobody could prove that it wasn't one. But people were bound to talk, and the longer she stayed here the riskier it became. She thought of Ben and George, and the welfare of the child she carried inside her.

Isabelle took the only course possible under the circumstances. She clicked her tongue and urged the horse forward. It would be business as usual as far as she was concerned.

When she was out of sight, the stable boy darted out of the lane and quickly went through Hannah's pockets, finding a few coins to reward him. He picked up the knife and was about to turn away when a faint glitter caught his attention.

Pulling the blood-soaked shawl aside, he whistled to himself when he saw the necklace.

It was a messy business removing it.

When he'd put some distance between himself and the corpse, he stopped to rinse his hands, along with the knife and the bauble, in a public horse trough. He held the headband up to the light, entranced by the way the dawning sun drew prisms of brilliant colour from the stones.

He nearly dropped it into the trough when a heavy hand descended on his shoulder.

21

The next day the feeling of doom surrounding them was too strong for Siana to ignore. As much as possible she kept Edward company.

He came and went during the day whilst the men searched for her missing horse or any trace of the felons. Finally, he came back, his face grave. 'I'm sorry, my love. Josh has been apprehended and will be handed over to the authorities.'

Her eyes widened and she placed a hand over her mouth to stop herself from screaming. 'Josh wouldn't steal from me.'

Edward ran a hand tiredly over his brow. 'I suspect he might have been an accomplice, but I cannot prove it. However, he's been carting my fish again.'

'Edward,' she pleaded, 'it's only a few fish. Let him go.'

'So he can do it again?' He shook his head. 'Josh is making a laughing stock out of me, Siana. I let him off without punishment last time.'

His memory was conveniently faulty considering he'd beaten Josh half to death, then exacted a further price from her. 'Please, Edward. If you love me, let him go. I'll talk to him and make him promise not to do it again.'

His face took on a stubborn set. 'Dishonesty must be punished.'

'Does that include your smuggled brandy?' she threw at him. 'You're a magistrate. How would you have yourself punished?'

He started. 'Damn you, Siana. You know exactly where to hit a man.'

Desperately she said, 'This will mean the end of all Josh's hopes and dreams. He's worked so hard. He'll be transported and I'll never see him again.'

'That will be no loss. He's a Skinner and the pack of them are low-born scum.'

'Daisy is a Skinner.'

Dispassionately, he said, 'She's young yet. Given time, no doubt her blood will out.'

'Sometimes I despise you,' she threw at him.

'I know, my dear.' He came and stood before her, looking down at her. 'It makes no difference to me whether you love me or hate me. You're mine, and will stay mine.'

'Let Josh go, Edward. Please.'

He slanted his head to one side, contemplating her through glittering eyes. Softly he hissed, 'I wonder, what exactly would you do to secure your brother's release, Siana mine?'

'Anything.'

'Anything? Would you, for instance, accept punishment in his place?'

Horrified, she stared at him. 'If that's what it takes, but I'll give you a valid reason for doing so.' And although she knew she might be taking her life in her hands, she slapped him on the face.

Taken aback, his eyes darkened with anger. Then he smiled, took both her wrists in his hands and pulled her close, kissing her until she weakened enough to respond to the caress. Finally, he released her and stroked a stray hair back from her heated face. 'I didn't expect you to become violent over such a trifle.'

'A trifle! What sort of man are you? It's a contemptible suggestion.'

'It proves you love me enough to trust me, my little peasant girl.'

Tears filled her eyes. 'I have told you I love you, why should I need to prove it? I cannot fathom your trickery. I'm going to my room to rest.'

He dangled a key from his finger. 'Don't you want to come and tell your brother why he is being set free?'

Longing leapt into her eyes, then it slowly faded. 'You must not tell him.'

'Perhaps you're right, my sweeting.' He was all solicitude. 'You look tired and must go and rest now. You can watch your brother depart from your window. Later I will join you. I'll expect to be properly compensated for setting the little thief free.'

She dare not insist on accompanying Edward to the cellar in case he changed his mind. Clinging to the bars in her window, her heart breaking, she watched Josh drive off. He looked taller than the last time she'd seen him, broader in the shoulders. She wished she could visit

366

Elizabeth again. She missed having a woman to talk to. She threw herself on the bed and wept a little before drifting off to sleep.

She woke when Edward entered later. In his hand he was carrying a whip made from several strands of plaited silk.

When she stared at it uncomprehendingly, he smiled. 'You once asked me what I'd do if you disobeyed me, Siana. You're about to find out because I believe you are due a little punishment. I will be lenient this time. Next time, the whip will be knotted and will mark you.'

She laughed with relief, wondering what pleasing game he'd thought of, and knowing he would not hurt her now she carried his child inside her. She found out. He was thorough in his punishment. The whip swished through the air and stung against her skin. After a while it became almost unbearable and she was forced to beg him to stop.

He made love to her then, with an exquisite finesse, so the silk-induced discomfort became a prolonged and almost unbearable pleasure.

When it was over, he smiled. 'Tell me how you feel now.'

Her body was hot and lethargic with satisfaction. He was a wickedly exciting man. He made her feel . . . taken. She blushed as she haltingly told him what he wanted to hear, that her times of intimacy with him were unforgettably sensuous.

The next morning Siana ached all over. She groaned softly as she seated herself opposite him at the breakfast table.

Edward's smile was intimate, his voice as smooth as cream. 'Sometimes we have to pay for our pleasure with a little pain.'

'Then why is it me who is groaning?'

He laughed. 'I experienced your pain, but you might like to reverse the process at some time.'

'Can I use a horsewhip on you?'

When she grinned at the thought, his eyes narrowed. 'You have yet to learn the finer points of pain in pursuit of pleasure – like when to stop.'

She stared at him, puzzled, not quite knowing what he meant.

He smiled his enigmatic smile. 'I meant to tell you yesterday, but quite forgot. Your stepsister, Hannah Collins, was found dead. She'd been run over by a cart.' He took her jewellery from his pocket and threw it on the table. 'These were found in a pawnbroker's establishment in Blandford. The headband is still missing, but no doubt it will turn up in time.'

How unimportant he made her stepsister's death sound. But then Hannah was just another peasant to Edward, who had never known any other life than this wealthy one he lived.

Siana stared at the adornments for a moment. They were a symbol of wealth she could never have contemplated when she was a child. Pretty as they were, they would never satisfy the hunger gnawing at a child's stomach and they couldn't cure a disease or stop a woman dying from childbirth when her body was too worn out to support and nourish another infant.

Much as she'd disliked Hannah, Siana couldn't help

feeling sorry for a life so wasted, when the cost of such baubles would have improved the lot of Edward's field labourers considerably.

Light streamed through the stained-glass window and touched on the jewels. It turned the pearls a deep red, like drops of blood.

Behind Edward, she thought she caught a glimpse of a woman standing. Her hands were on his shoulders and she was smiling. There was something inhuman about her. Siana gasped as she remembered Mrs Pawley telling her about Edward's first wife. In the blink of an eye the woman was gone. Goosebumps raced up Siana's arms to her neck as a feeling of doom swept over her once more. She could sense danger around Edward again. She rubbed the small cross at her throat between her forefinger and thumb.

'*You cannot stop fate,*' the voice of her great-grandmother whispered in her head.

Siana's hands went over her ears and she shook her head from side to side. '*Stop it! Stop it!*'

In an instant Edward was by her side, his expression revealing his concern. 'What is it, Siana? Are you in pain? Did I go too far yesterday?'

'I think . . .' She leaned against him. 'It's nothing except for a little dizziness. Will you stay home with me today, Edward?'

'Alas, I cannot, my love. I have some business to conduct and will be gone all day. I'll tell Rosie to sit with you.'

Her arms went round him, hugging him tight, keeping him with her. 'Please, Edward. I beg of you. Do not go out.'

His eyes were tender as he tipped her chin up and placed a loving kiss on the end of her nose. 'What is this, Siana mine?'

'I can't explain. I feel there is . . . danger around you.'

'You're unsettled because of the burglary, that's all. Would you like me to leave you my pistol?'

'No, I don't know how to use it,' she said shakily. She was convinced that the woman she'd seen at his shoulder was a warning as well as an apparition. The image had been so strong she didn't think a pistol would prove to be an effective deterrent.

He set her away from him and stood up. 'I promise to try to get back during the day, and you shall have the dogs inside to guard you, if you wish. Will that put your fears to rest?'

'It's not necessary. Just take care, Edward. Remember, you'll have a son to raise before too long.'

His smile was one of pure delight. 'So, our infant is to be a son, is it? How can you be so sure?'

'I'm his mother. I just know.'

He ran a finger down her nose. 'You little witch, there's a lot of the pagan in you. You must have inherited it from your Welsh ancestors. I promise to take care. If you present me with a son, I'll be the happiest man in the world. When the troubles die down, we'll spend a summer in Italy. You'll be able to see for yourself all those damned statues you read about when you sneak into the library instead of pandering to your husband. By now, I must have the cleverest woman in the district for a wife.'

'I would like to go to Italy with you.' So why did she

370

have the feeling she never would? She gave a fleeting thought to Daniel, wondering if he ever thought of her now.

Although Edward had grumbled, she was aware of the laughter in him. Still, she didn't want to let him out of her sight and followed him to the stables. The dogs greeted him with howls of delight.

The day was overcast and thunder rumbled in the distance. She gave Edward another loving hug before he left, with more instructions to be careful and not to get wet and catch cold. She had never loved him more than she did at that moment.

She watched him mount his great black horse and canter off with the steward into the light of the sultry day, his handsome figure full of vigour and life. The dogs took off after them as they always did. They would not be back until their energy was spent, which would not be for an hour or so.

When she got back to the house, she felt the weight of Edward's ancestry press down upon her. The portraits climbed the walls along the rise of the stairs, each squire similar, yet different, as their blood was diluted with the blood of their mothers, so although Edward greatly resembled his father, but not quite, he looked very little like the first squire.

There was a shifting on the shadowy upper reaches of the stairs and she remembered the portrait of Edward's first wife, Patricia.

Siana had never been to the attics before but her feet seemed to be drawn upwards as if she had no will of her own, until finally she stood before a stout door. It was unlocked. At her push the door swung back on its hinges with a long-drawn-out creak. As she advanced into the attic it closed behind her.

She didn't have to look far to find Patricia. There was a covered easel in front of one of the dormer windows. She gasped as she pulled away the cloth.

Mrs Pawley had told her she resembled Patricia.

'Nonsense,' she said, but a little uneasily, for she had to concede the woman's mouth displayed the same curve, and perhaps her eye shape and the long sweep of her lashes were similar. As for her hair, she agreed, they both had a dark abundance of it.

But there any similarity ended. This woman was exquisite. Her face was a classic oval and her mouth supported a wryly amused twist, which her own didn't. Patricia's eyes glittered pale green to match the gown she wore, and her expression was one of aristocratic indifference as she stared back at Siana.

Siana gazed at her for a long time before indulging in a moment of one-sided conversation. 'So, you do not like being usurped in Edward's affections,' she whispered.

Her heart picked up a beat when a floorboard creaked. 'You're a spirit and he's a man who needs to be surrounded with love and life. You're a danger to him. Let him go.'

A draught whistled from somewhere above and swirled in a circle around her feet, stinging her ankles with a gritty storm of dust particles and debris.

'Is that the worst you can do?' she murmured, but decided not to mention the child she carried inside her, in case it was tempting the unknown.

She spun round when the door creaked open, giving a little cry when she saw a figure in the doorway.

'Don't be afeared, it's only me, my lady,' Rosie said, and came to her side to stare at the portrait. 'That Patricia became right mazed after their child was lost. Sunk into a black melancholy, she did. The master had to lock her up when she kept trying to harm herself. Terrible disfiguring things she did to herself. She was there for years. The old doctor, Bede it were, said it would be easier for the squire if she went into a madhouse. Squire wouldn't countenance it, though. He said he married her for better or worse, and she didn't deserve to be cast aside because she was sick. The way she sobbed and cried made our hair stand on end. Most of us were right pleased when she died. When they brought her out she didn't look like that, but like a poor old crone with no sap left inside her.'

Siana made a murmur of distress. Someone chuckled against her ear and she clutched at Rosie's arm. 'Did you hear anything?'

'Only the wind. It's spooked you, hasn't it, you being as you are? This be a right draughty place.' Rosie threw the cloth back over the portrait. 'Now you come away from here. Looking into the past ain't healthy and the master wouldn't like it. The squire loves you true, else he wouldn't have married you. He doesn't pay no mind to her no more, and neither should you.'

'How did you know I was up here?'

'Saw you go past, didn't I? Thought you were going to the nursery but I hears the door creak. A right loud un it be, too. Never have been able to rid her of her squeak.

Kicks up a right old shindy sometimes, especially when a storm's brewing like this one. Rattle, rattle, rattle, like someone's shaking it to try and get out.'

Rosie led her down the stairs and into the nursery. 'You forgot to eat your breakfast. Left it on your plate, you did. Now you come and eat something with us. I'll send the nursery maid down for more.'

Siana spent a pleasant couple of hours with her sister but, although pleased to discover Daisy's sore throat had come to nothing, she was sorry she couldn't use it as an excuse to call Francis in. When it was time for Daisy to take her rest, Siana wandered down to the drawing room and started her piano practice. She should have been practising the piano exercises her teacher had set her but her mind kept drifting and her hands stopped in the middle of a scale. She caught herself staring out of the window at the darkening storm, at the shrubs and trees whipping violently about. She thought of Italy and sunshine and smiled.

Going into the library, she grabbed a book from the shelf and seated herself in the chair Edward always used by the window. Unable to concentrate and still uneasy, she put it aside and, laying her head against the comfort of the head-rest, looked around her.

It was a vast room, filled with storm gloom now, and lined with books from ceiling to floor. All this knowledge at her fingertips and she knew not which one to choose. She wanted to read them all at once. She began to drift into a reverie, but something intruded into her mind. An insistent rattle coming from above.

She knew exactly what it was. But how did the noise

reach her in the library which was two floors below? All she needed to do was open the attic door and put something in front of it so it wouldn't close.

She took a heavy, leather-bound book down from the shelf and made her way upstairs. The house was so dark from the storm it was like midnight. As she neared the attic door the rattling increased and she could see it shaking back and forth.

For a moment she hesitated, her skin prickling. Then, telling herself not to be so fanciful, she took a deep breath and turned the handle. For a moment there seemed to be resistance, then it suddenly gave, as if it had been snatched open. As she took a few steps forward lightning illuminated the attic. The sheet over the portrait billowed outwards, then was seized from the painting by the strong draught and hurled towards her. She caught a glimpse of Patricia's mad and staring eyes before the sheet wrapped around her own face and body like a shroud.

Giving a scream, she fought the dusty material, but the more she fought the tighter it wrapped around her. She couldn't breathe and panicked. Then something pushed her forward and the door banged shut behind her. There was silence, except for a low rumble of thunder. She felt as if she'd let something out.

She pulled the sheet aside and headed for the door, grasping the handle, her heart thundering and her breath coming in shallow gasps. The door wouldn't budge. She rattled it violently back and forth, shouting for Rosie. Then she staggered backwards as the handle came loose in her hands. There was a series of dull thuds at the other side as the handle dropped to the floor and went bouncing down a flight of stairs.

'Damn! damn! damn!' she muttered.

It was a while before she realized that the door was not going to open without outside intervention. She seated herself on a box and banged on the floor with a heavy cane she found, shouting for help at the same time. But the storm redoubled in fury, disguising the sound of her puny efforts.

It was an hour before someone found her, by which time she was almost totally exhausted.

'Siana.' It was Francis at the door.

'Francis!' she shouted in relief. 'I can't get out.'

'Push the shaft of the handle through the door.'

When it opened, she threw herself at him, her face streaked with tears and dust. 'I'm so glad to see you. The door slammed and I was scared.'

He hugged her against his chest and she felt his heart beat against hers. She stayed there after it had quieted, enjoying this moment of safety and rapport with him. He hadn't the excitement of Edward, but he was solid and comforting and his compassion was infinite.

'My love,' he finally said as they heard Rosie shout her name, 'whatever we feel for each other, we must not allow ourselves to become involved.'

'Just tell me you love me, Francis. I will live off that truth for the rest of my life.'

'Aye, I love you,' and his grey eyes shone with the honesty of his emotion. 'I will always love you.'

She was troubled. 'You know it's reciprocated, Francis, but I love Edward in a different way and I cannot fathom the fickleness of my nature.'

'You are young, Siana. When you are older you will see the truth of it.'

The dogs came bounding up the stairs, shaking water from their coats. When they saw Francis so close to her, they sniffed at him and growled a warning.

He pressed a brief, telling kiss against her mouth before stepping back, shouting out to Rosie. 'Your mistress was locked in the attic, but is not harmed.'

'Will you stay for refreshment?' she offered politely as they descended, but inside, all she really wanted to do was kiss him back with all the love she felt for him.

'I was caught in the storm and stopped for shelter. It sounds as if the worst is over so I must proceed on to my next patient. I will call in on the way back as there is something I want to discuss with Edward.'

She took a delicate lace handkerchief from her pocket and pressed it into his hand before he left. 'Will you laugh if I ask you to keep this close to your heart?'

He smiled at the romantic token. After holding it against his lips for a moment, he placed it carefully inside his waistcoat and directly against his heart.

Edward had done something he'd vowed not to do. He'd gone to the house Elizabeth occupied.

She had not been feeling well, the assistant at the shop had told him, and had given him an oddly calculating look.

He left Hawkins quaffing a tankard of Dorset scrumpy cider in the *Jolly Sailor* tavern on the quay. There, his steward would keep his ears canted for any local gossip he could pick up. He set off for the house, whistling to himself.

Edward felt nothing for Elizabeth now, except

admiration for the way she'd grasped the concept of merchandising. She'd repaid his loan in just over a quarter of the time he'd specified. He was about to inform her that the lease to the house would be renegotiated when next it was due to be renewed. No longer did he feel the obligation to subsidize her.

He'd made sure Daniel was well equipped to fend for himself, too. The boy would return from Europe with a career and his education considerably broadened. There would be a substantial amount of money placed in a bank account for his use, and an appropriate legacy on Edward's death. Had Daniel played his cards right he would also have a woman of means waiting in the wings.

Edward found Elizabeth's front door open, which was surprising after the storm. Then he caught sight of Siana's horse.

Keara was in a sorry state, her mane and tail bedraggled and tangled. She quivered when he ran a hand over her flank. Her flesh was heated and foamed. Somebody had slashed her badly with a willow switch. The bloodied stick had been thrown aside. Whoever had brought her here had not long arrived, he thought, as his gelding snickered and nudged gently up against his stable mate in comfort.

Then, in the muddy ground, he saw the pock mark from a peg leg and his blood ran chill. Tom Skinner!

There was not a sound when he silently let himself into the house. Elizabeth was standing in the middle of the drawing room. Blood trickled from the corner of her mouth and her nose. She was in her shift and robe. Her eyes were terrified. Her hands clutched across the mound of her stomach. *Elizabeth was with child!* His mind flashed back to Croxley Farm – to the day when he and Elizabeth had last made love. Was it his child?

'Of course it's your infant, Tom,' she said, and, much to her credit, although she must have seen Edward from the corner of her eye not a flicker of an eyelid betrayed his presence.

'So why did you leave me?' Tom shouted, his back towards Edward as he advanced on her.

'Because you kept hitting me and I thought I might lose the infant.'

'Why did Edward Forbes supply you with this fancy place then?' His hand shot out and tangled in her hair, twisting her head around. 'He wasn't content with Siana, was he? The mean sod gave me a few paltry shillings to set her up for the plucking, and her still a virgin. He never did pay me the rest.'

He took the diamond headband from his pocket and dangled it on his finger. 'I bet he never gave you anything as valuable as this for your services. I'm going to make Siana wear it when I kill her.' He stroked the thin-bladed boning knife he'd taken from the mute. 'But first, I'll deal with you.'

'No you don't, Skinner,' Edward shouted in alarm and launched himself at the man. The headband shot across the room in a glittering arc. There was a short struggle in which Edward realized that, peg leg or not, the younger man had the advantage.

A pain sliced through him and he clutched his stomach. Elizabeth screamed when blood seeped through his fingers. Edward fell to one knee, but he remembered

379

Siana was in danger. He managed to pull out his pistol, fumbling as he cocked it. Why the hell hadn't he thought to do it outside? He fired. A neat round hole appeared in Skinner's chest and he dropped like a stone. Right through the heart, Edward thought with satisfaction. He managed to pull himself upright. He had to get home to Siana. She'd been worried about his safety, and he'd promised.

Josh came running in at the sound of a shot. His glance went from the body of his brother to Edward's wound then to Elizabeth's shivering form. 'Oh, my God, what's happened?'

Edward shot orders at him from habit. 'Go and fetch the authorities, Josh. And tell Hawkins I'm on my way home. He's in the Jolly Sailor. Then come back and look after Elizabeth.' He fished a shilling out of his pocket and threw it to him. 'That dark bay outside belongs to your sister. Give it a feed and a rub down. Then bring it to the manor the next time you pass through.'

He allowed Elizabeth to pad and bind the wound. Stabbed in the gut, he thought. Of all the damned bad luck. There wasn't much pain, just a feeling of spreading heat. 'I've got to get back to Siana, she will need my reassurance,' he said when Elizabeth tried to make him stay.

Despite Elizabeth's protests, he pocketed the headband and made it onto his horse. He needed to be with the woman he loved now, and nothing was going to stop him.

The storm had bruised the shrubs and flattened the flowers. Siana was in the garden trying to rescue enough of the blooms to put in urns, when she heard the sound of the horses' hooves.

She glanced up as two riders rounded the bend in the carriageway, smiling with relief when she saw Edward. Then she noticed something was terribly wrong. Her husband was being supported by Jed Hawkins and the gelding's side was covered in blood.

She gave a small scream and, dropping the flower basket, trampled the blooms under foot as she hastened to his side. She followed after Jed when he carried Edward upstairs to lay him carefully on his bed, her breath coming in little sobs. Then she sent one of the hovering servants outside to the road to keep watch for Francis.

'Edward, my love,' she said, desperately trying to staunch the flowing blood with her hands.

He was deadly pale but Edward's eyes flickered open and he managed a smile. 'Do not fuss, my angel. Let me die in peace.'

'If you love me, you'll stay alive.'

His hand covered hers. 'Would that I could, for I have never loved another more deeply,' he whispered. 'But at least I'll not have to stand by and watch you fall in love with a younger man.'

She began to weep. 'It's you I love, Edward. I'll always love you.'

'In five years it will be different.' His voice strengthened a little. 'Look after our little squire.'

'He will be named after you.'

'He must have his own name. Call him Ashley if you would. Make him a better man than his father, and don't think too badly of me when you learn how truly unworthy of you I really was. Now, kiss me, my love.'

As she covered his mouth with hers, his last breath

was a whisper of sound against her tongue. Something dropped from his relaxed hand to thud on the floor. Giving a loud sob she threw herself on his body, entreating, 'Please don't die, Edward. Please! Francis will be here soon. He will save your life.'

But it was Francis who lifted her from Edward's body, covered in his blood. Francis who shook his head with finality when she gazed at him through hopeful eyes. It was Francis who held her close while she sobbed like a demented baby. She fell asleep in his arms, exhausted and wanting to die herself, because she couldn't stand the pain of what had happened to Edward.

When she woke, there was a sudden golden moment when all seemed as it was. Then she heard Edward's voice say, before grief crowded in on her again, '*Look after our little squire.*'

Later, she realized there was something different about her room. There was a lightness, as if Patricia's presence had gone now she'd got her husband back.

But Siana would still have the gift of his son to love. She went through the adjoining door to where Edward lay. He'd been changed into a nightshirt and cap whilst she slept. There was no trace of his blood anywhere. He looked like a stranger to her, older and diminished as if he'd shrunk. His skin was bloodless and waxy. His hands had been placed in an attitude of prayer on his chest. On his dressing tray her diamond headband glittered.

She kissed his cold forehead. 'Goodbye, my love. I will find you again in our son and will be content.'

22

Nothing seemed real to Siana. Inside her was a never-ending silent scream of anguish.

The day wore a mantle of bright blue. Trees were clothed in their prettiest shades of green, with enough of a breeze to make them resemble graceful dancers.

Flowers flourished in the lush grass spreading across the church grounds. Beneath it, the earth had opened its dark crumbling maw to accept the body of Edward Forbes.

They were laid in a row, the Forbes men. Around them in this fenced-off section were arranged their wives and children. *Josiah Forbes . . . Anne, wife of . . . William Forbes . . . Katherine, wife of . . . George Forbes, beloved son of . . . Patricia, wife of Edward Forbes. Charlotte, beloved daughter of Patricia and Edward Forbes.* As if they were there to welcome Edward to their midst.

Siana tried to be courageous but she couldn't stop crying. She was not like these people standing around her, trained from birth to be in control of their emotions. The women dabbed at imaginary tears with lace-edged handkerchiefs and leaned on the arms of their men, as if they were all Edward's widows. Siana stood alone, silently weeping.

As in life, not one of them spared a thought for the widow. The display of her grief embarrassed them. But Siana could not love somebody one moment, lose them the next and carry on living unscathed. Already there had been too much grief in her life.

Through a blur of tears, she watched Edward's coffin lowered into the grave. They had put him next in line in the row. At his feet lay his daughter, Charlotte, who had hardly lived, and Patricia who had fought her for possession of Edward, and who'd won. There was no room for Siana, his peasant bride, in this sad garden of stone flowers, only space for her son, who would lie next to his unknown father in the fullness of time.

Across from her, the Earl of Kylchester stood, brother to Francis Matheson. There was a large age difference between them. The earl was just beginning to stoop into old age, but it hadn't quite claimed him yet. His countess was younger. She was upright and odd-looking with eyes the colour of flint and twice as sharp.

Francis stood with them. Now and again she could feel his glance on her and knew he was watching her. She could not meet his eyes.

Dust to dust. Ashes to ashes. Would it never end?

Elizabeth had stayed away. Siana dropped a handful of earth into the hole. *Goodbye, my love.* She felt so alone.

Through the trees she could see her father. He stood there, tall and untidy. His white beard flowed in the breeze like fine strands of cotton. Such a strange man, so full of fire and passion. Did he feel her pain now? Yes, he must, for he was lonely too.

She gazed back at him and he moved towards her, coming across the grass in the long, ungainly strides that had taken him over the length and breadth of the country to find her. He stood beside her, taking her hand in his, making her feel less alone.

A smile touched Francis's mouth as he exchanged a glance with Richard White.

Then they were back at the manor, she and these strangers – the empty manor where she would raise the little squire for Edward. What did she know about raising squires?

'Damned fine gelding. Edward always did have a good eye for horseflesh. Must ask the steward if they'll part with him.'

Never! Edward's horse would go to Edward's right-hand man, Jed Hawkins. Edward would have wanted that.

'And a good eye for a filly. The marriage was a bit of a surprise, though. Still, Edward seems to have shaped her into something. Her peasantry isn't obvious and I heard she's directly descended from the Marcher Lords.'

Snobbish fools! Let them believe that if it made her easier to stomach, she thought. Personally, she'd set aside such childish fantasies.

How insensitive their laughter as they surreptitiously looked her over. They were drinking Edward's favourite brandy. Josh had told her the liquor was smuggled ashore in flat punts able to negotiate the several shallow channels of Poole Harbour, where the customs men couldn't go.

She took the servants aside and told them to serve an inferior brand. That she could control what these aristocrats drank made her feel a little better.

She slipped from the drawing room and went to the stairway to stand in front of Edward's portrait. 'See what power you have given me, Edward. The men are like horses at the trough so I have stopped them drinking the good brandy.'

His eyes twinkled approvingly at her and she chuckled. 'See, only you can make me laugh today. I'm quite cross with you for leaving me alone.'

There was a faint noise from the bottom of the stair and she spun round. There was the outline of a man in the doorway, the shape so familiar to her she knew exactly who it was.

'Edward,' she breathed, her heart beating so fast she felt sick and dizzy. But it was not Edward she saw as he stepped forward to gaze up at her. It was Daniel, tall and tanned and looking so much like his father she wanted to scream. But Daniel was not his father, he was his poor shadow. He had neither his father's elegant bearing nor his charisma.

'I have come for the reading of the will,' he said.

'I didn't see you at Edward's funeral, Daniel.'

'No,' he said. 'I considered it inappropriate to attend.'

'And you think it appropriate to attend the reading of the will?'

'I'm his son. As his only blood kin, I believe I'm to be a beneficiary, perhaps the main one.'

How petulant he looked. 'Is that all Edward meant to you, Daniel?'

Bitterly he said, 'It seems I was not the only one to take advantage of what he had to offer. You did not wait for me long, Siana.'

'Perhaps if you'd informed me of your intention to leave, or even sent me a letter, I might have waited longer before I broke off our agreement. As it was, I heard of your involvement with another quite by chance instead of directly from you. I would have preferred to tell you to your face that I'd fallen in love with Edward.'

'I wrote to you and didn't receive answers.'

'I didn't receive any letters.'

He looked slightly shocked. 'But I sent them to Richard White's address.'

'Perhaps they didn't arrive,' she said, somehow knowing Edward had persuaded Richard to keep them from her in his determination to have her himself.

'My father was an old man,' he scoffed. 'You took advantage of him. My mother tells me you loved my father, but I don't believe you wanted him for anything more than what he could give you materially.'

'That's untrue,' she stammered.

He didn't even listen to her protest. 'Be warned. When I take over this estate, I will expect every jewel and gift he ever gave you to be returned.'

She'd willingly give them to him now if it would bring Edward back.

'You will leave here with only the rags you arrived in.' He gazed around him, his face avid. 'My mother was not welcome in this house before. Now she is carrying an infant. He may carry the name Skinner, but I'll make sure my sibling grows up in its rightful place.'

How cold and ruthless he was now. 'Elizabeth is carrying Edward's child?' Siana felt sick as she stared at him, ashen-faced and unbelieving.

'I see she hasn't informed you.' He shrugged, slightly shame-faced. 'The infant is to be delivered very soon, I believe.'

Francis appeared at her elbow. 'Ah, there you are, Siana. My sister-in-law wishes to offer you her condolences before the will is read.' He gazed at Daniel and nodded, the expression in his eyes bleak. 'Mr Ayres. I believe congratulations should be offered on your recent engagement. The young lady is a very wealthy young woman, I understand. Your father would have approved of such a step to better your lot.'

Daniel turned a dull red.

Siana's knees gave way and she would have tumbled down the stairs if Francis had not been there to hold her up. 'Take heart,' he whispered. 'It will all be over soon and you can rest.'

The countess was kind. 'Allow me to call on you whilst you are mourning your husband, my dear. You are so young and there can be nothing worse than being alone at such a time.'

The earl gave her a searching glance, kissed her hand and exchanged a slight smile with Francis.

She was grateful to the countess and her husband for their attention. Soon she was surrounded by women murmuring insincere words of comfort before they drifted off to find a seat for the main event. The reading of the will.

What it contained came as a surprise to everyone

388

except Edward's lawyer, and Jed Hawkins, who had acted as witness to his master's signature. Siana was bestowed the house in Poole and an endowment for life. Daniel was awarded a lump sum. Richard White received a large grant to use however he saw fit for church restoration.

The lawyer smiled at her and cleared his throat. '"The remainder of the estate is to be entrusted to my dear wife, Siana Forbes, on behalf of my legitimate heir, as yet unborn, and whatever the gender. Should that heir not survive then the whole of the estate shall become the property of Siana Forbes and can be dispensed with by inheritance or sale at her discretion."'

Daniel shot to his feet amid the muttering and gasps. 'I object.'

'I haven't finished yet,' the lawyer said smoothly. '"From this moment on my obligations towards Elizabeth Skinner and her son, Daniel Ayres, are fully discharged. Should Daniel Ayres see fit to challenge my will his legacy shall be rendered null and void."'

Daniel walked out.

A long silence followed.

Eventually, Siana rose to her feet and nodded shakily to the lawyer. 'Thank you, Mr Beldon. That was all very clear.' She managed a small smile as she faced the stunned assembly. 'It's been a very long and trying day and I'm grateful for your kindness on this sad occasion.' Her voice broke and tears came. 'I hope you will all excuse me, but I must rest.'

Her legs felt as if they didn't want to support her as she moved through the mourners and away from them.

She went straight to her room, then through the dividing door into Edward's room.

It was gloomy. Dust sheets covered everything and the curtains were drawn. She pulled them back, allowing the light inside. The drawers in the dressers were empty of clothes. The blood-soaked mattress had been taken away and burned. She pulled the sheet from his chair and seated herself, drawing her knees up under her chin like a child.

She didn't know how long she sat there trying to find comfort from some thread of something Edward might have left behind. But when the afternoon light began to fade, she realized there was nothing left, not even a scent. Then suddenly, the infant inside her moved. It was just a soft flutter under her navel, but she knew immediately what had caused it.

'Thank you, Edward,' she whispered. She marvelled over this small sign of comfort. A few moments later, she glanced up when Francis came in, followed by an agitated-looking Rosie. She smiled delightedly at them. 'The baby moved. He moved! Edward would have been so proud.' She thought of Elizabeth's baby and began to cry and laugh at the same time.

'Of course he'd be proud,' Rosie said.

Siana allowed herself to be drawn through to her own room with its barred prison windows, the lavender decorations suggested by Elizabeth, Edward's mistress, and the memories of sad Patricia who'd selfishly taken Edward away from his unborn son.

She wondered. Had Edward made love to them all in this room? No, not Elizabeth. This had been

Patricia's shrine. For the short time Elizabeth had looked after Siana they had been allocated two of the upstairs guest rooms. Before that, Elizabeth had been kept out of sight in a house in Dorchester.

Ashamed, she realized that Elizabeth had been her friend. She'd loved her. She still loved her. She was jealous and ungrateful thinking of her so bitterly when Elizabeth had always been so kind.

Rosie touched her black-clad arm. 'You must let me put you to bed.'

Siana bit back her inclination to indulge in hysterical laughter. 'Not in this room. I'll never sleep in here again.' She picked up her skirts and hurried away from them to a room across the landing. It was small in comparison and had wallpaper the colour of almonds with garlands of pink roses on it. The hangings were dusty and the bed was lumpy. Siana didn't care. She fell into the middle of it, curled herself into a ball and was instantly asleep.

Rosie gazed down at her. 'Poor little moth. She's taking this business real hard. This room used to belong to the nurse of the first Lady Forbes. We can't have her moping in Sir Edward's room. I'll find her a nice room and have her things moved. It should be all ready for her by the time she wakes.'

Francis pulled a cover over the still form. His heart went out to her as he took in her tear-stained face and the dark rings under her eyes. 'Look after her, Rosie. Make sure she eats something for she has the baby to think of too. I'll drop by in a day or two, but if she needs me I'll come immediately.'

'Bless her. She be stronger than she knows. The

master knew what he was doing when he brought her here. Give her a week to get the hang of it and the estate will be in good hands, just you see.'

It took several days for Siana to regain a semblance of her wits and to get through the day without drowning in her own tears.

The change was brought about by Josh, who brought her horse back a fortnight after the funeral.

'Josh,' she murmured, and hugged him, 'I've missed you so much.'

When she let him go, he looked her up and down, grinning. 'There was nothing stopping you coming to see us, was there?'

Except Edward wouldn't have encouraged it.

'You're growing into a giant,' she accused. 'Look at those big feet of yours.'

'I know. I keep having to buy meself new boots. Got a second cart now and a proper horse to pull it. Found me a lad to help me out. Begging in the streets of Poole, he was. His master caught him doing a fiddle. Fetched him a clout round the ear and chucked him out on his arse. Good with horses and such, even though he be deaf and dumb.'

'Then how did you learn all this about him?'

'Just because he's dumb, it don't mean he be stupid. He can draw pictures a real treat.'

She had to ask. 'How's Elizabeth?'

'Tired. She gave birth to a little girl last week. Come early, she did. Not much Skinner in her, thank God. Bonny though. She looks like Elizabeth, and for such a little un she can squawk up a storm.'

Siana smiled.

'Elizabeth calls her Susannah. Pretty name, aye? I'm going to be godfather at her christening.' He looked morose for a moment. 'Means I've got to dress up like a fancy toff again.'

Tortured by the thought that Edward had been fatally wounded defending Elizabeth from Tom Skinner, Siana brought the conversation round to the events of that dreadful day.

'Didn't see anything until it were over,' Josh said. 'You should talk to Elizabeth about it. It were a real shock for her and she won't tell me what happened. Upset her, see. She might talk to you, though, seeing it was your husband who copped it in the brawl too. '

It would not harm her to visit Elizabeth. Of late, she hadn't been anywhere. Besides, she wouldn't be satisfied until she saw the child. It would give her an excuse. 'Will you deliver a note back to her from me?'

'She'll be glad to hear from you. Now, how about you send one of those fancy servants of your'n to bring your little brother a wedge of pie or two and a jug of ale to wash it down with?'

'A jug of ale, indeed! Our mother should rise from her grave and give you a clout around the ear. You can come up to the nursery and have tea with our Daisy. You'll be surprised how big she's getting.'

August had turned into a golden September when Siana set out in the carriage to visit Elizabeth. It was the first time she'd left the estate since the funeral. It had been hard to make the decision without consulting Edward, but part of her enjoyed the freedom of being able to please herself.

Jed Hawkins accompanied her because although George Loveless, the last of the Tolpuddle men, had now been been taken aboard the *William Metcalfe* and transported to Van Diemen's Land, others had taken up the unionists' cause, demanding they be pardoned.

So the unrest continued. Tolpuddle was used as an excuse, but much of the trouble was due to old grievances coming to light, the loss of common grazing land and vegetable plots now the enclosure system had been completed. Cheverton estate had lost nearly a whole field of wheat a couple of days previously when someone had deliberately stampeded a herd of cattle into it to trample it underfoot.

Knowing the poverty that the labourers constantly lived with, Siana had decided to order another shilling or two to be paid to them if the estate could afford it, and she was sure it could. She'd already discussed with Jed Hawkins the need to improve the state of the cottages before winter. Perhaps that would go a little way towards appeasing the trouble-makers, who seemed to have a different agenda to that of the labourers – which was to better their lot rather than destroy the source of their living.

Her grief over Edward's death had not lessened, but there were moments of contentment now. The infant inside her had grown stronger, even though the swelling of her stomach was still too slight to be discernible under her clothes. Edward would live on in the child they'd created. She must remember that.

It had been months since she'd been to Poole and the

fresh stinging breeze and odour of mud brought back memories of the happy time she'd spent here with Elizabeth as company.

Elizabeth was waiting for her on the porch. She was thin and pale, her eyes and hair lacking lustre. There was a strange watchfulness about her. The smile that came to her mouth was just as quickly withdrawn and, as Siana descended from the carriage, it seemed to her as if Elizabeth was dubious of her intent.

Siana didn't bother with preliminaries. 'Elizabeth, my dearest friend. I've missed you so much.' She was across to her in a trice, clasping her in a tight hug.

After a moment of hesitation, Elizabeth returned the hug. 'I'm so sorry for what happened to Edward, Siana. I should have sent you a note, at least. You lost a husband and I a dear friend.'

Arms around each other's waists, they strolled inside. Elizabeth arched an eyebrow as she gazed at her. 'Daniel has told me your good news. Congratulations. I'm so pleased for you, my dear. The child will go a long way to helping you cope with your loss.'

'Daniel was not too pleased at the time.'

'He regrets his behaviour now. Edward has been good to him in the past and he has always had expectations beyond the reality of his situation. I hope you'll find it in your heart to forgive him. He is to wed in London next month. With his legacy, he intends to buy a partnership in a legal office.'

The fact that Daniel had not seen fit to apologize personally didn't sit well with Siana. He was, she thought, as shallow as Francis had once indicated.

'And what of your daughter? I'm eager to see her.'

'Yes, I suppose you must be.' A slightly mischievous smile was slanted her way. 'We shall go to the nursery then, so you can satisfy your curiosity. She is not much like her father, by the way.'

Exactly who that father was became apparent to Siana the moment she set eyes on Susannah. Although the infant possessed Elizabeth's beauty, there was a faint look of the Skinners about her, especially in the light blue eyes and the flaxen colouring of her hair.

Relief cascaded through her and she let out a sigh. 'She's so sweet.'

'She's a demanding monster who keeps me awake all night,' Elizabeth caressed the infant's silky skin. 'Although she was not conceived in happy circumstances, I love her dearly.'

Siana met her eyes and said honestly. 'I thought Edward might have fathered her.'

'Of course he did not. The moment Edward set eyes on you, he had time for nobody else.' Which was not exactly the whole truth, but the nearest Elizabeth could come to it. Edward's heart had been constant, if not his urges. 'Now, let's go downstairs. We shall take some refreshment and I will tell you what occurred here that terrible day. Edward had come to see me about renego-tiating the lease agreement on this house, I believe. At the time, as you know, my life was in peril, and it was Edward who paid the consequences, an event which has been on my conscience ever since. But even so, I'm glad he got home alive. He was so desperate to be with you.'

By the time Elizabeth finished speaking, some of the colour had returned to her cheeks and the sparkle to her eyes, as if the unburdening had done her good. They cried a little over Edward together, sharing their grief for the death of a man they'd both loved, and parted the best of friends again.

Two months later, the Countess of Kylchester came to call. With her were Pansy and Maryse Matheson.

As they waited in the drawing room for their tea to arrive, Siana thought: What would you make of this then, Ma? Your daughter putting on airs and graces and entertaining a countess to tea.

'How are you coping, my dear?' the countess said and, without looking around or drawing a second breath, warned, 'A young lady should not fidget, Pansy Matheson. Kindly desist at once.'

When the girl stifled a giggle, Siana grinned at her.

The countess shrugged. 'My dear, boys are much less bothersome to raise. Give them a horse, a strict tutor and a good thrashing from time to time and they behave quite beautifully.'

'Papa said boys have no brains,' Pansy offered.

'He remembers being a brainless boy himself, no doubt,' the countess said caustically, and turned a cool eye on Maryse. 'Do stop picking at the seam of your glove, otherwise you will have to spend all day tomorrow repairing it.'

Maryse blushed and dropped her hands into her lap.

Siana felt sorry for them. So much energy and nowhere to expend it. 'It's a fine day. I will send for my young sister and the nursery maid can take the young ladies on a tour of the grounds, whilst we keep watch from the window.'

It was not long before the girls were running off down the path. The countess smiled at her. 'When is your child expected?'

'In February, my lady.'

'Edward Forbes was a rogue marrying someone as young as you.'

'I loved him,' she said, jumping instantly to his defence.

The countess laughed. 'Of course you loved him. All gels love a man as wicked in his ways as Edward. Were you a virgin when you took your vows?'

Siana's eyes flew wide open and she gave a nervous laugh. 'Uh . . . why yes.'

'He must have sensed you were just right for the plucking. Edward liked a little debauchery, I believe. Tell me, my dear, was he as wicked in the bedchamber as they say?'

She leaned forward when Siana blushed, saying softly, 'Ah . . . you see, spring and autumn. You were full of rising sap and malleable. Edward needed to plant his seed in fertile ground. How lovely you are, my dear. No wonder he chose you over Isabelle. As for Francis, he's totally captivated by you.'

Siana's blush became a fire in her cheeks. 'Francis is my friend.'

'Nonsense! Francis is in love with you. It's as plain as the nose on my face.'

Siana giggled, for the countess's nose was rather noticeable, in fact.

The countess grimaced. 'I'm not so fearsome as I pretend to be and you shall call me Prudence when we are alone. I was totally misnamed, of course. Do you intend to marry Francis when he asks you? It's about time he had a wife to warm his bed.'

Her forthright manner was rather disconcerting. Siana's smile faded and she grew sad again. 'My husband has not long died. It's too soon to consider—'

'Yes . . . yes . . . I understand convention all too well, but you're young. Once the child is born, you will crave the touch of a man again. Francis will sense that and he'll act on it. See, here he is now. He hasn't seen us yet. When he does, we will watch him smile, as he does every time he mentions your name.'

His girls intercepted him, dashing out from the trees to stop his horse.

He dismounted and hugged them tight against him.

Daisy freed herself from the grasp of the nursery maid, dashing after them to clasp tight to his knees. He swung her up to ride on his shoulders and the four of them started up the drive with the horse and maid following behind.

Francis glanced up and caught sight of them at the window. There was a moment of stillness in him. His eyes sought her out and he smiled – a slow, beautiful smile full of yearning.

'There,' Prudence said, almost purring with satisfaction. 'I told you so. He's in love with you.'

And Siana could only hope she was right, because if Francis never smiled like that at her again she knew she would die.

23

Time passed quickly for Siana.

Her childhood had made her aware of the basic facts of farming. She knew which crops were planted when, and the finer points of such essentials as muck spreading and harvesting.

She consulted regularly with the estate steward, Jed Hawkins. Although they didn't always agree, because Hawkins had been Edward's man since a young age and had absorbed Edward's overbearing attitude towards the local peasantry, he did make workable some of her suggestions. He managed to overturn her demand for a two-shilling raise in wages, though, and after a fierce argument in which he reminded her she was a trustee for Edward's unborn child, they'd compromised on one shilling a week and an extra pair of boots for the labourers.

Unbeknown to Hawkins, Siana came to an arrangement with her own midwife, which was to attend to the birth and after-care of those labourers' wives who wished to take advantage of her services. The midwife had been recommended by Francis, which was good enough for her. The service was paid for from the allowance Edward had left her.

There was a trickle of visitors that autumn, as if the women who'd ignored her when Edward lived were now eager to make amends. Most of them were tedious to entertain. It took Siana a while to realize their displeasure had been aimed at Edward, not her. The fact that he'd dared elevate a peasant to their ranks had not sat well with them. Now they had found her to be civilized, after all, they were curious about her.

As Christmas approached her baby grew in strength. Her belly swelled.

'It's growing as fat as a churn full of butter,' the midwife said. She took Siana's hands in hers and guided them over her stomach, using pressure to indicate. 'That there's its head. It should be pushed out first and will be the hardest and most painful part of the birth. Here's the curve of its back and its little arse. The legs be tucked under most of the time.'

Her infant surged against her palm and she laughed. 'He's kicking me.'

The midwife smiled. 'You're sure it's going to be a lad, then. Have you thought of a name?'

'Ashley Edward shall be his main names, and Joshua after my brother.'

Her mind full with the impending birth of her infant, Siana added little pieces to the layette and had the nursery wing redecorated.

Josh called in from time to time. He brought her gossip. Ben Collins had wed Isabelle a month after

Hannah's death. Shortly afterwards, Isabelle had given birth to a baby.

'A girl it were. Took everyone by surprise, except her. With all that flesh on her nobody knowed she had a belly full. Not like you, our Siana. You looks like a cow in clover.'

'And I feel like one.'

'Gonna be right handy being related to the next squire, especially if you calls him after me,' he said proudly.

'Not if you're still stealing his fish.'

Josh cocked his head to one side. ''Tis only a few trout and it's not me who's takin' 'em.'

'But you're makin' money out of the theft. That's the same thing. If they were being stolen to feed the poor, I might turn a blind eye to it, but they're not.'

Shrugging, Josh said cockily, 'Whatcher going to do about it, sis? Rat on your own brother? Nah, you haven't got it in you.'

Siana smiled and said nothing.

The next time Josh came back from market, his cart was confiscated by Jed Hawkins and he was forced to ride astride Jasper to get back to Poole.

Told to collect the cart from the side entrance a week hence, when he returned his nostrils were assailed by the strong smell of rotting fish. The secret compartment had been filled with trout and nailed shut.

'Who would have thought it of it but Siana?' he murmured, grinning at his sister's simple solution.

But it worked. On the way back to Poole, and for weeks afterwards, he was followed by a cloud of flies and felt sick every time he went near the cart.

*

Gruffydd Evans was as strong as he'd ever been. He hadn't experienced a seizure in weeks. As his body had filled out, his mind was filled with the burning desire to take the message of the Lord to the people again.

His good friend, Richard White, had promised him the pulpit on Sunday. Worldly goods meant nothing to him, but for the sake of his daughter – whose grief at the funeral of her husband had torn his heart apart – he intended to preach of love.

The reverend sang his praise to Siana when he visited. 'Gruffydd has regained his health and will be leaving the district shortly after the sermon.'

She nodded. 'I'll be there, Richard.'

'I was thinking that perhaps I should do something to honour Edward. Do you have any wishes regarding this?'

'He was a vain man who'd have preferred to have been honoured grandly.' She smiled at Richard's surprise, then said gently. 'You know that to be the truth. Is there room for a window to his memory?'

'There are several plain windows which could be replaced.'

'He was a brave man. He honoured me by making me his wife. He then lost his life saving Elizabeth's. Would St George rescuing a maiden from a dragon be inappropriate?'

'How very apt. You are a good girl, Siana. Sometimes I felt guilty keeping Daniel's letters from you, but it all turned out for the best.'

She drew in a deep breath. So he *had* kept Daniel's letters from her? 'It was wrong of you to interfere. Did Edward put you up to it?'

Richard nodded miserably. 'He loved you. He wanted you for himself.'

'He wanted me for his mistress. How could you countenance such an action? I trusted you, Richard. Didn't you stop to think how hurtful it might be to both Daniel and myself, or the danger you put me and my sister in? Do you still have the letters?'

He shook his head. 'I gave them to Edward.'

She found them later in Edward's writing desk. Three beautifully penned letters from Daniel. The first one expressing his everlasting love for her, the second describing Italy in a way that made it all so clear to her. He said he missed her and was looking forward to hearing from her.

The third one expressed his hurt because he'd just learned from Elizabeth that she'd wed his father. The fact that it had been sent via Richard White made her wonder if Elizabeth, too, had been involved in the scheme to keep them apart.

I am desolate, he wrote. I should have known my father was going to pursue you. I saw it in his eyes when he looked at you. My dearest Siana, I wish you every happiness and will keep you always in my heart.

Edward had told her on his deathbed that she'd discover things about him she didn't like. He'd had power over them all. Richard, Elizabeth, Daniel and herself. But she couldn't blame anyone because she knew now that her love for Daniel had been a vague and purely romantic notion. That she'd so easily pushed it aside for another told her how shallow it had been.

So she threw the letters into the fire and watched

tongues of flames curl the edges and consume them until they were blackened ashes that were sucked up the chimney.

Everybody was in church to hear the Welsh orator speak. Richard conducted the normal service, then seated himself beside Siana as Gruffydd Evans strode to the pulpit.

His piercing glance moved slowly over the congregation. The shuffling feet and coughs gradually silenced under that gaze until the expectant hush was a noiseless sound of its own. She jumped when his voice rang out, rich and resonant with Welsh cadences.

'I am here to tell you of one man's sin.' His glance came to where she sat and his expression was curiously humble. 'I'm here to tell you of my own sin – of the lust I felt for an innocent girl long ago. I'm here to tell you of the punishment she was forced to endure, because my pride told me my sin against her was justified.'

Tears pricked at Siana's eyes when he smiled at her. 'I have been on a journey into hell. I was lower than the beasts in the fields. I had no honour, no pride and was not fit to preach the word of the Lord.'

The congregation was spellbound as he continued, telling the story of Megan's downfall, describing the way the Welsh village women had shorn the hair from her head and her father had cast her from her home.

'For many years I sought the daughter I fathered.' Tears began to roll down his face. 'Finally I found her and I asked her for something she couldn't give. Forgiveness. I have been searching my soul these last

405

few weeks. Her answer renewed my faith, for out of that sin has come a rare gift. Eternal life.'

Whether the congregation understood his words didn't matter. They were mesmerized by the depth of his emotion and his humbleness. Women and men had tears in their eyes and when he stood before them, cleansed of his sin, they clapped and cheered.

She waited until the crowd dispersed. After he said his farewell to Richard White and Mrs Leeman, Siana went to where he stood.

They gazed at each other, father and daughter. She took the silver cross from around her neck and placed it in his hand. 'It belonged to my great-grandmother. If she is still alive, tell her I will visit her one day. Will you come back to see your grandson?'

'God willing, you have not seen the last of me, daughter.' He held out his carved stick to her. 'It has fulfilled its purpose. Keep it until my return. Your name is on it.'

'My mother would have forgiven you now, I think.'

He smiled. 'Bless you, Siana. Walk with God.'

'It's you who must walk with God. I am a child of the earth like my mother and great-grandmother. You must accept that.'

He stooped to kiss her cheek, then turned and walked away from her, his coat flapping loosely around his ankles, his beard flowing in the breeze.

'Papa,' she called out and ran after him to give him a hug. There was a moment of empathy between them, then they parted and he strode away, his step full of purpose.

She wondered as she watched him go. Will I ever see him again?

She turned to find Francis watching her from the church porch. Telling Jed Hawkins to wait, she hurried to where he stood.

'I love you,' she said, because she'd learned from her father that people needed love to survive. 'I've loved you from the moment we met.'

His smile warmed her. 'You must not say such things. You are still in mourning.'

'I'll always mourn Edward.' She gently touched his cheek. 'He brought out the pagan in me, Francis, but, instinctively, he knew what I felt for you was deeper. Before he died he said he didn't want to live to see me fall in love with a younger man.'

Francis began to walk her back to the carriage. He kissed her hand. 'Will you celebrate Christmas with my family and friends at the hall? Prudence said she would enjoy your company.'

'Not this year, Francis. I'll stay at home and be quiet for the sake of my child.'

'I don't like the thought of you being alone.'

Her hand touched her stomach and she smiled. 'I'm not alone. Josh is coming over with the orphaned lad he employs, and there is Daisy.'

'Perhaps I'll bring Maryse and Pansy over to visit you in the morning.'

'I would like that.' She nodded to Jed who told the coachman to set the horses in motion.

Francis watched her go, the smile broadening on his face. He felt so exhilarated he wanted to leap through the village like a scalded frog. But it would be too undignified for a man in his position.

Still, he felt the spring in his step as he headed for his horse. He was a patient man and she was still young. He would wait for her.

Ashley Edward Joshua Forbes was born six weeks later. Of a healthy size, he slipped from Siana with the minimum of fuss, making his presence felt and his position known with a demanding cry for attention.

'Thank you, Edward,' Siana whispered as soon as she set eyes on this handsome child of hers. She began to laugh. She should have known her late husband was too vain to allow her to produce a son who wasn't almost moulded in his image.

In fact, young Ashley would have been his father's double if it hadn't been for the green in his eyes – a colour which she knew would darken to match her own in time.

An hour and a half after his birth, Siana was propped up in bed, feeling anything but exhausted. The infant had suckled at her breast, his mouth seeking it out and closing around it in instant possession and gratification.

'A good sign,' the midwife told her. 'It says he knows what he wants from life and will go after it.'

Now her son lay in her arms, looking smugly like his father, and accepting homage from his servants who crept in one by one to marvel over him.

The first anniversary of Edward's death arrived. She placed some flowers on his grave and whispered goodbye to his memory.

Returning to the house, she discarded her mourning and donned a gown of pale green. Taking her mother's shawl from a drawer she pulled it around her shoulders. She hadn't worn it for a long time and enjoyed being surrounded in its familiar warmth.

It was a cold day, yet full of sunshine. She took her sister up on the hill, where they danced barefoot amongst the long grass. There was such joy in her, as if she were part of the sky, the sea and the hills.

The smell of the earth and the sharp sea air reminded her of her childhood. How different things were for her now.

'Here we are, then, Ma,' she shouted, her voice echoing over the hills. 'We've got this far, though it hasn't been without trouble. Daisy and I will always love you.'

The spirit of her mother seemed to reached out for them, surrounding them with love.

She and Daisy spun around laughing and giggling until they collapsed together to roll in the grass, the sky and hills still spinning around them.

The story of Siana Lewis will be continued in

BEYOND THE PLOUGH

Don't miss the enthralling sequel to *A Dorset Girl*

To be published in Pocket paperback in July, 2004

1

Dorset 1837

It was the first day of the New Year. The hallway of Cheverton Manor was decorated with ivy and prickly holly boughs, bright with blood-red berries. A huge log fire blazed in the hearth. Pine cones and needles had been added for the fragrance. Sparks exploded up the chimney as the pine resin heated.

Siana Forbes paused on the stairs for this, her second New Year without her husband. She was young to be a widow, barely twenty-two. Small and slim, she'd long ago discarded the black of mourning. Her burgundy coloured riding habit followed the curves of her waist and breasts. Beneath her skirt she wore white silk pantalettes, but not for warmth. Her late husband had introduced her to such undergarments on her wedding day and now they were part of her.

Edward Forbes gazed down at her from his portrait. Grey-haired and elegant, he appeared to be the essence of propriety. Actually, he'd been downright wicked in his ways. The painted twinkle in his eye and ironic twist to his mouth made her smile. The artist had captured it well. Siana's blood still ran hot if she thought of him for any length of time. Even now – now she'd come to understand that her love for him had been born from necessity, and his for her, from lust – Siana felt honoured to have been his wife.

Edward Forbes had lifted her from the depths of despair, educated her and given her a life so unlike the one her mother had known that she often had to pinch herself to believe it. She had enjoyed her short marriage, had enjoyed her husband in all his moods and ways. Her grief had been genuine when he'd died before he'd had a chance to see his son and heir.

The young baronet was upstairs in the nursery. Christened Ashley Edward, a name his father had indicated on his death-bed, the little squire was a strong child who resembled his father in feature. His hair was dark, containing the glossy raven blackness of her own. His eyes were the same hue too. A dark, mysterious green, the colour of pines, her husband had described them as. They'd been passed down through the blood of the Welsh ancestors she'd only been told about.

She loved Ashley with all the intensity a mother feels towards her first child. She loved him more because he would never know his father or experience his guidance, and more still because his future was not his own to decide. Cheverton Manor and the estate surrounding it would be his life work. Such a lot of responsibility for such a little boy to shoulder.

It was early as she made her way to the door, stopping only to greet the servant who came to tend the fire. Her own maid was still abed. No doubt Rosie would scold her for going out with her hair hanging in a loose braid down her back. Not that anybody would be abroad at this early hour on New Year's day to see her.

The morning was raw. The night mist still lingered, floating in shifting layers that writhed around the stark winter tree shapes and hid the sky. The air was sharpened by wood smoke, which rose from the manor's chimneys to be trapped within the damp blanket of vapour.

Siana slipped the bridle over her mount's head and led her from her stall. Her horse pocked impatiently at the stable floor with her hoof and snickered softly when she struggled to lift the saddle to her back. She was a pretty bay, with a dark tail and mane and soft brown eyes ringed with dark lashes.

'Stand still, Keara,' Siana told her as the saddle began to slip sideways.

She jumped when the steward took over the task, scolding, 'You should have had the groom kicked out of bed, Lady Forbes.'

Siana eyed Jed Hawkins warily. The steward was a big man, bigger than her late husband, to whom he'd been devoted. Grey-bearded, and weathered, with eyes like dark honey, the enigmatic and taciturn steward was totally to be relied on, but slightly intimidating on occasion. She hadn't noticed him much before Edward's death, and it seemed as if he'd suddenly stepped out of his shadow. She hadn't heard him coming up behind her.

'It's the first day of the New Year,' she said by way of an excuse.

'New Year or not, the groom still has his duties to perform. One of them is to escort you. Surely you were not thinking of going out alone?'

3

'Sometimes I need to be alone, Jed. I have a strong urge to visit the place I grew up in. I've not been back there since my mother died.'

As he tightened the cinch around her mount's belly his eyes softened. Gruffly, he said. 'All right, lass. I'll follow on after you and you won't even know I'm there.'

'You're not my father, you know,' she dared to say.

He gave her a level look. 'No, but I would have made a better one than that preacher man, Gruffydd Evans, ever was.'

She cocked her head to one side, trying to fathom him out. 'Perhaps you should wed and produce children of your own instead of trying to be a father to me.'

Jed chuckled at that. 'Before he died your husband told me to watch out for you. I intend to follow his orders to the letter.'

'Edward said that? It's odd that your loyalty to him stretches beyond the grave. What were you to him?'

He lowered his eyes. 'Childhood companion, comrade-at-arms, friend.'

'Why did he charge you with my care when you are no relation to him?'

'Because he knew he wouldn't be here himself.' Before she knew it, Jed's big hands had circled her waist and he'd lifted her on to the saddle. She hooked her knee around the horn and gazed angrily at him. 'I refuse to let Edward control me after death, so the order is rescinded. Wherever you were going at the crack of dawn, you can continue on.'

'I'm going nowhere. I've just come back.'

Her eyes flared with curiosity. 'From where?'

4

'You'd be surprised.' Jed grinned slightly to himself, a gesture which reminded Siana forcibly of her late husband when his mind had been absorbed by the ways and means of love.

Jed was unmarried, but, no doubt he would know how to take advantage of certain intimacies necessary to men. She clicked her tongue and rode out before he could see the colour flood to her cheeks, feeling sorry she'd embarrassed herself by asking. Her curiosity about Jed was now biting at her.

Half an hour later she stood under the bones of an oak tree. This was the spot where her mother had died giving birth to a still-born child. Her mother's blood had poured from her body to nourish this tree. A little way off stood the remains of a labourers' cottage. The walls were blackened by fire and grass grew amongst the tumbled bricks.

Her mother's bastard, Siana had been brought up in the cottage. Although she'd survived the constant brutality of the Skinner family, her mother had not. The last of the Skinners still living were Siana's half siblings, Josh and Daisy. They shared the blood of her own mother.

Despite his youth, at sixteen, Josh was well on his way to becoming a man of substance. Five-year-old Daisy lived at the manor.

Melancholy crept over her. She'd sworn never to come back to this place of sorrow again. For a day or two though, something had been pulling her back. The previous night she'd dreamed of her mother. The cottage had been whole, and her mother had beckoned her from the doorway. Siana had realized then, she could ignore the call no longer.

Sliding from her horse she strode across the grass and into the remains of the cottage. A glance back showed Jed a little way off, motionless inside the drifting breath of the mist. Her heart gave a little tug. Jed resembled Edward from this distance. But he would, she told herself. She'd given him Edward's horse, and Jed had the same way of riding, moving with his mount's gait instead of trying to force it to his own rhythm.

She closed her eyes, listening for the first sigh of wind over the hill. It usually came keening in from the sea at this time, travelling five miles over the land to bring with it the smell of brine and seaweed. It was too early perhaps, for the wind remained mute and the silence pressed tension against her ears.

There was something here in these sad ruins, something alien to it. She listened to its voice. It was the sound of a breath perhaps, but not a breath expelled. It was held inside, trapped within heart-beats thundering with panic. Whatever it was, it was scared of her. A stray dog? She stretched out her hands and could feel its presence tingling against her palms.

She smiled. The sight she'd inherited from her Welsh grandmother had not visited her for some time. In the past, sometimes it had brought her a warning, sometimes the gift of healing. This time, she sensed something both needful and precious.

'You needn't be afraid,' she murmured, and opening her eyes, gazed around the gloomy interior of the place. It was not a place of happy childhood memories. Here,

6

she'd known nothing but misery. It was still trapped within the burnt spaces, as if the heat of the fire had shrivelled it, but hadn't been fierce enough to kill it.

The kitchen had caved in long ago, the bricks piling in one on top of the other. The sky showed through the remains of charred roof timbers, which supported nothing but mist. Over to her left, where the second storey wall was still intact, a rough shelter had been built of the charred bricks. Inside, something moved a fraction.

It was not a dog but a small child, huddled against a bundle of grey rags. The girl whimpered in fear as Siana picked her way over the fallen bricks, ignoring the faint, sweet smell of death in the air.

Siana held out her arms. 'Don't cry, my sweet little angel. Come to me, I promise I won't hurt you.'

The waif came creeping into her arms, cold and quivering for comfort like a wretched runt of a kitten. Siana removed her jacket and cuddled the child within its warmth. The thin little body pressed against hers, a pair of pale blue eyes regarded her for a moment then closed. The child's honeyed hair clung in damp ringlets against her scalp.

'You have me now,' Siana whispered to her, her heart aching for the child's plight, for she'd been in the same position herself once.

As she left the cottage with her burden the first breath of wind came over the hill to push at the mist. Then it blasted with some force against her body, flattening her thin shirt against her shift and chilling her to the bone. She moved into the shelter of the trunk of the oak tree, waving for Jed to come forward.

7

He gazed down at the bundle in her arms. 'Not one of ours,' he said. Removing her jacket, he handed it back to her, then tucked the child cosily inside his topcoat. Siana used his bent knee as a mounting block to scramble into the saddle.

She gazed down at him. 'Her mother is dead.'

'I can smell it on her. The poor soul must have been there for several days. As soon as we get back I'll send some men out with a cart to take the body to the undertaker.'

She couldn't help but tease him a little. 'You're right, Jed. You'd make a good father.'

'Aye,' he said comfortably, and giving a quiet chuckle, mounted one-handed and brought his great, black gelding under control. They started back towards Cheverton Manor side by side, the child asleep against his chest.

Francis Matheson was pleased to discover it wasn't Siana who was ill. Her husband's death had been harder on her than he'd first thought it would be. It seemed that as soon as she recovered, the melancholy had set in again. At least she had young Ashley to take her mind off her widowhood, and her son's arrival had been the first real turning point.

Today, she greeted him with a spontaneous smile. 'I'm so happy to see you, Francis.'

Handing his topcoat and hat to a servant, he followed her up the stairs. There, on the landing, out of sight of the servants' prying eyes, he pulled her into his arms and kissed her. The ardent response from her soft lips displayed a new hunger, so he dared to ask. 'Have you decided when you'll wed me?'

'Soon.' Her eyes lit up with mischief. 'Soon, I will give you an answer.'

'My darling,' he murmured. 'If I have to wait for you, I will.'

Her arms slid around his waist and her eyes were dancing now. Pushing open the door to the nearest guest chamber she pulled him inside and invited. 'You could make love to me now.'

Even as he experienced shock his body reacted positively to the thought. Though tempted, he gazed down at her and regretfully shook his head. 'Unfortunately, I'm on my way to the infirmary, and wasn't there someone in need of medical attention? Is it Ashley or Daisy?'

She shrugged slightly. 'It is neither. Tell me, Francis. Will you be so cold with me after we are wed?'

He tried not to let his surprise show as he held her at arm's length to gaze at her flushed face. He could see his refusal had embarrassed her. He kissed the end of her nose. 'I love you, Siana. But I've loved you for too long, and respect you too much to take our relationship lightly. That doesn't mean I'm cold. I'm trying to keep some distance between us, for without a wedding day in sight the consequences could be disastrous for you.'

She nodded. 'You do not think too badly of me for being forward?'

'How could I?' Briefly, he kissed her lips, not daring to do more than that if he was to keep his mind on his work all day. 'Now, who is this mysterious patient?'

'It's a child I have found. Her mother is dead. The

men have gone to pick up the woman's body and take it to the undertakers.'

'A cadaver to examine,' he grumbled. 'Did you have to pick today to go to the cottage?'

'If I hadn't, the child would have spent another cold night in the dark with only her dead mother for company. Would you rather have that happen, Francis? I think not.'

A few minutes later he was gazing down at the child. Siana had possessed the sense to isolate her in case she was infectious. 'What's the child's name?'

'She is called Marigold.'

'A pretty name. Flowers seem to flourish in your family.'

'And yours. She's named for the colour of her hair, I think.'

'Was there anything on the mother's body to indicate who she is, or where she came from?'

'I didn't look, and she hasn't spoken yet.'

'Then how the devil do you know her name?'

She shrugged, and avoiding his eyes, fussed with a piece of lace at her cuff. 'Perhaps I was mistaken and she whispered it before she went to sleep.'

Francis knew evasiveness when he heard it, and was familiar with the strange way Siana had with her sometimes. 'And perhaps you just know, aye? I'll take her with me to the infirmary if she's fit to travel.'

'You can't, she's my child now.' Siana bit down on her lip. 'She has nobody else.'

Francis sighed, because he already knew he was going to lose this battle. 'The girl is a foundling, you can't just keep her.'

10

'Why not?'

'There are procedures.'

'Since you're on the board which runs the infirmary, I see no difficulty with procedures. Besides, Marigold will be your child when we are wed, so nobody will dare object. I thought the first day of spring might be a good month for the wedding. Does that suit you?'

Astounded by her blatant manipulation of him, he nodded. 'That's only three months away.'

'So it is.' She gently kissed his cheek, and judging from the laughter in her voice she knew she'd just dealt herself the winning hand. 'I'll go and play with Ashley and Daisy whilst you examine Marigold, shall I?'

'Please stay. She might wake and feel scared by the sight of a strange man.'

'She'll grow to love you as much as I do.'

He smiled, and wrote on his notebook with a graphite pencil. *Female foundling of unknown origin – to be known as Marigold Forbes (Matheson?) Aged about 4 years. Suffering from malnutrition.*

He took a good look at the child. He had visited just about everyone in the district over the past few years, and this little girl was certainly not one of his patients. She had a delicate and dainty air to her, like a porcelain figurine. Her limbs were thin, but without too much muscle wastage. He listened to her heart. It's beat was strong and regular. She was dirty and dehydrated and smelled of death.

She opened her eyes and stared at him. They were of the palest blue. Her hair was a mass of tangled gold curls and freckles were sparsely scattered across her nose. Her

11

gaze was direct, without curiosity, yet slightly assessing. Francis was disconcerted by it.

'Can you tell us your name?' he said to her.

Her gaze moved on to Siana and she gave a tentative smile. Her voice was a piping little lisp, like that of a bird. 'Mariglowed.'

He slid Siana a glance, absorbing the deceptively innocent expression on her face. There was a gleam of triumph in her eyes.

'Do you have a second name?'

The child shook her head.

Behind him, Siana expelled a sigh of a breath and reached out her hand to close the smaller one inside it. When Francis looked again, the child was asleep.

'She is free of external parasites,' he informed her. 'We don't know what the mother died of yet, so have her bathed as soon as possible. Feed her on milk-sops, oatmeal and chicken broth for a day or two. Inspect her for worms when she functions.'

'Yes, Doctor Matheson.'

'Her appetite will be small to begin with.' When she kissed him on the mouth he was forced to abandon his professional mantle.

'Thank you for not making a fuss about her, Francis.'

He gazed sternly at her. 'You do understand that you can't take in every child who is orphaned, don't you? As it is, we're going to start married life with five children to care for.'

A wide grin spread across her face. 'Don't look so horribly fierce about it. Be warned, as soon as possible I intend to present you with a son, then there will be six.

He can grow up with Ashley for companionship and you can teach him to be a fine doctor, like yourself.'

He pulled her against his body, murmuring with a grin. 'Now we have a wedding date I'm almost tempted to get some practice in for this son of ours.'

Her breath chuckled against his ear, making him shiver. 'Make your mind up to this, Doctor Matheson. Once I have you in my bed you will not escape easily. Now, as you pointed out earlier, you are expected at the infirmary. So, be gone.'

'So I am.' They sprang apart, laughing as a knock came on the door and Siana told whoever it was to enter.

Rosie came in carrying a large bowl and a jug of water.

'Leave them on the table, I'll bathe her myself,' Siana said, seeing him to the door. She was about to give him a chaste peck on the cheek when he gave a chuckle and swept her into his arms.

When he was finished kissing her entirely to his satisfaction, he strode off, laughing inside as she stood there, hot-faced and flustered.

Rosie was grinning from ear to ear when Siana turned towards the child. She couldn't quite meet her eyes. 'Indeed, I don't know what came over Doctor Matheson,' she said, fanning her face with her hand.

'Looks like he might be a lusty fella, the doctor, with the pair of you always kissing in corners where you think you can't be seen.'

Siana tried not to grin. 'You think so?'

'Stands to reason, don't it? Since his wife died he ain't

had time for a woman, until he sets eyes on you – or so I hears.' She lowered her voice. 'Built like a stud bull, too, but I supposed you'm noticed it.'

'Rosie!' Siana said, half in protest, half in laughter. She wouldn't have taken this familiarity from any other servant. But Rosie had been her maid since her first marriage, and had become her confidante and ally in her transformation from peasant girl to lady. 'You should not say such things.'

"Tis only the truth. You'll be walking around with a smile on your face from the word go. Now, when's the wedding going to be?'

'The first day of spring. And he doesn't mind about me keeping Marigold.'

'Have you told him you want him to move into the manor?'

She shrugged. 'I'm sure he won't mind.'

Rosie's look was measured. 'Best you ask him soon, with the wedding so close. The doctor has his pride. He'll want to provide for his wife and children himself.'

Siana promised herself she would ask him as soon as possible. After all, what objections could Francis possibly have to moving into Cheverton Manor?